Shadows

Thorne Moore

Acknowledgements.

Many thanks to Janet Thomas for her polishing, my agent Sara Keane for her belief, my friend Catherine Marshall for her enthusiasm and all the ghosts lurking in the shadows of the old houses of Pembrokeshire.

Keep your face always toward the sunshine, and the shadows will fall behind you.

Walt Whitman

1

I was sitting in an interrogation room when Leo Mardell hanged himself.

He died alone, but I shared it with him. I didn't realise I was doing so, because I was intent on D I Overly's questions.

'So, just to go over this again, Mrs Lawrence, you knew nothing at all about the handling of these funds?'

If Overly had been anything but a policeman, I might have found him droll and likeable. But he was a policeman, so I refused to melt. I was furious with my boss Leo for involving me in his mess, furious that I hadn't walked away the moment I realised something in the company was fishy. Now I was furious with D I Overly for his insinuations.

'I repeat: I've worked for Leo Mardell for less than three months, I deal with clients and I deliver the service they pay for. Period. I have no idea what happens to their money once it reaches the accounts department. It never occurred to me to ask.'

Which wasn't true. I'd nagged Leo about it from day one. The last time I'd spoken to him, I'd been so blunt, he was sweating and grey round the gills. Why on earth had the idiot chosen to mess up a perfectly good and thriving business? And worse, involve me?

For a moment, trapped in that police station, I was drowning in irrational despair, as if an endless succession of locks were snapping shut around me.

Don't be so bloody ridiculous, Kate Lawrence. You're not the one in the shit. This must be Overly's interrogation technique getting to you.

'All right, Mrs Lawrence.' Overly rocked back in his chair and pressed his thumbs together, grinning 'Or can

I call you Kate?'

'No, you can call me Mrs Lawrence.' Beneath my righteous indignation, I again felt that rising tsunami of hopelessness.

'Madam?' he suggested.

'You dare!'

Then it happened. For the smallest fraction of a second, the universe turned upside down, and when it righted itself, something was missing. The panic, the guilt, the trapped despair were gone, and with them Leo. As I sat there, facing D I Overly, Leo Mardell vanished from existence. The universe swung back round to hit me in the solar plexus. A familiar nausea swept through me. My hand shook on the coffee-stained interview table, though I fought to still it.

'Mrs Lawrence? Are you okay?'

The policewoman who was chaperoning us had her hand on the back of my neck, ready to force my head between my knees.

'Mrs Lawrence?' Overly's face was alarmingly close. I could see his consternation. 'Are you feeling faint?'

'What?' I shook myself free. 'No, I'm fine. Sorry. Just – it's hot.'

'I thought you were going to pass out.' Overly sighed with relief. 'All right, Mrs Lawrence, I don't think we need to continue this interview. Get yourself into the fresh air.' He opened the door for me. 'We may need to speak to you again, after we've re-interviewed Mr Mardell.'

'Yes.' *Good luck with that*, I thought. *You can interview Leo all you like but he won't reply. Because he's dead.*

I'd felt him die. That's what I did: I felt Death. It's not a party trick I'd recommend. Not remotely entertaining. All it had ever done was make my life a hell.

I walked out of the police station, my guts twisting themselves in knots, and I went home to wait for the news.

The police found him hanging. He left a suicide note. More of an extended essay, excusing his own fall from grace, blaming his ex-wife, the Inland Revenue, over-litigious clients and an international conspiracy of bankers. I suppose I was expected to be pleased because it exonerated me.

Legal exoneration. It's good in theory, but it never quite cuts through the smoke of innuendos and doubts that trail behind it. In the following days, I sat mourning the hopeless man and listlessly appraising my CV, wondering how to word the latest addition in something approaching a positive light.

I wasn't rushing to look for something new, while I had Leo's death to work through. Too late to realise that the despair I'd experienced at the police station had been his, echoing across the city to me in his last frantic moments. Could I have stopped him? I was sick to think that my harsh words might have helped push him to the edge. That was why I felt obliged to agree to the request to go to his home and sort out his things.

The fact that there was no one else, no family or close friend, just a temporary work colleague, to take on the duty, only increased the poignancy of his death.

The moment I turned the key in the lock of Leo's Pimlico apartment, I knew I'd made a mistake. The chaos created by Leo or the police, hunting for incriminating papers, was lost on me. All I could focus on was the wall where he'd been hanging.

I didn't need the chalk marks, the stain on the floor, to tell me where it was. That coil of panic and screaming regret, tightening around me in the police station, had burst from his body the moment he'd died, to career round the room, seeking dispersal on the wind. But there had been no escape, so it had turned back on itself and eaten like acid into the plaster and brick. It was enshrined now in the fabric of the building, waiting for me. No one else, just me. Because I was the one freak in the world who could feel it.

I didn't want to feel it. I'd already shared Leo's final pathetic spiral into the dark. I couldn't face reliving it, while he was dead and free. I turned and ran. Back to my clean, safe home, empty of shadows.

Empty of people, living or dead. All my life, I'd striven to keep my weird experiences buried so deep that no one would guess what I was feeling, and the result was this: I was alone in an empty house. I'd trained myself to keep quiet, but sometimes the need to share was so strong it left me sick with longing. Except that now there was no one left to share.

Not my husband Peter. I'd frozen him out of my life by my silence and he'd found solace elsewhere.

Friends? Absolutely not. They never stayed, once I'd let slip about my little peculiarities.

How about D I Overly? '*That day when you were interviewing me, when you thought I was going to faint? That was me feeling Leo Mardell die.*'

'*Yes, Mrs Lawrence, of course it was.*' An instant freezing of that flirtatious friendliness; Alert! Batty cow in the room. '*How about you have a nice cup of tea and we'll call a doctor.*'

And what would a doctor say if I tried to explain? '*I feel people die, Doctor, even if they're a hundred miles away. Or I stand where they stood and I share their last horrors, even if they're a hundred years dead.*' I could guess the reaction. It was probably the solution. Maybe

I'd be better off lobotomised.

I wanted someone to tell me that all would be well, and I had no one.

Except…

I had Sylvia! Of course. No matter what, there would always be Sylvia. In my chill loneliness, I ached for her blithe, unquenchable optimism.

I phoned and heard her voice, from a world away, in green and rural Pembrokeshire. 'Kate! How lovely! Mike, it's Kate. How are you, darling? How are you coping? I do wish—'

'Sylvia, I'm fine,' I cut my cousin off before she could drown me in her irrepressible chatter. 'You and Michael both well?'

'Oh we're wonderful, aren't we, Mike? Having a lovely time. It's a dream here. We've got such plans—'

I interrupted again. 'Is the job offer still open?'

'Job? You mean the partnership? You'll come here? Mike! Mike, she's going to come here. Isn't that wonderful? Kate's coming to join us.'

2

'*In one hundred yards, turn right. Turn right.*'

I turned right, over a narrow stone bridge and saw the pub sign, the Cemaes Arms. Sylvia had told me to watch out for it, but without my sat nav, I doubt if I would have found it in the maze of North Pembrokeshire. I took the next left fork, as instructed, along a narrow lane winding up through the trees from the river.

I wasn't running away, I told myself. I wasn't fleeing to the bosom of my family in a cloud of self-indulgent misery. I was doing what I was good at, embracing new and challenging avenues. This was a business opportunity and a chance to clean out all the chaotic irritations in my life. Like my wrecked marriage. Like my death thing. I was going to slap it in the face and put it back in its box, while I took control of Sylvia's business dreams and worked miracles. Order, organise, arrange. Passionless efficiency, oh yes, that was me.

'*In three hundred yards you will have reached your destination.*'

I rounded a bend and there was Sylvia, jumping up and down on the verge and waving her arms.

My cousin Sylvia. Billowing crushed-velvet skirt, voluminous mohair jumper and Wellington boots – Rossetti at Cold Comfort Farm. A comfortable middle-aged plumpness about her now, and a halo of silver in her unruly yellow hair, but still overflowing with life.

'Clever, clever girl! I knew you'd find us.' She tugged at my door as I pulled the handbrake. 'Any trouble? Of course not. You never get lost. Well then, come on, come on. Let me see you.' She swamped me in her bear hug, then held me at arm's length to take a long look at me. 'Too thin. We'll have to feed you up. How are you, darling? What a horrible time you've had, but you're going to love it here, I promise you. Come on, let's drive up to the house.'

'This isn't it then?' I nodded at a cottage, standing guard over rusting wrought-iron gates. Sylvia had promised me a mansion, but I knew her capacity for hyperbole, and the cottage did have Palladian pillars and a pediment. Four rooms could be a mansion in some books.

'No, no, this is just the lodge, but isn't it unbelievably

twee? I'm going to get working on it soon.'

'I am impressed.'

Sylvia, already clambering into the passenger seat, urged me on. 'Come on. Wait till you see the rest.'

I returned to the wheel and manoeuvred the car through the gates and up across steepening pasture, round banks of rhododendrons. As the neglected drive turned alongside low, stone estate buildings, Sylvia clutched my arm in mid gear change. 'There, there, look!'

The great house, Llys y Garn.

No hyperbole after all; it was a bona fide mansion, a dark confusion of wings, gables and chimneys, enfolded in its own shadow as the sun slipped down into the west. The track divided, the right fork circling to a terrace fronting the formal façade of the house, washed by evening light. The left passed through an archway into a dark cobbled courtyard.

'In there, in there,' urged Sylvia, as I edged in under the arch and parked up in the gloom between a Volvo estate and a Ford Fiesta.

Sylvia waved to figures at a lighted window. 'Here she is! Come on, here's Kate.' She turned back to me, face alight with enthusiasm. 'Didn't I tell you it was wonderful? You'll love it: it's oozing with atmosphere. Just your cup of tea.'

My cup of tea. Ah, yes. Five minutes after phoning Sylvia, I'd remembered that this house she and Michael had bought would be exactly the sort of place I'd always avoided. A house so old that echoes of death were guaranteed. For a moment I'd thought of crying off. Then I'd decided; if I really wanted to conquer it, this had to be my golden opportunity. I'd run in panic from Leo's apartment, just as I'd run from a hundred places before, but now I was going to stand my ground.

This house was going to be my Battle of Britain. I'd take it on and win.

I wouldn't be explaining this to Sylvia. She knew that I felt 'things,' and she'd decided it must be a wonderful gift. Everything was wonderful to Sylvia. But then, who could understand what a curse my 'gift' really was? Peter had claimed to understand, long ago before our romance froze to death, but Sylvia never. Curses weren't in her vocabulary – and that was what I loved about her. She was my refuge, my utterly uncomprehending cousin, with whom I could relax in undemanding intimacy, despite the fourteen-year difference in our ages.

Michael Bradley emerged from the house and proffered his hand. I took it, amused at the formality, and turned the gesture into a hug. It was impossible not to like Michael. Nothing big or loud, no star qualities, just a slightly neglected one-eared teddy bear, or a comfortable old slipper, quiet and affable. In his former existence, he'd been the senior chemist in a petroleum multinational, but he looked far better suited to life as a rural woodworker. He'd been with Sylvia for three years now, and they fitted together like an old married couple; lovers and business partners.

'Glad you could come,' he said, smiling, a little shy of my embrace.

'I am glad too. Really glad.'

'Hi, Kate.' Tamsin, Sylvia's youngest child, sidled round Michael to receive the obligatory peck on the cheek. She'd been the baby of the family for eighteen years, but a couple of terms at university had begun to break the bonds.

'Tammy, you're looking gorgeous. How's Bristol?'

'Great! Well, you know.' She whispered a correction. 'Taz.'

'Taz. Sorry.' I'd forgotten. 'I'll remember next time.'
She laughed self-consciously. 'Whatever.'

'Come and help with Kate's bags,' said Sylvia, heaving suitcases from the boot with Michael's aid. Rooks rose wheeling into the white sky, their caws echoing around us.

I followed Sylvia through the house, up a darkly grand staircase into a dim corridor. 'Here we are,' she shouted over her shoulder, as a door opened onto the last rays of the setting sun. 'I thought you'd like this one.' She ushered me in. 'Remember, it's all yours now, so do whatever you want with it. Express yourself!' She gave me a kiss on the cheek. 'Bathroom's just round the corner and through the arch. Take a deep breath and then come down.'

I sank onto the antique brass bed and tried a discreet bounce. The mattress was reassuringly comfortable.

A lofty room, with gracious fireplace, polished oak boards and two tall sash windows facing west over a leaded porch roof. Golden light flooded in, liquid as wine, streaming with motes of dust onto the white tulips Sylvia had placed on the massive chest of drawers. No other frills. I understood: I was to transform it into a purely Kate Lawrence room, minimalist and composed.

With what? I didn't do totemic trappings. There was nothing of deep significance in the heap of suitcases containing my thirty-four years. Did my lack of personal detritus make me challenging, positive and forward-looking, or just sad?

I knelt on the wide sill to look out. Beyond the gravel terrace, pasture rolled down into the forested valley, no hint of green yet on the tangled boughs. The far rim of the valley blazed as the sun disappeared from view and the depths were cast into darkness. The March sky, promising frost, faded from indigo to palest golden green, huge and cleansing.

It certainly wasn't London.

I surveyed the room again, open to any shadows that might come seeping through the plaster. But if anyone had died in this room, they'd done so peacefully, without fear, leaving nothing but a slight creak in the floorboards. I could live with this.

'Have a bit more,' said Sylvia. 'You need feeding up, doesn't she, Mike? Look at her, she's thin as a rake.'

'She looks fine,' smiled Michael.

'And really, I'm full,' I insisted. Michael had cooked the lamb casserole, as he did all things, with undemonstrative perfectionism, but the pear and almond tart was Sylvia's offering, and she was easily distracted. My arrival had been a major distraction. 'It was lovely though,' I lied.

'I think I might have added the sugar twice,' Sylvia laughed. 'It is rather sweet, isn't it?'

'Well I like it,' said Tamsin, helping herself to another slice.

'I'll make the coffee,' said Michael, squeezing Sylvia's hand and turning his attention to the espresso machine. It was the only contemporary touch in the Victorian kitchen. High ceiling the colour of nicotine, the walls arsenic green, a vast utilitarian pine dresser occupying the whole of one wall and an antique Rayburn roasting off the spring chill. Complete antithesis of the hygienic brushed steel of my London home, with my unappetising and uneaten microwave meals.

For a moment, despite the sugar overload, I felt a surge of happiness.

Then Sylvia said, 'We've been terribly worried about you, you know. The things that man put you through!'

I squirmed, recalling my last conversation with a disintegrating Leo. Surely the issue was what I'd put him through.

'Abandoning you for that – that hussy!'

I laughed. 'Oh, you mean Peter.'

'He's a bastard, he really is. I told Sarah to cut his balls off if she sees him.'

'Oh Mum!' complained Tamsin.

'Well why not? Men are all shits, the lot of them.'

I smiled at Michael, as he reached for four mugs, his brows raised in benign exasperation. 'Does she allow any exceptions?'

'No, but she can't afford to throw me out.'

Sylvia sighed. 'It's true. If it weren't for his money, he'd be living in the dog kennel.'

Tamsin glanced at me, screwing a finger into her forehead. 'Totally gaga, both of them.'

'It's the only way to be,' I said. Totally gaga in their sweet way, not in mine.

'You don't have to be mad to work here, but it helps,' said Sylvia. 'But poor you, all that trouble at work as well. What on earth was that Mardell man up to? So horrible for you, the police and all that. I know just what it's like, you know. They won't let go, they want to nose into everything, you don't have any privacy left.'

She was speaking from experience. Her ex-husband Ken was a crook too, but proficient with it. Leo had simply been foolish, one rash mistake compounded by the next, until he had no way out, whereas Ken was a dedicated professional. Sylvia had been married to him for eighteen years, never suspecting a thing, until the fraud squad descended on their home.

'It wasn't that bad for me,' I reassured her. 'I'd only been there a couple of months. They gave me a clean bill of health.'

'So I should think! The brutes. Of course you couldn't possibly have been involved.'

The disorientation at the moment of Leo's death swept back over me. That was involvement, Sylvia. As deep as it could get.

'Kate.' I found Michael watching me, his eyes expressing quiet sympathy. 'Black. You don't take sugar, do you?'

'No.' We shared a grimace.

He handed me a cup of pure caffeine to wash away the cloying sweetness of the tart and the bile of guilt. 'Just so you can relax, we're completely legal here. That's probably the best that can be said of us. We're chaotic, impractical and impossible, but we are strictly legal.'

I laughed. 'I'm sure.'

'And Kate will sort it all out,' said Sylvia, reaching round the table to hug me. 'You're so clever. And you're to leave all that horrible stuff behind.'

'I already have,' I promised. 'I've cast anchor and set sail, utterly free.'

Michael gave me a wry smile. He too had cast anchor and sailed away from everything; career, home, the life he'd built with his wife Annette, before cancer claimed her. But he'd cut the ties because there was nothing left to stay for.

'Anyway.' Tamsin scraped back her chair. 'Got to go.'

'Lots of texting to do?' suggested Sylvia.

'Since you haven't got broadband…,' With a pointed sigh, she trailed from the room.

Sylvia beamed after her. 'Kids, eh. Love 'em or loathe 'em, you can't live without them.'

There was a moment of mutual cringing as the casual

comment hit all three of us in different ways.

'Oh God,' said Sylvia. 'My big mouth. Get the brandy, Mike.'

Michael fetched the bottle from the battered dresser. 'Not for me.' He gave her a quick kiss. 'I'll take my coffee out to the workshop, leave you two to catch up.'

'You're a good dog,' Sylvia whispered.

'Woof.'

She leaned back and poured the cognac. 'Come on, let's drown our sorrows together and compare notes. Talk about the shits who've wrecked our lives.'

I looked at her, astonished, my thoughts still focused on the kids we couldn't live without. Her son Christian was the monster in her life, but I'd never heard her admit it before. How many times had I wished she could live without him?

'Husbands!' said Sylvia. 'String up the lot of them, I say.'

Ah yes, husbands. A much safer target for our coconut shy. I smiled. 'But we're not letting husbands wreck our lives, are we, Syl? Ken really was a shit, I grant you, but you're rid of him, and you've got Michael now. If you dare call him a shit, I'll fight you.'

She laughed. 'Mike's a darling. I don't know how I'd have coped without him. I don't deserve him. And his kids are such unspeakable beasts to him, it isn't fair. But Mike's one in a million. Let's face it, they're mostly like curdling Ken and poisonous Pete.'

'No. Please. Peter isn't poisonous. It didn't work out between us, that's all. At least as much my fault as his.'

'How can you say that? He ran off with his bloody secretary!'

'Gabrielle was his colleague, Sylvia, not his secretary, and truthfully, it really didn't matter that much.'

Sylvia glared. 'Yes it did! I'm not having you meekly

16

turning the other cheek!'

I didn't think I was, but of course Peter's dalliance struck her as the worst of sins, after what she'd been through with Ken. It hadn't been the law suits or the criminal charges that had wounded her. It had been the discovery of three mistresses. Three. Her divorce had been unpleasant and hysterical and she was still fighting Ken a decade on.

Peter's affair was such a tame little thing, and though it had hurt me, it merely put the seal on damage already done. 'We both had a lot to forgive. Peter's a lovely man, just not for me. We were in trouble long ago and Gabrielle was his way out. We'd already come apart.'

'Oh.' Her face crumpled with pain. 'Oh Kate. Not because of the baby.'

'Don't.' I raised a hand. 'Don't go there. Please.'

Eyes brimming with tears, she came round and hugged me. 'Not another word.'

'And no more being beastly to Peter?'

'Maybe a little bit. But no wax dolls and hot pins, I promise.'

Silence. No traffic. Someone screamed out there in the darkness, but Sylvia had warned me about foxes. I could cope with foxes. I sat on my bed, endlessly rearranging jumpers, underwear, makeup, pretending I was unpacking. Thinking. One thing my long chat with Sylvia had confirmed; I really didn't hate Peter.

We'd agreed to part, he'd gone to Gabrielle, I'd packed up his CDs. It hadn't been the most civilised of partings, but it hadn't been the most acrimonious, either. I had loved him once. Perhaps, in a mortifying way, I still did.

My phone began to drone. I flicked it open. Peter. On cue.

17

He was talking before I could say a word. 'Kate? What's happening? Are you okay? You're at Sylvia's, is that right? Sarah told me.'

Of course Sarah had told him. Sylvia's elder daughter, my very good friend, and wife of Peter's buddy Phil. My marital breakup created all manner of complications in our incestuous circle.

'I don't get it,' said Peter. 'Why didn't you tell me?'

'Hello Peter,' I said.

'You just upped and went? The house is on the market. What's going on? I thought you were looking for a new job. Partington's said they wanted you, and then there you were, gone. Why didn't you tell me?'

'I thought the deal was we didn't have to tell each other anything, anymore.'

'Oh, Kate. Don't be like that. You know I still worry about you.'

'Why on earth should you worry? Am I ill?'

A brief hesitation. 'No, of course not. But this move – it's just a visit, right?'

'No, I've gone into partnership with Sylvia and Mike. And what are you doing these days, Peter? Still setting the economy to rights? Do keep in touch occasionally. I'm sure I'll follow your career with interest.'

'All right, I deserve it. But you should have told me you were going to run away to the back of beyond.'

'I didn't run away, thank you. Where I choose to live and work now is my business.'

'But you could still have—'

I could hear the voice in the background. 'Petey darling, don't be all night.'

I could tell he had his hand over the phone, before coming back to me, his voice lowered. 'Look, Kate, I can't—'

I switched the phone off in mid-sentence and returned

it to my bag.

Okay, so maybe it wasn't love I still felt for him. But I really didn't wish him ill. I was just better off alone. No one to love, no one to hate. I was fine.

Outside, in the darkness, an owl hooted derision.

3

No!

I didn't hear the word, but I felt it, pushing me out of the cramped attic room, with its leaking dormer window among the chimney pots.

I'd been waiting for some shadow to spring out on me throughout our tour of inspection, as Sylvia led me up staircases, down corridors, through one derelict room after another, but this, high up under the eaves, was the first sense of death and dark emotion I'd felt. There was fear in this garret, and a lingering misery, but mostly there was a strident, fierce defiance, determined to push me out.

No!

So I pushed back, and followed Sylvia in.

I'd done it. I'd conquered. Not so difficult after all. I just had to be strong. It was still there, that melting pot of misery and resistance, but I could put it firmly to one side.

'…and perhaps the guttering.' While vanquishing my shadows, Sylvia was considering the large blooms of damp on the sloping ceiling. She looked at me anxiously. 'Could we?'

'Sure!' I felt absurdly all-conquering. 'Nothing to worry about.' I followed her, gleeful in my triumph, back down servants' stairs to the ground floor.

She flung open double doors. 'Ta-Ra! The drawing room. It's the only one we've seriously tackled so far. What do you think?'

'Hey.' I could see why the room had inspired her into action. It was all mock-medieval plasterwork, with a Gothic fireplace and touches of stained glass in the tall arched windows that opened onto the terrace. Sylvia had decked it out with William Morris wallpaper, a chaise longue upholstered in faded red velvet, an Oriental rug and a brass oil-lamp with Tiffany shade. The sagging 1950s sofa and the Ikea futon slightly dampened the effect, but it was hard not to be impressed.

'Wonderful. Creative. Just right.' I reeled off compliments. It certainly demonstrated the potential of the place. Every other room merely screamed 'Rewiring! Dry rot! Woodworm!'

'I love it,' said Sylvia. 'Well, I think that's it here. Now come outside.'

In the entrance hall, with its patterned tiles and mock-Tudor staircase, we struggled with the bolts of the towering front door, and emerged into the rinsing chill of a spring morning. Tissues of mist were clearing from the tree tops and the distant fields were already free from frost, though the sloping pasture below us was still crystalline grey.

From a mossy balustrade with crumbling urns, I surveyed the house. Solid Victorian, with heavy-handed touches of Gothic Revival; a pointed window here and there, a gargoyle or two, writhing vines on the woodwork.

'We were so lucky to find it,' said Sylvia happily.

'You'd have thought developers would have snapped it up, wouldn't you? But we just happened to be in the right place at the right time. An elderly spinster lived here for decades, in a couple of rooms downstairs, poor thing. That's how it got so run down. When it went up for auction, I expect most people were put off by the amount of work it needs. Listed building and all that.'

'But you and Mike didn't mind?'

'Of course not! I know there's masses to do, but it's such a dream and we've got money between us. Not endless money but you know, if we manage it carefully.'

I laughed. If Michael managed it carefully. Sylvia had never managed anything carefully in her life, least of all money.

'And if we can get the easy bits up and running, like the lodge, well, it will just pay for itself, won't it?'

I doubted it, but practicalities could come later.

'Of course it's a gamble,' she went on. 'But we both fell helplessly head over heels in love with it as soon as we saw it. And it does have incredible possibilities, doesn't it?'

'Oh God, yes.' If the initial financial nightmares could be sorted out. That was where I came in. Nothing like a challenge.

'Obviously guests,' Sylvia took my arm and led me along, scrunching on gravel. 'Music festivals perhaps. And a restaurant. You know, local organic produce, and our own herbs and vegetables. Themed weekends.'

We reached the end of the terrace. 'And of course this is the real pièce de résistance.'

I jumped. There had been something so comfortably bourgeois about the Victorian façade that I was unprepared for what lay round the corner. The remnant of an old house. Much older, crouching behind the new.

Nothing fake about this Gothic. Crumbling stonework, sagging beams, a small bush sprouting from a chimney.

'What do you think?' asked Sylvia, gleefully. 'I could have taken you in through the boot room, but it's so much more dramatic from this angle. Isn't it incredible?'

I stared into the darkness behind crooked mullioned windows. My victory over an odd twinge in a servant's attic was forgotten. This was altogether more forbidding. There were centuries upon centuries fossilised here.

'A pity there's so little of it,' Sylvia continued. 'Not much more than a hall, really, with a minstrel's gallery. Oh, *and* there's a dungeon. With a spiral stair! Lord knows how old it is. Mike's researched it all, says it was already here in 1540. The rest of the house was demolished and rebuilt in Queen Anne's time, and then again in Eighteen something.' She patted the neat Victorian stonework as we passed.

I shivered. Hardly surprising with the frost still intact on the shaded gravel. Shiver with cold if I must, but it was absurd to shiver because of what might lie within.

There might be nothing.

Then again… Dungeons, Sylvia said. I'd dealt with an attic. Did I really have to deal with a dungeon too, on my first day?

Yes, apparently. Sylvia turned the iron handle on the grey, studded, plank door. I took a deep breath and followed her inside.

Nothing seemed to have been touched here for centuries. Worn stone flags, huge beams smudged with cobwebs, tall leaded windows, a wide, arched fireplace.

The once noble hall was now just a barn. Mouldering harnesses and farm implements hung from the rafters, and a section of the roof had been patched with corrugated iron. Shrouded with dusty sacking, the lower walls were panelled, carving quietly rotting in its frames.

'Mike's working on this.' Sylvia's hand left a black print on one worm-eaten panel. 'Linenfold. He's using all the old techniques so that he can do a genuine job. A lot of it is salvageable, but some bits are just falling to pieces.'

'So I can see.' My voice echoed back at me.

'Criminal, isn't it? But can't you just see what we could do with the place? Elizabethan banquets. Wedding receptions.' Sylvia waved her arms to encompass the magnificence of her vision.

'Oh definitely.' Generations of memories were sealed into these walls, and somewhere in those memories there had to be nightmares, but Sylvia wanted banquets.

She climbed a stone stair to a creaking gallery at the end of the hall. 'And musicians up here. Harps and psalteries! What is a psaltery?'

The gallery, far too narrow for musicians, gave access to an upper chamber. I followed, ready for whatever might lie through the stone arch.

Ruin and decay. Nature had reclaimed any grandeur. Torn plastic was pinned over the remains of an ornate window and sodden boards patched gaping holes in the roof. Wind and rain had wrecked the place, rotting the woodwork, devouring the stone, dissolving traces of decorative plaster.

'I could weep,' said Sylvia, testing the rotten boards, cautiously, with one toe. 'So much work needed, but we're still waiting for an assessment. And of course you can't rush in and do what you like with a listed building. There are so many hoops to jump through.'

Her despondency lasted five seconds, then reverted to bouncy enthusiasm. 'Oh but come and see the dungeon.'

Down in the hall, we passed through one of two doors under the upper chamber into a small, low room.

'The buttery,' said Sylvia. 'Every hall would have had one, so I'm calling this the buttery. Would it be where they kept butter? I have no idea, but I like the name.' She opened another narrow door to the side. 'Be careful, it's dark.'

I peered down a spiral staircase. Sylvia unhooked a torch, hanging by the door. 'Watch your feet. It's a bit uneven.'

I groped the cold stonework for support and forced myself to follow. At the bottom, Sylvia grinned back at me, her upturned face ghoulishly underlit. 'Creepy, isn't it?'

'Very,' I agreed, heaving relief that I felt nothing worse than a twinge of claustrophobia. We were in a low undercroft, with an earthen floor. Barrel vaulting dripped minute stalactites of oozing lime.

'Oo-er,' she whispered. 'Imagine the poor prisoners chained up down here.'

I was fairly certain nothing had ever been kept there except barrels of beer and sacks of grain, but I was willing to play along. 'Don't tell me, a reconstructed torture chamber?'

Sylvia whooped with delight. 'Wouldn't it be wonderful?'

'Somewhere to send wedding guests if they get too rowdy?'

'Of course! Frighten them into sobriety. Because it must be haunted. Is it haunted, Kate?' She clapped her hands, like a child wanting ice-cream. 'Oh please, please say there's a ghost down here.'

'There's a ghost down here.'

'No seriously, please tell me. You'd sense one, I

know.'

What the hell. I closed my eyes solemnly. 'I detect – a definite shiver of fear.'

'Is that all? I was hoping for a white lady. If only we had battlements. I'm sure we'd have had a white lady, walking in the moonlight.'

'Perhaps we can persuade one to move in.'

'Yes!' Sylvia gripped my arm. 'A ghost hotel! We could get a licence to serve spirits!'

We were still laughing as we climbed back to the buttery. To finish, she led me on into the second small room, under the upper chamber.

As before, a low square room. One tiny window, two doors, stained walls, stone floor, just another empty room. 'Not sure what to call this one,' babbled my cousin. 'Think of a good name. The armoury! I wonder if we could get a suit of armour.' She was already opening the far door, into a panelled arch through deep masonry back into the Great Hall.

Just a doorway to Sylvia.

But not to me. Oh God, not to me.

'Come on,' she sang. 'Where next?'

I watched her pass through, amazed that she could sense nothing. Rigid in my determination to conquer, I followed her, trying to block out the shadow, to refuse it entry into my brain.

I couldn't. It overwhelmed my defences, enveloping me in a black cloud. Huge atavistic fear, searing thirst, gut-wrenching despair. I could feel the interweaving strands of emotion like filaments of rot, tightening around me, meshing in my lungs, my veins, my bones. How could Sylvia possibly not feel this?

I lurched for the open space beyond and swallowed my nausea, forcing my fists to unlock, my pulse to slow.

'Fascinating place,' I said, before Sylvia could comment. My voice was totally calm. 'I can see why you were captivated by it.'

'It could be a gold mine, don't you think?' She was utterly oblivious, because I'd had years of practice, learning how to show nothing. All I needed to learn now was how to feel nothing. It wasn't going to happen. I'd never learn to block out something this terrible.

'It has so much to offer,' continued Sylvia. 'We could do wonders.'

The hair still prickling on the nape of my neck, I followed her out into the chill relief of the open air. Outside was safe. No echoes, just cleansing wind, washing round the tumbled walls of an abandoned kitchen garden.

'I'm going to have all this for herbs.' Sylvia was off again, amidst a sea of last year's nettles. 'Isn't that a good idea? ... old recipes ... herbal remedies ... alternative medicine centre ... aromatherapy ... wine...,'

She chattered on while I was still struggling with the dark anguish behind us. No! I forced myself to tune in again to her enthusiasm.

'...yes I know that elderflower was awful, I don't know what went wrong, but Mike could do it, chemistry and all that. Oh, and there's a real well. Look.' She heaved at corrugated iron, on which "Caution!" had been scrawled in yellow paint.

I helped her shift the sheet, and found myself staring down into an abyss. Masonry, green with slime and sprouting ferns, descended into blackness. A pebble broke loose and clattered for a moment, finishing with an echoing splash.

I pulled back sharply.

'What is it?' Sylvia looked up, all consternation. 'Oh Kate, how awful! You're sensing something, aren't you?'

'Yes! A bloody big hole and I don't want to fall down it.'

'I thought, a ghost or something? It would be horrible if something nasty had happened here. Anyway, where next?' She turned to get her bearings, spoilt for choice. 'The orchard – oh I must restore that. Medlars and quinces and so on, you know. And there's a row of cottages through there – well, a couple are still habitable, so we can do them up, like the lodge, for holiday lets. And the pasture, down to the road. Dewi rents it at the moment but I was thinking, Jacobs sheep. And wild boar. Alpaca! But you must come and see the workshops at the back. You know, for a proper craft centre. We're a start, me and Mike. If we could get some others, basket makers and things like that – I'll show you. Let me think, what's quicker? Through the woods, or back through the old house—'

'The woods,' I said. 'I'm enjoying the fresh air.'

'Oh yes. The woods. I get hopelessly lost in there. Mike had to come and rescue me once.' Sylvia opened a gate at the top of the walled garden and we passed through, following one of the many tracks that wound between tangled oaks and holly and mossy boulders.

In a clearing, a sculpture, ten feet tall, perched on a rock over us. Glad to have something to distract me, I stopped to look at it. A reach of gnarled bough, transformed into an abstract image of soaring flight. 'Michael's? It's a falcon, isn't it?'

'Yes! That one's called "Windhover". He's put his pieces all over the place. That's what's so wonderful. Llys y Garn is just perfect for them, isn't it?'

She was right. Michael made a living, these days,

producing exquisitely crafted furniture, but his real delight lay in these massive chain-saw sculptures. I'd seen a couple before, in the tame surroundings of a Home Counties park, but out here, among the rocks and the trees of their origin, they came into their own, organic and complete.

'Hello.' Michael appeared, coming down from the woods, a freshly discovered length of wood in his hand. 'Doing the tour?'

'I've barely shown Kate half of it.' Sylvia bounded to him? 'What's that, darling? What's it going to be?'

Michael turned the piece of wood against the light, exploring its angles. 'I haven't decided yet. It will tell me when it's ready.'

Looking from the yearning sculpture, liberated on its rock, to Michael, studying wood for a spirit within that only he could feel, I understood why he'd risked the mockery of colleagues and his children's wrath, to follow his true calling, out here in the forsaken wilds. Perhaps his enthusiasm for this place really was as strong as Sylvia's, if more muted in its expression.

'You can show Kate our workshops, while I make a start on lunch,' she said, giving him a hug, which he returned with a peck on her cheek, holding his new find aside to avoid impaling her.

He smiled at me, as she skipped off. 'What do you make of it so far, Kate?'

I fell in beside him. 'It certainly is a huge undertaking.'

Michael chuckled. 'Sylvia wants solar panels, but she generates all the energy we need, don't you think? And the ideas, of course.' We were strolling towards the estate buildings whose backs lined the drive.

'Let me guess.' I peered into a two-storey coach house, currently housing crates and a wrecked tractor.

28

'Shop? Art gallery?'

'I believe so.' Michael smiled. 'Do you think you can manage all this, Kate? It's a monster, I know.'

'Can I rely on your backing? You know how business works. Sylvia believes the fairies do it all.'

'I never have the heart to rein her in. But you'll make it work for her. Here's her pottery.' He opened the door of the first workshop, with kiln and wheel, shelves laden with glazes, clay splattered on the stone walls and the concrete floor. Sylvia had dabbled with ceramics during her housewife years and after the divorce she had taken it up more seriously, almost making money.

'She's loving it here, isn't she,' I said.

'I hope so,' said Michael. He gazed fondly round the chaos.

'Thanks for all you've done for her.' We moved on to his workshop, rich with the scent of resin and fragrant wood chippings. 'She had such a shit time with Ken, but you've made her shine again.'

He looked embarrassed. 'I'm the one to be grateful, for what she's done for me.'

I thought of his widowhood, the awful nightmare of watching a wife slowly die. 'You must have been through hell,' I said.

'Yes, I got very low. Rock bottom.' He drew breath, then shrugged off the memories. 'But Sylvia pulled me up again, into the light. If she shines, she shines on me.' His glance fell on another of his sculptures, perched in the trees above his workshop.

I looked up at it, an arcing, leaping form. A hare? High-kicking, joyful chaos. I hugged Michael's free arm, laughing. 'It's Sylvia!'

Michael smiled.

The hare and the windhover. Joyous release was what Llys y Garn meant to them. The horror in the Great Hall came back to me, the hopeless sense of release denied, like a negative image of their affectionate delight. But I was going to fight it, and somehow I was going to clamber up onto that liberated plane with Sylvia and Michael. Until then, I dreaded to think what sculptural form my spirit would take.

4

Llys y Garn now had an office. It was the former library, adjoining the drawing room. Some of the lofty bookcases remained, but in place of antique volumes in hand-tooled calf-hide, mahogany desks and padded armchairs, I had box files, a computer – with broadband – and a telephone.

When it rang, I rushed to it, praying that one of the fifty builders I'd contacted was getting back to me, offering a date earlier than August. My first business goal had been to get the lodge cottage up and ready for letting by Whitsun, but our efforts with paint stripper and Polyfilla were going to be wasted without some professional input. Surely someone was available.

'Good morning. Llys y Garn Enterprises. Can—'

'Give me Chris.' The voice was deep and aggressive.

'Chris?'

'Yeah. Chris. Get him.'

'I'm sorry, you must have the wrong number.'

'Chris Callister.' He slowly enunciated each syllable. 'Tell him Tyro wants him. Now.'

'I'm afraid that isn't possible. Christian doesn't actually live here. This is his mother's house.'

A wheeze of sinister mockery. '*Actually*. His mother, eh? Then tell her—'

'Mr Callister isn't here, hasn't visited for months, and I have no idea where he is. London, probably. If you have any other contact numbers for him, I suggest you try those. Good morning.'

I put the phone down, ordering myself to laugh. Tyro. The name suggested a pantomime villain, but pantomimes involving my nephew Christian were never entertaining. I didn't want him or his sinister contacts anywhere near Llys y Garn. The idea that they had our number was enough to make me uneasy. For the first time, the isolation of the property unnerved me.

I was alone in the house, for once. Sylvia and Michael were delivering a consignment of pottery pigs and candle-snuffers to a shop in Pembroke, leaving me to hunt for stray receipts and builders.

There could be people out there, prowling in the woods, creeping up to the house, and what could I do about it? For that matter, they could be in the house, and I'd never know. There could be an army of Christian's underworld friends or enemies loping around its labyrinthine ways, slithering up to the office door…

The growl of a vehicle, turning in at the lodge, had my pulse quickening. Calm. It was probably Sylvia and Michael returning. But instead of rumbling on up the track, the engine stopped and a distant door slammed. I forced myself to laugh at my own fears, and marched resolutely down the long drive, to investigate.

A Land Rover was parked up by the open lodge door. I'd seen that Land Rover before. I recognised the owl painted on the door. It, and a garishly decorated campervan, had been standing outside a house down the valley, where a bunch of grubby, New Age travellers, in

31

patched leather jerkins and dreadlocks, had been repairing a porch.

Odd-job men. Builders, of sorts.

'Hello?' I looked into the lodge and called, in a tone of neutral authority. 'Someone here looking for me?'

A figure ducked under the kitchen lintel. 'Hi, I'm Al Taverner.' He proffered a hand in greeting. 'Sylvia asked me to do some work here.'

'She did?' I swallowed my exasperation with my cousin. 'She must have forgotten to mention it.'

'Well, she was just on her way to Pembroke, so maybe she didn't have time.'

'She asked you this morning? What about the Old Rectory? Weren't you working there?'

'Just finished.' He grinned. 'She caught us as we were packing up. Said we could come straight here. Gave us the key. Sounded pretty keen for us to get started.'

'Well… yes.'

'The others will be here soon. I was just taking a look at the work needed. Should be simple enough. No load-bearing walls involved, and the stonework's good. Sorry, and you are?'

'Kate Lawrence. Sylvia's cousin.'

'Nice to meet you.'

'And you.' A polite nothing, but it was, I discovered, quite true. Very nice to meet him. An eccentric wardrobe, maybe, even a hint of beads, but nothing remotely unsavoury. He was shaggy in a romantic, Cavalier way. Thirtyish, I guessed; not much younger than me. Long legs. Eyes to die for.

There it was. I found him attractive. Astonishing. It had been a long time since I'd allowed such feelings in. So I was still alive then.

Al was nursing an iPad, which didn't quite match the hippy image. 'So you're planning quite an enterprise here. Holiday cottages, crafts, rare breeds.'

'Sylvia told you her grand ideas.'

'She's a life-enhancing lady. Great aura. You can sense the life force in her. And in this place.' He thumped a lintel. 'Good vibes.' He caught me looking at him dubiously. 'Nice atmosphere,' he corrected.

'As long as holidaymakers think so.'

'They'll love it.'

'Well, I'm sure you can bring it up to standard.' Doubts had strangely evaporated. Al and his crew would be quite sufficient for our needs.

Whatever those needs were. I was amused and embarrassed by the warmth of my response, but what the hell. Peter and I were separated. Why shouldn't my libido assert itself again?

On the other hand, all that New Age gibberish about auras and vibes and feeling the force was discomforting. Llys y Garn already had a resident weirdo. It didn't need more.

The campervan, towing a clattering trailer, arrived and Al's gang emerged, just as I remembered them – grimy, hairy and generally suspect. Not in the same league, but then one has to take the rough with the smooth. The very smooth.

There was a burly stone mason called Thor, and a whiskery plumber called Nathan. A gangly, unfocussed youth, Pryderi, was something unspecified. Hod carrier, maybe. I understood there would have been more but Tim and Baggy and Gary were 'doing stuff' elsewhere and Joe and Padrig were hiking in Peru. Of course they were. There were two women, as well – Molly, a shamanesque earth mother in henna and beads and Kim, a waif with nose studs and a penny whistle. Neither were geared for heavy labour, so I guessed this alternative company wasn't quite so alternative in some

33

respects.

When Sylvia and Michael rolled up a few minutes later, Sylvia bounced out as if the circus had arrived in town. 'Oh wonderful, you found us. Now Al, do you think it will be all right? Have you looked up in the woods yet? For your camp? That's if you really want to. If you prefer to stay in the house, we have plenty of room—'

'A place to camp will be great,' said Al. 'We'll take a look around later.' He shook hands with Michael. 'You must be the artist.'

Michael chuckled. 'Joiner, maybe.'

'Artist!' insisted Sylvia. 'He's a genius, really. Now, you can camp anywhere you like. Absolutely anywhere. Don't worry about thinning out the undergrowth. It needs it anyway.'

'Excuse me, they're camping here?' I asked, because it was nice to be kept informed.

'Oh yes, well of course, why not?' Sylvia beamed. 'We have so much space.'

'They have a yurt,' Michael whispered in my ear.

'I should have guessed.'

'What will you do about water?' Sylvia was rubbing her hands. 'There's a tap—'

'Al said there's a stream,' said Molly. 'That's all we need. Earth, water and air.'

'What about fire?' I asked.

'We provide the sacred fire,' said Molly. Definitely a priestess.

'As long as you don't set the woods ablaze.'

'We do no harm,' said Molly. 'We honour the spirit in the trees.'

'But that's lovely,' said Sylvia. 'Worshipping trees rather than Mammon.'

'We don't worship trees,' said Molly. 'We worship

34

the spirit in them, in all things.'

'And so we should,' agreed Sylvia, promptly. 'The world would be much better if we could only feel the spirit. Kate knows better than anyone. She feels it all the time.'

I cringed.

'You feel things, don't you, ghosts and so on.'

Silent mind-control failed to shut her up, so I had to speak. 'What Sylvia means is that I sometimes have a feeling for atmosphere. Sort of feng shui. Like the lodge here. A lovely atmosphere, isn't it?'

They all agreed that it was very positive.

'It's a great relief,' said Sylvia. 'Because Kate feels quite weird things sometimes. If something awful has happened, you know. And I'm so glad nothing really horrible has ever happened at Llys y Garn.'

She was looking at the others, so she remained immune to my glare.

Al considered me, quizzically. 'You feel things? You pick up the vibes?'

'Oh, yes,' said Sylvia. 'Like that poor old man who burned...,' She caught my expression, at last, and hugged me contritely. 'I'm sorry, oh so sorry, darling. Kate hates to talk about all that.'

The gang regarded me with hungry interest. Michael, too, studied me with a puzzled smile, unacquainted with family gossip. As a corkscrew worked its way through my innards, I smiled with tolerant exasperation.

'What, you some kind of, like, medium?' asked Pryderi, aroused almost to animation.

'No. Sorry. I don't see ghosts; I don't talk to spirits; I can't tell the future. Feeling a place is nice or nasty is just about it. Lunch, anyone?'

Everyone seemed satisfied. As we trooped up to the big house, they turned to more mundane topics; the proper construction of yurts, the work needed on the lodge, recipes for sesame seeds, the correct use of the pole lathe...

I followed, trying to empty my mind of the sickening images Sylvia had resurrected. Apart from that unguarded faintness at the moment of Leo's suicide, I had learned to conceal my demonic feelings, but I hadn't possessed the same skill at the age of eight, when our old neighbour died in a fire. My response had been so obvious, the whole world knew about it. Sylvia learned that something very shocking and uncanny had happened, that I'd had a horrible time and I was terribly upset. She didn't know about all the guilt and fear, the bullying and shouting, the nightmares and bedwetting – and I was determined that she never would. Which I'd manage more easily if Sylvia stayed off the subject. The trouble with eternal buoyancy is that it has a very short memory.

When everyone finished the lunch Sylvia managed to conjure up out of nothing, I left them to inspect the workshops. I needed time and space to forgive her. I allowed myself one revenge bite, though, when she returned with Michael.

'Thanks for arranging builders for the lodge. I'll cancel the ones I called, shall I?'

'Oh. Oh! Oh dear, had you found someone else? I thought you were having so much trouble getting anyone – and there they were, ready to start.'

'You checked their references, of course?'

'Well, you know, Meg says they're just wonderful. And aren't they lovely? They have this wonderful idea of building a round house, you know, like an African hut, sort of thing, like they had in the Stone Age—'

'Iron Age,' amended Michael.

'Al's always wanted to try and this place is just

perfect, so it's working wonderfully for all of us. Can you just imagine? A thatched house up in the woods, with wattle and daub and hand-woven blankets and everyone round the fire eating wild boar. You know I had plans for wild boar, so we'd have a market on our doorstep.'

Michael laughed. 'Sylvia, if you kept wild boar, you know perfectly well you'd never let anyone eat them. Remember the chickens?'

'Oh but – yes well. We did start off with some chickens,' Sylvia explained. 'Sweet little things. I only wanted them for eggs.'

'So we didn't eat them, the fox did,' said Michael 'It killed two, and Syl was beside herself, so I bought a shotgun.'

'Ha!' said Sylvia.

He drew her into a hug. 'And then she wouldn't speak to me for two days, because I shot at the fox.'

'Butcher! It probably had cubs, poor thing.'

'I missed! And then the poor little fox ate the rest of the poor little chickens.'

'Oh dear.' I laughed, cruelly.

Sylvia sighed, then added brightly, 'Anyway, I'm sure Al's people are all vegetarians. And now we'll have the lodge ready, so everything's wonderful, isn't it?'

5

'Morning, Kate.' Al appeared at the kitchen door as I washed up the breakfast things. 'Michael asked me to take a look at the house. Extra work?'

'As much as you want.' I wiped my hands. 'Come in and I'll show you round.'

We examined the sagging plasterwork of a parlour and continued through to the dining room, with its pervasive perfume of damp.

'It's an incredible place.' Al strolled to the window to look out across the terrace, over the deep blue of the valley to the sea-brightened sky. A faint whine of distant traffic and the chug and clank of a tractor in a field somewhere near, but otherwise silence. 'The force is really strong here.'

Yes, I could see him as a Jedi knight. 'I'm sure it is.'

Al glanced at me sidelong. 'So you sense something else?'

'Oh.' I closed my eyes. 'Dear Sylvia.'

'Did she really get it wrong?'

'You must realise she likes to colour things.'

'Nothing wrong with that.'

'But she wants me shocking pink and I'm really only beige.'

Al laughed, eying me up and down. 'Beige you are not. So how is it? What do you feel?'

'All right. I feel death. That's what it seems to be. People dying, places where people have died, stuff that gets left behind when people have gone.'

Al stroked the back of his head.

'You're supposed to say I'm deranged.'

'No, no. It makes sense.'

'Does it? I wish it did to me. Why me? Do you have an answer? I'll believe anything that offers some sort of explanation.'

'Perhaps you're simply more receptive. Like having an ear for music. You're attuned to the life force. It's there, whether we acknowledge it or not, around us and in us. We die but the force remains. It has to go

38

somewhere.'

'It isn't life force I feel, though. It's the negative stuff. The overwhelming emotions that scream out, they're so violent. I feel people's misery while they die and then they're out of it, but I'm left with it, trapped, like radio waves that can't get out, can't just disperse on the ether, or whatever it is that radio waves do.'

'They propagate.'

'Well death horrors don't. They stagnate. And I get them in the gut.'

'And you've had to live with this, all your life?' He winced. I wasn't used to empathy.

I hesitated. I hadn't lived with it all my life, not quite. 'Ever since my father died. Which is as good as all. I was only four.'

Only four and I hadn't felt him die, even though I'd been holding his hand. Very little makes sense at four, but I knew that Daddy lived in bed, and Mrs Coley, the horrible witch from next door came in to look after us while Mummy went out. I couldn't remember my father refusing to wake up when I pulled and shook him, but I could remember Mrs Coley yanking me away, shouting 'Stupid girl, let go of his hand. Can't you see he's dead?'

No, I couldn't see that he was dead, but after that, I seemed to see death everywhere. I'd scream if I had to go into that room where my father died. The breathless fading blur of death was always there for me now.

'It opened the door, triggered your native gift,' said Al. A gift! So maybe not so empathetic. 'It makes sense, when you think about it. All those electric impulses in our brains – they connect, they have to go somewhere, they get earthed into stuff, clinging on. We just need to learn to tune into them. Sometimes I think they get me too.'

39

My heart missed a beat.

'Sometimes, in old places, you know, centuries of thoughts, feelings, dramas. There has to be something captured there.'

'Vibes?'

He shrugged. 'What would you call them?'

'Shadows.'

'Okay, shadows. All we have to do is open ourselves up.'

'I don't want to open! I want to close. They're vile!'

'That's because you're only attuned to the negative, Kate.' He seemed excited by it. 'But there's the positive, too. Hundreds of years of positive emotions and energy, all around us.' He patted the chimney breast as if to lap it up. 'It's here. You just need to learn to feel it.'

For a moment I was captivated. Of course there must be the positive too. I just needed to reverse my polarities. Sylvia could be my sonic screwdriver, and if there were someone with whom I could share at last... The end of solitary confinement.

I knew how to find out.

'Building repairs first. Come on.' I led him back through the service rooms: laundry, dairy, butler's pantry, where we kept endless junk, a twin tub, the once-used shotgun in its locker, a moth-eaten stag's head. Al examined tilting lintels and creaking timbers, brandishing a retractable steel rule like a wizard's wand, thumping old plaster with an experienced fist.

'There's this too.' I opened the last, unassuming door. 'But we need permission to do anything in here, and it requires a bit more than painting and plastering.' Studiously controlled, I stepped out into the Great Hall.

Al followed, and looked around hungrily. 'Ah yes, the famous hall.'

I'd hoped to take him by surprise, but of course he'd known about it. all the time.

He strode to the centre and turned slowly, taking in the linenfold panelling, the mullioned windows, the gallery, the huge beams up in the cobwebs of the roof. 'Okay.' He crossed to the cavernous fireplace and looked up. 'Got jackdaws.' A muffled squawk, and ash twigs showered down on him.

He ducked back under the stone lintel and crouched down to examine the panelling. 'Incredible survival.'

'Michael's working on some replacement panels. Do you think you're up to any of the basics? If we are allowed to restore it, we'll probably have to get experts in for the major work.'

Al shot me a sideways glance of sardonic amusement.

'Unless you know anything about old restoration,' I amended.

He stood up, brushing himself down. 'You could say. I cut my teeth on a project like this, while I was at university.'

'Seriously? Studying mediaeval building?'

'Biochemistry. I took a labouring job in the vacation and worked on a moated manor in Leicestershire. That was when I decided craftsmanship was better for my soul.'

'So our little hall is no problem.'

'Mm.' He grinned apologetically. 'The moated manor belonged to a millionaire.'

'Well, we don't have limitless resources, but what with shares and divorce settlements and platinum handshakes, Sylvia and Mike aren't paupers. Can you give us a vague idea of costs?'

'I reckon I could. How much of it is there?'

'This is about all that's left of the old house. There are those two rooms at the end and a cellar below us;

Sylvia thinks it's a dungeon. The bit up on the gallery is in a really bad way. I'm not sure anything up there can be salvaged.'

Al bounded up the stone stairs. I watched him peer into the upper room. He winced back down at me. 'Yip. Bad.'

'I'm convinced it's all going to crash down,' I said, as explanation for hanging back. He descended, entered the buttery, testing the low ceiling, then vanished from view. A few moments later he emerged from the dark panelled doorway of the empty armoury, the doorway that, to me, swam with horror.

He stood beside me, looking around, chewing his lip, in calculation I assumed. Then he said, 'There's something here, isn't there?'

I'd remained motionless, while he carried out his inspection.

'I feel something,' he continued. 'You do too, don't you?'

Go on, I thought, tell me. Prove to me you really feel it.

'Definitely something not good,' he added. 'Has to have been a few bad things in a place this old.'

Oh yes, there was definitely 'something not good.' Since my arrival at Llys y Garn I'd been in the Great Hall several times, challenging myself to confront the demon in that low arch. Mostly I'd chickened out. Twice, I'd braced myself and gone through. The first time I'd managed one step before fleeing. The second time I'd stood there, trying to fight it, singing, shouting, determined to master it, emerging five minutes later drenched in sweat, to lunge for the garden door and throw up. Whatever had happened in that place, a hundred, a thousand years ago, it had been unspeakable and it was always going to conquer me.

This time, though, I'd stayed well clear, at the far end of the hall, and I was certain I'd done nothing to alert Al.

'You do get it, don't you?' he insisted.

'Maybe there's a hint of something. But it's been empty so long. The thing that really disturbs me is the thought of it all collapsing. Do you think you'd be able to make it safe?'

'Oh sure. Do more than that. Bring in the right guys.'

'Come and have a coffee then, while I tell Sylvia the good news.'

Sylvia was wild with joy. Naturally. How long would it be, I wondered, before I could absorb this ability to enthuse over everything? If I were negative, she was positive plus.

'Kate's been showing me some of the work needed in the house,' Al explained.

'An awful lot, isn't there?' said Sylvia, quite unperturbed. 'But it'll be wonderful if you really can restore the hall, when we get permission. You have no idea what complications there are.'

'I have.'

'And I was really hoping to have an Elizabethan Fayre there this summer.'

'Okay,' said Al.

Sylvia took it as a fairy-godfather promise. 'Oh isn't that wonderful? I know exactly what we'll need.'

I met Al's eyes while she reeled off costumes, crafts, recipes. Dour realism could wait.

'So, any idea of the age of the house?' asked Al, rocking back in his chair.

'Mentioned in Owen and there are sixteenth century records,' said Michael. He'd acknowledged Al's expertise without surprise. 'Almost certainly older though.'

'Sure. At least fifteenth century I'd guess.'

'Oh it must be older than that,' added Sylvia eagerly. 'Norman. Roman. Prehistoric! We have standing stones. Did you tell him about those, Kate?'

'We have standing stones,' I said.

'Oh yes, up on the moors,' burst in Sylvia. 'Just above us. Neolithic – or was it Bronze Age? And all manner of lumps and bumps in the fields.'

'How interested are you in lumps and bumps and standing stones?' I asked.

'Very interested,' replied Al. 'Care to show me some time?'

'Now if you like.'

'Oh yes, let's all go,' said Sylvia. 'It's lovely weather for a walk on the hills.'

Michael declined the offer, with work to do, but Sylvia was eagerly clambering into outdoor gear.

Of course I didn't object. Her presence would shield me from complications I wasn't ready to deal with yet. I needed space to think.

We followed a path through the woods, pausing for Al to admire one of Michael's sculptures. A contorted inward-leaning knot, without beginning, without end.

'I've found five so far.' I'd concluded that this one was an image of depression, but I said, 'This one's Office Politics.'

'Is it?' said Sylvia, stroking it fondly. 'I thought it was a snake.'

Al ran a craftsman's fingers along the grain. 'Same thing? I saw another, on the way up to our camp. The Mother Goddess?'

'Hooded lady,' I suggested.

Sylvia thought about it, frowning. 'Oh! The whale. I thought that one was a whale. Don't ask me why. Mike will never explain them. He says they should touch, not

44

tell.'

'I'm all for touching,' said Al, glancing my way.

'Here's the track!' Sylvia was always surprised when paths led where she'd hoped. 'Farm track, really. Watch for the mud. Dewi brings his cows along here. And the tractor sometimes, so it's a bit of a mess.'

We followed her along deep ruts, hopping from tussock to tussock, zigzagging up the steep hillside. Sylvia regaled us with gossip, questions, ideas and delight, monopolizing Al's attention. No matter.

We emerged eventually onto open upland. To our left the trees marched on, but to our right a cluster of pocket-sized fields were cupped in a web of stone walls and high banks.

'These are ours,' said Sylvia, pausing by a gate. Lumps and bumps as Sylvia had promised, scattered rocks and mounds of turf. 'These three fields. The ones beyond are Dewi's. That's his house down there: Hendre Hywel. He's a darling.'

The sagging slates of an old farmhouse were just visible, tucked under a protective cluster of rowans. Our nearest neighbour.

'We've been told this might be an old village or something,' explained Sylvia.

Al scrambled up onto the stone wall and surveyed the field, his eyes shaded. 'Could be round houses.'

'And you are going to build one. How marvellous! Making the past come alive. Wait till you see the stones. Kate's felt extraordinary things there.'

Oh God. What hogwash had I come up with? Warrior cries? Druidic fervour? The problem with a lifelong habit of lying was that I couldn't always remember what I'd said.

We tramped over heathery moorland. The clouds billowed and sagged, then split apart in the sharp wind, shreds of blue peering through. We were free of the valley, the world vast and open around us. The sea was a white shimmer under a white horizon.

The stones stood by a ridge-top bridle track on an outlier of the long ragged parade of the Preselis. My first sight of them had been disappointing. No awesome monoliths in the Stonehenge mould, no tool marks that I could see, no miraculous balancing. A couple of the jagged rocks might be considered upright. One of them topped six feet, the other was shorter and a few more were tumbled and propped against each other, or flat, or just mounds of peaty turf. It could have been a mere outcrop, like the tors that pierced the adjoining hills.

'Okay!' said Al.

'It's a genuine ancient monument,' explained Sylvia. 'On the map. It's called… oh, what's it called, Kate?'

'Bedd y Blaidd?' suggested Al.

'That's right,' said Sylvia. 'I can never remember. I was talking to Ronnie about it. Ronnie Pryce-Roberts, Fran Garrick's brother. He's a professor of archaeology and he was fascinated, quite certain it was enormously significant.'

'Yes, there's power here!' Al sprang onto the pile of rocks and stroked the taller of the standing stones. Were there forces throbbing through the creeping lichen? He was silhouetted against the white sky, locks of his long hair whipping in the wind. Heathcliff. Mm. And didn't he know it.

He looked down at me. 'You feel it, don't you? There's something here.'

I smiled, touching the rock. Such wonderful, cleansing emptiness. There was no emotion trapped here. If the stones had some mysterious cosmic power, it was not to preserve but to wipe clean. A lightning rod, earthing all passion and turmoil, drawing it down, out of life and light into all-dissolving magma.

So what was it that Al felt? Something positive that evaded me?

'It's a good place,' I agreed.

He jumped down. 'It's been a sacred place. Still is.'

Sylvia was delighted. 'How lovely! Like a church. Our own chapel. Aren't you glad you found a place to camp so near? Is it near? In the woods, down there, isn't it? Can we see the yurt? Please?'

'Sure.' Al took one last look at the stones, then surveyed the hillside below us. 'By the stream,' he said.

Below us, the woods dipped where the rills and gullies of the rain-sodden hills accumulated. The resulting stream eventually gurgled under the road a few yards beyond our lodge.

Al pointed out a likely route. 'That should take us in the right direction.'

We tramped down off the ridge and into the trees. Al stole a few glances back at me, but mostly he was occupied with Sylvia, helping her over steep rocks and reaching out a hand whenever the path turned slippery.

I shrugged. There would be other times.

Sweet Jesus!

It hit me, a black cloud of nausea.

How? This never happened in the open air. My nightmare required stifling walls to trap the horror. But that was what Nature had created here – an enclosed basin, backed by an overhanging crag of dripping rock. The steep slopes to either side were banked with trees, lowering, mossy, still bare, branches writhing and contorted – or was it just my revulsion that painted them so? The path descended into this pit and skirted a carpet of lurid green hummocks among black pools of glistening peat, to reach the rocky ravine where the stream escaped. The bleached branches of a fallen tree thrust out of the mire, sinking slowly into an opaque depth.

Suffocating fear. I couldn't escape it. Frenzy, panic and furious snarling animal anger, yes I could recognise all those. And something else, something overwhelming in its fierceness and I had no idea what it was, only that it was turning everything upside down.

I swallowed. For a moment I blanked out. When I refocused, there was Al ahead of me, deep in conversation with Sylvia on the subject of comfrey poultices.

Unaware. Totally unaware.

He felt nothing. In the old hall, it must have been my very stillness that prompted him to claim he detected something. He'd felt something among the standing stones, because Sylvia told him I'd done so. He was a charlatan, that was all there was to it. Just another fake.

No. I was unfair. It wasn't trickery on his part. It was wishful thinking. He wanted to feel. He wanted to believe there was something under the drab surface of life. Could I blame him, when he couldn't begin to understand what a curse it was?

'Watch out, Kate.' His voice was coming from another world. 'The track's slippery here. Do you want a hand?'

'Thanks.' I reached out, and he clasped my hand, supporting me as I clambered over the mossy rocks, away from that horror.

'Just down here,' he said. 'Not far now.'

I could smell wood smoke drifting up. Dissipating into nothingness, like my hope of finding a kindred spirit.

Some way below, a plank, carved with Celtic swirls and the word "Annwfyn," had been hammered onto a post, and beyond it stood the yurt, round-bellied and maternal, squatting among the gnarled and spindly trees, like a fat lady trying to look inconspicuous in a crowd of anorexic teenagers. In the clearing beside it, shreds of smoke rose from a stone hearth. A few yards away, the stream gurgled innocently over a dam of rocks, constructed so recently that the shallow pool forming behind them was still murky with disturbed mud. I shuddered, thinking of its birth in that dark hollow.

We were ushered into a patchouli-scented interior of oriental carpets and wickerwork. The men were labouring down at the lodge, but earth-mother Molly was brewing herb tea. Sylvia, already enthroned among cushions on a camp bed, beamed around, admiring everything.

'It's wonderful. Wouldn't you just love to live like this, Kate?'

'If you tell me there's a Jacuzzi tucked behind that curtain.'

'We have a stream,' said Molly. 'Everything natural. Welcome to Annwfyn.' She offered me a plate of suspiciously wholesome cakes.

Kim rose from a pile of rugs, where she'd been darning a jumper, and sidled towards the door.

'Going?' asked Al, quietly.

She shrugged. 'Might as well.'

He didn't argue but gave her a one-armed hug and a quick kiss on the forehead.

A mere gesture. It could mean nothing – it could mean everything. An hour before, I would have cared deeply; I would have been seething with jealous intrigue. But now, I knew Al wasn't the kindred spirit I craved. Could I cope with anything less?

6

'Sorry, no cake.' I shielded a mug of tea against the dust of the dining room, while Al righted himself. He was on his back, prodding soft mortar with an old screwdriver, while his team was tidying up at the lodge.

He sat up, his Byronesque locks scraped back into a workmanlike ponytail. 'Not good enough. Got to keep the Proletariat happy.'

'There's gingerbread somewhere, but I've no idea where Sylvia put it. She's shopping.' I gritted my teeth. 'Sacrificing the fatted calf. We're expecting her son, Christian, so the whole world grinds to a halt.'

'Oh?' Al took the mug from me.

'Two in the morning, he rang!' My irritation boiled over. 'Just to tell us, casually, that he was on his way. Now, Sylvia will fill the pantries, exhaust herself preparing for him and then the little bugger probably won't turn up.'

'Undependable?'

'I wish! You can always depend on Chris to cause Sylvia grief, one way or another. He'll have her in tears before the day's out, whether he comes or not. And our first guests are arriving in three days. It is so typical of him to choose this moment to throw a spanner in the works!'

Al's eyebrows shot up at my vehemence. 'So what's with Sylvia and her son? Too much love or too little?'

I thought about it. 'Both? It's complicated. Christian's his father's son. No, that makes it sound like a simple tug of love. Sylvia's ex, Ken, is a text-book spiv. Calls himself an entrepreneur. He's a shitty husband and a lousy father; gets his secretary to buy his kids expensive presents, but never turns up for their birthdays. He was just a big sugar daddy with his girls, but Christian—'

'Son and heir?'

'Precisely. You can't blame the boy for playing along, I suppose. The schoolyard bully, Ken bailing him out of every scrap. Chris learned to despise Sylvia, which I can't forgive. She'd insist it was only boys being boys, but it made me want to…' I laughed ruefully.

'Clip him round the ear?'

'Yes! The divorce – Sylvia got custody, so, of course, Chris wanted to be with his dad. My God, Ken enjoyed having Chris as a fifth column in Sylvia's camp. She thought she could win the boy round with motherly love, but that just made him think she was weak. And Christian devours the weak.'

'I'm wildly guessing here – you really don't like him, do you?'

'The worst thing is the drugs. When Sylvia heard Chris was messing with them at school, she panicked. You know, innocent victim led astray by evil pushers at the gates. She refused to see he was the evil pusher, running the bloody school mafia. Just like Ken, eye for the main chance. His father encouraged him to quit college, supposedly to set up some internet business, the next Facebook or Ebay or something; there was a lot of talking the talk but it's the only one of his fairy tales that never fooled Sylvia. She was convinced drugs were involved and her poor boy was heading for an overdose in a gutter.' I glanced despairingly at Al and he nodded brooding understanding.

'She was desperate, tried everything to rescue him from himself – bribery, counselling, doctors. In the end she shopped him to the police.'

That brought Al's head up sharply.

'She had this idea a prison sentence might actually

51

help, he'd get treatment, sort himself out. I don't know if it ever really works like that, but of course Ken was there to screw things up. Brought in some hot-shot lawyer to prove it was all down to a vindictive mother, trying to get at her ex. Christian had a few nights in custody, then a suspended sentence. Certainly no treatment. And he's been making her pay ever since.'

'A mess.' Al put his mug down, examining his palm for splinters. 'Kim had a problem.' His confidences in exchange for mine. 'Heroin. She's clean now but I keep an eye out for her. She's off busking most days, so it can be hard to keep track of her.' He added, as if he had seen my ears pricking and my nose twitching, 'She's my baby sister.'

'Ah.' A sister, of course. 'So you understand what Sylvia was going through. But you never went to the lengths of handing her to the police?'

'No way!' He gave a short bark of indignation, then remembered himself. 'I can see why Sylvia thought it the best thing. She probably regards the fuzz as officers and gentlemen.'

'She'll never do it again. Trouble is, there's nothing else left to try, and she's so crucified with guilt, she lets Chris walk over her.'

I glanced around the derelict room, two floorboards raised, plaster in piles. If only it were always possible to take things apart and put them right. 'I shouldn't be telling you about Chris. Too biased. Last time we met, I caught him stealing his mother's credit cards. We got a little heated. He scratched obscenities on my car and I threw a Pyrex bowl at him. Full of hot soup.'

'Can't picture you losing your rag.' Al paused, seeing me wince. 'Wrong thing to say?'

I smiled. 'An inability to lose my rag has always been my problem. Maybe I should try it more often. Ironic that Chris, of all people, made me do it. Remind me to thank him.'

I doubted I would need the reminder, because I was convinced Christian wouldn't turn up.

It was a conviction Sylvia refused to share. She returned, laden with exotic goodies. 'He's not here yet then? But it's still early, isn't it? I've got vodka. He likes that. Fabulous cheeses from the Italian – is that the meat? I got a leg of lamb, this season's, and I thought we could start tonight with the trout – locally smoked, and—'

'Sylvia, how long is Christian staying?'

'Oh Lord, I don't know.' She released a punnet of strawberries and looked at me anxiously. 'You won't mind, will you, Kate? I know, last time, things got a bit awkward. He wasn't really trying to steal it, you know. He did explain, he was only…'

'Syl, don't worry. It's just that you've bought enough to feast an army for a month.'

Sylvia gazed guiltily at the mountain of bags still littering the table, the dresser and the floor. 'I have overdone it a bit, haven't I? I just wanted to celebrate. I hardly ever get to see him these days.'

'It all looks gorgeous,' I said. Christian was going to crush her spirits without any help from me.

The afternoon passed in preparation. Over the last month I'd helped Sylvia patch and decorate another guest bedroom – the Guinevere room, she called it – overlooking the rhododendrons, with lancet windows, stained glass and a pair of gargoyles by the canopied fireplace. My idea of a nightmare, and it would be even more so if she found the Elizabethan four-poster she was looking for. She aired the best linen and dragged up extra furniture, dusting and polishing as if we were expecting royalty. Then down to the kitchen to whip up cakes and puddings, as if a flood of tasty delicacies could wring some love out of him. Every few minutes, she rushed to the window in search of an approaching car.

Nothing.

Michael came in from his workshop at seven, exchanged kisses with Sylvia and a grimace of irritated despair with me.

'He's not going to come,' I said, as Sylvia dashed from the kitchen to check the phone for messages. No chance of calling him. Christian changed his number so often, she had no idea what it was.

'I'm afraid not.' Michael considered the pots and pans on the range. 'We'll probably be eating late. Are you hungry? I could make us some sandwiches.'

'Don't worry about me. Oh dear. Sylvia.'

Sylvia returned, looking stressed. 'Where could he have got to?'

'Now, now.' Michael gave her a hug. 'We don't even know where he was starting from. Could be Aberdeen. And he's never an early riser, is he?'

'No, that's true. Oh God, has that sauce spoiled?'

'I've taken it off. Come and sit down, out of the kitchen. Just relax for a bit.'

We retreated to the lounge. Michael drew the curtains and lit the oil lamp and the candles, so Sylvia wouldn't have her eyes fixed on the slow dipping of the sun. Then he poured us drinks and set out to divert Sylvia with one of her favourite films. I was convinced his efforts were wasted, she was so on edge, twitching back the curtains, straining for the sound of a motor, but somehow, in the final drama of *Casablanca*, we all missed the tell-tale crunch of the gravel, the amplified sound of an engine passing under the arch into the courtyard.

We did hear the final rev, the slam of a car door. Sylvia leapt up, her whisky flying, and ran out, into the kitchen, to fling the outer door open just as the knock came.

Following, we saw, over her shoulder, a short wiry figure, with a weather-beaten face under a cloth cap.

'Shwmae,' he said, raising a finger to his cap. A cock-eared, black and white sheep dog stood alert at his side, fixing us with a basilisk stare, poised for the command to round us up.

Sylvia said nothing, frozen to the spot.

'Evening, Dewi,' said Michael, gently easing her to one side. 'Come in.' His glance invited me to take charge of my cousin, while he dealt with our guest.

'Oh no, won't come in. Boots.' Our neighbour indicated his mud-caked Wellingtons. 'Murk! Lawr! Came to say I'll be moving the cattle—'

'Come on, Syl.' I put my arm round her, steering her away.

At the door she attempted to rally. 'Sorry, Dewi, I don't know what I—'

'Go and sit down,' ordered Michael. He explained to Dewi. 'A headache.'

'Oh, well I won't be staying. Just came to say I'll be moving the cows tomorrow.'

'Thanks for letting us know.' Michael stepped outside to talk in the courtyard and I led Sylvia out of the kitchen. As soon as we were in the hall, she put her face in her hands and burst into tears.

'Oh Kate. I know I'm stupid; it's silly, crying. Why am I making such a fuss? It's just that I'm so desperate for things to be right again, but nothing I say or do seems to work. Why do I always make it worse? Why can't I let it be?'

'Shh.' I hugged her back to the comfort of the sofa, where she curled up, sobbing into the cushions. I could only stand over her, cursing her son who could, with one off-hand phone call, reduce her to this.

At last she sat up, wiping her eyes. 'He's not going to come, is he?'

'No, I think probably not.'

She sniffed. 'I'm wet.'

'Wet?'

She shifted her weight. 'The sofa's wet.'

I sniffed in turn. 'It's the whisky.'

'Oh God, I spilt it, didn't I? I'll have to get the covers off.' She started heaving cushions, groping for zips.

'Leave it, Syl—'

'No, no, it will stain if I don't get it out.' She wouldn't normally care about whisky stains on the sofa, but the physical onslaught was a therapeutic outlet for her misery and frustration. Better than wrestling with the truth.

The next morning, while I tried not to rejoice too openly at Christian's absence, Sylvia retreated to her pottery, to thump clay. I assuaged my guilt by clearing up all vestiges of the largely uneaten feast, still congealing in the kitchen, and doing the dutiful builders' tea duty. The lodge was finally finished, in readiness for its first visitors, so the entire gang was now at work on the big house.

It took only a few moments to deliver tea and gingerbread to the crew, busy on the exterior wall of the dining room. A couple more to exchange a few nothings with Al. I returned, heading through the drawing room for the office.

Christian was sprawled on the chaise longue.

Sylvia's bleach-blond Adonis. Twenty-three and already going to seed. The smirking idol of a host of teenage girls had begun to look jaded, designer jeans and t-shirt unwashed and slept in. His face was pasty. Christian was a nocturnal animal, blinking now in daylight, as he flicked his cigarette ash on the carpet.

'Well, well. Cousin Kate.'

I would be good, for Sylvia's sake. 'Christian! What a lovely surprise. We heard you might be dropping by, sometime this summer.'

'Moved in with Titania and Doc Crippen then? Who'd have thought the old goat had it in him.'

'Sylvia, Michael and I are in partnership.' I was determined not be riled.

He grinned. 'Sure. So how's the Mater taking the competition?' His public school drawl had begun to alternate with unconvincing Cockney. 'Still squawking like a headless chicken, is she?'

'I'll tell her you're here.' I headed for the door, thankful that I had no hot soup within reach. 'And please put your cigarette out. We don't smoke.'

His drawl followed me. 'So he hasn't murdered her in her bed yet?'

'Surprisingly, no.'

'She takes up with a wife-killer, you have to wonder.'

I turned back, exasperated. 'That's a pretty sick joke, Chris.'

'Michael Bradley topped his wife, didn't you know?' Christian watched me through the haze. He laughed. 'Ever asked why his kids cold-shoulder him? He got bored with her, wanted to move on to silly Syl, but wifey wouldn't divorce him. Catholic, that crap. So he slipped her a little overdose in her cocoa. Everyone knows; that's why he lost his job. It was just never proven.'

'That is complete garbage and you know it.'

'And now you're here, maybe it's Mumsy's turn for

57

the chop.'

'Chris, I know rattlesnakes less poisonous than you.' I had to get out. Fast.

Sylvia was in the pottery, smocked and clay-splattered, looking unusually pugnacious, while Michael, taking a break from his own work, was trying to chivvy her into a good mood.

'He's here,' I said and watched Sylvia's jaw tremble.

'Oh he's here! I knew he'd come!' She ripped off her smock and was running before I could say another word.

Michael gave me a wry smile as we followed. I smiled back. Of course Michael hadn't murdered his wife. How preposterous. Anyway, Sylvia hadn't even met him until... Stop! Chris's slanders weren't worth rational argument.

'But darling, we thought you were coming yesterday!' Sylvia had her arms round her son, who hadn't stirred from the chaise longue. 'We were all so desperately worried about you.'

Christian shot me a triumphant look, and hooked his arm round his mother's neck. It could have been a gesture of affection, or of possession. 'Thought I'd do a bit of business on the way.'

'Christian.' Michael seized his hand in a manly shake, which coincidentally released Christian's neck lock. 'Good of you to come. Your mother looks forward to your visits, and we all want to see Sylvia happy.'

I'd only seen Michael with Christian once before, when he'd just met Sylvia. He'd skirted round her son with avuncular jollity, uncertain how to deal with this problematic relationship. Things had clearly progressed since then. I wondered if Michael had any inkling of what Christian had been saying about him.

'I am so happy to see you here,' babbled Sylvia.

'We'll have a wonderful time. I've bought all your favourite things, and Kate and I have prepared a lovely room for you. The one at the end, with the—'

'I've already got a room.' Christian rose to his feet. 'Over the porch. My room.'

'Oh yes, but this one's even nicer. We've made it—'

He flicked the remains of his cigarette away and looked down on her. 'Your own room, you said, so you can feel this is your home any time you want.' He mimicked her gushing tone.

'Yes, but what I meant was—'

'I was thinking of doing some business down here. With my own pad. Yes?'

'You are quite welcome to set up your new room as an office,' said Michael. 'But Kate has the room over the porch.'

Christian's eyes flickered to me. 'Give Kate the new room. You told me the one over the porch was mine. Okay? Mine.'

'Now darling, we can't just turn Kate out.'

'Kate won't mind.' He was challenging me. If I made a fuss, Sylvia would be distraught and he would win. And if I capitulated, he would win. Damn it, I would not capitulate. I didn't want the ghastly, Gothic fantasy. I wanted the simple room I'd made my own, over the porch.

'Oh but Chris – Kate?' Sylvia's look pleaded with me. 'Would you mind terribly?'

Michael interrupted. 'Kate is a partner here; that room is hers. You can have any of the others, Christian, but Kate stays where she is.'

I was accustomed to Michael following in Sylvia's fiery wake, quietly stilling the chaotic waves she raised. It was startling to hear him laying down the law.

'Okay, so I'll have that cottage by the gate.'

'That's holiday accommodation, for letting.'

'There's no one in it at the moment,' said Sylvia.

'We've got our first guests arriving in two days,' I reminded her.

'So move them,' said Christian.

Michael kept his temper. 'The lodge is not available.'

'Well I suppose, if you don't want me here, I can always find somewhere else.'

His challenge had the desired effect on Sylvia, who was on the point of tears, but Michael stood firm. 'If you prefer, there's the Cemaes Arms in the village. It has rooms, or there's plenty of bed and breakfast around.'

'Fuck that,' said Christian pleasantly. 'I suppose I'd better make do with the servant's quarters then, if that's all you're offering.'

'It's not the servant quarters, honestly,' pleaded Sylvia. 'They're up in the attics. Though they would make a lovely private pad, if that's what you really want.'

Yes, I thought, stick him up there, with that shadow of fear entombed under the sloping eaves. Push him in, lock the door and leave him there, please!

'We could convert them for you. Your own apartment, a proper office and everything. Just tell us what you want, for next time. Come and see...,' Sylvia begged and urged and he allowed himself to be drawn along.

Michael and I were left facing each other.

'Don't you dare even think about giving up your room,' he said.

I laughed, uncomfortably. 'Not to oblige Christian, certainly.'

'Don't imagine it would oblige Sylvia.' No sense of indulgence in Michael now. 'She always crumbles before him. We've got to be her backbone for her, Kate. I am not going to let him hurt her anymore.'

So, there was Christian, come amongst us, deliberately late, snidely malicious and conjuring an explosion out of nothing, within minutes of arrival. If I stood back, I could see he was just a silly brat, squealing for attention. He really wasn't worth hot soup or choler. If I kept out of his way whenever I could and kept quiet when I couldn't, all would be fine.

Still, I was taken aback when I returned from the bathroom, the following morning, and found him in my bedroom, stooping by the window.

'Forgotten where you are?' I asked, pulling my towelling gown around me.

He straightened himself, scratched his unshaven chin and yawned. 'Just taking a last look at the old view.'

I certainly preferred my clear view of valley and misted woods to a tangle of rhododendrons darkened by crimson and emerald glass, but I couldn't believe Christian had noticed either. 'I'll take a snap of it for you,' I suggested. I held the door open and he sauntered past, pausing to leer down my cleavage.

As I shut the door behind him, I noticed the key in the lock. It had never occurred to me to use it before.

My bag was on the chest of drawers. I checked. Phone, purse, cards were all still there. Nothing was different.

Or was it? A table with my laptop had shifted, under the window, catching the curtain. Beneath it, the carpet was rucked slightly. I walked across to check the table's contents and caught the squeak of the floorboard.

I shifted the table further, flicked back the carpet and found a short section of flooring cut through. Two empty screw holes. I locked my door hastily, then crouched down, armed with a nail file, and prised the loose board up. Underneath were joists, wires, a startled spider and a few plastic bags of powder, brown and white assorted.

I sat back on my heels. No wonder Christian had been so eager to have his old room back. I knew I should be concerned, for Sylvia's sake, but as I carefully removed his stash, I gloated at the thought of smacking him where it hurt.

Flush it down the toilet? God knows what that would do to our country plumbing. For the moment, I concealed the bags in the bottom of a drawer and went down to breakfast, locking my door behind me. Later that day, I sauntered out to one of the workshops, where we stored a couple of freezers and decorating gear, and dropped the packages into a rusting paint tin. A police dog might be able to sniff them out, but I doubted if Christian would.

7

That afternoon, Sylvia was in maternal heaven with two children under her roof. Tamsin came home for the Whitsun weekend, recovering from exams and delightfully alleviating the strain of Christian's presence.

'Hi, Krizo.' Giving us all a hug and her mother a bag of laundry, Tamsin plonked herself down beside her brother. 'Thought you were going to Thailand.'

'Na. Stuff came up.'

'Were you going to Thailand?' asked Sylvia.

'Yeah, well, that's kinda difficult when mater's made sure every shit in uniform thinks I must have nefarious motives.'

'Oh Chris…,'

'And did you have nefarious motives?' I asked.

He fired two fingers at me, an amusing, boyish gesture.

'You can help with the guests at the lodge, Taz,' I suggested. 'They arrive tomorrow.'

'Looks cool.' Tamsin airily acknowledged our weeks of hard labour.

'We've worked miracles,' said Sylvia. 'The builders have done wonders. You'll have to meet them. Lovely people. They live in a yurt.'

'Cool!' repeated Tamsin.

'Sounds interesting,' said Christian. 'Maybe I'll check them out.'

I thought of Kim, ex-heroin addict, and my heart sank.

Tamsin dragged me to her room, supposedly to examine her latest purchases from Top Shop and Next. 'I've got a sort of problem, Kate.'

'Serious?'

'No. Well, yes, maybe. You know what Mum can be like.'

'Something to do with your father?'

'Yes!' Her astonishment at my telepathic powers lasted only a second. 'Well yeah, it's always Dad, isn't it? The thing is, he's asked me over to Spain for the summer.'

'Oh.'

'Yes, oh.' She sat back, pouting. 'It's not my fault they don't get on, is it? But you know exactly what she'll say. If I go, she'll be all over the place again and—'

'Now wait.' Tamsin was right: Sylvia would be hysterical, but I could handle it. 'You know your mother's never wanted a breach between you kids and Ken. Even that time when you wouldn't talk to him.'

'I know, but that won't stop her being all hurt now, like I'm betraying her and taking his side.'

'She'll understand. It's the summer vacation; who wouldn't want to go to Spain? And he is your father.'

'Right,' agreed Tamsin. 'And I mean, he invited me at Christmas but I came here instead.' She pulled a face. 'Chris said he'd come too, and Mum prepared everything, then Dad phoned on Christmas Eve to say Chris was staying with him. It was awful.'

'It must have been. Look, are you really keen on this trip, Tam?'

'Yes. Sort of. Dad said I could bring friends. It wouldn't be for the whole summer. Just a month.'

I smiled. 'Leave it to me. I can manage Sylvia.'

Of course I could manage Sylvia. My partisan instinct was to sow discord between Ken and his children, but Sylvia had always insisted that his divorce was from her, not from their children. Alas, her noble intentions to maintain the father/child relationship were inevitably scuppered by her own histrionic diatribes, but at least she had noble intentions. It wasn't for me to undermine them.

Whitsun set fireworks under the quiet countryside. Traffic flooded the narrow lanes, craft shops and cafes came alive, exotic fruits appeared in the supermarkets. Cottages woke from their winter slumber, opened their doors and drew back their curtains, including our lodge, as our first guests arrived.

The Fergusons from Leicester were very pleasant, appreciative of the lodge and the gift of fruit and wine that Sylvia had arranged on the table. While she was still buzzing with satisfied glee, I raised the issue of holidays.

'Taz has ideas of spending some of the summer with friends,' I said, as the three of us gathered in the kitchen.

Tamsin looked alarmed.

'That's lovely,' said Sylvia. 'Bring them here. We have plenty of room.'

'Oh but—'

I laughed. 'Come on, Syl. She's at university now. They'll want to see the world, do Europe. It's a long, long break, you know.'

I watched Sylvia's expression work through alarm, puzzlement, enthusiasm. 'Oh, well, yes of course, that's a wonderful idea. It really it is. There is so much to see. Venice. You must see Venice.'

'Venice?' Tamsin was preparing to argue.

'Have you fixed on your route yet?' I asked. 'You mentioned Europe but you can't do it all in a couple of weeks. What have you settled on? East or west?'

'I, er, oh, west. Yeah. Like, west.' Tamsin finally took the hint.

'France, Spain, Portugal.' I nodded.

'Yeah – sort of.'

'But that's wonderful,' said Sylvia. 'Gives you the chance to see those countries properly.' She paused, bit her lip, then braced herself. 'Now Tammy, I'm sure you'll be making your own plans, but if you are going to Spain, I really think you should try and see your father. It's only right. You needn't visit for long if it's really out of your way, but do call on him, promise?'

Tamsin was wide-eyed. 'Oh, yeah, right, if you really think I should. No, I don't mind. It'll be fine.'

'Your friends will understand. You hardly ever get the chance to see him.'

'Oh they won't mind,' said Tamsin earnestly. 'Don't worry, Mum, I'll go see Dad, if that's what you really want.'

'Of course she'll see him,' said Christian, from the kitchen doorway. 'He's the one who invited her over there. That's why you're going, ain't it, sis? To stay at Dad's villa? Got to be better than summer in a soggy, Welsh dump.'

Sylvia looked as if she'd been slapped in the face. 'Is that true?'

Tamsin, caught in the lie that I had perpetrated, exploded. 'I knew you wouldn't understand! Chris, shut up, you pig! What's it got to do with you?'

'Ken asked you to go to him?' Sylvia wrung a dishcloth as if it were a chicken's neck. 'To Spain, instead of coming to me?'

'I knew you'd be like this!'

'He couldn't resist it, could he? He just has to try and prise you away from me. The bastard! Can't rest until he's messed things up for me as much as he can. You know what he really wants, don't you—?'

'Now wait.' I thought fast. 'You said you were planning a holiday for a fortnight or so with your friends, Taz. Three or four weeks at most. Wasn't that it?'

Tamsin glowered, but I went on, 'And you were coming back here for the rest of the summer, weren't you?'

'Oh, if that bastard's willing to fling me the scraps,' said Sylvia scornfully.

'Sylvia.' I ignored Christian's derisive hoots from the

doorway. 'Tam wants a holiday with her friends and they want to go abroad. Isn't that what every student wants? Yes, I bet Ken was quick to put in an offer. Typical of him, I know, but look at it from their point of view. They need to travel as cheaply as possible, and take any free accommodation on offer. If a parent has a villa just sitting there, of course they'll jump at it.'

'And we're going to Jason's place.' Tamsin seethed. 'His parents have a time share on the Algarve and we're going there too. So what? Anything wrong with that?'

'Oh, you're going to Jason's too?' Sylvia grasped at this.

'Yes, and maybe we'll stay six weeks instead of four, if you're going to be so shitty about it.' Tamsin pushed back her chair and stormed from the room.

'Oh Tammy, now don't be like that.' Sylvia followed her, leaving me facing Christian and his mocking laughter.

He came in, slumped down on a chair and groped for his cigarettes, grinning at me. 'Nearly screwed that one up, didn't you?'

'So you've met the kids?' I was inspecting the building works – any excuse to chat to Al. Chris and Tamsin had sloped off down the Cemaes Arms to join the gang the previous evening and burst back into the house, loudly, at 3 a.m. Tamsin was utterly smitten with Al. She'd raved about him for half an hour until I begged for earplugs.

'We met them. Taz is a nice kid.'

'She is. Tends to slip into baby mode when she's around Sylvia, but she's doing fine. Actually works hard when she thinks we're not looking. What about Chris?'

'Chris isn't a kid.' Al scrutinised the re-pointed wall.

'No, old as sin. Horns in there somewhere. Did he behave?'

'Generous guy. He figures he could bring some business our way.' Al's lips twisted.

'Construction? Chris?'

'It wasn't building work he had in mind. More like transport. Imports. Mobile phones, apparently. He's arranging a shipment from the Far East.'

'Mobile phones, my eye.' I sniffed derision, then realised that the tilt of Al's mouth was anger, not amusement. 'If you want to tell him where to shove his mobile phones, please go ahead. But I guarantee he won't be here more than a week. There'll be a flaming row and he'll storm off.' I hesitated. 'Did he meet Kim?'

'Oh yes.' Al looked at me, his eyes hard, no sign of the questing spirit. 'And I won't ask permission for what I'll do to him, if he gets her screwed up again.' His tone was cold and measured.

No contest, I thought, as I returned to the house. If there were a confrontation, my money was all on Al. Christian had weight, increasingly more of it in the last year or two, but it was all flab, whereas Al was pure, lean muscle and sinew.

I was considering said muscle and sinew with some complacency as I skipped up the grand staircase and flung open my bedroom door, intending to change.

Christian was standing there. He had his back to me, surveying the empty cache by the window and as he turned, I prepared for his snarling petulance. I could deal with it. No need to throw things. Let him foam at the mouth, if he wanted. I would just keep calm.

But Christian wasn't in a rage. He was smiling. With his mouth, but not with his eyes. It was a neat trick, unnerving and menacing.

'Where is it, Kate?'

'Where's what?'

'You know what I mean.' His tone was almost pleasant as he approached.

'No I don't.'

Without warning, his hand closed round my throat and he thrust me back against the door. 'I think you do.'

'Don't be ridiculous, Christian.' I shifted, but his grip was unrelenting. He was stronger than me. A struggle would have been futile, not to mention undignified, so I tried to relax. 'If you're talking about the cocaine or whatever it was, it went down the pan weeks ago.'

His face was very close to mine, his breath foul. 'You'd better be lying, Kate.'

'Of course I'm not. Did you seriously think I'd leave it there as insulation? Llys y Garn is a business, Christian. A legitimate business. You don't run a legitimate business by stashing narcotics under the floorboards.'

The act of ice-cool malevolence was failing. I could feel his hand trembling. For a moment I thought he was going to throttle me. One of his eyelids twitched uncontrollably; sweat gleamed on his upper lip.

And I wondered, was it my panic and fear I was feeling, or his?

He stepped back with a falsetto laugh, his grip relaxing. 'You're a stupid woman, Kate. You threw away – you have any idea what that stuff was worth?' He sneered round the room. 'Legitimate business? You're a joke, you know that? You couldn't make money out of this crap, if it poked out of the woodwork.'

'If that's your judgement, I can live with it.'

'I reckon maybe I should be looking for compensation, don't you?'

69

'Get a job, Chris. You'll find it much healthier.'

'I had a market for that stuff. Customers queuing up, right on your prissy doorstep. Now figuring on what I could have made—'

'If you have any ideas of supplying Al's sister, Chris, he'll break your legs. And I'll be there to cheer him on.' Where was my dignified resolve now?

'Oh yes?' Christian's grip became an obnoxious caress, his finger stroking my jaw. 'The builder, eh? Got you hot, has he? Petey too soft for you? But then you do have a taste for violence don't you, Katie? Bet you've done more than throw crockery in your time. Killer Queen. That's what they call you. People do just drop round you like flies. How d'you do it, Kate?'

My joints locked rigid, the blood pounding in my ears. Did they really call me Killer Queen?

'Go on, tell me. Everyone knows you did for Leo Mardell. What's your technique? Drug his tea? Poison him with words? Or just give him the evil eye. Ma thinks you're a witch. Maybe that's it. You just mutter a little curse. Is that what you did with your baby, or did you have to resort to gin and a hot bath? Got rid of it either way, didn't you?'

It was no longer his hand around my throat that stopped me breathing. I couldn't have said a word. My brain was numb with shock.

'No wonder you fall for killers like Al Taverner,' whispered Christian, lapping up my obvious distress. 'But I don't think he's much of a threat to me. He only whacks girls.'

What was he saying, now? I could no longer hear, or think.

Christian giggled. 'Didn't you know about the woman he beat to a pulp? Would be handy with a crowbar, wouldn't he? Oh, and I don't think he'll be too fussed about his little sis, just as long as I don't mess up her earning potential. More of a pimp than a brother. You do know what she gets up to when she goes out each day?'

His mistake. He'd thought he could carry on shovelling his malice on me until I drowned, but he'd miscalculated. He'd talked too long, giving me time to still my pulse and my brain. I was going to take back control if it killed me.

'Chris.' I was amazed to hear myself almost casual in my dismissal. 'Do you have any idea how pathetic you are? I don't know if this sort of behaviour impresses your buddies like Tyro… He's phoned a couple of times, by the way, looking for you? Did he ever catch up with you?'

I'd done it, wrong-footed him. I felt the gust of a child's helpless terror as his malice crumbled. He just managed an unconvincing laugh. Then his grip tightened. Seriously tightened, his thumb biting into my throat so I began to gag. 'One of these days, when you're not expecting it, I'll be waiting for you, Killer Queen.' His hand dropped and he sidled past me, out of my room.

I nonchalantly shut the door on him, flicked my hair back, straightened my clothing, then my knees buckled. I was in a state of near liquefaction, ready to vomit. Why in God's name had I come here? Christian had become a demon, more monstrous than any shadow.

Killer Queen. Just one of Christian's spiteful lies. But I'd let the canker in.

My baby. I'd felt him die, that was all. A stream of life within me suddenly ceased to exist. I hadn't killed him. Only Christian could think it – except that it hadn't only been Christian. When I felt my baby die, I'd wrapped myself in iron self-control as I'd told my husband. 'Peter, the baby's dead.' And I could read, amidst his panic and distress, his instant thought, even though he pushed it away the moment it seethed into his mind: she's killed it, she's willed it dead.

I'd never forgiven him for that. But what if he'd been right and I did kill? Death had stalked me so long, maybe it had burrowed into my entrails, until I'd become its instrument, releasing it on others in murderous barbs. If it poured into me, it had to go somewhere. I thought back to the sickening moment of Leo's death, how it came just as I'd been silently cursing him for involving me in his troubles. I hadn't wished my baby dead, but what if death was all I had to give a child?

I lost my lunch. Afterwards, swilling my face with icy water, sanity began to reassert itself. Ridiculous. My thoughts had never killed anyone. I stared at myself in the bathroom mirror, forcing myself to repeat it. Christian was the lethal poisoner, not me. Spit it out now, before it burns through you. You're not a killer, Kate. Al's not a killer, Michael's not a killer. Stamp it all out.

I was in control again. I could see Christian for what he was. It didn't mean I could face the thought of him in the house, but what was I to do? Raise hell? Report his drugs to the police? Or pretend to forget the whole thing and keep smiling for Sylvia's sake? I couldn't do it, not any more. The bruises on my neck showed he was moving beyond poisonous words. The fear that had pounded round me while I'd been with him was his, and it was very real. He'd got himself entangled in something horrendous and I could still feel his panic, clawing at my innards, his frantic sense of falling. If he grew truly desperate, God knows what he'd do.

I sat on the edge of my mattress, trying to recall the

cooing infant Sylvia had placed in my arms; the bright-eyed little boy in his first prep school uniform, the lad on the beach, eagerly showing off his cricketing skills. How had it all got so warped and twisted? Sylvia's son, of all people.

All right. I would gather all my reserves and play it cool for the next day or two if I could possibly manage it. But if Christian stayed, I would have to find an excuse to go.

8

I had to face Christian at dinner, but his attention was all on his mother and Michael.

'Got a spot of business.' He interrupted Sylvia's enthusiastic plans for her vineyard. 'New line. Smart phones.'

'How exciting, darling. You have such good ideas. I'm sure it will be—'

'Thought you might be interested in investing.'

'Well…,' Sylvia floundered. I could tell she'd had this conversation many times before. 'Well of course—'

'We'll certainly consider it,' said Michael. 'Let us have a look at your business plan, market research, so forth, and if it's viable, I am sure we'll be happy to invest.'

'Right. I don't have the paperwork with me. I'll send it to you. But this sort of deal, you don't waste time, you get in there before the competition. Practically on its feet already, customers lined up. I've got a shipment in the pipeline. Just a bit of a cash flow problem at the moment.' His blue eyes flickered over me for a moment. 'Still waiting for a payment. You know how it is. I figured you could lend me a bit to tide me over for the next couple of weeks, just as payment down.'

'Well, of course, darling, I'll help if I can. How much do you need?'

'Peanuts. Five grand would clinch it.'

'Five thousand! But Chris, darling, I haven't – I don't think I—'

'We're undergoing extensive renovations at the moment,' said Michael. 'It's a costly business. You mother doesn't have five thousand to spare.'

'Make it two, then. Christ, it's just a loan. You'll have it back in a couple of days when the deal goes through.'

'I know, darling,' said Sylvia. 'I'm sure I can lend you a few hundred, but—'

'And see the whole deal go down the drain? Thanks!'

'You could ask Dad,' suggested Tamsin.

'I'm asking my mother,' said Christian, with that tone of cold pleasantness.

'I'll see what I can do,' said Sylvia. Michael squeezed her shoulder, pushed his chair back and went to the dresser. I wanted to scream 'Don't!' but I held my tongue and watched as he opened a drawer, produced a cheque book. The room was silent while he wrote, tore the cheque loose and handed it to the hungry Christian.

Chris's eyes gleamed with victory, then narrowed. 'One K. I said—'

'Have the other thousand when you show us the business plans.'

'Oh thank you, sweetheart.' Sylvia threw her arms round Michael.

Christian pocketed the cheque and dismissed my disgust with a smirk. 'Okay. I'll just have to make do.

So sis. You back to Bristol tomorrow?'

'Yeah.' Tamsin looked hopeful. 'Can you give me a lift to the station?'

'I'll take you the whole way. I've got to get back to London.'

'So soon?' asked, Sylvia.

'Great!' said Tamsin.

'Early start,' said Christian. 'Can't hang around.'

'If you prefer to go later, Tammy, I can take you to the station,' said Michael. 'You already have your train ticket.'

I hoped Tamsin would remember how much she valued her weekend lie-ins. A train would be a lot safer than Christian at the wheel of that outrageous red Lotus Elan, currently sprawled across the yard.

But Tamsin didn't hesitate. 'No, thanks. I'll go with Chris. Cool! If that's okay with you.'

'Of course it is, darling,' said Sylvia. Her two children were behaving like proper siblings. What more could she want?

Sickened by the whole scene, I went back to work. Christian was going. Whatever it had cost, at least it was taking him far away from Llys y Garn. Preferably forever. The world could only be cleaner without his parasitical nastiness.

The early morning start Christian demanded was ten o'clock. We watched the red Lotus choke into life, screech out of the yard and swerve off down the track, Tamsin waving from the open window, Christian extending his hand in a casual gesture that might have been a farewell salute or a single finger.

'Such a pity they had to go so soon,' said Sylvia.

Michael kissed her cheek. I fancied his eyes avoided mine, and for a moment I wondered. Shades of guilt?

Christian's snide insinuations kept encroaching.

Total garbage. I hadn't killed my baby and Michael hadn't killed his wife.

'He'll be back soon, won't he?' Sylvia was ever hopeful. 'With this business scheme. I'd love to help him if I can.'

'Mm,' was all I could manage. I bolted for the office, determined not to think about Christian and his slimy games. Work. I messed for a while with the layout of the website that had already brought us three bookings for the lodge. Then there was a letter to the planning department about the restoration of the hall. Soon, with luck, I'd be able to give Al the go ahead. We were just waiting for—

Blood.

For one flashing second, it blotted out everything else.

Blood and guts. The image was so strong, I could almost smell it. I could see it, spattering, pooling on tarmac. A thud of distress hit me hard in the chest.

I bolted outside. No one was there. Michael was in his workshop, Sylvia probably at her pottery.

God, God, had I really wished him dead? Tammy was with him! What had I done? All my rational denials dissolved. What if I really could kill with thoughts? Had I channelled that horror, lurking in the Great Hall, and unleashed it on Sylvia's children?

No. Tamsin wasn't dead. I would feel it if she were. But she was deeply distressed, I knew that much, and there was blood.

They'd been gone twenty minutes maybe. No more. I tried her phone. No response. In panic, I started running down the drive, without stopping to think how pointless it was. They must be miles from our lane by now. I'd need the car if I intended to follow them.

On cue, I heard the chug of a diesel engine. Al was

coming down the track in his Land Rover. He stopped. 'Hi. You're out of breath. You want a lift to the village?'

'Yes. No. Wait.' I ran round, wrenched open the passenger door and climbed in. 'Will you drive me?'

'Sure. I was going to Pembroke Dock. Right route?'

'No. Wrong route.'

'Where then?'

'I don't know.' Stupid answer. I took a deep breath. 'Tamsin's in trouble. Don't ask me to explain. I think she might be hurt.' I couldn't get the image of blood out of my head.

'Okay.' Al pushed into gear. 'Where is she?'

'I don't know! Christian was taking her back to college. They can't have got far. '

'Didn't she say where she was?'

'Say?'

'Did she phone or something?'

'No. No she didn't phone.' I stared at the dashboard. 'Just trust me.'

There was only a fractional hesitation. 'Yes, okay.' Al's hand closed reassuringly over mine, as we rolled down to the lodge. 'Which way?'

'Right.'

We bumped along the rutted road. 'Not the village,' I said. 'Straight on.' Al followed my directions. He must have assumed I had some sort of divination. It wasn't true. I was using my knowledge of Christian. He wanted the motorway, so he'd make for the main road. Tamsin wouldn't persuade him onto the narrow lanes that offered short-cuts through the wooded hills and valleys. Come down from fifth gear? No way. But he'd go with it if she suggested the turning at Prenford because it seemed to offer a straight, two-lane route.

'Left here,' I said, and Al obediently turned.

77

We found Tamsin a mile along the road. Her head was up and she was walking. Not limping, but her face was streaked with tears, two panda eyes where her mascara had smudged. When she saw us, as Al eased to a halt, tight against the hedgerow, her resolution crumbled and she sat down on the verge with a sob.

I leapt out and put my arms round her. 'Tammy, are you hurt?'

'He… it was… I…' Her burst of tears left her incoherent.

Al hurried round to join us. 'What's happened, Taz? Has there been an accident?'

She nodded, her verbal response incomprehensible.

'Is your brother hurt?'

'No!' That was clear enough. Her initial distress gave way to spitting outrage. 'I don't know where he is, lousy shit! He hit a fox!'

'A fox,' I repeated.

'It was horrible…' She dissolved again.

A fox. The blood and guts of a fox. I hadn't killed Christian or Tamsin. Relief exploded in me. I managed to meet Al's eye. 'I think we'd better just get her home. Was the car damaged, Tam?'

She shook her head. 'I don't think so.' Raw anger now. 'He did it deliberately! It saw us, it was running out of the way but he swerved deliberately to hit it. It crunched…' She clenched at the memory. 'And he laughed. I shouted to stop and go back and he just laughed. Then I screamed at him and I was hammering on the window, so he stopped, and I said go back, and he was like, no way, so I said I'd run back and see if it was still alive, but when I got out, he drove off. He just drove off! He's got my bag and my phone and my money and everything! I walked back and it was – it was horrible.'

'Come on, Tam,' I said. 'We'll take you home.'

By the time we were nearing Rhyd y Groes, Tamsin had cleaned her face with the tissue I proffered, and was even attempting a laugh at her embarrassing situation.

'God, I'm so stupid. Sorry you had to come out. I feel such an idiot. How did you find me? Did Chris phone?'

'No.'

Al took his eyes off the road to look at me.

'We were going to Pembroke,' I said. 'Just pure luck we found you. We can go tomorrow instead, can't we?'

'Sure,' said Al, without batting an eyelid. 'Let's just get you home.'

Sylvia was in the yard, hands and forearms wet and white with clay.

'Al, I didn't think you'd be so quick. Did you get the – and Kate? Do you know, I didn't even realise you'd – Tammy?' Panic set in at the sight of her daughter. 'What's happened? Oh God, there's been an accident. He's dead, isn't he? I knew it! I knew something terrible was going to happen. Oh God!'

When our denials finally got through, she calmed down enough to burst into tears, which set Tamsin off again. 'I'll fetch Michael,' I said, and left them outbidding each other in histrionics.

9

'Are you going to tell me what happened back there?'

I'd given Michael a brief account of Tamsin's drama, and he'd hurried back to the house from his workshop, leaving me with Al and the questions he had so politely not asked until now.

'I wish I could. I don't know what happened.'

'You felt something. Is that it?'

'I don't know. I pick up…' What? Not death, this time. Unless it was the death of the fox, and God help me if I'd started to tune into the death throes of animals. 'I think it's when someone experiences something that jolts their brain somehow. I get their shock. Sometimes, I see things. This time it was blood.'

'You connected with Tamsin seeing it.'

'I think so.' Al's restrained curiosity had a strangely liberating effect on me. He wasn't pushing, so I didn't resist. I just talked. 'There was an old man.' The image that had haunted my adolescent years. 'He saw his cat burning.'

'Nasty.'

Al took my arm and guided me on, into the labyrinth of the trees. The heavy green silence of the woods had the feel of a confessional.

'I think it was probably already dead,' I added, more for my benefit than his. For years I'd imagined a cat burning alive, with its owner. 'He lived in our street. Mr Jackson. His house caught fire, and he died. He shouldn't have died but he went back in to find his cat. He must have found her burning. He saw it, so I saw it.'

'And you have to live with this.' Al's arm slipped round me. 'Every horror in the world knocking at your door.'

'Not every one, thank God. I feel things when I'm there, physically, in the place where something happened in the past, but presents things, at a distance – I only feel those when I have some sort of emotional link. Otherwise I really would be insane.'

'Sure. Anyone would. You were close to the old man,

80

were you?'

'I was – connected. He was just an old man, who lived alone and talked to his cat, and didn't like children very much, probably because they didn't like him. I was walking past his house that morning – to my lift to school – and some older kids were there. One of them ran up to his door and wrote something on it. Then he rapped on the window and they started shouting at him. I was terrified because he'd think I was with them and he'd tell my mum. That was what I was worrying about, when I came home from school. And that's when his house was burning down and I saw the burning cat.'

Al sat down on a fallen log, and pulled me down beside him. 'You've been nursing guilt about it ever since, haven't you?'

'Stupid, isn't it. I was convinced for years that the image of the cat had been sent to haunt me as punishment.' It was surprisingly calming to get it off my chest. Clarifying, even. 'I was feeling guilty about leaving Tam with Chris this morning. He's a crap driver, even when he's not bent on deliberate mayhem. Not surprising I imagined things.'

Al's arm tightened around me. 'You didn't imagine it, you felt it. You see, Kate, you're convinced you only feel the negative, but think about it. If you'd felt nothing, Taz would still be wandering along the road, crying her eyes out. That's positive. You felt a cry for help and you responded.'

'You think?' Al might see it that way, but I could only think of Leo's cry for help that I'd refused to acknowledge until it was too late. 'It was hardly a major crisis. A girl left high and dry on the side of the road. She is nineteen, after all.'

'But a very young nineteen.'

'Yes, still Sylvia's baby. But she'd have hitched a lift home before long. She wasn't hurt or in danger, just upset.' Not broken and impaled on a shattered windscreen. I pushed away the ghastly thought.

'You wouldn't want her upset, though. You love her.'

'Yes. I do.'

'So you did fine. You helped her through a transition. She's growing up, got a lot of travelling still to do, and she travelled some today.'

'Yes. Of course. And I'm just thankful she's not travelling down the same road as Chris. In every sense. She can be petulant sometimes, silly, lazy, all sorts of healthy immature things, but she'll never finish up like Christian.'

No one was like Christian. Pure poison.

Just above us, on a bank of mossy boulders, sunlight filtered down onto one of Michael's chainsaw sculptures. The Mother Goddess, Al had called it; someone had left flowers at its foot. To me it was a hooded woman, purely abstract of course, like all Michael's sculptures, but undeniably a hooded woman, fading slowly from womanhood into primeval matter. Dust to dust. Annette. His dead wife.

Christian's spiteful lies came back to me, about me, about Michael, about everything. 'To Hell with Christian. He's an evil little brat and I wish Sylvia would throw him out for good!'

Al followed my gaze. The connection was not obvious. 'He's manipulative. He knows how to pull his mother's strings. He thinks he can do it with everyone.'

'Has he tried pulling yours?'

'Of course. He believes he has to play people to get what he wants, and in the end just playing with them is an end in itself. Gets pally, slips in a few drops of vitriol, stands back to watch them squirm.' Al caught my expression, and laughed. 'You recognise the technique.'

'It rings a bell.'

'I suppose he's been feeding you venom about me?'

'Oh, about everyone! He's universally generous.'

'Maybe it's a compulsion. Just another drug for him. So come on then, what did he whisper about me?'

'Nothing! Nothing that I was prepared to listen to.'

Al smiled. 'Of course not. Come on, we're behind the bike shed. Tell me what he said about me and I'll tell you what he said about you.'

I managed an unconvincing laugh. 'He came up with all sorts of nonsense about you having a criminal record. About a woman being hurt.' I preferred to leave it vague. Beaten to a pulp, Christian had said. Whacking girls. What did whacking mean? Could Al really have killed someone? I knew so little about him, and I was sitting alone with him in a wood, taunting him with his secret. Not the wisest move – if there was the slightest truth in Christian's sly allegations, which of course there wasn't. 'I know it's not true.'

'Ah, but do you?' Al smiled darkly. 'He's right, you see. I do have a record, for resisting arrest at a protest. And I did have a set-to with a woman who annoyed me. She was Kim's supplier, and when she seemed disinclined to leave my house, I removed her.'

'Well there you are.' I took a deep breath. 'I don't have to ask what he said about me. I murdered my baby.'

Al's eyes widened a fraction. I'd got it wrong.

'All right, what then?'

He was still taking in what I'd said. Then he smiled. 'Only that you're insane, your husband had you sectioned, and you murdered your boss.' His hand, squeezing mine, turned it into a joke. Ha ha.

I tried to smile. 'Yes. That's Christian. My boss committed suicide. He was about to be sent down for fraud. As for the rest, when I lost the baby, I had some counselling.'

Al nodded.

'And I lost it. A miscarriage. I didn't kill it.' My eyes prickled with tears.

Al drew me close, hugging me, and we sat a moment in silence.

'Look.' I pulled free. 'I've got to go back.'

'They can't manage without you?'

I can't manage with you, I thought. I'm not used to all this sharing. It's not what I do. 'If I leave Sylvia to her own devices, she'll find a way of excusing Christian, and then I'll have to shout at her. Sorry.'

'I'll save your place,' he called after me.

I needn't have worried about Sylvia's reaction. She was a mother tigress to Tamsin, and when Christian hurt his little sister, he'd gone beyond her tolerance pale.

'I'll kill him!' she said, fierce as I'd ever seen her. 'How could he be so irresponsible? He's taken all her things, and he just left her there! Well! She's all right, thank God. And at least she didn't bring her laptop home, with all her work, but he's got her bag with everything else in it. Mike's taking her to Swansea and I'm going to contact the bank, stop her card.'

'Good idea.' I hadn't expected such common-sense efficiency, even less her willingness to see Christian for what he was.

She slammed the bread knife down on the table. 'When he comes back here—'

'*If* he comes back, he can find lodgings elsewhere,' said Michael, leaning against the Rayburn, arms folded.

'Yes,' said Sylvia, and I could see her resolve

wavering before my eyes. 'Or at least—'

'Elsewhere,' repeated Michael.

'Oh hell, how could he be such a…' She began to cry again. 'He's my son. I try and I try. Why can't I do anything right?'

'Sylvia.' Michael gave her a reassuring shake. 'You are far more than he deserves.'

'Mike's so sweet to me,' said Sylvia, when he'd gone. 'I don't know how he puts up with me. And giving Christian that money. I know we'll never see it again. He was paying him off, wasn't he?'

'I think so.'

'He shouldn't have to do that for me. Not with all he has to put up with from his own children.'

I hesitated. 'Why don't Michael's children speak to him?'

'Oh.' She sniffed. 'Just a sad family thing. About their mother, you know.'

'Her dying?'

'Yes, isn't that awful? Annette didn't want all that long drawn-out agony, so she asked Mike to help her. She had pills.'

'Ah. Of course! So he gave her—'

'No! That's the point. Mike refused. Couldn't bring himself to do it, poor lamb. He felt so guilty afterwards. He told me if only she'd asked a second time, he'd have done it, but she never asked again. Then, of course, his kids blamed him for making her suffer, all those horrible weeks in hospital when she could have died quickly and painlessly at home.'

'Oh. Poor Mike.'

'And then there was the funeral. Annette was an atheist, like Mike, you know. But when she died, he was in pieces. Terribly depressed. He just let the undertakers arrange things. A vicar, the full works. He wasn't in a mood to make an issue of it. But then his children made a big fuss because he hadn't arranged a proper humanist funeral. I mean, if they felt that strongly about it, why didn't they arrange it themselves instead of leaving it to Mike?'

'Quite,' I said, remembering my mother's funeral, arranged by others because I couldn't face it. One more little stab of guilt.

'And then Mike gave up his career, sold up and we came here, and anyone would think he was threatening to disinherit them.'

'They think he's squandering the family inheritance?'

'Horrible brats. Barely speak to him anymore. But then, considering how my son behaves... Oh Kate, what are we going to do about Christian?'

'We're going to get on with life and stop worrying about him,' I said. It may have convinced her. It didn't convince me.

'Mike.' I surprised him in his workshop as he was doing last minute work for his London exhibition.

He straightened from eying along the flawless gleaming plane of a table top. 'Kate. Hello.'

'I've brought you a present.' I held out a set of antique tools I'd picked up on a market stall in Cardigan. A token of penance for giving a moment's thought to Christian's slanders.

He looked understandably surprised, picking out a fine chisel, the only tool I could identify by name, and examining its well-honed tip. 'Well.'

'I expect you already have them.'

He studied the bundle. 'Not all. They're beautiful pieces. Craftsman's tools.' He looked up at me. 'I'm delighted, but why?'

'For paying Chris off and getting rid of him.'

'Oh.' He looked amused. 'And I thought you'd blame me. I just can't bear to watch her being used and abused by him. I shouldn't have done it, I know.'

'You shouldn't have had to. It's my fault the little beast was asking for money. You remember that fuss about having my room. It wasn't just bloody-mindedness. He was expecting to reclaim some drugs he'd hidden there. I found them, told him I'd flushed them away.'

'Thank God for that.'

'But I think he really needed the money.'

'Smart phones!' Michael scoffed.

'I know, but he did need money, badly. He's got creditors and he's afraid. Unsurprisingly; I've spoken to them a couple of times on the phone. They're looking for him, and they don't sound the sort to bother with solicitor's letters or the small claims court. If he can't pay them off, he'll be in real trouble. I'm sure he wouldn't have badgered you if he'd had this.' I produced a carrier bag with the contents of the old paint tin.

Michael took it and looked inside, picking out the packets, one by one. 'Better he took all our money than put this lot on the streets.'

'Do you know what it is? I've always steered clear of drugs.' I had enough to contend with, without additional hallucinations.

Michael opened a packet, shook its contents. 'Haven't a clue.'

'You're a chemist.'

He gave an ironic smile. 'Doesn't mean I can identify every crystal with the naked eye.'

'No, sorry, I suppose not.'

He raised the packet to his nose, then thought better of it. 'I'll make an educated guess if you like.

Benzoylmethylecgonine?　　　　Diacetylmorphine? Whatever's the latest craze on the streets?'

'I didn't like to flush it down our drains. And I'm not sure burning it would be a good idea. If the wind's in the wrong direction we might have the whole parish tripping.'

Michael nodded. 'Leave it to me. I'll dispose of it. You haven't told Sylvia about it, have you?'

'No! She deludes herself he's clean now.'

'That boy will never be clean.'

The sound of an engine brought our heads up. Michael met my eye and we laughed painfully. Three days since Christian had left, and we were still on edge.

A vehicle rolled to a halt in the yard, and a loud bray warned us it was Fran Garrick, self-styled queen of Rhyd y Groes parish.

Sylvia was at the kitchen door, arms full of sage and rosemary. 'Fran! How are you?'

'Thoroughly thriving.' Fran eased her tweedy, strapping limbs from her Range Rover. 'You know there are yobs swarming all over your lodge?'

'Yes, they're our first guests.'

'That's all right then. As long as they're not squatters. Thought you might want me to let the dogs loose on them. I've brought Ronnie. You remember Ronnie, don't you? Wanted to take another sniff at your fields, or something. Archaeological claptrap, don't ask me. Ah, Pat. Is it Pat? I can't remember.'

'Kate,' I corrected.

'Something of that ilk. Sylvia's cousin Kate, Ronnie. Kate, this is my brother, the prof. Ronald Pryce-Roberts.'

The professor was a stick insect, a very large nose being his only memorable feature. He was pleasant enough in an academically preoccupied way, rather beyond retirement age and quietly shy, unlike his sister Fran, who boomed like a brigadier.

We shook hands and I left Sylvia and Michael to show them our lumpy, bumpy fields. When Sylvia returned, she was in a state of such hyper-enthusiasm that I could see guilt hovering around her.

'Ronnie's going to hold a summer school. A dig. Isn't that wonderful? He organises them for his students and enthusiastic amateurs, just to get the feel of it, you know. Just imagine, a real archaeological site. Howard Carter? Prizing open a long lost tomb—'

'A summer school here?

'Yes. Isn't it thrilling? In our top fields. He's looked at aerial photos and he's really keen. I was hoping they might excavate around the standing stones, but there was some sort of difficulty about that.'

'Meaning it being an ancient monument and us not owning that bit of land,' explained Michael.

'And he said it wouldn't be as productive as the fields anyway,' said Sylvia. 'He thinks there's definitely some sort of settlement there. Just think, that means Llys y Garn is thousands of years old. Can you imagine, we had people sitting on this very spot, gnawing dinosaur bones—'

'Sylvia.' Michael massaged her shoulders affectionately. 'Not dinosaurs.'

'Well, hairy mammoths or something. I thought it was a good idea,' she ended, plaintively.

'I suppose a couple of weeks of upheaval won't be so bad,' I conceded.

'A couple or so.'

I caught Michael raising his eyes to the ceiling. 'A couple or how many?' I asked.

'Well, the whole summer really. They'd need that if they want to get anywhere, won't they. A succession of schools actually. A relay of students. It's a public service, isn't that a good thing? And –What?'

'How much is he paying us?'

'Oh. I said he could come for free.'

'Sylvia!'

'No, but seriously, I was thinking of it as promotion. Aren't you always telling us we should promote this place more? And that's what this would be. Ronnie will be publishing. In academic journals. Maybe even a book. It will put us on the map. And they won't be in the way, right up there in the top fields.'

'And where exactly will they be living?'

'Camping. In the paddock by the orchard and using those old cottages. Don't you see, it's perfect. Their own entrance, everything. We can carry on running this place as if nothing's happening. Please don't look at me like that, Kate. Is it so bad? I thought it was such a wonderful idea.'

'Maybe,' suggested Michael, 'Kate is thinking, if this is a partnership, shouldn't we *all* discuss things before we make decisions?'

'Oh.' Sylvia was instantly contrite. 'Kate, I'm so sorry. Yes of course we should have discussed it with you first. Now I feel awful. We weren't trying to exclude you. Of course we're partners. Oh dear.'

Forgiveness is divine, but I couldn't resist one small jab. 'As long as you and Mike discussed it fully, that's all right.'

Behind her, Michael was having a silent chuckle. I doubted he'd been able to say a word before Sylvia jumped in with her offer.

She looked at me brightly, working on the premise that the brighter she looked, the less she'd have to compromise herself.

Michael came to her rescue. 'The summer school was

supposed to be at an existing excavation in Cumbria, but there were last minute problems, so Ronnie needed an alternative, urgently.'

'And he says there'll be extra educational value in starting an excavation from scratch,' said Sylvia, eagerly. 'It's a public service, really, isn't it? Doing our bit?'

Michael and I smiled at each other, in surrender. 'There is the promotional factor,' he added.

I doubted that a few pot shards, dug up on a Welsh hillside, would have much publicity value, but I was done with being a wet blanket. I could still be a hard-nosed business woman, though. 'If they're having it all for free, I want our lodge booked solidly, all the way to October, by dons and professors. That's the least he can do.'

'What a good idea,' said Sylvia. 'I'll give him a pile of our leaflets.'

'And you'll get your Tenby order done *before* you go to London,' I commanded. 'Now we've got the go-ahead for the hall, we need all the money we can get.'

10

Michael and Sylvia set off for his London exhibition a week later. I stayed to deal with our second guests and the work on the Great Hall. Scaffolding had gone up, the moment we received permission from the planning Tsars, and I very quickly learned that any woman in Al's life would have to accommodate his overriding enthusiasm for antique Lego. So much for my idle dreams of having to fight him off.

On the eve of Sylvia and Michael's return, I was alone in the house, listening to the whining and moaning of distant silage-making as I dried my hair, when the doorbell rang.

The brass bell of the front door. It reverberated through the house with the impact of an air-raid siren.

I peered out of my bedroom window, but the caller was invisible.

The bell rang again and my skin crawled at the thought that it might be Christian.

Clang!

Stop it! I refused to be cowed by fear of my nephew. I went downstairs as the bell clanged a fourth time. The louder it rang, the slower and more deliberate my actions. I drew back the bolts and calmly opened the door.

He was standing on the wide slate step, hands in pockets, gazing out across the valley in the limpid evening light. He turned as the door creaked open.

Sophisticated. Handsome. Witty. Athletic…

At least that's what I'd thought when I first met him, twelve years before. I noticed the beginning of middle-aged girth. 'Hello, Mr Lawrence.'

'Hello, Mrs Lawrence.'

'So. You found me.' I stepped back. 'You'd better come in.'

'Thank you.' Peter followed me through to the drawing room and stopped short, shaking his head over the Gothic fireplace. 'My God. Pure Strawberry Hill. Where did Sylvia find this place?'

'It found her, I think. Sit down, it's not a museum.'

He hesitated. I took solitary possession of the chaise longue to avoid any misunderstanding. Peter perched on the sofa's edge. 'I wasn't sure what sort of reception I'd get. Thought you might just slam the door in my face.'

'Am I that petty?'

'I didn't mean that. But I kept leaving messages on your phone and you never got back to me.'

'Sorry. Crap signal round here.' I rested my chin on my hand and looked him over. He needn't know I'd nearly thrown my arms around him in relief when I found he wasn't Christian. 'Okay, so now I'm listening. To what?'

He opened his mouth to reply and then neatly sidestepped the issue. 'So where's Sylvia? I'm sure I can rely on her to throw something at me, can't I?'

'You're safe. She's in London with Mike. I'll throw something if it'll make you feel better. Would a cushion do, or do you want a full dinner service?'

'Rain check, maybe?'

'How is Gabrielle?'

'We parted company.' He gave a wry smile. 'She decided I was too married.'

'Poor you.'

'You see, I'd already realised the same thing. I was still far too married.'

'So you came all this way to ask for a divorce?'

'No.' Peter sat back at last, head on one side, squinting at me quizzically. 'Unless that's what you want. Is it?'

What did I want? Of course divorce was the logical conclusion to our separation, but no one was going to descend on me, without warning, last thing at night, and expect me to give a simple answer. Least of all Peter. 'It's getting late. Where are you staying?'

'Haven't fixed anything yet. I suppose there's a hotel or something nearby?'

'Don't be stupid. You can stay here.'

He looked hopeful, even slightly complacent. He

wasn't going to have it that easy. 'We have a spare room.'

'That's – fine. Right. Thanks.'

'Go and get your things then.'

When he returned with his bag, I had a whisky waiting for him. 'As you're not driving on. You weren't really expecting to, were you.'

'Hoping, Kate. Hoping.' He gave an impish smile, then he cradled the whisky in his hand and swirled it. 'We need to talk, don't we?'

'Do we?'

'It's about the only thing we haven't done.'

Very true. We'd fought, sulked, needled; we'd maintained stiff, dignified silences, but we hadn't talked. Yes, we needed to, but not like this, out of the blue.

'Sorry, Peter. You need to give me a couple of day's warning before I can settle down to a meaningful heart-to-heart.'

'I tried but you never answered my calls. No rush then, but perhaps we should make one last effort to behave like rational grown-ups, before we say goodbye forever?'

Too reasonable for me to object. 'Tomorrow.'

We went, I in my private nun's cell, he in the Guinevere room overlooking the rhododendrons, with the sheets I'd hastily aired and a polite 'goodnight then' exchanged down the dim corridor.

Why did he have to do this to me? I lay in the dark, thinking back over the years of our marriage, the disappointments, the small pathetic betrayals. And the good times. Did the bad really outweigh them? I didn't know but good and bad were still following me around. Would a talk be sufficient to cut the threads and release us?

Peter had arrived just as I was appreciating he wasn't the only fish in the sea. Not the only sleek, silver, sparkling fish. I fell asleep and dreamed of swimming beside him, weaving through weeds, as he glided inexorably towards an underwater yurt.

'I see you've come dressed for the country.' I eyed Peter's pale grey suit as we finished breakfast in the kitchen.

'I didn't realise quite how country this place would be.' He tapped the Rayburn. 'Hotel, Sarah said. I thought maybe genteel suburban. Fawlty Towers.'

'Pembrokeshire doesn't really do suburban. Wash or dry?'

'Wash.' He plunged our mugs. 'Seriously, what are you doing in a place like this? I know you're fond of Sylvia, but you're a city girl and this is the ultimate sticks.'

'I'm multi-facetted.'

'Was it the business with Mardell? The police couldn't have found anything to implicate you. Could they?'

I concentrated on drying a mug, thoroughly, inside and out. 'Thanks for your resounding vote of confidence.'

'Some people were suggesting…' Peter stopped.

'Gabrielle perhaps? Let me guess. My professional reputation was so mired that I must have run here to hide.'

'Look, I know it's not true.'

'I am not hiding. Quite the reverse. I came here to escape the rut, to broaden my horizons.'

'Obviously! Talk about leaving your comfort zone! Look at the place.' He stared out at the cobbled yard, the stone walls and narrow windows beyond. 'A year ago I wouldn't have been able to drag you within a hundred yards of a house like this. It must be riddled with demonic shivers.'

'How long are you staying? No lectures to get back for? No desperate deadline for *The Economist*?'

'I am allowed the occasional break. Still avoiding awkward subjects, Kate?'

'Still avoiding stupid comments. I warn you, Peter, if you put those grouts down the sink, you'll be the one probing the septic tank with a Dyno-rod.'

'Ye Gods. Time you moved back to civilisation and mains drainage.'

I laughed. 'Drainage aside, what do you think of our new business then? Impressed?'

'Certainly an impressive house. Just as long as anyone can find it. It's off the map, just about. What is the business exactly?'

'Anything that crosses Sylvia's fermenting mind. Holiday cottages for starters; you drove in past one of them last night. Mike has his woodwork and Sylvia pots away merrily, when she can remember. I keep a gentle managerial hand on it all. Project manager, guiding it in sensible and hopefully profitable directions.'

'What's the next project?'

'The craft collective. I'm sorting out proper electrics for the workshops. At the moment, there's one trailing cable and a couple of Bakelite sockets. We should be renovating a couple more holiday cottages, but they'll have to keep for the autumn. Sylvia's offered them to a bunch of archaeologists for a summer dig. Her pet professor thinks we're on a Bronze Age site.'

'Serious stuff.'

'Sylvia is excited – well of course, when isn't she? I'm not so convinced.'

'This is because you hate history of any description.'

'No I don't. Why should I hate history? That's a typically illogical male generalisation from random observations.'

'I was always told it was women who were illogical.'

'See, there's another one.'

Peter opened his mouth, decided against it and raised his hands in surrender. 'All right, you love history.'

'I don't love or hate it. It's just what put us where we are. End of story.'

'All right.'

'We're working on an historical project right now, as it happens.' I arranged the mugs and plates on the dresser. 'This is a listed building, you know, with a mediaeval hall. We're restoring it, using the original techniques and materials at monstrous expense. Mike's working on some beautiful linen-fold panelling. We've got men in, replacing oak beams and repairing the roof and the stonework.'

'Mighty stuff. Do I get to have a peek before they arrive?'

'They're already at work. Early risers.'

'I haven't heard a van.'

'They're staying on the estate.' I smiled. 'Yes, come and meet them.'

We could have gone through the boot-room to reach the Great Hall, but it was so much more dramatic seeing it for the first time from the outside. Peter stood open-mouthed, just as I had, on the gravel terrace, staring at the crumbling gable end and the arched doorway.

'You weren't kidding.' He reached round me before I could grapple with the iron handle. The door swung open. 'After you.'

It was the closest we'd been since he arrived. I felt his hand gently on the small of my back, drawing me in.

'So this is it.' I stepped free from his touch, and realised I'd walked into my own trap. Before me, from the low armoury door, shadows writhed at me. Behind me, Peter's presence nagged me with questions and regrets. And in the arch of the massive fireplace, Al, like some Prospero in command of this island of dust and rubble, billowing plans in hand, directed his Ariel and Caliban – Pryderi and Thor – as they gathered up tools.

'Hi, Al, how's it going?'

Al strolled across to join me, relinquishing his papers to Thor. 'Morning, Kate. Come to see the demolition start? We're ready to get smashing, we reckon.' He eyed Peter, waiting for an introduction.

'This is Peter Lawrence,' I said.

'Planning?' Al had probably never taken note of my surname and Peter was certainly dressed like a planning officer.

'No. A family friend. Just visiting.'

'Hi.' Al held out his hand.

Peter took it, with polite formality. 'How do you do?' Very restrained as he considered my words, our friendliness, Al's ponytail.

Al's eyes suggested the same spirit of enquiry.

I hoped mild chatter would get me through, with the minimum of embarrassment. 'So, the real work starts today. Do you really think we'll have it presentable for Sylvia's fair? There's far too much to be done, surely.'

'I'm hopeful. A lot of the panelling is sound enough. Just needs a little TLC. We're going to begin stripping out the worst of it. Go on, guys.'

Of course. It had to be now, with me standing there.

Of all the panels, corners, stones and timbers in this hall, Pryderi and Thor had to head for the wall by my nightmare doorway, armed with crowbars. I watched, my heart pounding, as they heaved and prised. In a flurry of foul dust and blackened splinters, a section of rotten panelling came loose, crashing to the flag floor, revealing stone wall, stained green with seeping damp. Al bounded to join them, examining the exposed masonry with scholarly interest.

Off came the next panel, and the next, and with each one I found myself edging backwards. I hadn't even realised I was doing it, until I found Peter beside me. 'Okay? You're white as a sheet.'

The final panel, into the armoury doorway. From pounding, my heart began to slow, till I thought it was going to stop completely. My lungs refused to function.

Creak, whine, wrench, crash, and then—

'Jeez!'

'Fucking hell!'

'Hey!'

Out flowed tentacles of horror, seething through the sour clouds of dust.

Al dropped on his knee, in the gaping mouth of a dark opening, too excited by the find to remember he was supposed to be attuned to spiritual vibrations. 'Priest's Hole! Yes!'

Pryderi and Thor were stooping round him, peering in. I tried to concentrate on Peter's face, as his eyes moved from me to the fascinating discovery, but his features were swimming. I was going to be sick. I bolted, out into the open air, stumbling across the weedy gravel, and reached for a shattered urn on the parapet to support me, before my knees gave way entirely.

Deep breaths. The sun, after a night of rain, played hide and seek among drifting flocks of clouds. A breeze ruffled the long grass in the meadow. Just like the cold rippling through me. Get a grip, woman!

'Kate? Are you all right?' Peter had followed. 'Here. Sit down.' He sat me on the parapet. 'You look terrible.'

'It's just the dust. I don't know how they cope with it—'

'It's not the dust. You felt something. Something about that priest hole or whatever it is. You knew it was there?'

'No! No I didn't know there was anything, anywhere.'

'But you did feel something.'

'No! Yes. Maybe. Well what do you expect? Anyone would find that place creepy.'

'Oh come on, Kate. I know you, remember.'

'Kate!' Al emerged from the hall, slapping dust and cobwebs from his arms. 'Work's going to have to go on hold, I'm afraid. Have to make some phone calls.' He was close enough now to take in my expression and pallor. He didn't ask, didn't need to, but he paused, putting the brakes on his enthusiasm. 'Sorry. A bit of a problem. We've opened a priest's hole and it's – not empty.'

'Not a priest!' Peter couldn't resist.

Al grimaced. 'God knows what he was. Or she. Definitely human though. Bones.'

'I see.' I rose to my feet, nails digging into my palms to stop my trembling. I'd known that death had happened there and was still screaming its terror and agony from the fabric. It had been screaming for centuries probably, but now that I'd arrived, it just had to erupt and spring a rotting corpse on me. 'Yes, of course work stops. What is the procedure? Do you know? Ever uncovered remains before?'

Al nodded, scrutinising me surreptitiously. 'Yes. It happens. You want me to handle it? I know the ropes.

100

Police, coroner's licence, bone specialist. They're old, that's all I can say for certain. If you want to see—'

'No!' I said.

'Yes!' said Peter, at the same moment.

'Show Peter,' I said. 'And I'll call the police.'

The two cheery police officers who drove up looked in on the gruesome find with as much prurient curiosity as Peter. It was obviously not a case of recent murder. The skeleton, probably male and partly dismantled by rats, was green and mouldering. A few shreds of rotting clothing remained, along with a leather belt and shoes, with buckles. Al guessed seventeenth century. Everyone was keen to take a look, except me.

'We'll pass it on to the coroner's office.' PC Evans finished his mug of tea and smacked his lips. 'Nothing for you to worry about. Soon have it off your hands.'

'Good,' I said. 'The sooner the better. Then they can get the restoration work back on track.'

'Yes.' Evans drew the word out. 'Your builders. Mm hmmm. Taverner. You chose him, why?'

'Because he's an expert in this sort of work.'

'You reckon?'

'Yes, I reckon.'

'You've got your doubts about them?' asked Peter, unhelpfully.

Evans straightened his hi vis vest, ready to leave. 'Wouldn't like to comment, Mr Lawrence. Suffice it to say, we knew his gang was in the area. Lost sight of them for a while, but here they are. Well, well. Just keeping tabs. Right then. We'll be on our way. You'll hear from the coroner soon, I hope.'

As soon as they'd driven away, Peter poured me a brandy. 'How are you feeling? You're not quite so green any more. Come on, sit down.'

'Don't fuss. I'm fine.' I didn't want him clucking over me. 'I don't do hysterics, remember. Save the sedatives for Sylvia. She and Mike are on their way and I'm not looking forward to telling her.'

He watched me, head cocked on one side. 'Will she be surprised?'

'Of course! It was a complete surprise to everyone, wasn't it?'

'Except you. I thought you might have mentioned what you'd felt in there to Sylvia.'

'Of course I didn't. You know I don't talk about these things.'

He gave a short pained laugh. 'I know you don't talk about them with *me*. I thought maybe Sylvia had more of your confidence.'

'I wouldn't inflict it on her.'

'Or maybe somebody else. Your new builder chum, perhaps? You seem pretty pally with him. Al, is it?'

'Yes, Al's working on the Great Hall. You think that's enough to make me unbutton my soul?'

'Looks like he's capable of unbuttoning more than that.'

'Peter, don't,' I warned him.

'Never imagined you developing a taste for rough trade, Kate.'

'Oh for God's sake!' I walked out, furious.

Peter caught up with me, on the stairs. 'Sorry. I don't know why I said that.'

'I really don't think you have any grounds for playing the jealous husband, do you?'

'No.' He agreed, so contritely I stopped in my tracks and sighed. 'Sorry, Kate. I know, I have no right to an opinion, whatever, whoever you choose to – but this Al. What do you know about him? The police seem pretty wary of him. Why?'

'It's probably his ponytail.'

'Maybe they know something. How did you find him? Did he come knocking on your door?'

'No, we knocked on his. All right?'

'You did get references?'

'Of course I did!' I wasn't going to let Peter question my professionalism, even if Al's arrival had been a case of pure serendipity. We'd had a reference of sorts. Meg, at the rectory, had assured us they were very good. 'Stop worrying about Al, or me, and start worrying about how Sylvia will react when she gets home to this.'

The Volvo pulled into the courtyard and Sylvia burst from the car to hug me. 'How *are* you? You're looking tired, isn't she, Mike?'

'She's looking fine,' said Mike. 'Hello Kate.'

'Oh I didn't mean – yes of course you're looking fabulous, you always do. I was just worried it would all be too much for you. London was wonderful, wasn't it, Mike, and people were saying such marvellous things about his work, royalty too, and he has commissions and everything, but do you know I'm really glad to be back home, it can all get a bit too much. So how is the Great Hall? I must go and see what's happening. Is Al managing all right? I was wondering, all the time, if they had the roof on yet, oh and how were the Baxters? I was so worried we might have forgotten something, wasn't I, Mike? Did I tell you we saw Sarah and Phil and darling Liam and they're coming in the autumn, oh I did, didn't I, and Sarah told me, now I don't want to put my foot in it or anything, but I thought you'd want to know that Peter, that rat, has split up with his secretary, she threw him out apparently and it serves him right, I say, because he deserves—'

I put a hand over her mouth. 'No the hall roof isn't on, but the oak for the beams has come, the Baxters are no trouble, and I know all about Peter. He's here.'

'What, here? At Llys y Garn? Oh darling, that's wonderful! No, really. Oh I'm so glad. Isn't that good news, Mike?'

Michael gave me a quizzical smile. 'Is it good news?'

'He's just visiting. Actually I've got some rather more important news for you.'

Sylvia gazed brightly at me.

'Al's started work in the hall, and they've found a concealed priest hole.'

Sylvia's mouth gathered to a perfect O. 'How exciting!'

'Interesting,' agreed Michael.

'And unfortunately, they've found human remains inside.'

In an instant, just as I had suspected, Sylvia's excitement turned to horror. 'Oh no, how awful. Oh that's horrible.'

'Just some very old bones, Sylvia. Nothing too ghastly. They'll be taken away very soon, for examination, and then Al can get on with the work.'

'But bones! Oh Kate.'

'Now, now.' Michael led her into the kitchen, while I prepared to deal with a prolonged session of weeping hysteria, by administering hot tea, spirits and words of reassurance. But Sylvia managed to confound me. I'd barely switched the kettle on when she grabbed my arm.

'Oh Kate!'

'Don't worry.'

'No but Kate, just think. Bones in a priest hole! What a story! Won't it be just perfect publicity!'

I stared at her, as Michael rolled his eyes and winced.

Then for the first time that day, I laughed.

11

Now that the gods of the hearth had returned to the house, all was alive and bubbling. Green bones, even a green skull, were too impersonal for Sylvia to feel real distress. She inspected them, with exclamations of comfortable horror, and invited the Baxters from the Lodge to come and see, which they did, armed with cameras, until official visitors arrived to bustle them out.

Michael stayed with Al to answer questions and witness, while our unsuspected lodger was dealt with, leaving me free to put as much distance as I could between myself and the horror.

'Fancy a walk?' I suggested.

'You don't want to hang around and keep an eye on things?' Peter, who was already reinstalled as Sylvia's golden boy, was clearly hoping to join the audience in the hall.

'No, I don't.' I'd spent the night in nightmares about the man trapped in that vile, claustrophobic hole. The desperate, screaming emotions I'd already felt had been given concrete form and, now it was daylight, I wanted to be well away.

And I needed to prise Peter away, before Sylvia had us up the aisle, renewing our vows. It wasn't that I wanted to slam the door on his overtures. I just wasn't ready to fling it wide open, either. Not yet.

'You came for a talk, didn't you, and the only place

we're going to manage it, with any privacy, is out there, so let's walk. I'll find you some boots. Come on, I'll show you our Stonehenge.'

As we set out, I heard another vehicle arriving, doors slamming. Soon, I trusted, the bones would be gone, but I could sense their sickening shadow creeping up behind me. I needed to be up on the hilltop, by my standing stones, and feel the clean, cold emptiness eating all my turmoil away.

Peter trudged beside me. 'So what about us then, Kate? How did it all go wrong?'

'That's an original opener.'

'Sometimes the obvious is the best.'

'Yes. I suppose I'm not the easiest person to live with.'

'Which of us is?'

'No, Peter. The correct response is "You were wonderful to live with, Kate."'

He laughed. 'And you were. Wonderful. Just not necessarily easy.'

'Yes. Sorry. I do appreciate the efforts you took to make allowances. Like pretending there was something wrong with the car so that we'd be late for Sarah's wedding and I wouldn't have to sit around in an old church—'

'You knew I was lying? You did a good job of pretending to be exasperated.'

'That's what I'm good at, Peter. Pretending. I learned it so young, it's become second nature. Sometimes I can't help myself. It's meant to protect me, but as often as not, it just ruins everything.'

For once he didn't jump in with a soothing platitude. We walked on.

'Are old churches so very bad?' he asked at last. 'A bit spooky, maybe, but are they really riddled with ghostly agony?'

'They're riddled with graves, tombs, crypts. The dead. Which is fine if they really were dead when they were put there. How many people have been buried alive down the centuries?'

'You're kidding!'

'If people had nothing to go on but pulse and a feather, I expect it was an easy mistake to make. Not so easy for the dying if they came round to find themselves suffocating in their own tomb.'

'Jesus! You've put me off churches now. No wonder you won't go in. And I suppose the guy in the priest's hole went through just the same.'

'Don't! Please. We're walking away from that.'

'Ah. Is that what we're doing? So you really have no idea—'

'No, I have no idea what he was doing in there.' I'd sat through dinner and breakfast listening to Sylvia and Peter's endless speculation, with only Michael's occasional suggestion, that we should wait for a bit more evidence, to add a touch of sanity. I'd had enough of the subject.

Peter hopped to avoid a puddle. 'Sorry. But you did know something was there. Okay, you felt something there, because that's what you do. That's why you avoid churches, ruins, old houses. That's why I can't understand why you chose to come here. An old place like this, with enough creaks and groans to spook anyone into thinking they see ghosts—'

'I have never claimed to see ghosts!'

'You know what I mean. Your shadows. Don't tell me Llys y Garn isn't crawling with them. It must be. Look at it.' We looked back on the muddle of chimneys, Victorian, Georgian, Elizabethan, neat brick, crumbling stone, buried in the woods. 'Don't tell me those bones are its only secret. Are there others?'

I thought of that waft of fear in the servants' attics. 'No.'

'No? Well, the bones are more than enough. So maybe you've come here to prove something.'

'Very perceptive of you.' I walked on.

Peter followed. 'And? Have you managed to convince yourself that it's all a figment of your imagination?'

'Oh that would be lovely, wouldn't it?' I glared at him. 'Discovering that I'm just a delusional basket-case.'

'Whoa! I'm not suggesting it. I was just wondering if that was what you wanted it to be.'

'No, I'm not hoping I'm insane. I can't stop feeling the things I feel, so I just want to learn to live with it. Look. Here's our archaeological site. Excited?' We'd reached the top fields. 'All manner of treasures under these humps, apparently.'

Peter leaned on the dry stone wall to look. 'Serious archaeological theory, or local folklore?'

'Serious archaeology. I told you, we have a professor who's going to dig it up. Professor Ronald Pryce-Roberts, BSc, PhD, MIFA—'

'RPR! Good God. Small world. I know Ronnie Pryce-Roberts!'

'You do?'

'Dour guy, big nose, smells of moth balls. Yes, we met – where was it? Henry introduced us. Don't you remember?'

'I've never met him before. Maybe you were with Gabrielle?'

He winced, then relief lit his face. 'No, I remember now. I was just with Phil. The conference on academic funding. I remember RPR. Totally out of place. Should have been in a solar-tope in Mesopotamia, directing native bearers.'

'Well, this is his Mesopotamia for the summer. He was keen, this was cheap, and his sister lives round here. She's on every committee and quango in the county, which means that we'll get permission for the camp, without having to resort to bribery.'

'What are they're expecting to find? More bodies?'

'No idea.' The thought didn't disturb me. The bones of the quiet dead, buried under the wide sky, held no terror. They were just organic matter. 'It's "An Introduction to Excavation Techniques" for undergraduates and aspiring students. Probably hoping for a few bits of pottery as a bonus. Ask Mike. He actually listened when Ronnie explained it.'

'You can't sense anything?'

'Out here in the open? Of course not. Come on.'

We climbed onto the open moor. 'Look, there are our stones. Be impressed, please.'

'Not exactly Stonehenge,' said Peter, as we reached the tumbled mass of Bedd y Blaidd. 'But still, very nice.'

We sat down on the springy turf, leaning against the upright stones, gazing out over the sweep and buckle of valley, forest and farmland, to the milky light of the distant sea.

For Peter that was it. A bunch of rocks to lean against. For Al, it had been a place of mystical intensity – or mystical claptrap. For me, the stones held sanctuary, their calming silence a refuge. What I felt, the sense of passion earthed, was mine alone. I knew I was always going to be alone. No point in wishing otherwise.

'So.' Peter stretched, making himself comfortable. 'How's it going? Your one-to-one combat with the grim reaper.'

I was jolted by his flippant tone. 'My what?'

'The thing that dogs you. Death.' Realising that his attempt at rephrasing it only made it worse, he stopped, then he leaned forward, determined to finish the point. 'I mean you feel death the way no one else can. Sorry, but there it is. It's never going to leave us alone, is it? It's our little problem.'

I didn't need psychic powers to know he was thinking about the baby. '*My* little problem.' I pulled up a tuft of heather and began shredding it. 'I'm the one who feels it.'

Peter got up, took a few steps along the ridge, hands in pockets, eyes on the glinting horizon. Then he did an about turn and looked down at me. 'That's the point, Kate. You make it all yours. You won't share. You shut everyone out, even me. Why?'

'Because it's the only way to survive. I did share with you, didn't I?' I pictured his face, the moment I'd told him the baby was dead, and I looked away. 'I told you how weird I was, on our very first date. You thought it quite sexy back then.'

'All right yes, no, not sexy. Interesting. But then you stopped talking about it.'

'I stopped because it isn't sexy, or interesting. It's vile, and I realised you'd never be able to understand that.' I stood up. 'You really don't want to share it, Peter. Believe me, you don't want to be constantly enmeshed in death, every way you turn!' I slipped past him, pained and angry, at him, at myself, at the whole of bloody life. Before he could pull me back, I charged on, slithering down the steep slope, slipping, almost tumbling into a sheltered cup among the rocks. I teetered on its brink, looking down.

A dead sheep was lying there.

Dead, rotting, eyeless, one limb torn off by scavengers.

Why did it have to turn up at my feet?

Because an irresistible force had brought me directly to it, because death was my shadow and I was never going to escape it.

Death had been with us from the start, sealing our marriage and then sealing its fate. I'd been courting Peter when my mother died. She went into hospital for a heart operation. A potentially serious condition, but a supposedly routine procedure. I went with her, packing her nightgowns and slippers. I paced the corridor while they operated, worrying about her, but all the while, guiltily, thinking 'I want to be with Peter.' I was with her as she came round, groggy and smiling. 'Successful,' they said. 'It all went very well.'

And amidst my joy and relief, there had been the shame-faced satisfaction that with her on the mend, I'd soon be able to go to my man. She knew, of course, pretending to shoo me away. 'Now off you go, to that Peter.'

'I'm not going anywhere,' I said, and meant it.

But by the second day, she was stronger, more colour in her cheek, and when she said 'Go on now. You're not doing any good hanging round here,' I kissed her and went.

Peter was working in Southampton. It was two hundred miles away, but a quick visit couldn't hurt. I phoned the hospital the next day and all was well, Peter was fun and life was good and I didn't phone again.

I didn't phone again.

I was ambling back up north, two days later, pausing at a craft shop in the Cotswolds, when I felt her confused panic, her urgent longing for me and then – nothing. A piece vanished from the jigsaw of my life. Between one breath and the next she'd gone.

I dropped a vase I hadn't even liked. £17.50. I threw

111

them a twenty pound note and didn't wait for the change. I drove north, blindly, flooring the accelerator, until a police car pulled me over. 'I have to get home,' I said. 'My mother's just died.'

They calmed me down, then let me go. I drove more carefully then. Why rush? It was too late.

Unexpected deterioration. Unforeseen complications. The hospital had tried to contact me but no one was sure where I was. I hadn't left a number.

They took me in to see her and say goodbye, as if the pallid, hollow thing under the white sheet was my mother. It wasn't her. She was already gone. She'd gone, wanting me, while I was cradling a vase I didn't like, in a shop I hadn't needed to visit, and that was the only goodbye I had.

Peter rushed to join me as soon as he heard. He hugged me while I sobbed, and when he said 'Marry me,' I held onto him and never wanted to let go.

Nine years later, I told him our baby was dead, and the marriage was over. That was how it worked, death marking my every turn. Peter had lived with me, watched me, touched me, listened to my rare explanations, but he could never truly understand. No one could.

I could demonstrate this to him.

'You've seen our bones, you've seen our stones. Now, do you want to see a yurt?'

'I don't know. Do I want to see a yurt?'

'Of course you do. And a round house. A genuine Celtic round house. Well, a genuine Nuclear Age round house, I should say. They're building it in the woods.'

'Why?'

'Why not?' I led him down in the direction of the Annwfyn camp.

'We did have good times.' Peter gave a wistful sigh

as he followed.

'I know we did.'

'Couldn't we—'

'I'm still the same, Peter.'

'Couldn't we learn how to deal with that?'

'How? I can't share because I don't dare. I've built a wall up round myself that keeps everyone out, even you. I know it's wrong, I know I'm to blame, but it's the way I am, and it's no basis for a relationship. It can't work.'

'Learn to talk.'

'How do I talk, Peter? I can use words, but they will never be enough for you or anyone to understand.'

'So you won't even try?'

'All right.' We were there, at the gloomy, overhung hollow, by the stagnant pools of foetid darkness. 'I'll talk. I'll share. This place. I feel something here.'

'You do? What?' Peter scrambled down, edging round on the narrow path as if to protect me from unseen spectres. He stood, waiting for some monster to rise from the waters. But nothing rose. There was nothing to see except, bizarrely, an offering of petals and grain on a rock in the midst of the shadowy horror.

'Something bad?'

'Yes. Very bad.' My voice was steady, however much my gut recoiled. 'Resentment. Terror. Animal fury. A Spaghetti Junction of blaring emotions. There. I am talking about it. But all I have to share is words, because you can't feel what I'm feeling, so you can't really believe.'

'Oh I believe!' Peter pulled a loose branch from the undergrowth and began to poke the oily surface of the nearest black puddle.

'What are you doing?' The unearthing of bones in the hall was bad enough. Now here was my husband, prodding mud in search of more. 'Leave it alone!'

'I just want to see…' The tip went down. And down. He let it go, and the branch slumped sideways into the glutinous mire. 'I can believe something bad happened here, all right. Well, look at it. Someone fell in, or fought, or was pushed. They died. That makes perfect sense. There's a body in there. They find bog bodies, don't they? Ancient sacrificial victims. Is that it? Is that what happened?'

'Don't you get it? I don't know! Is there a body in there? Yes, probably, a dozen. A hundred. I don't know any more than you. I knew someone died horribly in the hall, but I didn't know there'd be a body there. I can feel the emotions that came screaming out of people here. Death gave them escape, but what they felt is still here and when I'm here, I have to eat it, drink it, suffocate in it. So as far as I'm concerned, it isn't an interesting puzzle, it's a nauseating cancer. Can we get out of here now?'

Peter stifled the question on his lips and held out his hand to lead me on, out of the dell. 'I'm sorry, I really am. I know that when you get it, it totally messes you up. But I think you only make it worse for yourself by keeping it inside, putting on such an act of feeling nothing. If you just explained—'

I laughed bitterly. 'If I went round explaining what I felt, Peter, they'd lock me up. People don't want to understand. Do you have any idea what it's like when the whole world is pointing at you, calling you mad or bad?'

'Oh look, that old man, you were a child—'

'Yes, children learn. And I learned what I had to do to survive.' The aroma of wood smoke reached us. 'Look, here's the yurt.'

Annwfyn was a serious building site. The last time I'd

been up here, a pile of long stripped poles had been the only evidence of an incipient round house. Now a wide ring of sturdy short posts were in place and longer poles were waiting to one side, with an elaborate crown, in a vast and complicated jigsaw. It was going to be huge, dwarfing the yurt, which sat squat and homely under the trees.

Molly was alone, busy weaving wands purposefully into the wide circle of posts, with the help of good solid boots under a long embroidered kaftan, fringed scarf and a dozen strings of beads.

'It's going to be a palace,' I said, taken aback by the size of it. 'You must have cut down a forest to make room for it.'

Molly's brow clouded with regret. 'Mostly saplings. We did seek permission—'

'Oh don't worry, Sylvia wouldn't object. She's been enthusiastic about the whole project from the start.'

'The trees,' corrected Molly. 'We asked permission of the trees.'

'Did they give it?' Peter shot me a grin.

'They recognise us as non-confrontational spirits.' Molly selected another long supple rod and raised it like a druidic staff. 'They know we create, we do not destroy. We've planted new seedlings as appeasement.'

'Sustainability,' said Peter, gravely.

'We take nothing that we don't replace. And we worship with them.'

'I hadn't thought of trees worshipping,' I said.

'They worship by being. They draw strength from the force beneath us. They are its expression. There's a very strong ley line here. That's why we chose it.'

Peter shut his eyes as if to sense the earth energy, and nodded. I could feel the derision bursting within him.

'You can feel the force,' said Molly. 'It comes down

115

from the stones, through the spring. That's our harmony line. We tread it each day so that the trees know we understand.'

'A real ley line!' said Peter.

'You're interested? I have books.' She was wiping her hands clean, leading us towards the yurt. 'Would you like some tea?'

I would have said no, but Peter was enjoying himself. 'So you feel the force, what, in your fingers? Your feet?'

I sat back on a pile of rugs, drinking a tisane and cautiously nibbling little cakes, while Molly talked, earnestly, in full druidic mode, and Peter egged her on, struggling not to laugh.

'We ought to go,' I said at last, as he crossed his eyes over Molly's explanation of the temperamental difference between the ash and the beech. 'I really need to get back and see what's happening. Thanks, Molly.'

Peter followed reluctantly, but once we were free of the camp he was almost dancing, shouting his laughter. 'My God, she's a gem. Ley lines. Earth forces. She is one loopy lady.' He clapped his hands. 'Hey! I suppose this is their totem pole!' He slithered down the slope to a jutting rock where a single shaft of bleached wood speared up at the sky. 'Do you reckon they dance round it?' He was about to demonstrate.

'It's one of Michael's sculptures,' I said. 'A new one. Hasn't been here long.'

'Yes? Right. Yes, okay.' Peter did a double take. He stepped back to look at it, teetering, oblivious, on the edge of the rock. 'Yes, well, art. A bit stark, isn't it? What's it mean, then?'

'Does it have to mean something? Molly calls it Taranis. The force of lightning vitalising the earth.'

'Well there you are! A bit of minimalist artwork and

she has to turn it into an earth god thing. I bet they'll be dancing round it. You wait till the next thunderstorm. They'll be out here, chanting.' He started laughing again, mockingly worshipping the white shaft, while I flinched.

An austere white shaft, untouched, desolate, solitary. Thank you, Michael.

'I take it Molly hasn't converted you,' I said.

She might not have converted him, but she had offered him a lot of cake. He clearly hadn't realised what was in it. 'Oh, come on Kate. Don't tell me you believe any of that clap-trap? Where did you get these people? They're crazy, Kate. Totally bonkers.'

'Thank you for making my point, Peter.'

'What point? You don't believe that stuff any more than I do.'

'No, but they do. They feel something. Or they think they do, or they want to. It's not something I feel, but maybe Molly really does. Whatever it is, you don't feel it, so when she talks about it, you call her crazy.'

'Oh.' He sobered up quickly, scrambling back to join me. 'It's not the same as your thing. You feel something real, I know you do.'

'Why is it that you believe me, but not her?'

'Because I know you, I trust you, because your feelings make sense—'

'No they don't. They make no sense at all. You believe me because, when we met, you wanted to get in my knickers, so it paid to take me seriously. You don't fancy Molly, so you call her crazy.'

'Don't be daft. That wasn't it at all.'

'Yes it was.'

'No it wasn't.'

'This is an adult conversation?'

'God, you can be infuriating!' He slapped a tree in

frustration. 'And that's just what you want to be, isn't it. You don't want to trust people, you don't want to share because deep down, secretly, you've always enjoyed being misunderstood.'

'Don't be so puerile.'

'It's the kudos, isn't it? I'm your real problem, me, your husband, wanting to understand, wanting to share, wanting to spoil your magnificent isolation and mess up your life.'

'Bullshit. I never thought you'd messed up anything!'

'No? You've always blamed me for you not being there when your mother died.'

'And you blamed me for killing the baby!'

He flinched as if I'd slapped him. For a moment he stood motionless, struggling to speak without shouting. 'I did not blame you,' he said at last, through clenched teeth.

I put my face in my hands. What was wrong with me? 'Sorry. I shouldn't have said that.' How could I have said it? How could I blame him for that terrible thought? Hadn't he loyally rejected it as quickly as it hit him? He'd behaved impeccably after that split-second treachery. He'd taken care of me, demanded action at the hospital when they told him I was just being paranoid. He'd held my hand when their tests confirmed what I already knew. He'd cried and brought me flowers, he'd done everything he could to console me. He'd never said a word of blame or criticism, even though, for one small second, he'd thought I'd wished it dead.

Christian's vile innuendos came back to me. Killer Queen. No!

'I'm sorry!' I blurted.

Peter leaned back against an oak tree, staring up at the leaves. 'Kate – Oh God, this isn't going to work. This

118

isn't how I meant it to be when I came here.'

'I know. I'm sorry. It's my fault.'

'No it isn't. It was a stupid idea, that's all. My stupid idea.' He sighed, took my hand and led me on, down towards the house. 'Look, I'll go. Coming here without phoning, without warning you; it was madness. I should never have just landed myself on you, challenging you like this.'

'No it's me. I shouldn't have been so resistant. So argumentative.'

'Shall we quarrel over the right to take the blame? It's just bad timing. With this priest hole business, on top of everything, a body turning up. Christ, I chose the worst moment.'

'It's not the best.'

'I'm going to go.'

'You don't have to.'

'Better if I do. For now.'

Sylvia had gone to join Michael at the hall, which relieved us of the need for explanations. It took Peter five minutes to repack his bag and he came back down with a sad smile. 'Sorry, Kate. That stuff going on over there really screwed up yesterday for you, and now I've managed to screw up today as well. You deserve better.'

'Peter. Listen.' I stopped him at the door. 'You will come back, won't you? You're the one who deserves better. I really do want to talk. Let's give ourselves one last chance to be adults.'

He nodded. 'You know I never blamed you for the baby, Kate. I swear to God.'

'I know,' I lied. 'And I never blamed you for my mother. I blamed myself for that, never you.'

'Mutual paranoid sensitivity?'

'That's what it is. Promise you'll return.'

119

'I promise.' He hesitated, not sure whether to shake hands, or kiss me on the cheek.

I kissed him properly. It had been a long time. We hugged, hard. 'Take care,' I said.

The house was quiet when he drove away. Quiet as a tomb. I tiptoed upstairs, shutting my bedroom door. Al and his gang could sort out their own tea and sandwiches for once. I didn't want to see them. Not today. I wanted to be alone. Just as Michael had portrayed me; a white shaft, isolated, rejecting, closed, reaching into nothingness. I curled up on my bed and let the solitude feed my old grief.

12

Our bones were removed to a lab, to be studied with scholarly interest. The verdict, as Al guessed, was that they were of a male, from the seventeenth century. A young adult and, apart from being dead, in good health. Cause of death unspecified, identity unknown, presence unexplained, mystery unsolved.

Michael revisited his researches on the house in the records office, but found no clue. There was a crabbily written ledger, citing monies spent on everything from the demolition of a tower to the purchase of servants' liveries, but nothing about a priest's hole. A civil war atrocity perhaps? Whoever he was, our skeleton was doomed to be buried a second time, in the stories that were soon in circulation at the Cemaes Arms.

The starting favourite was that he was a gardener's boy from Llys y Garn, who had gone missing in 1922, amidst rumours of Satanic happenings at the house. But the story that won, soon cited as gospel fact, was that "she" was the low-born wife of a lord's son, murdered by her father-in-law on her wedding night, and that she had been found still shrouded in her wedding gown.

'It's what people want him to be.' Michael laughed as I ground my teeth when the postman mentioned it. 'You can't fight wishful thinking.'

'You're a scientist. You should fight it.'

'I'm a scientist, so I observe, and study the phenomenon.'

He was right of course. We were stuck with the smothered bride. Even Sylvia embraced the tale, so I gave up, and found better things to worry about. Professor Pryce-Roberts arrived to set up his summer school. In the paddock beyond the orchard, a camp was erected, with tents, a dining marquee and Portaloos. The two labourers' cottages, recently inhabited, with plumbing and electricity, would be acting as cookhouse and bathrooms, with beds for a select few. I directed deliveries and found Ronnie contemplating his camp bed, in Cottage No.1, with quiet ascetic pleasure. His sister had a comfortable sprung mattress for him, down the valley, but apparently he preferred a narrow canvas hammock in a draughty cottage.

At Annwfyn there was movement too. Nathan left, but plasterers Tim and Baggy arrived from Chester, Gary the glazier came from Bath, and Pete from East Anglia was going to thatch the round house. Joe and Padrig, something to do with metal working, were due back from Peru sometime in the next couple of months.

They were professionals. Anyone could see that. I hadn't demanded full references, or checked them out properly, but they so obviously knew their business, it would be absurd to sneak in an on-line search now. I refused to be nudged by Peter and the police, into doubting my own judgement.

Michael's beautifully crafted panelling was soon in place, covering the scar of the rotted sections, and the entrance to the priest's hole. I had hoped it would be fastened securely in place, forever sealing that revolting tomb, but Sylvia was determined that a priest's hole should be preserved and Al had contrived cunningly concealed hinges and a catch in the last panel, so that guests could enjoy the thrill. I put my foot down at the idea of posing a skeleton inside, wrapped in lace and illuminated by green lighting, but I couldn't stop Sylvia commissioning a picture of the tragic bride from a local artist. It, like the hall itself, promised to be ready for Sylvia's Elizabethan Fayre. She didn't doubt it for a moment.

The first archaeology students were bussed in, pleasantly rowdy, all keen to view the priest hole and speculate on its occupant, before settling into their canvas accommodation. By the end of the day they'd taken surgical possession of our lumps and bumps in the top fields and turned the paddock into a chaotic, booming, shanty town. Ronnie invited me to inspect the work so I strolled over to see what they were up to.

I pushed open the door of No.1 cottage and found my way blocked by a young woman carrying a tray of mugs.

'Yes?' She was occupied with the tray, but I could feel her, mentally, extending her arms to keep me out until I'd passed inspection.

'It's all right, I've just come to see Ronnie.'

'The professor is very busy. I don't know that he'll be able to see you just now.'

'I'm sure he will.' I called over her shoulder. 'Ronnie!'

His door opened and he peered round nervously. 'Ah, yes, er, Mrs Lawrence. Indeed, thank you.'

The young woman rushed him with belligerent eagerness. 'Professor, I've made your tea.'

'Thank you, yes, Hannah, er, Miss Quigley. Thank you.' He took a cup, peering into its pale, milky depths. 'Um, I'm just going to show Mrs Lawrence the trenches.'

'I'll fetch your notes,' said Hannah Quigley.

'No! No, thank you, if you could just, er, gather C group in the lecture room, so that I can, er... Mrs Lawrence, please.' He put down the untouched tea and earnestly gestured to me to precede him from the cottage. Hannah stood on the threshold, staring after us as we headed up the track.

'You have a very efficient secretary,' I said.

'Ah, yes, no, Miss Quigley is one of the students. She was not very, er, comfortable with the tents, so she has a bed in the, er, house. Very, um, keen. Yes.'

Keen, and he was trapped with her in No.1. I sympathised. As we climbed the track and left the camp behind, he brightened and treated me to a short dissertation on aerial photography and radiocarbon dating.

'... combined, of course, with dendro-chronology. Ah, here we are. You see we've already made progress with the surface layer of our primary dig, based on initial geophysical exploration.'

I surveyed mud and a cat's cradle of pegged-out string, where two long strips of turf had already been removed by a small mechanical digger. It looked far more industrial than I had expected.

There were to be two trenches at this primary site, and he had high hopes of uncovering the post holes of one or more round houses.

'The originals,' he added with a disparaging sniff. 'We are not going to be indulging in amateur reconstruction.'

'We've been checking out the one in the woods,' said one of his students, with a grin. 'Mega!'

'I can't imagine what they hope to achieve,' said Ronnie, acerbically.

'I think their aim is just to build something eco-friendly to live in,' I suggested.

Ronnie was unimpressed. 'There is no validated evidence for their techniques – that roof crown... Ah, now, Matthew, are you using that theodolite as I instructed? Who is mapping? You are recording properly?' He strode off among the mature amateurs, while the younger students hung back to ply me with questions about the woodland camp.

'So, what, they really going to live in it, for real?'

'Like, permanently?'

'I'm not sure.' I realised I had no idea what Al's long term plans were.

'Methodology is everything,' Ronnie returned from his tour of the incipient trench. 'Please remember, everyone, that this is an educational project. The techniques of excavation will be completely different at our secondary site, but the need for care, accuracy and precise record keeping will remain the same.'

'Your secondary site? You do know the standing stones are out of bounds, don't you?'

'Yes, indeed, Dr Bradley did explain the limits of our explorations. There is, however, a rather interesting bog.' He produced an ordnance survey map from his pocket, and showed me. 'It offers scope for a more novel approach. I think we have evidence that it is significantly old.'

I stared at the map. Contours, trees and a couple of

marsh symbols. How innocent on a map. The bog. Why? What, in God's name, had induced him to winkle it out and go poking about in it? 'I didn't realise that area was included in your plans.'

'Mrs Callister gave permission.'

'But – through the woods. Won't it be difficult to get at?'

'It will be a challenge, certainly, but I am reserving it for my more experienced students. The principle exercise will be to map it.' Ronnie's lip curled. 'If the, er, beatnik persons will permit.'

I thought of Molly's ley line, her withered flowers and grain. 'They have their beliefs, their rituals. The ancient people who lived here would understand that, wouldn't they?'

'I hardly think you can compare the religious and ceremonial customs of our remote ancestors with the antics of that strange woman in beads, who is harassing my students. The young can be very impressionable. I trust she'll not be allowed to inveigle them into some disagreeable cult. She seems to have erected the most bizarre idols, all over your woods.'

'Actually, they're Dr Bradley's sculptures. They're just supposed to be art.'

'Ah,' said Ronnie, groping for a way out. 'Ah, indeed. Of course.' I wondered what hapless form he would take, if Michael ever tried to capture his spiritual essence in knotted wood.

Ronnie's students were going to map the bog. I couldn't stop them, but mapping wouldn't be so bad, would it? It wouldn't stir the waters? I'd keep calm and hope that the professor's embarrassment over Michael's sculptures would be the only source of discomfort during the dig.

It wasn't. Two days later, there was a knock on the front door. The front door that nobody used. I wrenched it open to find Hannah Quigley standing there, chin raised and jaw set.

'Hello, Hannah, what can I do for you?'

'There are men.' She didn't bother with the niceties. But plenty of things did bother her. She was no teenager; late twenties I guessed, and fretfulness hung upon her, like her limp, pale hair. What could have been a pretty face was grooved by anxious disapproval. 'They're in the trees, lurking.'

'In the orchard, you mean?' The orchard separated the cottages and paddock from the walled garden by the Great Hall. 'I expect it's our builders. They often take their break there when it's hot.'

'They look at us. I've seen them. Trying to look in the windows.'

'The cottage windows? I don't think they'd see much from the orchard.'

'They shouldn't be there! This is our site.'

'No, I'm sorry, Hannah, this is our site. You archaeologists have the cottages and the paddock, the builders have the garden, and the orchard is common ground, for everyone. I'm sure we can all learn to live and work together.'

She was not pleased.

The next evening she was back. 'Professor Pryce-Roberts wishes to speak with you. If you could come, please.'

'What's this about?'

'You'll have to ask him that.' She was a hair's breadth from rudeness so blatant that I'd be obliged to shout at her. 'Now, if you don't mind.'

I glanced at my watch. 'I'll see if I can find a moment later on.'

I did stroll over, a few minutes after she departed in high dudgeon. There might, after all, be a genuine crisis. Ronnie looked up in surprise when I arrived.

'I've been summoned,' I said.

'Ah. Oh, oh dear, Hannah, yes, I said I would speak to you.'

'If it's about the builders using the orchard—'

'Orchard? Er, no, but we are encountering a little difficulty, up at the secondary dig. I did understand we would be permitted to survey the site.'

'So Mrs Callister agreed.'

'Without hindrance. From the beatniks?'

'Oh Lord. What have they been doing?'

'They seem determined to undermine our activities, with acts of sabotage.'

'Sabotage! That sounds a bit extreme.'

'Well… Tramping through while we're trying to work. Cutting our guide lines. I did consider calling the police.'

'No need for that. I'm sure we can work things out.'

'It's that very odd woman,' said Ronnie. 'She does seem bent on disrupting us.'

'I'll have a word, see if we can come to some sort of a compromise. We don't want the police called in, and everything stopped, do we? Much better to keep the summer school going.'

'Oh! Yes, absolutely,' said Ronnie.

I found Al tidying up in the walled garden. Sylvia's pots and herb beds occupied one sunny corner, but the rest was an open-air builder's workshop.

'How's it going?'

'Good.' He stooped for the last of the tools. 'Looking good.'

With the day's work over, a drowsy silence

descended, as the exquisite radiance of the summer evening washed over us. The deep blue-green of the wooded valley was hazed with gold. The horizon rang with the reflected blaze of the sea. It was the wrong time for territorial negotiations.

'Do you have to rush back to your tofu stew?' I asked.

Al smiled. 'I fancied a steak at the pub. The others are off to a gig. I'm giving it a miss, so Kim doesn't think I'm crowding her.'

'Do you fancy a walk? Up onto the hills?'

'Sure.' Al fell in beside me, as I headed for the gate into the woods.

'You take care of your sister, don't you? Not like some brothers.'

Al winced. 'I take care because I'm – I was her guardian. We lost our parents when she was twelve.'

'Oh God, I'm sorry. What happened?'

'A car crash.' He held the gate open for me and we passed into the cathedral hush of the trees. 'Just a Sunday drive with the dog. A maniac, coming home from the pub, smashed into them. The dog died too.' He shrugged, painfully. 'Not so bad for me. I'm nine years older.'

'Did that really make it any better?'

'Better able to cope. Kim couldn't. She went a bit crazy.'

'Is that why you dropped your course, took up building? To look after her?'

'No, I liked the work, that's all. Maybe too much. Maybe I'd have made a better guardian if I'd spent more time at home.'

'No one watching you with her could think you were a bad guardian.'

'Guilt-ridden possessiveness? Not always a recipe for success. But I'm learning to let go.' He smiled at me, his eyes narrow. 'At least as long as the likes of Christian Callister keep away. They're like sharks scenting blood. They can sense vulnerability.'

'I'm sure we won't see him again for months. He's got the money he wanted and after what he did to Tamsin—'

'She's recovered?'

'Oh yes, India rubber, she bounces back. Coming home soon.'

'She's okay. I like her.'

'I'll tell her you said that.'

Al laughed, then glanced at me sidelong. Still interested. Very forgiving of him, considering that I had paraded my husband before him and made it plain that I was still annoyingly confused on the subject.

So confused that I side-stepped to business. 'I've had Professor Ronnie chewing my ear, about you. You're beatniks, by the way.'

'Love it!'

'Thought you might. Anyway, he's worried about his dig.'

'I'm worried about his dig,' said Al.

'I assume Molly's upset that they're messing up the bog.'

'Pretty upset, yes. But you've given them permission to be there, and it is your land. You'd like us to keep away, I suppose. Are we banned from it?'

'I really don't want to set up demarcation lines round the place. You're not banned – but neither are the archaeologists. Can we live and let live? Ask Molly for a bit of forbearance. They'll only be here for a few weeks.'

Al nodded. 'We might be moving our camp on before then.'

'What! You can't! What about the hall?'

'Don't worry. We don't have to camp here to get the job done.'

'But the round house – you've got everything settled there.'

'Except that our water's being fouled up.'

'Oh hell, of course, the stream. You don't actually drink it, do you?'

He shrugged. 'No, mostly we use your well. That's still clean. All right, you want me to calm things down? Just as long as the professor does the same. The aggravation isn't all from our side, you know. He's got a mad woman, constantly haranguing us.'

'Hannah!' I laughed. Hannah and Molly; we certainly had our share of mad women. 'Haranguing is her thing. She harangues me whenever she sees me – I've started hiding when I see her coming. But she'll be gone in a fortnight. Can we keep things calm till then?'

Al grinned. 'You're in the middle here, aren't you?'

'Yip. Poor Sylvia. She had no idea letting them work on the bog would cause trouble. I wish she'd asked me. I'd have put it completely off limits.'

'So it wasn't your idea?'

'No it certainly was not! God, no!'

'Ah. I assumed, seeing as your professor was told about it by a colleague, Peter Lawrence—'

'What!'

'Mr Lawrence advised him to investigate the bog.'

'No!'

'This is what I was told.'

'I...,' I was spitting. Peter had told Ronnie to investigate the bog? Had my reactions sparked off a curiosity that was so much more important to him than my feelings? 'How could he!'

'You didn't suggest it then?'

'No! Never. Believe me!' Peter knew exactly how I

130

felt about it. He knew how I felt about the discovery of the bones in the hall and yet – and yet – 'I'll kill him!'

'Don't worry about it,' said Al. 'I don't suppose he realised it would create problems.'

'He's not stupid. Anything but. Oh, how could he!'

Al slipped an arm round me. 'Don't get worked up.'

'And I actually asked him to come back!'

'For a reconciliation?'

'Reconciliation? After this? Ha! What's the point of deep and meaningful talks, if he just sneaks off behind my back and—'

'Shhh.' I felt Al's arm enclosing me, his body absorbing my anger and frustration. Slight stubble against my brow. The smell of plaster dust and faint male sweat.

Peter really wasn't stupid. He was quite capable of calculating that the bog excavation would create friction with the camp below. Could it have been a sideswipe at my rough-trade builder friend? My anger doubled, and with it came the lightness of liberation. Had I really been hanging back all these months because I still felt too married to Peter?

Suddenly I felt very much divorced. 'Yes, let's forget all about my bloody husband.'

Annwfyn. A mystical Otherworld. A place to pass in and out of reality, just as the stars glinted, in and out of the fluttering shimmer of leaves over us, and the red glow of embers on the hearth set phantoms dancing in the creaking undergrowth. A vast sheepskin rug, wide enough to cradle the Celtic knot of entwined limbs, owls bearing our gasps into an echoing void.

Al kissed the hair from my cheek. 'Still hungry?' he asked.

'Ravenous,' I said.

'Well, you took your time coming to the table, but now that you're here…,'

There really is nothing like furious sex for sorting out the grims.

13

'How are you, Taz?' Al climbed down from a ladder to take a mug from Tamsin. 'No lasting damage, I see.'

She'd arrived from college barely an hour before, unmarked by the fox incident. Her first demand had been to see the priest hole, since she'd missed the bones. Her second, unspoken but equally obvious, was to see Al, and as he was working in the Great Hall, she was able to do both, by helping me with the tea duty.

'I'm fine. I hope my pig of a brother rots. But I'm so glad you found me, that day, Al. I don't know what I'd have done.' She'd have coped perfectly well, but if she wanted to play the helpless damsel card, who was I to deter her?

Al gave her a playful hug. 'Couldn't have you lost in the wilderness, Taz.' His eyes met mine, over the rim of his mug.

'Show me where the skeleton was, please, please?'

I let Al do the honours while I continued passing the tray round for six sweaty men to help themselves to mugs and cake. All right. That was more than enough time for my niece to relish the horror.

I raised my voice to reclaim their attention. 'Taz is leaving us in a week or so, Al. Off to Spain, tickets booked.'

'Oh – yeah.' Al's magnetism complicated Tamsin's holiday enthusiasm. 'It won't be for long. I'm meeting up with friends at Heathrow. Just friends. No one special.'

'Heathrow? In a week or so, you say?'

'Yeah, next Thursday.'

'Well, I need to go to London sometime in the next few weeks. You fancy a lift to the airport?'

'Really?'

'Why not?'

'Mega!' Tamsin gave him a hugely physical hug. 'Michael said he'd take me, but this would be, you know…,'

Al grinned at me over her head, keeping his balance with difficulty. 'How about you, Kate? Fancy a trip to London, to chaperone your niece?'

'You kidding?' Tamsin was appalled.

'Hey, I just thought your mother would want someone with you, at the airport.'

'I don't need anyone. Tell him, Kate.'

'I think it's a clever idea. Listen.' I drew her aside. 'You know Sylvia will worry. She still tries to hold your hand, crossing the road. Once she starts thinking about your flight, she'll probably want to come herself, make a big fuss, dig out a nice old biddy to sit with you on the plane.'

Tamsin groaned.

'If I tell her I'm going, she'll stop fretting and you can trust me to stand clear and leave you to it.'

'I suppose.' Tamsin heaved an exasperated sigh. 'But you won't—'

'Oh, er, Mrs Lawrence, hello?' With much flapping and panting, an archaeology student burst into the hall.

'Yes, what is it?'

The boy ground to a halt, stooping to recover his

breath. 'We've found something. RPR says to let you know at once, so you can see.'

'Found what?'

'A body! At least, I dunno. I think it's a body. I was on the other site. They just said to run down and tell you. They're getting equipment and stuff. So—'

'Right. Where have they found it?'

'It's in the bog.'

Of course it was in the bog. The blood turned sluggish in my veins, as I stood staring at the secret panel Al had left ajar. It was all as inevitable as a Greek tragedy. The dead of past centuries were going to keep rising from their unsuspected tombs, because I had arrived on the scene, a magnet for death, drawing them inexorably to me.

'Yes. That's very interesting. I see.' My automaton calmness was an island in a chaotic sea. Uproar. Tools and mugs were dropped. Al, Tamsin, the boy, everyone was speaking.

'What is it? Is this for real? Ooh, another one! You mean they've dug up a body? Let's go!' Everyone was excited, keen to see. In the general exodus from the hall I found myself left behind. Switched off.

'Kate. You okay?' Al returned, with Tamsin, torn two ways, in tow.

'Yes.' Switch on, Kate. 'We'd better go and take a look, hadn't we.'

'No rush,' said Al. 'Would you prefer not to come? I can go and see what this fuss is about.'

'No. I'm coming.' I pulled myself together and marched out, up into the woods, accompanied by Tamsin's excited babble.

And then I stopped. Ahead of us, Hannah Quigley was advancing, a hand raised. 'I'm sorry, I can't let you go any further. Turn back please.'

134

'Have they pulled it out?' asked Tamsin eagerly.

'I'm afraid I can't discuss it,' said Hannah, her self-importance so ridiculous that, in other circumstances, it would have had me laughing. 'It's a very important find and you must leave it to Professor Pryce-Roberts. He mustn't be disturbed. There have already been people making trouble. I am going to call the police, have them arrested.'

'No, you are not calling the police, Hannah. If anyone does that on this property, it will be me, do you understand that? Now, what sort of trouble?'

'That woman! She needs to be arrested. I told her—'

I wasn't going to learn anything by listening to Hannah's diatribes, so I side-stepped her.

She thrust out her arm to stop me, thumping into my chest. I could feel her quivering. Was she seriously going to fight me?

'Off you go!' Before I could react, Al had hold of her wrist and spun her round like a doll. 'Come on, Kate.'

Hannah was left staring after us, near to tears and nursing her wrist.

'You didn't hurt her, did you?' I asked.

'Did she hurt you?'

'No.'

'That's all right then. Look, if there's trouble, I'd better get to Molly. You don't mind?'

'Yes, go.' I let him bound on, at a run, Tamsin eager on his heels.

Around me, students were running around through the woods as if they'd found the holy grail. Did anyone understand that this wasn't just some academic artefact? They were dealing with someone's horrific death. They had no right to go dragging it up into cruel daylight as some fascinating exhibit. Leave the dead where they had come to rest.

I followed at my own pace, which was slow whenever I thought of what lay ahead, and faster whenever I thought of Hannah, left to her own devices, calling in the riot squad. I was just within sight of the milling crowd that had gathered around the excavation, when Al emerged from it and waved.

We met half way. 'Don't worry,' he said. 'Nothing really to see and the riot's over. I've persuaded Molly to walk away. She's gone up to the stones, to appease the spirits.'

'Screaming curses?'

'Almost. She thinks we shouldn't be taking something back, once it's been given to the Goddess. Even a human sacrifice.'

'Tell the archaeologists that.'

'Archaeologists! Call this an excavation?' Al shook his head. 'One of the stupid prats fell in. Left a boot under a submerged log, so they decided to rig up a hoist, drag the log out and retrieve the boot. Of course they managed to stir up the whole soup and up it bobbed. Your friend Ronnie can't decide whether to crucify them for unscientific procedure or give them medals.'

I stared up towards the dark hollow. 'Have they got it out yet?'

'No. I don't think the Professor would have the first idea how. He doesn't know any more idea about excavating bogs than his students.'

'How would you do it?'

'I wouldn't do it.'

'Nor I.'

'Because we knew there was something there, didn't we?'

'What on earth are you talking about?'

'Come on.' Al linked his arm in mine. 'I've seen your

eyes fix and your fists clench, up there. You've sensed it.' He swept his hair back, frowning. 'Me too, definitely—'

'Al.' I stilled his claims with a finger on his lips. 'No you haven't. I know you want to feel something. But you really don't want to feel what I feel. You can't imagine what it's like.'

He frowned. 'Is it really that bad?'

'I've felt everything bad up there. Anger. Fear. Monstrous rage. Emotions like a tornado, sucking the life out of me. I'm telling you because I trust you not to go broadcasting what I say to the world. And because you won't call me a lunatic or a liar.'

'Is that how it is?'

'How would you expect people to react if you told them you felt something nasty in the woodshed? There are only three responses: I'm batty, or I'm a lying charlatan, or could I please put them in touch with dead Fido.'

'Mostly the first?'

'Mostly the second.' I took a deep breath. Bad girls tell stories. That's what people think.

I'd been coming home from school when Mr Jackson died. I felt his panic for his cat. I saw the cat, burning. And I felt Mr Jackson die. A feeling guaranteed to derange any eight year old, so I was already in a state of shock when I turned the corner into the chaos and babble, the acrid fumes, shooting flames and billowing smoke of our street. Fire-engines, crowds gathering, people jostling to see.

I remember a neighbour explaining that they were looking for Mr Jackson. Mrs Coley had seen him in the garden, but he must have wandered off in confusion because no one could find him. Had we seen him?

My mother was watching the flames in horror. No, we

hadn't passed him.

And I knew why. He'd gone back into the burning house to rescue his cat and he was dead and the cat was dead.

I blurted it out. I couldn't recall the sequence of events after that, only a series of images, of big men in uniforms, anxious firemen, puzzled policemen, impatient policemen, and then, once the charred bodies had been found, highly suspicious policemen. What had I seen? I kept trying to tell them and they kept trying to make something different out of it. Had I spied on Mr Jackson? How did I know he was dead? Was I one of the children who taunted him, threw stones at his cat, daubed paint on his door? How did I know about the cat? Had I been there at the house when the fire broke out? Had I started it? How else could I know so much?

The more I stuck to my fantastical explanation, the angrier they became.

'Do you know what we do to wicked girls who tell lies? We put them in prison!'

My mother was furious with them, insisting I'd been at school and anyway I never told lies, but even she couldn't make head or tail of my story. Was I holding something back? Or imagining things? It couldn't be true, so she took the only way out of the impasse. 'Let's not talk about it anymore,' she said, when the police gave up on me. And we never did. Ever.

I learned that day never to tell. It could only ever lead to disaster. If I hadn't told Peter about the bog…

Al was looking at me thoughtfully. 'You felt the trapped emotions in there. You must have guessed there was a body.'

'Probably. There are such strange feelings there, I don't know what—'

I stopped as the sound of a siren brought us both to

our feet.

'That girl!' I clutched my hair. 'She's really called them in!'

'The professor called them,' said Al, shaking his head. 'He managed to get that bit right. Hardly calls for sirens, though. Are you okay to deal with them? I'd better get back to the camp, make sure everyone behaves in case the plod come barging through.'

'Yes, go. I need to get back to the house anyway. God knows what Sylvia is making of all this.'

I was a lot more content to go down the hill than up it, making my way through clusters of archaeology students, as they gleefully compared notes and photographs, or busily worked their phones. Not all were enjoying the drama. One girl was on her knees before the Hooded Woman, saying her rosary, and another was shaking with sobs. I offered a half-hearted smile of encouragement, and hurried on.

I found Sylvia pacing, hands clasped, by an empty police car parked at the bottom of the rutted track through the woods.

'Oh Kate. There you are. Oh Lord. Have you heard? Isn't it awful? Ronnie's found a body, up at the holy well.'

'It's a bog, Sylvia. Not a bloody shrine.'

'It's such a horrible thought,' said Sylvia, looking sick. 'A murderer prowling around, here. And no one seems to know who—'

'It's probably hundreds of years old.' I led her back towards the house. 'Just like the bones in the hall, remember?'

'Yes, but this isn't bones. Ronnie said it's a body! Face and hair and everything.'

'Really?' The idea of bloated human flesh emerging out of that peaty water stopped me short again. I had no

139

way of telling how long those savage emotions had been trapped in that dell. Centuries or months? No wonder the police had come with sirens, this time. This could be the start of a full-scale murder investigation.

'Come on into the kitchen,' I said 'No point us standing here. Let me pour you a brandy.'

'Oh, give me the bottle,' she said, in despair.

I filled two glasses and sipped mine, as Sylvia downed hers in one go.

'Ronnie called in the police.' She refilled her glass.

'Just like we did with the bones. You have to. Just in case.'

'Oh Kate, a murder! I wish Mike would come down and tell me what's happening. He went up with Ronnie. I couldn't face it, but I wish I knew.'

'Look, don't have any more.' I retrieved the bottle from her. 'I'll find Michael, and meanwhile, there's at least one girl out there in tears. Why don't you see if you can take care of her?'

'Oh! Poor thing.' The moment Sylvia had someone to mother, she got a grip. I pointed her in the right direction and set off again. One way or another, fate was forcing me to go and see the bloody thing.

In a brief fit of cowardice, I made the executive decision to divert via Annwfyn. As manager of the site, I had a duty to check that all was well, and I could see, instantly, that it wasn't. The whole crew were standing round the open hearth, just standing, but doing it in an unmistakably obstreperous manner. A couple of policemen faced them, looking as if they were just waiting for riot gear. Between them stood Al, polite as a king cobra.

'We'll be wanting statements,' said one of the policemen, eying Al from head to toe.

'By all means ask for them,' said Al. 'And when you

140

have a warrant—'

'What's happening here?' I asked.

'Don't worry about this, Kate.'

A third policeman appeared from the side of the yurt, which he'd been circling like a jackal, looking for a weak spot. 'And you are?'

'I'm Mrs Lawrence. I'm in partnership with Mrs Callister and Dr Bradley.'

'I see. Were you aware that these people were camping here?'

'Of course. They're here by invitation. I thought you were here to investigate a body up in the bog.'

'Indeed we are, madam. Investigating. Taverner seems reluctant to let us see inside this tent. His property, apparently. But then I understand Llys y Garn is actually the property of—'

'Mrs Callister and Dr Bradley, yes. If you have a warrant, you can show it to them. I think Dr Bradley is up here somewhere? Shall we find him – and leave these people to get on? They're here to work on our hall.'

'He already knows that,' said Al.

'Your hall. Yes, we've heard all about the hall,' said the policeman, as if its mere existence were deeply suspect.

'Well then, constable—'

'Sergeant Jenkins, ma'am.'

'If you have no actual business here…,'

'We'll go up and find Dr Bradley, ma'am.' Sergeant Jenkins had moved across from the yurt to survey the round house. It was as good as complete now, daubed, lime-washed and thatched, a great organic beast, growling quietly on the hillside. He peered in through the open doorway, without putting so much as a toe across the threshold. Heaps of bedding were clearly visible.

'In occupation. Permanent structure. You do have planning permission for this?'

Al turned to quieten the murmur of rebellion behind him.

'Oh for God's sake!' I snapped. 'We've got a body up there. Can we just concentrate on establishing whether it's old or new and get on with our lives? We have a business to run here.'

Sergeant Jenkins grudgingly stepped back and gestured to me to precede him. I, in turn, gestured to his two henchmen to go first. We were followed by muttered expletives and Al's hushes.

Up at the bog, Tamsin waved at me from the trees, with a gaggle of students, all trying to get good camera shots. I waved back and found Michael, who was standing at the brink of the dell with a plain-clothed policeman. He introduced him as Inspector Wiles.

'What's happening?' I asked, as Wiles and Jenkins stepped aside, to compare notes.

'They've established it's definitely human, but it's going to take them a while to get it out,' said Michael.

The far end of the dell, under the steep slope climbing up to the moors, was being covered with a plastic tent. I could see and hear cameras flashing but that was all.

'Have you seen it?'

'Ronnie showed me. Nothing much to see. The side of a head. You can just about make out an ear and an eye and I think it still has hair.'

I shivered, nauseated. 'So it really is recent? I wondered why we were swarming with police. Just two of them came last time. This time they're all over the place.'

'Yes.' Michael frowned. 'I'm surprised they arrived so quickly – and in such force. But I'm sure it's just a formality. The body's almost certainly old. The anaerobic environment would preserve it. I hope it's old, if only for Ronnie's sake. He's ecstatic.'

'I hope it's old for Sylvia's sake. She's convinced we've had a murder victim dumped on us.'

'I'll go down.' Michael caught Inspector Wiles' attention. 'If you don't need me…,'

'Well sir, nothing much doing just yet. No need to hang around here. We'll have to wait for forensics to examine the scene and get the body out before we can do much else. Perhaps it would be better if we all go back to the house and leave them to it.'

'Are you treating this as a murder?' I asked.

'Can't rule anything out,' said Wiles, unhelpfully.

'Your sergeant seemed very keen to search the camp over there.'

Michael frowned. 'No call to disturb them, is there?'

'You mean the travellers, sir?' asked Wiles, his tone carefully non-committal.

Careful non-committal had connotations, which Michael understood perfectly. 'I mean the craftsmen I've hired to work on the house.' He could do dignified authority when he chose. 'They've caused no trouble–'

'Oh I don't know about that, sir. We've had our eye on them for quite a while. Perhaps you're not aware of their criminal records. Drugs amongst other things.'

I was furious. 'Kim *used* to have a heroin problem,' I explained to Michael.

Michael laid a calming hand on my arm and addressed Wiles. 'You're quite correct. I don't *know* that any of them have records, and I don't *know* if any of them use drugs. I do know, however, that they have an excellent reputation, that they work well and extremely hard, and have been no trouble to us whatsoever.'

143

'Not quite what Professor Pryce-Roberts thinks,' said Wiles.

'Ronnie thinks anyone who builds a roundhouse with questionable king posts is a barbarian and scoundrel,' said Michael.

Wiles very nearly smiled. 'Very well, sir. I just thought you ought to be advised. After all, the law will hold you liable for anything happening on your property.'

'I'm aware of my responsibilities,' said Michael. If Wiles couldn't sense the irritation in him, I certainly could.

We parted company with our escort at a vacant workshop that had been appointed the incident room.

'I swear they're more interested in Al's crew than in the body,' I said. 'They did seem pleased to have tracked them down when they came last time. Do you think they've been waiting for this opportunity? They're very keen to search the yurt and the round house. I shooed them away, but they're probably back by now.'

Michael laughed. 'I hope Al and his crew had the sense to clean the place up. Do you think they have anything that shouldn't be there?'

'A bit of weed, probably. Al wouldn't countenance anything more than that. He's too concerned for his baby sister. And she's clean now, he makes sure of that.'

Michael waved the issue aside. 'If she has problems and wants to come to me for help, fine. Otherwise, I don't want to hear about it. They're a legitimate business and while they're on my property, doing nothing wrong, that's good enough for me. Sylvia.' He stopped to give her a kiss as she came into the kitchen, refilled glass in hand.

144

'Oh Mike,' she wailed.

'There's nothing to worry about. Everything's fine.'

The idea of murder, without being specifically eliminated, seemed to be quietly shelved. The police continued prowling, while a forensic team were at work, but there was no frenetic investigation, which was a relief at least to Sylvia.

Up at the bog, the body was slowly, carefully disinterred to be shipped off elsewhere for detailed study, Ronnie fluttering over it like a mother hen.

Poor Ronnie. I discovered that after years of being in charge of the excavation in Cumbria, his university had finally eased him into retirement. An insignificant holiday dig for amateurs in a Welsh field was the university's sop to get him out of their hair. This barbaric find in the bog could turn out to be his triumphant epitaph. But it seemed he wasn't sufficiently qualified or trusted to complete the task of removing the body. He could only stand and pretend to supervise.

Sylvia turned pale every time a vehicle rumbled down the track, in case it carried the mortal remains. 'When will we know how old it is?' she asked, repeatedly. 'Clive Taylor told Fran that Gethin Williams had a fight with a biker last year and it could be him!'

'Sylvia, I'm sure it isn't.'

'And Brian at the Cemaes says a girl went missing from a farm in Pen-y-bont on Bonfire Night—'

'Listen, the biker went home and the girl probably ran off to the bright lights of Crymych. I'm sure it's old. Just try to think of it as extra advertising.'

'Like Bridie? Of course! But do you think it's too much, Kate? Two bodies? People will think it's a charnel house. They might be afraid to come here. '

'I doubt it!' Students and regulars at the Cemaes

Arms had already spread the word, and a small crowd was massing at the gates of Llys y Garn. First a smothered bride, now a bog body, and the whole world simply loved bog bodies.

Bertie the Bogman. Someone came up with the name, and the press soon had hold of it. I was going to be kept busy again, though I had assistance this time. Tamsin revelled in the ghastly business, guiding reporters and photographing everything to be uploaded to Facebook and YouTube. She was welcome to take over the publicity as far as I was concerned. And I finally quietened Sylvia's last fears.

'The BBC is coming. They're sending a van.'

'Oh Lord!' Her hands flew to her wild hair. 'I look a sight! Will they want to speak to me?'

'Especially to you.'

The six o'clock news, that evening, reported on our big event, poor Ronnie side-lined yet again in favour of a more photogenic archaeologist with greater street cred. There were ten seconds of Sylvia sounding anxious, a shot of the tent shrouding the extraction and a good two minutes of Molly, standing on the overhanging rocks, in full druidic regalia, like a cross between Galadriel and a bag lady. They gave her incantations full coverage.

'If we take that which has been given to the Goddess,' she intoned to the smirking interviewer, 'the Goddess will take another in recompense. All will come full circle!' We were promised hundreds of fellow believers, already on their way to Pembrokeshire, to reinforce the sanctity of the site. I was not pleased.

At least one good thing had come of it. No sign of Hannah. Since our altercation she'd sulked in her room.

The police left, Bertie left and Ronnie was ecstatically

energised. He insisted on keeping me informed, plying me with details I didn't want to hear and photographs I didn't want to see. A blackened leathery face, twisted in an apparent snarl of rage – though immersion in a bog would probably do that to any face. The body of a large man, still dressed in leather and rough cloth, had been lying face down, hands bound and (I was supposed to be especially thrilled by this) very deliberately weighed down with stones.

'Clear indications of ritual practice,' said Ronnie.

'You mean a human sacrifice?' I asked.

'Now we mustn't judge the past by the moral standards of our day.' Ronnie mistook my disdain for outrage. 'One must understand the culture, the beliefs. Of course we're not certain yet of the exact era, but it was undoubtedly an intensely ceremonial society. We'll know more when we've completed our analysis. We haven't yet dated the bog itself, which was the exercise I had in mind for my students prior to this discovery.'

As soon as the police finally packed up their gear and left, he herded his students back to work. Phone calls from the press kept coming and I continued to answer politely. Yes, it was surprising to uncover two bodies. No, we didn't expect to find any more.

I certainly hoped not. Quietly, while no one was watching, I climbed up to the empty attic with its flutter of fear and defiance.

The defiance was unmistakable. Get out! The room was screaming at me. Out, out! But having coped with the hall and the bog, I was determined to be absolutely sure no more corpses were waiting to spring out.

I tapped on walls and floors, in search of cavities and concealed tombs.

'What are you doing?' Tamsin poked her head round the door. 'I heard knocking. Thought it was a ghost.'

'No ghosts!' I laughed, with relief. Everything was solid. Not even a creak in the floorboards. 'Just seeing everything's sound, for when we convert these attics.'

'Oh that's all right then. Cool.'

Yes, very cool. There would be no more bodies.

14

Bertie was Mediaeval. Not even Dark Ages, let alone pre-Roman. Ronnie couldn't be doing with anything so ridiculously modern. He tried to redirect his students back to the plotting of post holes, but he'd lost them. They wanted bodies, or nothing.

What Molly wanted was mollification of the Goddess. Fortunately, only a dozen fellow believers turned up and, before I could raise objections, Al shunted them off to a camp site in Newport.

'Can't have them here: it's a matter of sanitation,' he explained. 'Once Molly's done her thing at the holy well, they'll be out of your hair, I promise.'

We went to watch the Thing being done, standing in solemn silence as Molly's chanting entourage filed into the gloomy hollow and cast compensatory offerings into the foetid water. Some of the archaeology students attended, drinking up the awe of the moment. Others, further up the slope, added derisive cat calls, but they were largely ignored.

Sylvia stood with hands clasped. Tamsin, by Al's side, surreptitiously filmed on her phone. Michael shook his head over the scene.

I watched with relief. Oak leaves, a gold bangle, a

burning brand. I had wondered if Molly might try offering herself.

Everyone accepted that Bertie had been a sacrifice. No one except me suspected a miserable common-place murder, unrecorded and probably unpunished. When everyone else had gone, I crept back to the site, to see what difference any of it had made to the horror captured there.

What I felt, instantly, was extreme frustration, and it all emanated from Hannah Quigley, who was on her knees at the water's edge, groping for the still-smouldering wood that Molly had presented to the oily waters.

'Hannah, I hope you're not trying to get the bracelet.'

She snorted indignation. 'I don't want it!'

'Good. I doubt if it's real gold, so not worth drowning for. Can you leave that wood be, please? It's been offered to the Goddess.'

'It's an archaeological site! They have no right!'

'Yes they do have the right, because we gave it to them.'

'It's devil worship. That's against the law. I'll report them!'

'I'm not sure worshipping anything is against the law, Hannah. We don't burn witches anymore.' Fortunately for me.

Hannah managed to touch the smouldering branch. It sparked, she shrank back, a dainty plume of smoke rose and the wood sank from view with a faint hiss.

'Leave it,' I said, beginning to feel sorry for her.

She got to her feet, dishevelled and distressed, facing me in a gale of hostility. 'This is Professor Pryce-Roberts' excavation. You're just trying to spoil things for him.'

I noticed the bandage on her wrist, where Al had

grabbed her. Had he really hurt her? He'd swung her arm around with enough force to dislocate her shoulder, maybe, but she was obviously nursing a lot more than physical wounds. 'Come on Hannah, the excavation is going fine and Ronnie is very pleased with it. You want to be a part of his work, don't you? Leave this be and go and help him.'

'No thanks to you!' she said, brushing past me and storming off down the path. From the heaving of her shoulders as she ran, I suspected she was crying.

Ronnie's problem, not mine.

I turned back to the dark dell and listened to its silence, now that it was free of Hannah's turmoil.

A clean breeze filtered through the trees. Mud had been stirred, water defiled, flowers strewn, and with the upheaval, that shadow of raging anger had been churned free of its tomb in the stinking mire. Perhaps there was purpose to Molly's cleansing ritual, after all.

But she hadn't cleansed all away. One thread of that knot of trapped emotions still remained. One sensation, etched in the rocks, that wasn't fear or anger or despair; but an unidentifiable see-sawing - something. What else was it that a person could feel at the moment of death, other than fear, anger and despair? Whatever it was, it eluded me and I had no wish to penetrate its secret.

London beckoned. With phone calls still bombarding us about Bertie, and the great Elizabethan Fayre fast approaching, I felt guilty about absconding, but I needed my illicit interlude with Al more than ever.

July, and there was thunder in the air. Heavy rain began to splatter in huge drops as we dragged bags and cases from the capacious Volvo and bundled Tamsin into the terminal at Heathrow. I kept my promise of discretion, and diligently browsed the shelves of W H

Smith's, while she met up with her rowdy friends and paraded Al before them. We drove on into the city, with the windscreen wipers going for gold, but the storm passed, the sun came out and the glass and concrete shimmered, the air heavy with carbon monoxide and the smell of diesel and deep-frying.

'I presume you've fixed up somewhere to stay?' I asked, as Al changed lanes on the Cromwell Road. It had belatedly occurred to me that we might be bunking down in some New Age squat.

He grinned. 'A hotel – I did some work there; they give me a discount.'

We stopped in Kensington at a gracious terraced house, sash windows, classical pillars and sculptured bay trees at the door. Al was greeted like an old friend, and I gazed up at the elegant plasterwork, wondering how much of it was his.

'We're going Dutch,' I whispered, as we were ushered to our elegant room.

Al laughed. 'Forget it. I rifled the petty cash.'

I obediently forgot about it, as he slipped his arms round me. 'Eat out? Or in?'

'In,' I said.

He'd warned me he had business to see to the next day. 'Lawyers?' I'd asked. He'd dropped a mention of Kim's trust fund on the journey. 'Do you have to make yourself look smart?'

'Clean T shirt?' he suggested.

'I think so.'

But when I emerged from the shower, after a decadent breakfast in bed, I found him in a suit. Suited him surprisingly well. Worn, of course, with a clean T shirt.

'You're a different man.'

'I try to be, at least once a day. You're not going to be

bored, are you?'

'In London? Of course not. You go and charm your lawyers. I'll be fine. You've got my number.'

I waved him off, then paused on the kerbside. I had friends to meet, shops to visit… Instead, I found myself heading for the Pimlico street where Leo had lived and died. I stood on the pavement, gazing up at his balcony. A child's voice babbled through the open window. New tenants. The mess had been cleaned up, decorators had freshened the place and none of them would feel what was locked in that wall.

Emotions that wouldn't be locked in that wall, if I had responded to Leo's desperation in time. Instead, I'd sat in the interview room, glowering at the coffee stains, thinking 'Damn you, Leo, for dropping me in this,' while Leo hanged himself.

Killer Queen. Christian's insidious words whispered at me. Had I somehow channelled death at my baby? My mother? Mr Jackson? Leo?

Behind me, a taxi hooted exasperation at a van. A blare of reason. A kamikaze cyclist scooted past. The noise and bustle of London shouted at me, 'Reality, Kate: clamour and energy and life getting on with itself. There's no time and place for your whimsical delusions and your moping guilt trips. Leo died up there, and now there's a child, doing what children do. Get over it.'

Whimsical delusions. It was all so ridiculous. Bones and bog bodies – just good publicity for Llys y Garn. I needed to laugh at it all, and at myself. I needed to move on.

The problem, I realized, as I prepared to while away a day in the metropolis that had been my home, was that I had already moved on. From London. What was I to do here? Meet up for a morning of idle bitching with old colleagues I couldn't say anything meaningful to? Gaze at a house, contract pending, that I no longer shared with Peter? Stroll among towering offices where I might once have worked? I didn't belong here anymore. The only thing in London I wanted was Al, so I mooched, alone, and I waited for him to return.

He sent me a text to say his meeting was done, but he had to see some people over in Battersea, and he'd be back at the hotel by seven.

I was there, waiting for him, glass of wine in hand. 'How has your day been, dear?'

'Not too bad, dear. And yours?'

'Delightful. So who were these Battersea dogs who kept you occupied all this time?'

'No one you'd want to meet.'

'You know that's just going to make me more curious.'

He shook his head, warning me off. 'Just a bunch of junkies. Some of Kim's old contacts.' He dumped the case he'd been carrying. A long narrow case.

'Is that a violin, or a machine gun for your next bank robbery?'

'Kim's.' He flicked it open to show the violin, before depositing it in the wardrobe. 'I promised to collect it for her.'

'Is she as good on the violin as she is on the penny whistle?'

'Better.'

He wasn't refusing to answer my questions, just not eager to discuss Kim's affairs. I respected that. 'So do I have you to myself tomorrow?'

'Almost.' He sipped his wine, beginning to relax into the evening. 'Got to see a man in Kent first thing, but–'

'A man in Kent!'

'A possible job, sorry.'

'You've got a job! You're working on our hall.'

'And when that's finished?' he laughed. 'Sorry, Kate. Promise, I'll see him first thing, be back in time for lunch, and then I'll be all yours.'

'You haven't got a man from Essex or somewhere to see tonight?'

'Not tonight, no.'

'Good,' I said, refilling his glass.

He slipped quietly from the room while I was still blearily trying to decide whether to wake fully, or drift back into sleep. I opted for sleep, but before it came, his absence prodded me into wakefulness. Why did he need to look for another job? The work on Llys y Garn could go on forever if I played it right; always some plaster to smooth and screw to tighten. Wasn't that enough for him?

I sat up, fighting my pillows. Kent. About as far from West Wales as he could get. Did he have to be such a nomad? I pictured his yurt in the middle of Kensington, while he'd worked on this hotel. A different man at least once a day, he'd said, and how many of them were involved with me?

I wasn't demanding to have him all. Just one version of him, for the summer. I wasn't asking for commitment, or marriage. Just a brief interlude of idle play, a chance to pretend I wasn't alone in the world.

And sex, of course. Hugely satisfactory sex.

So what was I complaining about? I got up and sauntered out to another morning of retail therapy.

I bought nothing.

He returned for lunch, and we spent the afternoon seeking out a little gallery displaying some of Michael's pieces. Then we strolled round the Serpentine.

'Ice-cream,' said Al, and raced off to get some. I sought some shade, listening to the babble, the distant traffic, the subterranean hum of a city that had, just a few months ago, been so much part of my life that I barely noticed it. Now I noticed it.

A sharp yank and my bag was off my shoulder, jerking me backwards. I swivelled to find a boy in a grey hoody trying to run, while I clung on for dear life. 'Get off, you little sod!'

The boy raised his free hand. What if he had a knife?

He didn't. Or if he did, it was thrown wide as he went flying. I hadn't noticed Al return. He moved so fast I didn't see what he did, but there was the boy, sprawled on his face, trying to figure out how he'd got there. Al reached down, snapped him to his feet and whispered something in his ear.

'Gerroff,' whined the boy, a dribble of blood running from his nose.

Al's grip on his collar tightened, and the boy choked, almost off his feet. Al whispered again, dropped him, and the boy loped off, on wobbling legs.

'Are you okay?'

'Fine.' I wasn't sure whether to laugh or tremble. 'I'd like to think I could have fought him off, but thanks for the intervention.'

'My pleasure. You still want an ice-cream?' Coolly, he offered me a cone, which had miraculously remained intact. The other one was a splatter of goo on the ground. 'Or would you prefer a stiff drink after that?'

'Maybe a drink,' I agreed, and we sought a bar.

'We can stay another day if you like.' Al handed me my glass.

I thought about it. 'I don't think so.'

'That little thug shook you up, didn't he?' He reached for my wrist, feeling my pulse. 'I didn't think you could really be that cool about it.'

I laughed. 'Maybe not totally cool, but stirred more

155

than shaken. It's not the first teenage highwayman I've run into.' Truthfully, I was more disturbed by Al's reaction than the attempted theft. That swift meting out of violence. It was too primal for comfort. Looking at him now, relaxed and unconcerned, I couldn't quite get my head round it, so I looked out across the park instead. Across city haze that suggested illusion, deception, sleight of hand. 'I know it seems impossible, but I'm not sure London does it for me anymore. It all seems a bit hollow. I want proper fresh air again. I want real woods and owls.'

Al laughed. 'We'll have you hugging trees yet.'

I could think of better things to hug. Not all things primal were discomforting. But in the morning, I was happy to be heading for home. That's what Llys y Garn was, even with its shadows. Llys y Garn with its deep woods and meadows of long grass, the espresso machine hissing in the nicotine kitchen and a sea-charged sky overhead. Most of all, Llys y Garn with its people.

All of which seemed a long way off as we shunted our way to the M4. The motorway was surging, heavy lorries grinding around us, the sun pulsating, the tarmac at melting point.

'How about getting off this and going across country?' said Al as we slowed into a jam at a Reading exit.

I sensed hesitation in the suggestion, but there was none in my answer. 'Oh God, yes, anything's better than this.'

So we headed up through Oxfordshire. I offered to map read, but Al knew where he was going. Way off the motorway. The Cotswolds.

Yes, beautiful countryside and pretty villages, and I really had to stop cringing every time I saw a sign to

Stow on the Wold, just because I'd been there when my mother died.

Al probably had a cosy little pub in mind for lunch, and why not? I'd have to forgive the area sometime. But Al didn't head for a pub. Again, I sensed his hesitation, then decision, as he turned onto a side road, up into thick woods and over the brow of a hill. He pulled into a farm gateway and turned to me.

'Let's stretch our legs, take a walk,' he suggested, as if the idea had just struck him. I could tell it was anything but spontaneous.

'All right. Why not?'

It wasn't a particularly inviting spot for a stroll, along a stubbly verge. I kept to the tarmac.

A sharp corner lay ahead. Al's long legs carried him ahead, out of sight, but as I rounded the bend, I found him waiting for me. Watching me, intently.

The road plunged down a steep hill into a picturesque green valley, where a church and village of pale golden stone clustered by a brook that twinkled in the bright light.

A charming view, but still no explanation for our little walk.

'Very pretty,' I said. 'Why are we here?'

'Good to get out of the car.'

'Is this a game? If it is, tell me how to play.'

'No, I was just stiff driving. I thought there might be a …' He gestured towards the village, then stopped, pushed his hair back and squinted back up the hill. 'Sorry. This was stupid.'

'Was it?' I kept pace with him, this time, as we returned to the car. 'If I knew what we were doing, I might judge.'

'It's nothing. I'm out of my mind. Let's find a pub, get some lunch.' But I could feel his eyes on me still, watching for the slightest sign of – what?

I stopped him, a hand on his arm. 'Was I supposed to feel something?'

'No, I'm sorry, I shouldn't – did you feel anything?'

'No. What was it I was supposed to feel?'

'Nothing. No, if you felt nothing, that's fine.'

'Al. Why here?'

He paused before replying, staring back at the sharp bend. 'That was where my parents were killed. I just wondered—'

'Oh Al.'

'Yes, I know, it was stupid. But you say you feel emotions that get left behind. I thought you'd feel if there was anything there. I have this nightmare they died screaming.'

I swallowed. There was no breeze. There were no shadows. There was nothing, to see or to feel. Just July heat and dust and the suspicion of another thunderstorm approaching.

'I felt nothing,' I said. 'It's all quite empty. Nothing there.'

'That's all right then. Sorry. I shouldn't have done it.' Contrition, but enormous relief.

I felt nothing because shadows never lingered out in the open, and my mind had been so focussed on memories of my own mother's death, I would probably have felt nothing anyway. 'I do understand. Don't fret about it. Come on. It's my turn to drive.'

He tossed me the keys, then leaned back against the car and laughed. 'Sorry, Kate. You did warn me how people reacted, and I slipped right into line, expecting you to reach out to the dead for me.'

'That's the one reaction I can forgive. You couldn't have passed this by. I wouldn't, if I'd been you.' I turned the key in the ignition. 'And there really is

158

nothing here. Nothing but peace and the quiet earth.'

'That's all I wanted to know.' He took a deep breath, satisfied.

What else could I have said?

Pembrokeshire, when we reached it, was unbelievably busy. The school holidays had begun and the roads were clogged with traffic, caravans and camper vans lurching up hills, cars creeping cautiously along winding lanes. Pedestrians too: the road up from the Cemaes Arms was littered with students I didn't recognise.

'Of course!' I said. 'This was their change-over weekend. Ronnie's got his new gang of eager beavers.'

'And they've already discovered the pub.' Al edged the car round an unsteady threesome.

'He tried to put it off limits with the last lot. Fat chance. Looks as if he hasn't even bothered this time. Poor Ronnie. Still, he'll be glad to be free of Hannah Quigley.'

'Not the only one.' Al turned in by the lodge, its new residents happily knocking sand from their shoes on the door step.

I waved, then shrank down in the passenger seat.

Hannah Quigley, laden with shopping bags, was plodding up the drive.

'You were saying?' said Al.

Hannah turned at the sound of the engine, recognised us, and raised a laden arm to stop us.

'Drive on!' I squeaked.

Al's foot hit the accelerator, till we were safely past.

We laughed. 'Oh Lord,' I said. 'What's she still doing here?'

'She's the Prof's assistant?'

'No. She's not even a full-time student. I have it on

good authority – well, gossip – that she dropped out of college. She does a job she won't talk about. What do you think it could be? My money's on traffic warden.'

Al shook his head. 'Whatever she does, she'd better start doing it away from me. If she tells me off again, I may have to teach her a lesson.'

How primal a lesson? I'd had a frequent desire to throw her bodily out of my way, myself – but I wouldn't dream of acting on it. Just as well it was me she'd be wanting, not Al. 'Quick,' I said, as we pulled into the courtyard. 'Let me run and hide.'

I failed. I was still hauling bags from the boot when Hannah came huffing into the yard. Al treacherously grinned and beat a retreat, with Kim's violin.

'I need to speak to you about the facilities,' said Hannah, by way of a greeting.

'Hello Hannah. I'm surprised to see you still here.'

'I'm staying the whole summer,' she announced, as if I should have recognised her preferential status. 'It's the bathrooms. I don't know when you last inspected them, but one of them is disgusting. It hasn't been cleaned for ages. The sink's blocked.'

'Sorry, Hannah, but the state of the cottages is the responsibility of the students – although I do expect them to be vacated in a reasonable state. Has anyone mentioned cleaning duties?'

'Well I don't think that's good enough. You are responsible for the facilities, aren't you? What are we paying for?'

'Nobody is paying us anything. Mrs Callister and Dr Bradley have very generously allowed you all to camp on their land and excavate their fields for free. I'm afraid you'll have to take it up with Ronnie. He's the one responsible.'

'The professor has quite enough to think about,

160

already.'

'So he'd probably be very grateful if you sorted it out for him.'

'Obviously someone will have to. Not that anyone listens to me.'

'Kate!' Sylvia was at the kitchen door. 'You're home! Had a wonderful time?'

'Wonderful,' I said, remembering with an effort. The delights of London were on the far side of Hannah Quigley.

15

My holiday was forgotten. Summer meant an end to relaxation for several weeks. Life outside Llys y Garn became one endless queue, one long struggle to find a parking space, shopping at dawn to avoid families, screaming babies, men in shorts, English voices deriding the lack of okra.

Within our grounds, I had the Fayre to cope with. Now it was clear that the Hall would be presentable in time, there was no stopping it. Sylvia's networking conjured up spinners, weavers, leather workers, candle makers and jewellers. I arranged the insurance, found a costume supplier, advertised brazenly and sorted out a licence to serve mead, cider and sweet white wine to accompany Sylvia's Tudor recipes. I'd persuaded her that our kitchen didn't meet health and safety requirements, so a nearby restaurant would be producing the food. With Al's assistance, I found jugglers, puppeteers, a fire-eater, folk dancers, a harpist and assorted musicians. Molly was going to tell fortunes and do things with crystals; I didn't argue.

One by one, items on the endless checklist were ticked off. On the day before the Fayre, I was satisfied that everything was under control.

The postman's van rolled into the courtyard mid-morning with a bundle of mail, including a postcard from Tamsin.

'Your daughter's having fun.' I offered the card to Sylvia, who was busy with floral arrangements. She wiped petals from her hands and read Tamsin's scant lines as if they were Holy Writ.

'Oh, how wonderful. They've gone on to Jason's place. Isn't that good? Should I phone her, do you think, just to say—'

'No. She'll think you don't trust her. Just concentrate on the flowers.'

'Yes, you're right. I don't want her to think… What about – no, not the stocks. It's impossible to find something that goes with marigolds. Oh God, and it's tomorrow. I'll never manage to sort this out!'

Yes she would.

'I'll get it,' I said as the phone rang. I took the call in the hall, giving a tourist office directions to our gate, as I sorted the remaining mail. Fliers went in the bin. Michael's woodworking magazine went on the shelf. That left an invoice and a letter from the local authority. I opened it, reading it on my way to the office.

A demand for the demolition of the round house, which didn't have planning permission.

Just as well I was out of the kitchen, I thought, hot with anger as I shut the door. How petty! I couldn't discuss this piece of bureaucratic spite now, with Sylvia already so fraught. Get the Fayre out of the way first. I slipped the letter in the desk drawer and returned to the kitchen, all smiles, to help Sylvia with her garlands.

The costumes arrived and Sylvia's eyes lit up. Dressing up time! Something subdued in dark green, Anne Boleyn style for me, but a full virgin queen outfit for her. Sylvia was the one more likely to lose her head, but only she could carry off that pneumatic creation without a flicker of embarrassment. There were eight yeomen and damsel outfits for the local teenagers we'd hired to help. The girls at least would love them. We had court gowns in crimson, peacock and amber for Sylvia's willing friends and half a dozen gents' outfits for any volunteers.

The heat had subsided and the sky was cloudy. Rain would be disappointing, but no point worrying about it. I inspected the Great Hall one last time, cluttered with folding tables, piled up in readiness.

Al had done a superb job. Old beams had been treated, new ones carved, hauled and pegged into position, chimney cleared, stonework cleaned, carving restored. Panelling was as new, the windows a miracle of re-engineered antique glass and lead-work. There was still a vast amount of work to be done in the end rooms and the cellar, but the hall itself was superficially complete.

A shadow still lurked behind the locked door of the priest hole. The removal of the bones hadn't cleansed it, as the bog had been cleansed. An agony borne too long, perhaps. It let me feel its cold breath as I stood alone in the hall, but I hoped the noise and bustle of the fair would drown it out.

I was wearing my Boleyn gown, so I experimented to see if I could negotiate folds of velvet round corners, without bringing stalls down. There was a knack to walking in Tudor garb and I wasn't sure I'd mastered it.

At least I could hide trainers under the long skirt.

I found an open space, took a wide sweep, in order to disentangle myself, and found myself face to face with my husband.

Peter applauded. 'Wow!'

'What are you doing here?' I snapped.

'Sylvia told me to come through. You did say I should come back.'

'You were going to phone first, weren't you? Then I could have told you not to bother.'

Peter's face fell. 'You never answered.' Which was true. 'What's the matter, Kate? I thought—'

'Peter, I don't want to talk to you, after what you did. Come on out of here. I want to change.' I flounced – there was no other option in long velvet – out of the hall and stormed upstairs, to retrieve my jeans and t-shirt. It was impossible to sustain a serious quarrel in Tudor lacing.

Back in the drawing room, Peter was looking upset. So he should be.

'What's wrong, Kate? What have I done?'

'You contacted Ronnie. You told him to excavate the bog. Didn't you!' I glared at him.

'Well, yes, but I thought—'

'Why? I can't believe you'd do it. Why?'

'Because you felt something there.' Peter floundered. 'They found it, didn't they? The bog body, just as you said they would.'

'I said no such thing! And I certainly didn't want you repeating whatever it was I did say.'

'But—'

'They dug up another body. Wasn't one enough? You seriously think I want corpses dropping on me, every time I feel something?'

'I just wanted to prove you right.'

'I don't need proof, Peter! I know if I'm right and I'm not interested in convincing anyone else.'

He groped for some kind of silver lining. 'At least it must have been extra publicity? Sylvia was so keen about the other one.'

'Bugger the publicity. We had police swarming everywhere. They must have been waiting to pounce on the place. Itching to arrest Al and his crowd for something. And now!' I stormed into the office and returned with the letter I'd hidden in the desk. 'Now this!'

Peter frowned at the paper. 'Planning permission? Didn't you get it?'

'For a wattle and daub round house? Somehow I don't think it would have met building regs, do you? And how could it possibly have mattered? It's hidden in the woods. It's not hurting anyone. No one would have known it was there, if the police hadn't come marching through, because Ronnie found a body, because you just had to tell him to go poking around in that bog. Why did you have to interfere?'

Peter held out his hands, then sank down on the sofa with a groan. 'I didn't mean this to happen.'

'Not just sneakily making trouble for my rough trade?'

'No! Of course not. I didn't even think about your New Age buddies. All I meant...' He got up, walked to the window and groaned a second time. He looked desperate. 'Kate, I know you don't talk about your feelings because you think people will laugh—'

'Laugh! That's the least of it.'

'All right. I know what happened when you were a child. You think no one will believe you, so you say nothing. I just wanted to prove I did believe. I wanted to show that people can believe and act on what you say. Sorry. I really didn't foresee all the ramifications.'

I almost felt sorry for him. Not good; I needed to be angry with him. 'You told Ronnie that your wife had odd feelings about the bog?'

'Of course not. I just mentioned it being there. I found an article about bog bodies in Ireland and I floated the suggestion. That's all.'

'Well it certainly floated. Like a bloody turd that won't flush away.'

'Sorry.'

I sighed. How could I be angry and resentful while he wilted like a slapped child who'd only wanted to please mummy.

'Couldn't we just start again?' he pleaded.

'Start what again?'

He hesitated for just a second. 'This visit. I promise, no matter what you tell me, I will not breathe a word about it to anyone else.'

I thought of all I might tell – torrid nights in London, naughty interludes in the woods… 'How's Gabrielle?' I asked.

'I promise you, that's all over. Now.'

I smiled at that extra word. 'It's just an enquiry. I'm not gloating over another woman's misery.'

'Gabrielle doesn't do misery. She's fine. I'm not really likely to run into her any more. She's found herself a sub-editor position.'

'Well that's nice. Anyone else on your horizon?'

'No. There's only one woman I'm interested in, Kate, and she's a lot closer than the horizon.'

Confrontation was impossible. I sat down. 'Since you're here, we'll have that soul-searching talk. But first we've got to get through Sylvia's Elizabethan Fayre, God help us. How would you like to be a waiter?'

'I brought a bottle of champagne.'

'You'll be passing round flagons of mulled ale.'

'Yes, fine, anything.'

'And you'll dress up. We don't have enough costumes, but you can just strap on a codpiece.'

'Fine.' It took a second to sink in. 'You're joking! Oh. You are joking.'

'Don't worry, we do have enough costumes. You will wear one.'

Peter swallowed. 'All right.'

Sylvia appeared, all smiles and hugs, and anxious, encouraging glances at me. I didn't have time to put her in the picture just then. I had calls to make, tables to arrange, signs to put up, parking to organise, deliveries to unpack – and the planning letter, which was waiting for me.

I took Peter back to the hall. Tables needed to be unfolded, clicked into upright position and placed where my blueprint dictated.

'How many are there?' Peter examined pinched fingers after unfolding the fourth.

'Don't worry, only sixteen. We have to leave room for performances in the middle, and we—'

Al sauntered in. 'Hi, Kate.'

He'd have to learn about Peter's return sooner or later, but I'd have preferred to choose my own moment. 'Hello, Al. You remember Peter, don't you?'

'Sure,' said Al easily.

'The family friend,' added Peter.

Al grinned. 'Need a hand?' He swept up a table and flicked its legs into place with one easy movement. 'Where do you want it?'

'That corner.' I pointed. Peter was unfolding the next table, with an air of indifference to mask any clumsiness. Poor Peter. Al could turn his hand to

167

anything, and Peter had created chaos with one Ikea flat pack. But then Peter was an academic economist and financial journalist, not a builder, so the comparison was unfair. Peter was very good with his hands, in some respects. As was...

'Where does this one go?' asked Peter.

'There.' I stood and watched. No antagonism. Peter concealed any jealousy – he knew I hated it. But then he'd never had just cause for jealousy before. Al joked, talked casually and, when Peter's back was turned, gave me a smile of benediction, suggesting a willingness to fall back with good grace, whenever I wanted.

Good. I certainly didn't want two grown men spitting and snarling at each other over me. And yet – did Al have to surrender quite so willingly? Surely I was worth one small competitive growl.

'There,' said Peter, putting the last table in place. 'How have we done?'

'Just perfect,' I said dryly.

16

The day of the Fayre dawned and Sylvia was in a state of dementia from the moment she opened her eyes, but I knew she thrived on hysteria. I was quietly confident that everything would fall into place when the time came.

Craftsmen arrived to set up their stalls. Besides the sixteen in the hall, eight others, selling herbs, garden pottery and such delights, were set up on the gravel terrace. Michael organised a sensible parking plan.

Molly came down with the Annwfyn contingent, to fetch and carry as required.

She'd kept her word that they would dress for the occasion. Not exactly authentic Tudor, but I expect their hand weaving, tie-dye silks and painted leather wouldn't have looked any odder in 1588.

'Oh Kate, there's absolutely no sign of the food!' Sylvia was in wild panic. 'I knew we should have done it here. What if it doesn't come?'

I looked at my watch. 'Sylvia, it's only just gone eight.'

'But if they leave it any longer, we won't have time–'

'The Fayre opens at eleven. We will have time. Go and check on the jewellers. They're worried they're not in the best position. Persuade them that it's just perfect.'

'But what if the food—'

'If the food arrives, we'll deal with it.'

The food did arrive, in ample time, and was duly sorted into bowls and platters. No swan or peacock, but we were having an ox roast in the meadow, well clear of the archery butts.

The local boys and girls arrived and, as I expected, the girls were keener on the fancy dress than the boys, who found a football and entertained themselves in the car parking zone, to distance themselves nonchalantly from the absurdity of their doublets and breeches.

The drinks needed organising. Barrels of ale had been delivered to the old boot room, courtesy of the Cemaes Arms, along with crates of wine and cider. The adjoining pantry was being laid out for inauthentic tea and coffee.

'Peter, go and dress yourself in manly array, then come and help me carry this lot over. We're going to make the punch.'

169

He'd been desperately trying to prove himself helpful and considerate – but the costume – rich gold-trimmed plum purple with scarlet hose – had him wilting.

'I feel a complete prat.' He looked down at himself in disbelief. 'Are you sure it does up like this?'

I sailed around him in my green velvet, checking his laces. 'It's more the way you're standing. Try to enjoy it.'

'How?'

'Think swash-buckling thoughts.' I swept a curtsey and waited. 'You're supposed to bow.'

'I daren't. I don't know what will split.'

I laughed. 'Well we'll soon find out. Can you carry that crate of oranges?'

'Of course. Anything.'

Poor Peter. I began to wish I hadn't forced the costume on him. He might settle into it as the day wore on, but for the moment, he was so self-conscious it hurt.

Queen Elizabeth made her regal appearance and everyone else faded into insignificance. She paraded round the grounds, dispensing benediction on the stalls, the refreshment tables, the St. John's ambulance contingent, the musicians, the archers and the performing dogs. Peter and I trailed in her wake.

We were progressing back up through the newly mown meadow, when Al appeared, at the top of the terrace steps.

'Your majesty, Lord Peter, Mistress Kate.' Alone among the gang from Annwfyn, he had accepted my offer of a costume, so he'd had the first pick. White shirt, black doublet and hose, and a plumed cap that he doffed with a graceful sweep. Errol bloody Flynn. Mistress Kate indeed! He appeared just as Peter was hoisting his tights in an un-genteel manner. And where had he found that rapier?

'Al, you look delicious.' Sylvia engulfed him. 'Isn't this wonderful? Is it going to rain, do you think? That would be awful.'

Clouds were rolling across the sky, but there was no sign of rain. It was in fact perfect weather for the Fayre; just overcast enough to keep people off the beach. 'Your Majesty has ordered sunshine,' said Al. 'Sunshine it shall be.' He handed her up the steps with a bow.

'You're doing fine,' I assured Peter, who was beginning to sulk.

The Fayre opened promptly at eleven, and an initial steady stream of visitors became a healthy flood. First port of call invariably was our charnel house display, or Meet the Bodies as Sylvia called it. In pride of place was the still wet painting of the bride, in lace crinoline, screaming as she was locked in the priest hole. As a poster for a horror B movie, it was perfect. A local folk singer had found a mournful ballad to accompany it, and there was a photograph of the priest hole, gaping open, with suitably eerie lighting. No pictures of the bones or any reference to the actual truth.

The photographs of Bertie the Bogman were at least more honest. There he was, blackened face perpetually snarling. Michael produced a factually correct account of the find, and an amateur historian provided us with quotes from mediaeval annals and the Mabinogion, none of which helped to explain why a man had been bound and dumped under stones in our bog.

The grisly exhibition brought our visitors on to the stalls and the entertainments and Sylvia's animated welcome. I patrolled, watching and listening for hitches, but apart from minor whinges, all seemed to be going well.

'You were worried no one would find the place,' said Al, as I stopped my rounds for a gulp of ice-cold punch in the open air at the hall door.

'Now I'm just worried that we haven't catered for enough. Will cheese and onion crisps pass for Elizabethan nibbles if we run out?'

'You won't run out. The ox roast will feed a thousand. Just think of the takings.'

'I'll feel more confident about them when I know how many are actually paying. Sylvia's told the students they can come for free.'

Al laughed. 'The Queen's bounty.'

'I'm sure Hannah will add to the joy of the occasion. Except that I haven't seen her. Have you?'

'No. Probably thinks Elizabethan festivities are an insult to archaeological integrity.'

'Ronnie doesn't. I saw him quaffing. And I think I saw some hooded figures lurking around too. Spanish Inquisition, or did Molly invite her fellow druids?'

'One or two, maybe. Most of them have gone to pay homage to the bluestone quarry, while they're in the area.'

'Not tempted to go with them?'

Al grinned. 'The doublet and hose won. How could I resist?'

The costume did suit him extraordinarily well. I scowled down at his waist. 'You realise we're probably breaking all manner of byelaws with you brandishing that offensive weapon.'

He followed my gaze down and his eyebrows rose. 'What dost thou speak of, prithee?'

'The sword, and don't you prithee me. Go and make yourself useful, instead of standing around like God's gift to damsels. See if the archers can sober up. They're on after the juggler.'

Al laughed and sauntered away, the rapier giving a twitch of farewell. He exchanged brotherly nothings with the gipsy girl on the terrace parapet, with her fiddle. Kim was happy to sit there playing folksy airs, and the outdoor stall holders seemed to like it.

I turned back to my duties. All was fine in the Hall. Even the jewellers had stopped frowning. The only unhappiness hovered around Peter. I kept him busy but his cruel discomfort with fancy dress was obvious.

Michael was doing better, carrying off his Lord Melchett costume with oblivious unconcern. He was the sort of man who let his wife buy his sweaters – turtle neck, polo neck, lace ruff, it was all one to Michael. Peter couldn't emulate his sublime indifference, any more than he could emulate Al's seductive Tudor gallantry. Peter was a hopeless actor, whereas Al was a natural. A different man every day.

I crossed the hall to Peter's side. 'I'll take over,' I whispered. 'Have a break. You look as if you're hating every minute.'

'No! Not at all. It's good fun. Honestly.'

'Oh isn't it!' Sylvia, out of nowhere, embraced us both. 'Kate, you've done a brilliant job. Hasn't she, Peter? Didn't those Florentine tarts turn out well?'

'Very well. Peter, when that platter's empty, can you slip over to the kitchen and see if they need any help?'

My heart bled for him as I marshalled the crowds back from the centre of the hall in readiness for the juggler, and convinced a photographer from the local paper that he couldn't climb up to the gallery, because it might collapse under him.

'Ladies and gentlemen, we have more entertainment for you all.' Sylvia swirled in the empty space. 'What Elizabethan festivity would be complete without a juggler!'

'Your turn,' I whispered, waking our juggler from his snooze.

'Oh right.' He ambled into the arena to polite applause, sniffed, and began his tricks.

He was very good. Even too good. I'd anticipated coloured balls or skittles, but not blazing brands. I glanced nervously at Michael, who nodded meaningfully at the fire extinguisher in the corner. Sylvia, unperturbed by the small print of insurance cover, gasped with the rest of the audience, mesmerised by the spinning flames.

It had to happen then. At any other time, the noise of the milling crowd would have drowned it out, but the Hall was hushed as eyes were riveted on the swirling brands.

'What the fuck's going on here?' Christian dropped each word with loud deliberation into the expectant silence as he stepped into the central space. The juggler staggered back to avoid him, tripped, dropped a brand and struggled to retrieve the others as he sprawled.

Instant chaos. There was a scream from someone too near the burning brands. A couple of resourceful men were stamping on the flames and sparks. There was outrage at Christian's language and his obnoxious state, but Christian drowned them all. He was giggling uncontrollably. 'Jesus Christ. What wankers, the fucking lot of you.' His unfocussed eyes lighted on me. 'Kate! Hey, It's the Killer Queen. Shee-it!' He stumbled over the juggler and farted loudly. 'What's the loony cow got you all doing now? Jeez, you look a bunch of twats.' Seemingly stoned and oblivious to the consternation he had caused.

Sylvia wailed 'Oh Chris!' – torn between pleading and hurling her pewter goblet at him, her eyes brimming. Peter bounded across the hall to stand in front of me, as if to shield me from a dragon.

'Listen, you little punk!' he began, warning finger raised.

Christian managed a manic cackle in response, but that was all. His cheeks swelled. I could see the unpleasant, green tinge in his complexion as he began to gag; Sylvia's regal magnificence was about to be targeted by perfectly aimed projectile vomiting.

'Sylvia!' I shouted, waving her back as she reached anxiously for her son. Christian's victim was whirled from his sight as Al and Michael seized his arms and frog-marched him from the hall.

'Are you all right?' Peter asked me, urgently.

'Yes, yes.' I'd barely registered Christian's insult, far more concerned about damage to our Fayre. 'Just check and make sure nothing's on fire. Sylvia! It's all right.'

'Oh Kate.' She was a hair's breadth from full-scale sobbing.

'Come on,' I said with calm force. 'We all know Christian. And we're not going to let his little surprises spoil things. People are worried. Let's smile, right?'

With a miraculous effort she pulled herself together and forced a smile. 'It's all right, everyone!'

'Someone had a little too much sun and fine ale.' I watched the sea of faces around me. 'But don't worry, we've got the stocks prepared. You can all throw rotten eggs at him later.' Me first. 'Simon…' I looked at the juggler, but he'd had enough. He gathered up his props, muttering under his breath. 'Thank you, Simon, that was a thrilling show.'

Taking up my cue, Peter began to applaud and the audience joined in.

'Archery,' I whispered to Sylvia.

'Oh yes!' She was back in control now. 'Don't forget the archery exhibition, everyone. It starts in ten minutes down in the meadow.'

Had we managed to limit the damage? The crowd began to drift out of the hall onto the terrace. One silly interruption from a drunken lout was surely not going to spoil the day.

Peter was watching me with consternation. Ridiculous. Did he really imagine I'd collapse in a heap because Christian called me names? Michael and Al's rapid response had been far more to the point. Christian might be genuinely sky high or just trying to spoil his mother's day, but either way he'd have relished Sylvia's vomit-soaked distress. A slanging match with Peter in front of the watching crowd would have suited him perfectly.

'Come on, let's get out of here,' I said impatiently. Then I realised that, for the first time, Peter had forgotten his ridiculous clothes. His concern for me might be pointless but it was heart-felt. How could I blame him for that? I let him put his arm around me.

'I could kill him,' said Peter. Egad sir!

'Couldn't we all.' I stopped, biting my tongue. 'Where is he?' We were out on the gravel now, in the wake of the crowds. I held up my velvet skirts in case I found them trailing in vomit. 'What have they done with him?'

'That obnoxious thug?' asked the herb lady, sweeping up the compost from several smashed pots. 'They took him off round the back of the hall. Turning the air blue.'

'Oh Lord.' I sighed.

She beamed at me. 'Don't worry. I've seen and heard much worse. You're doing all right.'

'Of course you are,' said Peter. 'Do you want me to go and find them?'

'I would like to know.' I blew him a kiss and ran after

Sylvia, directing her down the meadow despite her repeated attempts to look back.

The archery took people's minds off the brief unpleasantness, and the visitors were buoyant, some even joining in the folk dances that followed. I persuaded Sylvia to set an example; anything to stop her fleeing back to the house in search of her son. While she whirled and skipped, I did a quick tour of the grounds, checking for damage that Christian might have done on his way in. There was a felt-tip moustache drawn on one of the photos of Bertie the Bogman, but that seemed a bit too tame for Christian. No other vandalism that I could identify.

All I did find was Hannah, standing on the track leading to the cottages, engrossed in a book, her back ostentatiously turned on the festivities.

'Not coming to the Fayre, Hannah?' I couldn't just ignore her.

'I wasn't invited.' She primly turned a page.

'Everyone was invited.'

'Well, no one told me.'

Christian's presence had drained my tolerance. I wasn't in the mood to indulge her. 'Suit yourself.' I turned on my heel.

I caught a sob as I walked away. I decided she'd meant me to hear it, so I kept walking.

Peter hurried up to join me from the walled garden. 'I found them. They took him to the carriage house round the back.'

'Left him gagged and tied, I hope.'

'Michael was reasoning with him, when I left.'

'Please tell me you mean Corleone reasoning. Sending him to sleep with the fishes?'

'No, but I bloody well might!'

'Because he called me Killer Queen? Don't rise to it.

Christian uses words like hypodermics. It's taken me time, but I've learned to ignore them.'

'Your builder friend hasn't. He wanted Chris to tell him where his sister's got to. Chris found that very funny.'

'Oh God.' The girl had gone from the terrace when we emerged. Had she met Christian on his way in? 'Kim is Chris's perfect prey. Did he say anything?'

'Plenty. All innuendo. Until Taverner hit him. Then he just rolled on the floor and made a big show of being crippled for life.'

'Was he really hurt?'

'Not enough. Your guy went off to find his sister and Mike told Chris to stop arsing around and start talking sense. I left them to it.'

'I hope Mike's okay on his own. Chris doesn't talk sense when he's in that state.'

'Don't be so sure.' Peter scowled. 'Mention money and he talks sense, whatever state he's in. Seems to think Mike is his private banker. How does he get away with it? Mike's not stupid. He must know Chris is just a thieving little toe-rag.'

'Of course he knows, but he'll do anything to make things easier for Syl. Chris knows Mike will do whatever it takes to keep him quiet until the Fayre's over.'

Peter looked round at the crowds and grudgingly admitted the situation. 'Now is not the time to put up a fight, is it?'

'No. We save the scene for later.' I forced myself back into positive thoughts. 'Come on, we've got work to do.'

The Fayre had many more hours to run, into the summer evening, with a bonfire, fireworks, music and vaguely pagan happenings. I spent it all on the look-out for Christian, but he remained blissfully absent.

The last car rolled away down our lane just before midnight. We'd been informed, almost universally, that it had been a thoroughly enjoyable day. Gratifying, but it didn't ease our dread of the confrontation to come.

To our general relief, it was postponed, at least for that night. Christian, bribed to lie low in the house, had discovered the bottles in the drawing room. We found him dead to the world and snoring like a pig in the Guinevere room. At least it allowed Peter and me to creep around him and retrieve Peter's gear.

'I'd better fish out another duvet,' I whispered, though there seemed little likelihood of waking the monster. I paused. The simplest solution was to take Peter back to my room. He'd worked like a Trojan, endured embarrassed torment and flown to my defence. He deserved more than a cold shoulder.

But he was feeling noble. He plucked a blanket from the linen cupboard and gave me an affectionate goodnight kiss. 'Don't worry about me. You've got enough on your plate. I'll go and sleep on the sofa, that'll be the easiest.'

'But—'

'Don't worry, Kate. Right now I could fall asleep anywhere.'

I watched him descend into the dark well of the stairs, and I felt – confused. Peter. Al. Peter… Was I going to count lovers like sheep? Fortunately, sheer exhaustion was enough to send me quickly sound asleep.

When, seven hours later, I came down to say good morning to my husband, I found Sylvia sitting in the kitchen, wiping the last of the dishes. 'What time did you get up?' I asked.

'Early. I couldn't sleep. We were on the local radio.'

'Really?'

'Near disaster as drunken guest sets fire to ancient hall.'

'Oh no.'

It had been too good a story to pass over. Sylvia was naturally deflated after the hyper-tension of the fair, and Christian's mere presence, let alone his behaviour, undermined her usual spirits, but she managed a laugh. 'They say any publicity is better than none, don't they? And they did mention it being an ancient hall. It was quite good, really. Comments about the ox roast and the musicians, all very nice. It's just that...' She had tears in her eyes.

'Sylvia, we had one tiny disaster. Do you realise we didn't have a single punch-up? No stalls collapsing. No heart attacks. No pickpocket alert.'

'I know.' She swallowed, forcing a smile. 'I'd never have managed any of it without you, Kate. It's just that, if there had to be one miserable moment, why did it have to be down to my son?'

Because that's what Christian did.

His drunken slumbers continued through the day, which was a relief; I had other business to attend to. Michael was organising some of the local lads in a mammoth litter patrol and Peter volunteered to join them. Before they set off, black plastic bags in hand, I took Michael to one side and showed him the planning letter.

He read it in silence, then thrust it back at me with exasperation. 'Sheer bloody bureaucratic nonsense.'

'We didn't ask permission for the round house though. Maybe I should have.'

'It's not a proper dwelling. It's...' He shook his head. 'Leave it with me. I'll speak to someone about it. Someone out there must see reason.'

'Okay, but I really need to tell Al. I can't put it off. I have to warn him what they're threatening to do.'

I climbed up to Annwfyn and found the gang in such a relaxed mood that I didn't even know how to begin.

'Come in,' said Molly. 'You're exhausted. This is restorative. Try it.'

'Thanks.' I took the proffered cup, hot and herbal. 'Did you have a successful day?'

'It was good. Positive energy; you could feel it.'

'I want to thank you all for your help. We'd never have managed without you.'

'Fair payment for this,' said Al, dumping a pile of wood as he joined Molly and me in the round house.

I looked around. This house was weeks of painstaking and loving labour, every slip of willow, every handful of clay selected and gathered and placed with care. It was alive, this house.

'Thank you,' I said. Where to begin?

Al came to my rescue. 'Fancy a walk?'

'Yes.' I sprang up, a little too eagerly. 'Yes, why not?'

'Tread the path.' Molly nodded. 'Get your balance right.'

'Up to the stones?' suggested Al as we set off, the air heavy with the smell of wet leaves, damp earth and wood smoke. 'If you don't mind passing the spring.'

'I don't mind; it's cleaner now. And the stones will do just fine.' I followed him. 'Where's Kim?'

'Off, without big brother breathing down her neck.' Al smiled thinly. 'I'm in the dog house for throwing my weight around yesterday.' He turned to face me. 'Where's Christian?'

'When I left, still in bed. Completely out of it.'

'Is he staying?'

'Not if Michael pays him off again. What was he was

181

asking for, this time?'

'Fifteen thousand.' Al picked up a twig and snapped it.

'An opening gambit. Michael won't have promised him anything like that.'

'The doc shouldn't have promised him anything at all.'

'I know. Everyone knows. But—'

'He should smack him back into the gutter where he belongs. I'll do it for him, if you like.' Al's smile was grim and meaningful.

I shrugged, helplessly. 'What can we do? It's Sylvia. Sometimes she screams at Chris, sometimes she throws things at him, but she can't stop being his mother, and Michael will shift heaven and earth to keep her happy.'

Al shook his head. 'Does it keep her happy?'

'No. Nothing about Christian will ever make her happy. He just gets worse. First it was verbal abuse, then vandalism, then stealing, then drugs, then blackmail. What's the next step? Violence?' I said it with disdain, then blushed. Why did violence in someone like Christian strike me as contemptible, irrational, wrong, whereas, with Al, I felt strangely equivocal? My willingness to bend in his favour was worrying; my principles were getting in a twist.

Al wasn't affected by similar moral qualms. 'He'd better be careful who he sets out to hurt. There are people out there more than happy to get violent with him, and they're not just spiteful little bullies. They mean business and they won't have any compunction about crushing an insignificant worm like him. He's got a lot less friends in that world than he needs.'

'Have you been investigating him?'

'I know people,' said Al darkly.

'Then you probably know more about his squalid life

than we do. But look, let's forget my horrible nephew. That wasn't why I wanted to talk with you.'

'Ah. You wanted to talk with me.' Al smiled. 'Your husband's back.'

'Oh. Yes. You know he really didn't realise how stupid he was, telling Ronnie about the bog. I was so furious with him for doing it—'

'I know you were.' He laughed softly. 'And now you're not?'

'Now – I don't know. He and I need to talk things through.'

'Yes, of course you do.'

Was Al's cheerful resignation a subtle way of fighting his own corner? I could have sworn he'd relished outshining my husband at the Fayre. But relationships are not built on an ability to look sexy in doublet and hose.

I was letting myself be diverted again. 'I didn't come to talk about Peter either. At least, not directly. I've had a letter from Planning. The police must have reported the round house.'

Al clasped his hands behind his head and took a deep breath.

'They said it has to be…,' I couldn't bring myself to say the word.

'I can guess.' He snatched off a leafy wand and thrashed the undergrowth that had thickened as we emerged from the trees.

'I haven't told Sylvia yet, but I've discussed it with Michael. He's furious, but he thinks he can talk some sense into them.'

Al laughed.

'He's going to see them. We should have sorted something out, but if the archaeologists hadn't started messing in the bog, no one would ever have noticed it.'

'Don't worry about it. It was just an experiment.'

'I'd hate to see all that effort come to nothing.'

'It's designed to be reabsorbed into the earth. Not quite so soon, maybe, but that was the idea. I didn't intend it as my Ozymandias moment.'

'Yes, but you're living in it.'

'So, we have the yurt. And the yurt moves. I doubt if we'll be around here much longer. Can't stand still, can we?'

'But – what about the hall?' I asked weakly.

Al laughed at my absurdly inane response. 'Don't worry. We'll see the summer out, I expect. And I'll make sure the hall gets finished.' He casually gathered me in to kiss me. Just to demonstrate what I'd be missing.

What was I supposed to do, give them marks out of ten?

17

Christian woke. Not quite the Kraken. He emerged, in the evening, surprisingly subdued and even, by his standards, polite.

'Hi.' He flopped down on the chaise longue, as we were having coffee. 'Christ, I'm shattered.' He groped for his cigarettes, then stopped. 'Oh, not in the house, right?'

'But it's a lovely evening,' said Sylvia. 'We could all go out and sit on the terrace.' No matter what had passed before, the smallest word or gesture of goodwill from her son had her desperate to preserve the moment of grace.

The rest of us were less impressed. Peter and I regarded him in stony silence, but Michael, with a visible effort, responded to Sylvia's aching wishes and did his best. 'Yes, let's get the chairs out.'

So we all trooped out onto the terrace. Christian even obliged by carrying a couple of cushions for the slightly damp chairs that stood on the gravel. I decided that the mossy parapet was preferable and my husband sat by me, protective and alert for the first hint of malice. His gallantry was both touching and irritating.

Christian lit his cigarette. 'Suppose I missed dinner. Anything to eat?'

'Oh of course! You must be starving.' Sylvia jumped up. 'I could make you a sandwich. Would you like that?'

'Yeah, sure.'

'Ham? Or ham and cheese? Would you like it toasted? Or there's some beef—'

'Whatever,' said Christian.

'I'll get it,' said Michael, pushing Sylvia firmly back into her seat.

Christian glanced at us and I felt Peter stiffen. 'So you've got your fair out of the way, then.'

'Yes,' I said.

'Must have taken some organising.'

'Oh it did!' Sylvia smiled coyly at her son. 'But Kate was wonderful. She had everything sorted out and under control. Things I wouldn't even have thought about.'

He nodded with a grin. 'But you have to admit, you did look a bunch of wankers.' He laughed, but it wasn't malicious, more a schoolboy snigger, and I suppose, to a schoolboy, we had looked absurd.

'I never mind making a fool of myself,' beamed

Sylvia.

I looked at her fondly. 'We live only to make sport for our neighbours.'

Christian flicked his ash onto the gravel. 'I suppose Tam's in Spain?'

'Yes.' Sylvia hesitated. She couldn't leave that offence entirely unrebuked. 'You know she was very upset, Chris, when you left her behind.'

'Left her behind?' He looked surprised. It was a look he'd been preparing. Over-rehearsed. 'She got all excited about some rabbit or something. When she jumped out, I waited for her, but she wouldn't come back to the car. What was I supposed to do?'

'All her things were in your car. Her phone—'

'Yeah, well I realised that, didn't I? So I dumped them all on the roadside. I thought if she wouldn't get back in the car, at least she'd come and pick them up, call a taxi or something. She did, didn't she?'

'No. Well, it was all a great muddle and very unfortunate, but it can't be helped now.'

Michael returned with the sandwich and handed it to Christian with an inscrutable expression.

'Thanks, Mike.' Christian responded with a sardonic twitch of an eyebrow and an innocent smile.

I understood that this pleasant humour would last until the second Michael gave Christian what he wanted. I was on edge. I felt much safer when Christian was showing his true colours.

'Let's take a walk,' I suggested to Peter, the following lunchtime. 'Down to the pub.'

'Yes!' He was just as eager to escape. Whichever way we turned, there was Christian, waiting for his tête a tête with Michael. But Michael had gone out, probably to withdraw the protection money and hunt down a planning officer, so Christian had to behave for another day. I could feel the gnawing boredom and frustration, oozing through that innocent façade. How much longer would he be able to keep it up? Constructive occupation was beyond him so he loafed around, doing nothing. His mother descended on him whenever he settled for five minutes, offering him drinks, biscuits, attempts at conversation, plans for a proper apartment, up in the attics 'so you can move in permanently, if you like.'

She was too busy worrying over him, like a warbler tending a fledgling cuckoo, to notice my horror. The thought of Christian in permanent residence made me desperate – but mine wasn't the only desperation. I could feel it swilling around the house. Sylvia's, desperate to redeem her relationship with her son? Or Chris's? I didn't want to think what he might be desperate about.

'I prefer it when he's being outrageous,' I said, as Peter and I strolled down the drive. 'Then at least I can scream at him.'

'What did happen with Tamsin?' he asked.

I told him.

'And Sylvia lets him back in the house?'

'You know how it is with them. Sylvia can't let go.'

'All right, he's her son. But Tammy's her daughter.'

'The conundrum of parenthood?'

'Yes…' We both fell silent.

As we started down the lane towards the village, I took his arm resolutely. 'We need to talk about the conundrum of our non-parenthood, don't we?'

'Kate—'

'We lost a baby, Peter, and that's at the heart of all our problems. Not the beginning or the end of them, but it's at the heart. Everything that was wrong with us was there. If you really want to discuss things properly, we have to start with the one issue we've always avoided.'

He steeled himself. 'All right. I just want you to know – the last time I was here, what you said – I have never blamed you. I know you wanted the baby as much as I did.'

I was determined to be honest. 'No, you didn't know. You couldn't know, because I wouldn't let you. Every day you showed how much you wanted a child, but I showed nothing. I kept it all inside me. I felt the baby die, just like I felt my mother die, and all I could think was that if I didn't hold myself together, keep it under lock and key, a tidal wave would come down on me. So when I told you the baby was dead, I looked as if I didn't care.'

'Yes, but I knew—'

'You *hoped*, Peter. You hoped I cared. But because I seemed so callous, there was a moment when you thought, "She's done this thing." You can't deny it, Peter. Don't deny it. Because there have been terrible, dark moments when I've wondered it myself.' I studied the road ahead of me. 'Not if I wanted my child dead, but if death was all I had to give.'

'No!' said Peter. 'That's not true. That was depression talking. I never seriously thought you'd done anything bad. You couldn't.'

'But the thought came to you, Peter. I watched you fight against it, I watched you do everything right, comfort me, grieve for me, and I couldn't respond. I'd frozen everything out of me.'

I could feel his arm trembling. 'You're always telling me you're not a clairvoyant, and yet you say you know what I was thinking?'

'Only because I know you so well. Just like later, when you were pouring your heart out to Gabrielle. The more she sympathised, the guiltier you felt. I could read

188

it in every smile and gesture you gave me. All women recognise guilt.'

Peter snorted. He always did, when he wanted to deny the truth. 'I still say it's witchcraft.'

I laughed. 'Womancraft.'

'Same thing.'

'That's what men have always said.'

He sighed. 'Even if I did have stupid moments, it didn't mean I stopped loving you.'

'I know. That's what made it so awful. You were trying so hard and I still couldn't respond. The more I faced the awfulness of it, the more I froze. The more you reached out, the lonelier I felt.'

'I failed you.'

'Good God, no. Neither of us could cope with the way I am – was. I have to change. I can't deal with life, or death, by sealing myself up inside an iceberg. That's why I came here: to force a thaw. I came to learn how to feel, to respond, to block out the shadows and embrace the light, the positive, get on with life, like a normal person.'

'And have you?'

'Yes, perhaps I am learning the art of balance. Getting my rational self back. Perhaps I've learned not to freeze up quite so completely.'

'Why don't you just talk about your odd feelings honestly? If you're among friends, how could it hurt?'

'I told you about my odd feelings at the bog,' I reminded him, and he grimaced. 'You didn't think it could possibly hurt to pass it on, but I know that to open my mouth is to release bedlam. There's no predicting and no controlling what happens.'

'Are you so desperate to be in control?'

'Shouldn't I be?'

'Maybe not so much.'

I thought about it. 'I'm surrounded by the chaos of the universe. There seem so many more dimensions than people realise. Control is the only way I can deal with it.'

'What you need is one person you can confide in, without fear. One person who promises never to repeat a word of it, to anyone. Not even to professors met once at a conference. Absolute silence.'

'My God, Peter, you make marriage to me sound like membership of a secret sect.'

He laughed. 'I could build a chapel, I suppose, with all your mysterious revelations encoded in cryptic carvings.'

'You see, you're itching to leave clues already.'

'Okay. Tell me one small thing that I can safely pass on; what do you want to drink?' We'd reached the Cemaes Arms and he gestured to the door. The low, dark, beamed interior was packed, and the larch-shaded beer garden was heaving too.

'You do the valiant thing and fight to the bar. I'll sit on the bridge and fan myself like a lady. And a mineral water, please.'

Peter smiled. 'Because alcohol weakens your defences? Loosen your control a little.'

'All right, then. A white wine.'

We sat, with a dozen others, on the parapet of the old bridge that arched over the shallow river. The low Welsh murmurs of the somnolent low season were buried under a babble of English, Dutch, Japanese, probably Martian. One world superimposed on another. In a month or so the tourists would be gone and this deep valley would be a silent, forgotten backwater, the rain falling on sodden yellow leaves, the roads deserted but for an occasional tractor, the bar of the Cemaes Arms empty of all but a couple of farmers watching

190

football over a lunchtime pint. The solid reality beneath the raucous trivia of the present.

Was there a solid reality underlying the raucous trivia of my marriage? 'You want to try again, don't you?' I watched ducks circling under us, ready to pounce on falling crisps.

Peter gasped. 'You see. Clairvoyance!'

'All right.' I laughed. 'Yes, you want to try again.'

'I don't like giving up so easily.'

'Nothing easy about me though, is there?'

'Nothing is easy if it's worth trying for.'

'You've been reading cracker mottoes again.'

'Just because I found it in a cracker, doesn't mean it isn't true. Yes, I want us to – to think about trying again.' He stopped me before I could interrupt. 'I'm not asking you to say yes and swoon into my arms, this very moment. I just want you to think about it. Reverently, discreetly, soberly.'

'Soberly? And he gives me wine?'

'Tipsily then.'

'Tipsy or sober, yes, I am thinking about it.'

'That's all right then.'

We finished our drinks and started back along the valley, up the wooded lane towards Llys y Garn. 'If we were to start again, we'd need to sort out some house rules first,' I said.

'Of course. I promise that in future I won't—'

'No! Rules for me. I'm the problem.' As the perfect bullet point, a distant shotgun shattered the green silence of the lane. Rooks cawed in indignation.

'You're not a problem,' Peter insisted. He took my hands. 'Kate, you're—'

Two more booms of the gun and another wild flutter of outraged birds.

'It's the peace of the country.' I laughed at his

exasperated frown. 'Farmers red in tooth and claw.'

'Couldn't they choose another moment to slaughter the local rabbit population? What I was trying to say—'

More shots. A cacophony of birds erupted from the trees. 'Those are our woods.'

Peter looked up. 'Yes?'

'Dewi wouldn't be shooting in our woods!' My stomach tightened. 'Let's get back. Find out what's happening.'

We hurried, our footsteps punctuated by continuing booms. The valley reverberated.

'Kate!' Sylvia was out on the drive, as we hurried up. 'There you are. I don't suppose Christian's with you?'

'No.'

'I couldn't find him. I thought maybe he'd gone with you.' She flinched at the sound of another double shot.

I seized her arm. 'Sylvia, have you checked the gun locker?'

'I thought maybe Michael had taken it. He was talking about getting rid of it.'

I spelled it out. 'Christian's got hold of the shotgun!'

'I don't know. He was trying so hard to be nice. It's my fault. I should have left him alone. He went off and locked himself in his room for a bit, and when he came down again he seemed so much livelier, you know—'

'Stoned, you mean. We'd better find him.'

'He wouldn't do any harm, really.'

'Sylvia, stop it!' For once I had to shout at her. 'If Christian's out of his tiny mind, he's capable of anything.'

'I'll call the police,' said Peter.

'No!' pleaded Sylvia.

'Then I'd better go and find him.'

'Al's gone to look, with Thor and Baggy. I asked them if they'd seen Chris and then we started hearing gunshots.'

'All right.' Peter turned to me. 'You stay in the house—'

'Don't be stupid.'

'Take Sylvia in,' he ordered, and set off up the track into the woods. It wasn't difficult to tell where Christian was. The gun bursts were still coming, sporadically.

'Come on Sylvia, no use you standing out here.' I shepherded her to the courtyard.

'I should never have nagged him.'

'Don't indulge in guilt! How do we deal with this? You don't want us to call the police, so what? My husband gets shot?'

'He wouldn't! I know he was a little high, but not out of his mind. He was just bored. He wouldn't shoot someone. He couldn't!'

'Oh couldn't he!' Christian had been a monster before. Now he was a monster with a gun. I pushed her into the kitchen and ran to the archaeology camp. Several dozen students were probably innocently wandering through the woods and my fingers twitched on my phone, regardless of Sylvia's wishes.

But by pure chance, Ronnie had his entire flock assembled at HQ, for a lecture on something microscopic. Hannah saw me and bustled forward to keep me at bay, but I'd already turned on my heel. They were safe, one major worry less, and now I could concentrate on my husband. I set off up into the woods, listening for the next shot to guide me.

Boom.

Looking up, I saw the harvest of an earlier shot. Michael's Windhover sculpture, soaring out from its rock, was stunted, one of its limbs splintered to matchwood. Evil little bastard! I wanted to spit in fury.

I ran up the track, listening for guidance. The shouts came first. Wild and urgent, but drowned by another boom from the gun, a shrill laugh and a woman's scream. I stopped, hand on my pounding heart. The shouts came louder, angrier, far up through the trees. I ran, ripping myself clear of brambles, up any pathway that opened in the direction of the raging voices.

They were up where the trees gave way to heathery moorland. I passed a sapling, shattered into white shards, then I saw Christian, spluttering and laughing, wrestled to the ground by Thor and Al, who were furiously pinioning him down. Thor, red with anger, aimed a kick at him. Baggy was comforting a weeping Molly. Peter, white-faced, was holding the shot gun as if it were a dangerous animal.

'Has he shot anyone?' I called, panting up to them.

Peter turned, almost pointing the gun at me as he did so. 'Go back, Kate!'

Al got to his feet and took the gun from Peter, breaking it to prevent any further harm. He handed it back, looked at me, shaking with anger, then bounded up out of the trees into the open.

'Don't come up here,' said Peter.

'What's he done?' Ignoring the order, I followed in Al's wake.

A sheep lay dead and twisted in the heather, gouts of blood everywhere. The crimson against the white wool held my eye first, but then I looked further, following Al as he climbed.

Our neighbour Dewi was standing in the heather, looking down at his feet. At something black and white.

'Oh no.' I shook Peter loose as he tried to hold me back.

The dog, Murk, was lying on her side. Not quite dead. She gave little whimpers as she twitched.

'You leave her,' ordered Dewi, as Al bent down to touch her. 'I don't want you touching her.'

Al took a step back.

Dewi bent down and stroked the shivering dog's ear. He straightened. 'I'll have the gun.'

We were silent, sickened. For a moment, no one moved. Then Al took the shotgun from Peter again and offered it to Dewi. We watched the old man grope in the pockets of his tweed jacket for a cartridge.

'Don't look,' whispered Peter fiercely, and this time I obeyed. One boom of the gun. I put my hands to my face.

There was silence, but for the rustle of the wind in the trees, the bleating of distant sheep. I turned back.

Al was holding the gun again. Dewi gathered up the dog in his arms.

'Let me—' began Peter.

'My dog, I'll deal with her,' said Dewi, from beyond a wall of absolute rejection. He was a farmer, accustomed to the death of livestock. A trailer load of sheep off to the abattoir. A chicken having its neck wrung for dinner. One dead dog. We were the weak and sentimental ones, horrified by the tragedy. He merely took it in his stride.

Except that I could feel, inside that mask of impassive taciturnity, the overwhelming, lonely grief of the man. It rose out of him, a cloud of pain, suffocating in my own lungs, wrenching my heart.

What could I say? He didn't want any of us to say anything. He wanted to be left alone, free of our insulting platitudes. We watched him, weighed down by the dog's limp body, plodding his way along the heather, back to his lonely farmhouse.

'Oh God, what a mess,' said Peter.

'What's happened?' Michael, back from his

expedition, was panting his way up through the trees. He gave one cursory glance at Christian, still pinned down by Thor, then climbed up to us. 'What other damage has he done?' He must have seen the Windhover, and the sheep lay now before him, but as he finished the question, his eyes followed ours, along the hillside, to Dewi's receding back and Murk's lolling head. I saw his lips, white and tight, work as he fought to control himself. 'Is the dog dead?'

'Yes,' said Al.

Michael closed his eyes. When he opened them, he looked at me. 'Kate, Peter, take Christian back to the house, please. Make sure he goes nowhere, does nothing, until I come down.'

'Yes,' I said.

'Al, take charge of the shotgun. Put it somewhere, well away from him, until I can dispose of it.'

Al nodded.

'I'm going to speak to Dewi.'

'I don't think he'll thank you,' said Peter.

The anger burst from Michael. 'It isn't thanks I'm after.' He pointed a shaking finger in Christian's direction, still without looking at him. 'Get him out of here!'

I tugged Peter's hand. 'Let's take him down.'

Together, we stood over Christian's squirming form.

'Get up, Christian.'

'How can I fucking get up, with this oaf on me?' Christian giggled. Thor removed his weight, but Christian made no attempt to stir.

'Get up.' Peter seized him by the collar and hoisted him to his knees. 'You disgusting little sod.'

'Oh come on. It was just target practice. I thought it was a rabbit.'

'Save it!' I glanced at Al. 'You'd better look after

196

Molly. I'm so sorry about all this.'

'It wasn't your fault.' He shot a look of loathing at Christian's back. 'Tell Michael I've got the gun safe, till he wants it back.'

I nodded. Peter and I took Christian's arms and dragged him down the track. He laughed all the way.

'Pack,' said Michael.

Sylvia's eyes were tear-filled, but she said nothing to remonstrate.

Christian, lolling on the sofa, had come down to earth sufficiently to be aware of his cuts and bruises. For a moment, interested in a graze on his jaw, he didn't seem aware that Michael had addressed him. Then he blinked.

'Are you talking to me?'

'Pack and get out of this house. I want you out, now!'

Christian laughed. 'And I thought it was my mother's house. Are you throwing me out, Mummy?'

Sylvia folded her arms, gripping herself tightly, and turned away.

'She won't want me thrown out,' said Christian.

'Your mother and I have agreed you're no longer welcome in this house.' Michael's anger was under control, but only Christian could be stupid enough to think there'd be a chink in his resolution. 'You will leave now.'

'Or what? You'll make me?'

'If necessary.'

'Is that how you keep her in tow, then? Whack her, if she doesn't do what you want?'

'Christian!' pleaded Sylvia.

Michael didn't deign to respond

'No one pushes me around. What you going to do? Call the police to do your heavy work?'

197

Christian knew exactly how to find his mother's fault line. At the mention of the police, Sylvia flinched. 'No one is going to—'

'If Michael needs a hand, throwing you off the property, I'll be delighted to help,' offered Peter.

I touched his arm, aware of Sylvia's distress. Now that she was struggling against all her maternal instincts and siding with Michael, I could only feel sympathy for her.

Michael remained impassive, as Christian continued to finger his jaw and his bruised cheek. 'I am waiting,' he said at last.

'Wait on, old man.'

Michael swooped, seized Christian's arm and plucked him up like a doll.

'Okay! You want to wreck my mother's home?'

'You're the wrecker, Christian, and now you're leaving. You can pack or I'll pack for you.'

'We had a deal.' Did he really believe that their arrangement could withstand this? 'I stayed out of the way. You owe me.'

'Mike?' Sylvia was bewildered.

He patted her on the shoulder, his attention still on her son. 'Any interest I might have had in your latest business proposal was void, the moment you decided to amuse yourself with a shotgun.'

'You said—'

'I've given the money to Dewi. Compensation for the sheep and the dog you killed. Compensation that you should be paying, if you had an ounce of grace.'

'You gave my money away for a fucking mutt!' For a moment it looked as if Christian would explode. Peter stepped forward.

Sylvia spoke up, at last. 'Oh Christian, how could you do it? How could you shoot that poor dog?'

'Hey, what was I supposed to do? Okay so I shot a sheep. I didn't know. I thought it was a badger or something. Then the dog went wild. I thought it was going to attack me. You're allowed to shoot in self-defence, aren't you?'

'The dog was nowhere near you.' Peter's fists clenched. 'You were having fun. You'd have probably shot the farmer, too, if they hadn't jumped on you.'

'Scared the shit out of you though, didn't I?' Christian was laughing again.

'A maniac with a shotgun would scare the shit out of anyone!'

'Yeah well, you know all about maniacs, being married to one. Watch out she doesn't throttle you in the dark, just like she throttled her foetus.'

Michael caught Peter's fist in mid-air. Sylvia cried out, aghast, and rushed to embrace me, though I hadn't reacted. I'd tasted this toxin before.

'You'll not achieve anything by vomiting your filth around this house,' said Michael, forcefully enough to silence everyone's incipient outbursts. 'You have fifteen minutes to empty your room, pack your bags and be out of here. Understand?'

Coming to the kitchen door, Al found us gathered in stony silence. Sylvia still had her arm around me. Michael had taken his watch off and laid it on the table. Fifteen minutes, he'd said, and he wasn't going to permit a second more.

'Came to say I've got the gun safe. You all okay?'

'Christian is leaving.' Michael picked up his watch and turned to the hall door.

'I'll drag him down,' said Peter. But he didn't have to. Christian was sitting on the bottom rung of the stairs, calmly smoking and listening to everything we said. He shouldered his bag and blew smoke in Peter's face. After that, his attention was all for his mother.

'So long then, Mummy.'

Her arm dropped from my waist as she stepped forward. 'Christian, I'm sorry—'

'Hey, you've got to do what your lord and master says, okay? Don't want him slipping you an overdose, like he did his last one.'

'Christian! Please, Christian, don't—'

'Oh, I won't be going far, by the way. Business in the area, clients to see.' He glanced round at the rest of us, with a taunting sneer. 'Got to keep my customers satisfied.' I saw Al stiffen.

'Do what you want,' said Michael. 'Find accommodation with anyone who'll have you. But you will not come back on this property.'

Christian leered at him, then gave his shell-shocked mother a hug. 'Don't worry, Mumsy. I'll be back.'

With that Parthian shot, he sauntered out into the yard, got into his car and screeched off down the lane.

Sylvia drew a shuddering breath, then leaned on the dresser, looking sick.

Michael gripped her shoulders, but she shook him off. 'I'm all right. I'll be all right.' Then she burst into tears.

He hugged her. 'I'm sorry, Sylvie. We couldn't let him—'

'I know, I know.' She wiped her eyes. 'We can't have him here. But it doesn't make it any easier.' She sniffed. 'Oh God, poor Dewi. That poor dog. Did you speak with him, Mike? Did you give him money?'

'He refused. I'll speak to him again, tomorrow.'

'I don't think he loves any of us,' said Peter. 'Can't blame him, I suppose.'

'No I don't blame him.' Michael slumped down at the kitchen table, and leaned his head on his hand.

'He's hurting,' said Al. 'Tomorrow, maybe—'

'Yes, tomorrow I'll speak to him again. Today he's too angry. He wouldn't even let me help him bury the dog.'

I was glad Dewi was angry. Anger was better than that hopeless grief.

Michael looked up, from Al to Peter. 'Was anyone wounded?'

'No, I snatched the gun away,' said Peter.

'A few bruises,' said Al. 'Thor was grazed by a pellet, that's all.' He shrugged it off, leaving us to shudder at the possibilities.

'Molly wasn't hurt?' I asked.

'No, just shocked. Wondering if she's misread the forces round here.'

'Christian is a dark force all of his own. What about Kim? Where's she?'

'Out.' Al grimaced. 'I can't force her to stay at home. Counter-productive.'

And Christian was on the loose, looking for prey.

Sylvia was grey. 'He's my son, but sometimes I think it would be better for everyone if he just…' She paused for an age, before adding 'Moved abroad, with Ken.'

Too late. In my head I'd already finished the sentence for her. '*If he just died.*'

Hell. Expulsion. A black void, pitiless, unforgiving. For a moment, I teetered on the brink of an abyss and beheld absolute damnation. Why? What was so wrong with wishing him dead?

The idea gushed out of me – and echoed back, bringing me up with a cold shudder. My thoughts might be unpardonable, but they were shared, probably, by everyone in the room.

If thoughts could really kill, Christian must be dead by now.

18

If thoughts could kill. It was a notion I couldn't push aside. All evening and through the night, I listened, for a phone call or a knock, a police siren. Waiting for someone to tell Sylvia her son was dead. A crash, a fit, a lightning bolt.

Looking out, at last, on morning drizzle, I swore. There had been no call, he was alive, and he'd won that round. Enough. I was going to put this stupid idea out of my head now, or I'd be forever at his mercy, wherever he was.

At breakfast I was monosyllabic, so Peter wisely gave me space and strolled down to the village for milk and the local paper. He returned, looking abashed. 'I walked in and the whole shop fell silent. We don't seem to be the flavour of the month at the moment.'

'We're the people who shoot dogs. Sorry you've got embroiled in it. I expect we'll live it down.' I picked up the paper and flicked through it. There was a lively account of our Fayre, dominated by a photograph of the tumbling juggler. It was taken over Christian's shoulder, his expression hidden so he seemed no more than a mischievous prankster. But Sylvia was in full focus, beyond the juggler, her face aghast, as if the sky had fallen around her. The headline: 'Knave steals the show from Good Queen Bess.'

'Have you seen this?'

'Yes. The article's not bad really. Quite appreciative. Pity about the picture.'

'I wonder if Christian's seen it. Probably laughing his head off.'

Sylvia came in, glanced at the article, heaved a sigh of exasperation and pushed it aside. She looked old.

Against our joint advice, she'd gone to see Dewi and had come back in tears. 'Let's have a drink. The boys must need their tea. Have you seen Michael?'

Michael. Not Mike. Things must be strained between them.

'In his workshop probably. I'll fetch him.' I wanted them back on purring terms. Sylvia would recover from these latest bruises – she always did – but she would do it sooner with Michael's comfort.

When I reached his workshop, he wasn't in comforting mode. The Volvo was parked by the door, its tailgate up, the shotgun lying inside. I heard the sound of clinking, within the workshop.

'Al's returned the gun then,' I said.

Michael was gathering jars into a crate. Dusty brown, ribbed jars, with stained illegible labels. Chemicals of various shades and descriptions.

'Yes.' He sniffed the contents of a jar. 'It's going. Even when we had the chickens I never managed to hit anything.' He pulled a biro from his pocket and scrawled on the label. To what end, I don't know. His handwriting was as illegible as the acid-chewed printing.

'What do you use them all for?' I peered into the crate.

'Nothing. Just mementoes of a past life. Things accumulate. I'd more or less forgotten them. But they're going too; I want them out of temptation's way.'

I could see a skull and crossed bones on one yellow label, where Michael's thumb had smudged away the dust. 'Christian's gone,' I reminded him.

'For today.' Michael lifted the crate and carried it to the car. 'How long do you think he'll stay away?'

'He can't come back if you won't let him.'

203

'What do you expect me to do?' He dropped the tail shut and gave me a sad smile. 'You want me to tell Sylvia she can't see her own son?'

'She agrees with you.'

'Her head agrees. Sylvia isn't a head person.'

'No. She's making tea. Won't you come and join us?'

'Later. First, I'm getting rid of this lot.' He opened the driver's door, then paused. 'Sorry things are such a mess, Kate. This wasn't what you came for, was it?'

'I've known Christian longer than you, Mike. I never had any illusions about the devastation he can wreak. We mustn't let him win.'

'No.' He smiled, more warmly. 'We won't. Tell Sylvia I'll bring a bottle back, and something for dinner. She can light the sandalwood candles.'

Sylvia nodded at the message, and almost smiled. 'I've made the tea for everyone else.'

I looked at the tray of mugs. It was understood that I took the tea to the Hall. What was I to do, with Peter hovering? I made no move.

Sylvia gave us a bright unconvincing smile. 'I'll take these over, leave you two to talk.'

'Right.'

'She's almost her old self,' said Peter.

'No she isn't, but she will be. Mike will bring her round. He'll relax, once he's disposed of all that lethal stuff.'

'It should have been locked up. Especially with Chris around.'

'The gun was locked up. That didn't stop him.' I sipped my tea. 'To hell with Chris. Let's not talk about him anymore.'

'How do you fancy dining out tonight?'

'Us two?'

'I think maybe Sylvia and Michael would benefit

from a quiet dinner on their own.'

'Yes, of course they would.'

'And it's been a long time since I took you out to dinner.'

'You won't find anywhere. They'll all be fully booked.'

'If I find somewhere, will you come?'

'Yes – yes, of course.'

He did find somewhere, eventually: a restaurant fifteen miles away. I retreated to my room, to survey my wardrobe. What should one wear for a romantic dinner with an estranged husband?

I dragged out a forgotten designer dress and held it up, to see myself in the mirror, ready to be shocked. No, not the scarlet woman I'd expected. Just puzzled. Worried. So I should be. Not long ago, I'd been nursing desperate disappointment that Al was thinking of leaving, plotting to keep him here indefinitely. And now here I was, feeling a frisson of pleasure at the thought of a date with Peter. If he really wanted us to start again, adults, knowing our strengths and weaknesses…

There were words for women like me.

I decided that I might as well enjoy it. As Peter escorted me gallantly to the car, Michael was in the kitchen, a composer surveying his orchestra, as he arranged the contents of a dozen delicatessen bags, while Sylvia happily toyed with a breadstick and a glass of wine. 'Be good, children.'

'And you.' We all laughed. As if the shadows had been dispelled.

*

'How are you, this morning?' Sylvia looked radiant, presiding over croissants and toast, like her old joyous self.

'I am just fine.' I helped her lay the breakfast table.

'I didn't hear you come in. Were you very late?'

'I suppose so. We went for a moonlit walk on the beach.'

'And did you…?' Sylvia was all benign curiosity. 'Peter and you, you know. Have you got back together?'

I laughed. 'Do you mean, are we back together for keeps? We're thinking about it. In a mature and sensible manner.'

'Oh that's wonderful. I did wonder. I mean, I was never sure how things were, what with, you know, you and Al.' She caught my wince and immediately sympathised. 'They're both lovely men of course.'

'I know, it's so difficult to choose. Peter has such an agreeable bank balance, but then Al is so good with a screwdriver.'

'Kate! Really. Be serious.'

'All right.' I gave her a kiss on the cheek. 'Don't rush me. I take it all is well with you and Mike?'

She beamed. 'We had an early night.'

'You need your sleep at your age.'

'Good morning!' Peter came in, fresh from his shower. 'Just ready for a good hearty breakfast.'

'Would you like egg and bacon?' proposed Sylvia.

'Sausage, tomato, mushrooms, fried bread,' enthused Peter. 'Hash browns – what else? Black pudding!'

'Shut up and have a croissant,' I said.

'But if he'd like—' began Sylvia.

'No he wouldn't. It will take more than a walk on the beach just to burn off that meal last night. I'll have to book him into a gym, if you start giving him full English fry-ups.'

Peter pouted. 'It was the beach that gave me an appetite. Walking – or something. Let's go back there.

206

See it in the pearly light of dawn.'

'Dawn was hours ago. But—' I ignored Sylvia, egging me on. 'We could take another stroll on the sands.'

'Yes, do go,' said Sylvia. 'It's such beautiful weather.'

Peter found room for three croissants and a bacon roll. Then, at Sylvia's insistence, we left her with the washing up. Peter picked up his jacket, abandoned in the drawing room. As a matter of course, he checked his phone in the pocket.

'Text from Jill. She wants me to phone, urgent.'

'They can't do without you. Go on, make your phone call. The beach will still be there in half an hour. I'll go and help Sylvia.'

I left him to it and returned to the kitchen to wipe while Sylvia washed. 'He's probably missing a deadline, by being here. Isn't it annoying, when work gets in the way of life?'

'Aren't we lucky to have our work here? Carmen said she was very keen on one of the workshops, so you see, our little craft centre could be a reality soon.'

'That's encouraging.' I heard Peter dash upstairs, two at a time. 'I'll start sniffing around and see if there are any grants available.'

'We'll need to get the shop going too, won't we?'

We discussed business until the kitchen was clear. Still no sign of Peter, so I strolled over to the archaeology camp to check that all was well. No Hannah warding me off for once, but another student, actually enthusiastic about his subject, showed me a burnt bone, a spindle whorl and a photo of a dark smudge that he explained was a hearth. I strove to be impressed.

When I returned, Sylvia had gone to her pottery. Peter

must surely be off the phone by now.

I found him in the drawing room.

I had spent much of the preceding night wondering if I would agree to start again with him. I'd told myself I still needed to think it all through, but as I walked into the room and saw Peter's face, I knew there was no doubt. I would have said yes. I knew it, the moment it was too late. Peter's face told me it was too late, though I didn't yet know why. It was finished.

'Kate—'

'What's happened?'

'Jill – she asked me to call.'

'I know. What's happened?'

'She thought I should know.' He was pacing the room, looking everywhere except at me. 'She's a friend of – Gabrielle. They met up at the weekend. Gabrielle is – It seems that Gab is—'

'Pregnant.'

'Yes. How did you know?' He met my eyes for the first time. 'Jill only found out—'

'An inspired guess,' I said. 'Yours, I assume?'

He spread his hands helplessly.

'How very careless of you.'

'It must have been that last—'

'Spare me the precise details!'

'I'm so sorry, Kate.' He was, too. There was no feigning his pain.

'Well.' I sat down, primly. 'A bit of a shock for you. But I can't see Gabrielle demanding a shotgun wedding. Does she even want you involved?'

'No. She's not asking me to marry her. Anything but. She's debating whether to have an abortion.'

I felt the knife twisting in my gut. His distress, writhing in me. Another child. His child. About to die. 'And you want to dissuade her?'

'She won't talk to me on the phone.'

'No. So you'd better go.'

'I've got to.'

'Of course you do.'

'If she – I mean, you and I, if—'

'You and I are over, Peter. We have to be. You know that. You want to persuade her to keep your child, marry you, make a family. You can't do that if you're keeping other commitments in your back packet. You go prepared to give it your all, or you don't go.'

'I've got to go,' he repeated.

'I know.' I smiled. 'So do it properly.'

He left. If Gabrielle had decided on an abortion, she'd probably already made the arrangements. I told him not to waste time on goodbyes. Less painful for both of us. His anguish was evident, but so was his determination. Could I seriously ask him to stay, to lose the child he'd always wanted? The child I hadn't been able to give him?

I watched his silver Peugeot disappear through the lodge gates, from my bedroom window. Our first separation had been a tear, a nagging ache. This was a sharp, swift amputation. Finished.

A baby. The perfect surgical knife. I stared at myself in my mirror as I gulped down a couple of Migraleve. How strange that sunlight surrounded me. I ought to live in perpetual darkness. That was all I was. Maybe I didn't kill, not physically, but I was doomed to murder all relationships. I was as Michael had portrayed me. Empty, desolate, meaningless.

Forget this stupid idea of learning to embrace life. Cold and callous, that was the only way to be.

'So your husband's gone again?' Al smiled, a smile of

quizzical sympathy.

'Yup. For good this time.' How good was I at playing it cool?

'What happened to the turtle doves?'

'Someone shot them, put them in a pie.'

'Sylvia's wringing her hands over you.'

'We make a good pair, don't we? The drama queen and the frigid princess.'

'Hardly that. If he really—'

'Al, I don't want to talk about it. It's over. I just want to think about something else.'

'I could offer you consolation. Or would that be the pinnacle of insensitivity, at the moment?'

I laughed, bitterly. 'Insensitive is exactly what I need. How's the work going?'

'Just fine. The gallery's coming along. Timbers all in place. Thor's working on replacement stonework for the oriel window.'

'Good. That's good. Michael did speak to the planners about the round house, you know. And Fran Garrick.'

'Yes, he told us. Didn't get anywhere.'

'No. Not yet. Fran was happy to pull strings for her brother's dig—'

'But not for a bunch of travellers.'

'No, well – Michael hasn't given up. There's the Assembly, M.P – he knows other people. He's so reasonable and surely they can't hold out on a petty point of principle?'

Al laughed. 'You haven't dealt with many planning departments, have you?'

'Not personally. I'm trying to be optimistic. Hoping that you won't just vanish with the first rains of autumn.'

'Nothing's ever fixed in my life.'

I got on with my work and with my free and easy life, faintly disgusted with myself. I hadn't imagined myself capable of falling straight into Al's arms, with Peter barely out of the door, but it was what I did. A means of slamming the vault shut. If I were another person, watching, I would have been appalled and amused in equal measure, but charging brazenly forward seemed the only thing to do.

19

The world moved on. Llys y Garn was gearing itself for another changeover weekend. Michael arranged a formal meeting with planning officers. Sylvia met Dewi in the post office and he nodded a greeting, the hostility fading. He wasn't the same. I saw him on the hills, diminished without his dog; a little old man, mournfully trudging among his sheep. Perhaps he would accept compensation now, ease our guilt a little. In the Cemaes Arms, the locals stopped treating us like lepers. Brian the landlord asked if the Fayre would be an annual event.

The weekend arrived with predicable bustle but no major crisis. The happy Waterstons from Hertfordshire moved out of the lodge, Sylvia and I zoomed over it with our buckets and mops, and the Pretty family from Kent moved in, with a trailer of surf boards and wet suits. Minibuses ferried Ronnie's students away and returned with the third battalion, most of whom headed straight for the bog, in hope of the odd arm or leg. Michael collected Tamsin from the station, with a golden tan, a bag of bizarre presents and plenty to say.

Sylvia hugged her for the twentieth time. 'I suppose I had better ask, how's your father?'

'Dad? Oh, you know. Have there been any more bodies at the dig? That was so cool. I'd scream if I'd missed him, like I missed the bride. Have there been any more?'

'No more,' I said. 'But you missed our Fayre.'

'Yeah? How did it go?'

'It was wonderful, darling,' said Sylvia. 'Such fun. You'd have loved it. We were in the paper and we got a mention on the local radio.'

'Cool. Did I tell you, Ben's putting my Bertie pictures on his Goth site?'

'And you missed Christian,' added Sylvia.

Tamsin's expression curdled. 'Big deal.'

'I know, darling, I could have killed him for what he did, but he did say he was very sorry.'

Tamsin shrugged. 'Yeah, whatever.'

Michael and I exchanged forced smiles. Clearly, nothing negative was to be mentioned.

'She smothers Tam with motherly love,' I said, as Al and I walked in the cool of the evening. 'Compensation for the child she's lost, I suppose.'

'She hasn't lost Christian. Kim saw them in Cardigan on Friday. Having coffee together.'

'Sylvia! She's hopeless. It will only make him think he's winning.'

'He probably is. Kim said Sylvia was giving him money.'

'Aagh!' I glanced at Al, taking in what, to my mind, was the secondary import of his revelation. 'Did he see Kim?'

'I guess so. When I ask, she bites my throat. Says I don't trust her.'

'Why can't he just go away? Better Cardigan than here at Llys y Garn, but it's still too close for comfort.'

'Oh he's closer than that. Staying at a B&B in Pen-y-bont.' The next village along the valley. 'They wouldn't have him at the Cemaes, or he'd be there.'

'What's he doing?'

'What do you think? He's probably established a customer base, and where else could he irritate so many people with so little effort?'

'He doesn't still think he can squeeze money out of Sylvia and Mike, can he? If she's buying him coffee and slipping him used fivers, he's already laid the groundwork. Oh, Sylvia!'

I received a card from Peter. The single word 'Sorry.' More than enough. I dreaded a fuller explanation, riddled with apologies and obstetrics. Whatever he was negotiating with the fecund Gabrielle, I didn't want to hear about it.

To put it out of my mind, I paid my regular visit to Ronnie. He wasn't at No.1 but Hannah, inevitably, was. Too much to hope she'd left with the second contingent.

She was hovering just outside, looking more demented than ever.

'Hello,' I said, resolutely cheerful. 'Is Ronnie up in the fields?'

'Professor Pryce-Roberts is inspecting the dig, yes.' She turned her back on me, then swivelled to face me. 'Someone's been stealing my things!'

'Oh dear. I don't like the sound of that. What's missing?'

'My brush! And someone used my toothpaste.'

'Right.'

The cottage door opened and a woman emerged,

213

slight and sprightly, but ancient by student standards. 'Would you be Mrs Lawrence? I'm Vicky Ives. How do you do.' She shook hands warmly. 'Hannah, dear, I'm sure the professor will look into it as soon as he comes down.'

'He said I could speak to him this morning.'

'Well, yes, I don't think he'll be long. Why don't you come in and wait?'

'No! I'm not allowed in!' Hannah was taut with distress.

'Now that's not what he meant, dear,' said Vicky, but Hannah stormed off.

'You'd best let her go,' I said, as Vicky seemed in half a mind to follow her. 'This is how Hannah always is.'

'So I've heard.' Vicky looked guilty. 'Oh dear. This is my fault, I'm afraid.'

I laughed. 'I doubt it. What does she think you've done?'

She ushered me into the cottage. 'I'm not as young as most of the others, you see. RPR thought I ought to have a bed here. I understand Hannah's been staying here from the start. I really didn't want her to be asked to move out. I'm fine under canvas - go every year with the grandchildren. If it weren't for my arthritic knees. RPR insisted.'

I tried not to smile. Of course Ronnie insisted. Anything to get Hannah out of his thinning hair. 'Quite right too. It won't hurt Hannah to slum it with the other students for another couple of weeks.'

'But I don't think she's really suited to camping. She's having to share a tent, you see, and she obviously had the idea she was going to have a room here for the whole of the summer.'

'Please. Don't try and fathom Hannah's paranoia. The

truth, if you ask me, is that she's smitten with the Prof.'

Vicky beamed. 'I did wonder. Poor girl, I think he's terrified of her. Now, would you like a cup of tea while you're here?' She already had the kettle on. 'I expect you'd like to inspect things, make sure we're not creating too much havoc. It must be quite a nuisance, having all us students on your doorstep.'

'It's been stimulating.' I looked around. The room was tidy and suddenly much friendlier, as if a poltergeist had been exorcised. 'I'm sure everything here is fine. How are the bathrooms? I gather they'd got into a bit of a state.'

'They had, rather. I told RPR we'd better do something or you wouldn't have us back again, so we've sorted out a rota.'

I smiled. Vicky obviously knew how to handle her professor. 'Any interesting finds since you arrived?'

'Well, nothing like Bertie, although I mustn't call him that in front of RPR.' Vicky handed me a mug. 'Poor man, you know what students are like. He wants them to study his spindle whorl and they just want to talk about the Bogman. Well of course they do. A real body is extraordinarily fascinating, whatever its date, isn't it?'

'Yes, fascinating.'

'How do you think he came to be there?'

'Who can say? So, what brought you on this dig, Vicky?'

'Oh, you know, keeping up with the grandchildren. I didn't want to them to think their granny's stagnating quietly in the corner. We all went to Pompeii last year. Saw the bodies there, of course. Well, the plaster casts. Not quite the same as the real thing, is it?' She caught my wince. 'I don't suppose you see it in the same exciting light, living here. Didn't you have some walled-up bones too? Bodies right on your doorstep – can't have been very pleasant.'

'Not exactly pleasant. I'll be quite happy if all you find from now on is pottery.'

Vicky laughed. 'And Hannah's brush, I hope, or we'll be in real trouble.'

'Hannah's been turned out of Ronnie's H.Q.' I was taking a furtive break with Al, up in the woods. 'And she is not a happy bunny.'

'She never was.' He shook his head. 'Not happy, and definitely not a bunny. Something scaly. Maybe if she's obsessing over lost brushes, she'll quit berating Molly about the sacred well.'

'Still at daggers drawn, then?'

'Hannah is. Molly's decided she's a wounded soul, needs healing.'

'Needs to go home, more like it. Why on earth does she stay, when everything makes her so miserable?'

'Beats me.' Al was sitting beside me on a log, while I idly plaited blades of grass and he worked on a detailed architectural drawing, on his laptop.

'She wouldn't come to our Fayre,' I said, tossing the plait away. 'So with any luck she won't turn up at your party.'

'Party?'

'Tamsin tells me you're expecting Joe and Padrig back from Peru, and you're planning on throwing a wild celebration.'

Al glanced at me, almost apologetically. 'How do you feel about that?'

'Fine. Should I mind?'

'Not if you don't.'

'I'm sure Sylvia and Mike will be delighted. Sylvia loves a party.'

Al opened his mouth to say more, then changed his mind.

'At least it will give Hannah something to complain about; a wild bacchanalian orgy in the woods. Are we all invited? Dancing naked round the bonfire?'

'Do I sense a lack of proper reverence, Mrs Lawrence?' asked Al. 'It's our festival of Lughnasadh. A bit late but you have to allow for Peruvian adjustments.'

'So is it a harvest festival, sort of thing? We could bring bread and wine?'

'Perfect.' Al shut his laptop, fished out a sheet of paper, and stood up. 'I've got a drawing for Mike. Come on.'

I eyed the solar-charged state-of-the-art laptop under his arm and thought of solemn pagan festivals. 'Just how much of it do you believe, Al? Lughna-whatever and all that. Do you really believe in earth forces and ley lines and sacred springs?'

'I've heard worse ideas. Is it any crazier than Creationism? Or a heavenly father inviting Abraham to cut his son's throat?'

'I suppose not.' I smiled. I'd already known the answer; Al was a man who hoped to believe.

'I'm not a dogmatic guy,' he said.

'You're willing to try on every coat for size.'

'Maybe.' Above us, on its rock, as we walked down through the woods, stood the white Taranis shaft, greening now in the dampness of the wood. 'I wonder what coat Mike would show me in?' said Al, glancing up at it. 'He does that, doesn't he? Sculpt people. I always think of that one as you.'

'Cold isolation?'

'No. Reaching up to the light, out of the shadows.'

'Oh. Thanks, I prefer that. Reaching up, even if I

can't quite touch it.'

'Yes you can. Touch it and fly. You can, you know.'

'Maybe.'

'So how do you reckon he'd sculpt me? I suppose he'd have me as…' Al stopped as the trees thinned, offering a clear view down the track to the end of the workshops.

A red sports car hovered there, a haze of fumes pulsating from its exhaust.

Christian. My heart sank in anticipation of another explosion. Then I realised that he wasn't alone in the car. Kim was sitting by him.

Al thrust the laptop into my hands, then started forward again, not running but striding so fast I was left behind. Christian handed something to Kim as she opened the door. A package? She got out, turning with a look both guilty and defiant, as her brother descended on her.

I heard a squeal of laughter from Christian as he pulled the door shut, revved up yet more, then spun the car round, churning the grass beside the drive, and roared away back to the lodge gates, while Al was still yards away.

Al didn't stop in his stride. Without a word or hesitation, he plucked the paper bag from Kim's hand. Then he came to a halt and looked inside.

She glared at him. The air burned between them. She held out her hand, and he returned the package.

'He gave me a lift, okay? Leave me alone, Alistair!' She pushed the packet in her coat and ran past me without another word, her face like thunder.

Al looked up at the sky, raised his hands in a gesture of prayer and thumped the crown of his head.

'Not drugs?' I suggested.

'Violin strings.'

'Oh no. At least, that's good of course, but—'

He silenced me with a look.

So it was just a man giving a girl a lift, and Chris hadn't lingered. But he had entered the forbidden land again. Not to stay, not to beg or demand, just to demonstrate that he could.

'You'd better go and make your peace with her,' I said.

'Can't see that's going to be too easy, with Christian Callister in the neighbourhood,' said Al. 'One of us is going to have to go.'

'Christian was here.' I watched Sylvia's expression run the gamut of pain, worry, guilt and nervousness.

'Did he – where—'

'He didn't stay. He was dropping someone off. How is he? I expect you've been keeping an eye on him?'

Sylvia looked sad. 'Yes. I had to make sure he at least had a roof over his head. He can't go home, you see, because, well, I think he has money problems. Debts. Quite serious. But he can't come here. Not again.'

I must have shown my surprise that Sylvia was so reconciled to the ban. I had suspected her maternal instincts were proof against any calamity.

'Not after what he did, this time.' Her wry smile made me want to weep for her. 'I feel so guilty about that.'

'Does Christian, though?'

'He claims he really thought the dog was going to…' She gave up. 'No, he doesn't feel guilty. Do you think he's capable of it? Have I produced a monster, Kate?'

'No,' I said, which was absurd, because we were both internally screaming yes.

At least, I thought, Llys y Garn was safe for a while longer. I had reckoned without the determination of the monster himself.

219

At eleven on Friday night he was back.

For once he must have driven up sedately, without a screech or crunch, because we heard nothing until he walked into the drawing room, bag on his shoulder, hands in his pocket. Perfect timing; we were all about to go to bed. None of us were geared up for a fight with a sneering puppy.

Michael frowned, his jaw stiffening, but he had no time to speak before Sylvia jumped up, her hand at her throat, already in an attitude of supplication.

'Oh Chris, what are you doing here?'

'And where's my phone?' demanded Tamsin. 'Pig.'

Christian gave a shrug and an almost conciliatory smile. 'Got chucked out of my lodgings.'

'Oh Chris! What have you done now?'

'Nothing.' He looked wounded. 'They had other people booked in. Needed my room.'

Michael looked pointedly at his watch. 'You've had ample time to find somewhere else, I'd have thought.'

'Yeah, well, it's Bank Holiday, innit? Everywhere's full up.'

'Then go back to London.'

'Sure, right.' A touch of sarcasm. 'In the morning. What do I do tonight?'

I saw Sylvia's hand close on Michael's arm, the pleading squeeze.

'You could sleep on the side of the road,' suggested Tamsin. 'Like where you dumped me.'

Christian ignored her. He too had seen Sylvia's gesture. 'All I need is somewhere to kip for a few hours. I'm dead tired, okay? Otherwise I'd drive through the night. You don't want me to cause an accident.'

Michael's lips were pressed together, but Sylvia was already lowering the drawbridge. 'One night. That's all.

We meant what we said last time, Chris. We can't have you back here.'

Her caveats were irrelevant. Christian had the surrender he'd been angling for. She turned to Michael. 'One night?'

'Take your bag back to the car,' said Michael. 'Sylvia can find you a toothbrush, assuming you use one. No need to clutter the house with your luggage, whatever it contains. You leave first thing.'

Christian grinned. 'Sure. First thing.'

Of course, he didn't. First thing the following morning, Sylvia was at his bedroom door with a cup of tea, only to find the room empty, his crumpled bed abandoned.

'He's gone,' she said, the tea slopping as her hand shook.

'I didn't hear his car.' I joined her on the landing and we peered, through the tall stair window, at the red Lotus, still parked in the courtyard. 'Wherever he's gone, he hasn't gone far.'

Michael surveyed the car, his expression inscrutable.

'I can't imagine where he's got to,' said Sylvia. 'Maybe he's gone for a walk, to clear his head.'

Michael's mouth twitched into a smile, despite himself. 'I'm sure he'll reappear. When he's had his exercise.'

'I'll make him a packed lunch,' said Sylvia. 'To see him on his way.'

But Christian wasn't around to eat the packed lunch. Nor dinner. I knew exactly what he was doing. Nothing. He finally turned up at nine, threw himself on a couch and yawned. 'Shit, I'm exhausted.'

'You were leaving first thing.' Michael didn't waste time asking for the explanation Christian was clearly itching to give. 'You've left it a little late, but you can

221

be on your way now.'

'You kidding? Have you seen the holiday traffic?'

'Any traffic is coming this way, not going. Go now, please.'

'Where have you been?' asked Sylvia. She had to give him his opening.

Christian looked hurt. 'I had to get some cash, didn't I? Someone's nicked my cards, I've got one quid left and I'm just about out of petrol.'

'You could have asked me,' said Sylvia. I ground my teeth.

'People owed me money, okay. I thought I'd collect – but I didn't want to waste the little juice I'd got, so I walked.'

'Oh you silly boy.'

How far had he walked? Up into the trees, safely out of sight and spent the day gently snoozing, most likely.

'Anyway, I've got cash for gas now, so I'll go first thing tomorrow, okay?'

And of course he didn't. The poor soul was so exhausted by his efforts that he slept on. It delayed his departure, but it also gave Michael the opportunity to rummage through the pockets of Christian's discarded jeans for his car keys. I found him in the Lotus, starting the motor. I peered in. The petrol gauge twitched into life. The tank wasn't full, but neither was it empty.

'You're not surprised, are you?' I asked.

'No.' Michael switched off. 'Is he capable of telling the truth about anything?'

'I doubt it.'

Sylvia was at the kitchen door, watching as Michael climbed out. Clearly steeling herself.

'I've been having a word with him, Mike.'

'He's awake, is he? Good. He has more than enough

petrol to make it to the motorway.'

'Now, I – has he? Oh good. But listen. He's right, you know. It is the bank holiday. The roads will be terrible.'

I laughed. 'The roads will be terrible because people are on them. If families with screaming kids can manage, I'm sure Christian can.'

'But that's not the point, is it? He'll only add to the traffic, and why make it worse for everyone else?'

Michael tutted in exasperation. 'That is ridiculous.'

'All I'm suggesting is that he stay here until Tuesday. The weekend traffic will have eased by then.' She must have realised the feebleness of her own argument, because her face crumpled as she took Michael's hands. 'Please, Mike. Don't make me beg.'

He heaved a sigh, pulled her to him and kissed her forehead. 'Sylvia Callister, what am I going to do with you?'

'Just till Tuesday.'

'What you doing with my car?' asked Christian. The bronchitic growl of the ill-used engine had hauled him down, half-dressed. He was still playing on his mother's goodwill, so he tried to make it sound mere polite curiosity.

Michael looked at him impassively. 'I gather you are staying until Tuesday.'

'Yeah, well, Mumsy suggested it.'

'Oh I—' began Sylvia, but Michael hushed her.

'Assuming you behave, you can stay till then.' He shut the car door, and locked it. 'You won't be needing the car until you leave, so I'll hold onto the keys.'

'You…' Christian started and stopped. 'What about my bag and stuff?'

'We can let you have clean linen if you want it. The rest you can manage without.'

Sylvia opened her mouth to object, then changed her

mind. It was enough that Michael had been persuaded to let him stay.

I could have crowed at the sight of Christian wrong-footed at last. But somehow it wasn't enough. We were committed to having him on our hands for another two days. At least another two days. Would he really leave on Tuesday? I doubted it.

20

I was sitting in the twilight, beside the sculpture of the leaping hare. Michael was in the house; there was no one to overlook me. A scouring pad might do it. No, it didn't. I would have to try something else. Sandpaper? There must be some in Michael's workshop. I got up and slithered down the slope.

Al was standing on the drive, shielding his eyes as he gazed down towards the lodge.

'Hello,' I called softly.

He turned, raised a hand and strolled towards me. 'You haven't seen Kim, have you?'

'No, not today. Is she missing?'

Al shrugged off any suggestion of panic. 'Molly wants to discuss the festival with her. She's usually back by now, but she was talking about going to Aber.' He glanced at the pad in my hand. 'What are you doing with that?'

'Surreptitious repairs.' I nodded up towards the arching hare. 'Someone has done a bit of defacing. Started off with a penknife and finished off with felt tip. I've got rid of the T and most of the N. The C and U are defeating me.'

'Show me.' We clambered up and Al examined the vandalism with disgust. 'Let's guess who did this.'

I met his eyes apologetically. 'Yes, Chris is here. The deal is that he leaves on Tuesday.'

Al laughed angrily.

'I know. What can I say? Michael's confiscated his car keys till then, so I suppose this is Chris's revenge.'

Al took a deep breath, running the tips of his fingers over the damage. 'He's sick. But too lazy to make a good job of it. I think I can smooth it out.'

He had, predictably, a Ray Mears knife in his pocket and he set to work, delicately shaving away the wood around the scars and scratches. 'Not so bad.'

'Thanks. I hoped Michael wouldn't have to see it.'

'No saving the other one, I imagine.'

'The Windhover? No. Michael's brought it back to the workshop, but half of it's just matchwood now. God, what a mess.' I watched Al eliminate the last scratch, then stand back to survey the job. 'Can you come back to the house? Have a coffee?'

'I really ought—'

'Please. I'm beginning to dread stepping across the threshold, with Chris around. Give me some moral support.'

He smiled in surrender. 'Okay.' He gave the repair a last wipe over, then took my hand and helped me back down to the drive.

The kitchen was empty; no Christian. Of such brief moments of relief did happiness now consist. I filled the espresso machine, and took mugs down from the dresser.

Sylvia's voice wafted through from the drawing room. Judging by her tone – desperately jolly – Christian was with her. I paused, hand clasping a mug

225

like a defensive weapon.

Al delivered his moral support with a kiss on the back of my neck. 'I'll stand guard,' he whispered.

I laughed softly, leaning back against him. Then jumped as the doorbell clanged.

'Front door.' I put the mug down.

'Jehovah's Witnesses?' suggested Al. He understood no one used the front door, but I knew one who did.

'Hannah, more likely.' I reluctantly made for the entrance hall, but Sylvia was already there, struggling with the door, so I shamelessly hung back.

'Hello! Hannah, isn't it? What a nice surprise.' Sylvia was the only person who could say that and not sound witheringly sarcastic.

I could hear Ronnie's voice, out of breath, approaching at breakneck speed. 'Ah, Mrs Callister, yes, er, Miss Quigley here has – ah.'

Hannah stood on the wide step, Ronnie hurrying up behind her, like an anxious circus master chasing a loose tiger.

'You're not going to stop me! I don't care!' Hannah was aquiver, finely poised between tears and rage.

'Come in.' Sylvia ushered them both through. 'How are things going at the dig? So exciting, isn't it? And you've been so lucky with the weather. Hardly any rain. Come in, Ronnie.'

Embarrassed, the professor followed his student into the hall. Michael had come forward to join Sylvia, but Al and I remained in the kitchen doorway, as standby reinforcements. Hannah's whinging was normally dreary and sour, like a constant hum of irritation to be swatted away, but everything about her tonight spoke of Apocalypse. She was dishevelled, as if she had fought free to get to us. Her cheeks were flushed crimson and even Sylvia's benign soothing might not be enough to calm those flared nostrils.

'I want to make a complaint.' Hannah rushed on as if she couldn't hold the words back. 'It's disgusting, all of it, what's been going on. Disgusting. You shouldn't allow it! I'm going to tell!'

'Really, this is – oh dear.' The wretched Ronnie writhed apologetically. 'I'm sure we don't want to interrupt your evening. If you've already retired—'

'Oh no. We were just having a drink. Can I offer—'

'No! You're not listening!' Hannah licked her lips and swallowed convulsively, her fists clenched. 'You should stop it. It's disgusting!'

'What is the problem, my dear?' asked Sylvia with motherly concern.

'I hasten to point out that there has been no actual proof,' floundered Ronnie.

'Him,' said Hannah, swelling. 'He's a beast! I've seen him. I know what he's doing. Drugs. Yes! I've seen him. No! Leave me be! I've seen him at it, giving them to people. I've seen him!'

'Seen who?' asked Sylvia, tensing.

'Him!' Hannah, like an avenging angel, pointed at the drawing room doorway, where Christian lounged, grinning broadly.

'Oh, surely not.' Sylvia was aflutter now.

'I'm going to tell. No one will do anything. It's not good enough. I'm going to report him to the police.'

'No!' cried Sylvia. I felt Al's grip tighten on my shoulder.

'Ah, now, Miss Quigley, I hardly think—' Ronnie was flapping.

'Are you saying that Mr Callister offered you drugs?' asked Michael calmly.

'No! Not me! Of course not me. How dare you! Don't you look at me! I wouldn't touch filthy stuff like that!

Filthy!'

'Sorry darling, feeling left out?' sneered Christian. 'Come and see me in the morning. I'll find you a diazepam.'

Watching Hannah work herself up like a whistling kettle coming to the boil, it had crossed my mind that a couple of spliffs might do her the world of good.

'I'm not taking anything! It's filthy! You're filthy! You're not coming near me!' Hannah screamed, her hysteria out of control.

'Calm down. Here, take a chair.' Michael drew one up for her.

Sylvia pulled herself together and stepped forward to encourage Hannah to sit before she collapsed. But Hannah raised her arms to fend them off as if they were attackers.

Instinctively, everyone stepped back and she stood there panting, like an animal cornered.

'Water?' Sylvia mouthed at me.

I filled a glass and brought it forwards, but Hannah snarled at the offering.

Michael shook his head at me. Keep it calm, don't set her off. 'Don't upset yourself, Miss Quigley. No one's going to do anything to you.'

'No! No one does anything. It's not right! You just – you just let him!'

'All right, let's deal with this.' Michael folded his arms. 'You saw Christian selling drugs?' It should be the proof positive that would justify him kicking Christian out, without another moment's delay, but Hannah, in her present state, was not a persuasive witness.

His reasonable tone quietened her. For a moment she was back to her officious, prim self. 'Oh yes, I saw him, all right. I know exactly what he's up to, and I'm going to tell the police.'

'Oh, but can you be absolutely certain?' Sylvia just had to say.

It was enough to set Hannah off again. 'I know what I saw! Why will nobody ever listen to me?'

''Cos you're a stupid cow?' suggested Christian.

'He's filthy! Disgusting!' Her cheeks were flushing again. 'He touched me!'

'I wouldn't touch you with a fucking barge pole,' jeered Christian, while the rest of us hastily adjusted to this new allegation.

'He touched me! I've seen him. Lurking, watching me!'

'Stupid fucking—'

'Hold your tongue.' Michael pushed Christian firmly back into the drawing room. 'Please accept my apologies for his language, Miss Quigley. He'll be gone from here soon. Very soon, believe me.'

But Hannah was beyond calming now. 'I've seen them all! All of them, at it all the time. I've seen them!' She was pointing at Al and me now. 'Rutting like animals! Filthy! Filthy!' Christian laughed, and her attention snapped back to him. 'I know what he wants! He follows me! But he's not touching me! I'm not letting him! I'm going to the police.'

'Oh please, my dear, there's no need for that,' pleaded Sylvia.

'Come now,' said Ronnie. 'Let's not—'

'And them.' Hannah was looking at Al again. 'Those disgusting gypsies. They're all in it together. All of them!'

'What's going on?' asked Tamsin, drifting down the stairs, pulling earphones loose.

I waved her silent, but she'd detected an insult to Al, so she came to stand stoutly by his side.

Al merely sighed, with a droll smile.

'You must stop flinging accusations around, Miss Quigley,' said Michael steadily. 'Though I'm not sure exactly what your accusations are, now.'

'I saw them! Him.' She stabbed a finger towards Christian. 'And that gipsy girl. I saw them, in the trees! Filthy!'

Al stiffened. 'You saw what, exactly?' Another squeal of laughter from Christian.

'You know!' shrilled Hannah. 'I saw him giving her things! Filthy stuff! I know what I saw! She laughed. She laughed at me. I'm going to report her too!'

'Hannah, you need to calm down.' Michael raised a hand to hold Al back.

'You can't stop me! You're not going to stop me!'

'Miss Quigley, we can all see you're very upset and yes, you need to talk to someone, but first you've got to calm yourself. I think it would be best—'

'Don't you talk to me!' said Hannah. 'You're in it with them. You're disgusting. I've seen you spying on us! You should be locked up!'

'Oh!' said Sylvia. Any sympathy for the girl's psychotic distress turned to anger. 'I'm not having you talk to Mike like that.'

'I've seen him! Lurking in the woods! Looking at me! Trying to touch me! Dirty! Nobody's going to touch me! You hear? Nobody's going to touch me!' Her emotions, like her accusations, were careering round the room like debris in a hurricane – panic, fear, anger, suspicion, desperation.

Michael drew Sylvia back. We could all see the girl was far beyond rational argument. 'Hannah, I think you should go back to the camp now. We'll discuss this in the morning. Meanwhile, the Professor needs to get you some help.'

'Oh, er, yes,' said Ronnie. His fingers twitched in readiness to grab the woman, but he was obviously terrified of touching her. 'Yes, of course.'

'A doctor,' suggested Michael.

'Oh – indeed. Miss Quigley, please—'

'Don't touch me!' she squealed, then, without warning, ran out, down the steps and off along the terrace, gravel flying up behind her.

'Don't forget I'm following you!' Christian shouted after her. 'Coming to get you in the night.'

I stepped forward and pulled the drawing room door shut in his face.

'Ah, I am so sorry.' Ronnie was wringing his hands. 'Forgive us, I can only apologise. Miss Quigley is a little – I assure you—'

'She needs help,' said Michael, pointedly.

'Yes, yes, of course.' This was a notion beyond the Professor. 'I shouldn't have allowed her to speak – if it hadn't been for some of the other students mentioning your young man and, er, substances...,'

'Oh no,' whispered Sylvia.

Michael took a deep breath, his anger welling an inch below the surface. 'I see. Well, I'm sorry that it's come to this, of course, and we can discuss it further in the morning if you wish, but you needn't worry. I shall be dealing with the matter here. It's over. Now.'

'Yes, of course. It is so very difficult. I do apologise for...,' Ronnie offered a vague hand in Sylvia's direction, but she was incapable of responding. Hands clasped over her mouth, she watched him follow Hannah, then she turned to Michael, appalled.

'You don't think Hannah will go to the police, do you?'

'It's about time someone did. You're not seriously questioning the story, are you? Chris has been dealing here.'

'Well, I – he promised. We don't know for sure—'

'Sylvia! He's been selling drugs. Accept it, please. We should be encouraging Hannah to take her story to the police.'

'If she does, she'll start accusing all of us,' said Al. 'You heard her. We're all disgusting.'

Michael made to brush the objection aside, then frowned. Some of us were clearly more vulnerable to wild allegations than others.

'I know she's obviously demented,' I said, 'but put her in a police station, with a sympathetic officer, and God knows what she'll dream up. Drugs, gang rape, kiddie porn, terrorist cells. Do we want them swarming over Llys y Garn again?'

'What are we going to do?' Sylvia groped for the chair Hannah had refused.

Michael took her hands. 'All right. Hannah needs to see a doctor, not the police, and most of what she was saying was delusional. But we know there's a kernel of truth at the heart of her hallucinations, don't we?' He waited for Sylvia's reluctant nod. 'I'm sorry, darling, but it stops now. He has to go.'

Michael threw open the drawing room door. We trooped in behind him.

Christian was standing, all innocence, by the gothic arch of the fireplace. 'She one crazy bitch or what?'

'You've been selling drugs to the students,' stated Michael. 'On my property.'

'You're not going to believe anything that freaked-out cow tells you?'

'Hannah Quigley isn't the only witness, so don't waste your breath on any more lies.' Michael nodded to Al, who caught Christian's wrist, whirled him round and frisked him, plucking a packet from his denim jacket with casual ease. I'd have admired his graceful dexterity if I hadn't known that he had done it so many times before that the movement came all too naturally.

'Hey, that's mine,' snarled Christian, as Al tossed the packet to Michael.

'You're leaving,' said Michael.

'That's mine,' insisted Christian. 'And maybe I shared. I'm generous. Where's your proof I sold anything?'

'Don't treat us like idiots, Christian. Your mother has put heart and soul into this place, trying to make it work, and I'm not going to see you jeopardising it all for your pathetic entertainment.'

'Yeah, she's put everything in, all right, all my father's money, and what do I get out of it?'

'Oh shut up, Chris,' said Tamsin.

'You be a good baby,' sneered Christian, 'and wait for the old cow to drop dead before you get your hands on any of it. Fuck that. I want my share. Now, okay? You promised me backing. I've got commitments. I've got people who want paying. You don't cough up, what do you expect me to do? I have to make money somehow.'

'Oh Chris.' Sylvia stared at him, hollow-eyed. 'How could you?'

'How do you fucking think? They want to buy, I sell. That's business. Real business, not this fucking stupid enterprise, you pissing around in stupid fucking fancy dress. You're a joke, you make me sick. Look at you. You couldn't run a business to save your life. All you do is take my father's money, and pour it into this shit hole. And you give it to this dirty old goat, and that fucking lunatic baby-killer, but you don't—'

Christian's diatribe was brought to a halt by the back of Michael's hand. For a moment the room was silent.

Nothing that Christian had said could equal the shock of Michael, the sane and reasonable Michael, resorting to violence. Even he seemed stunned.

Sylvia wept, Tamsin's comforting arms round her. 'Oh Chris. Oh Mike.'

'You leave now,' said Michael.

'Not till I get what I came for.' Christian made a show of wiping non-existent blood from his lip. 'You promised me cash. Pay me and I'll go.'

'You'll go and I will pay you nothing.'

'I want—'

'What you want is none of our business. Get out and don't come back.'

'You think you can take my father's money, and chuck it down this fucking drain and I get nothing? Right. Fuck you.'

Christian moved, faster than any of us had thought him capable. It was Sylvia's romanticism that gave him his opportunity: the Tiffany oil lamp on the mantelpiece, and the flowing drapes at the windows. He turned, seized, threw, and the next moment the curtains were up in oil-fuelled flames. Tamsin screamed.

'Fuck you!' He had a candle now, brandishing it at the throw on the sofa beside Sylvia, who was begging him with clasped hands.

'Stop it, please, Christian, stop it!'

Michael wrestled the candle from him, while Al plucked one of the flaming curtains from its pole. 'Stamp on it,' he ordered me, turning to the next. I did my best, overcoming the panic induced by the rush of the flames.

Christian fought back, although Tamsin, still screaming, came to Michael's aid, thumping her brother on the back. With a monumental effort he broke free from Michael's grasp, staggered back, tripped, and

234

collapsed into the folds of the last burning drape.

Now Sylvia screamed too, rushing to free him from the blazing folds. The flames had got him, licking his arms, singeing his hair. Michael pulled the curtain from him, rolling it deftly into a ball that extinguished the flames, but he made no effort to assist Christian. He was more concerned with the curtains that Al and I were still stamping on. He appeared behind me with a fire extinguisher, and in a moment the last smoulders and sparks were reduced to congealed foam and sodden char.

Michael threw the windows open, the freshness of the evening air only exaggerating the acrid smell of fire. Al followed him in tossing the blackened curtains out onto the gravel, then they shifted the furniture to ensure that no glowing embers were lurking unseen. We had scorch marks on cushions and rugs, blistering paintwork and blackened streaks of soot trailing up the walls and across the ceiling, but that was all. No splintered glass or burning timbers. Pushing back the panic and the fear, I felt a deep, dull throb of anger, a sickening realisation of what might have happened – what could yet happen if Christian could do this.

Sylvia was on her knees, tearing scorched clothing from her son. His face registered shock, and there were red burns on his arms and one cheek, but no worse than I'd received occasionally from the cooker and the iron. Let him hurt. For a moment, in the midst of the anger, I felt a surge of resentment that Sylvia had rushed to his aid so quickly. Wouldn't it have been better for the whole world if we'd just let him burn to a crisp?

No. Of course it wouldn't. 'Can I get something?' I forced myself to ask.

'Cold water.' Sylvia was trembling, but determined to be practical. 'And there are bandages in the cupboard by the range.'

Christian was already recovering from his stunned paralysis. He pushed her off with a snarl, and when she persisted, he spat at her.

He spat at her.

I was almost winded by the deathly wrath that nauseating gesture unleashed. It filled the room like black sludge.

'Fuck off. Take your fucking hands off me. I don't want your fucking mother love. I want what's mine. Give it me, or next time I'll burn the lot of you in your fucking beds.'

I expected Sylvia to weep, beg, cajole, do what Sylvia always did, but instead she sat back on her haunches, stony faced. She wiped the spittle off her cheek then looked up at me. 'Just cold water and bandages.'

I fetched them, feeling the darkness creep around me, wings spread to encompass us all. He'd spat at Sylvia while she tried to tend him. He would always spit at her, never letting her free as long as he lived, always there, always waiting in the wings to poison her life, to destroy her dreams and her happiness. As long as he lived.

I handed Sylvia the bowl and the bandages and stepped back. Michael was no longer in the room. Al stood by the window, Tamsin by the door, both of them watching with disgust. Christian had no one left to manipulate or torment, except his mother. She took his arm and bandaged it as if it had been an inanimate thing, a thing of no concern to her. Christian's vicious spite evolved, too late, into a calculating appeal. He whimpered when she touched a burn, but she paid no attention. He must have seen in her eyes that he had burned more than the curtains. His whimpers turned to sullen impatience.

At last, Sylvia was done. She got to her feet and wiped her hands. 'You'd better see a doctor when you get home, Christian. I don't think they're serious, but–'

'I'm not going to piss around in a fucking surgery.'

'Then don't. You make your own choices, Christian. I don't care anymore.'

'Fine. You can get rid of me any time you like. Just give me my share of this crap, and you can write me out of your life. Till then, I'm going to be waiting round every corner.'

'No, you will leave this district, and stay away.' Michael appeared at the door. 'The key is in the ignition of your car. Get in it and go.' His voice was cold and expressionless. 'If I find, tomorrow, that you are still in the vicinity, still in the county, I will personally see to it the police charge you with arson, attempted murder, drug dealing, criminal damage, cruelty to animals and anything else they can think of.'

'Oh yeah?' Christian's laughter dried, as he looked at his mother and realised that this time she wouldn't lift a finger to protect him.

'Yes.' Michael held up a toilet bag, full to bursting. 'I've taken this from your car if they want physical evidence.'

'Give that—' He lunged but Michael whisked it away, as Al caught Christian's collar.

'The police aren't going to find talcum powder and aspirin, are they?'

'You fucking bastard, I'm gonna—'

'Go,' repeated Michael, icily.

'Don't think you shits can get rid of me that easily.' Snarling, Christian pushed past Michael and on through the kitchen. In silence we watched him kick open the outer door, and lope across the stygian shadows of the courtyard. The car door slammed, the engine roared into tormented life. The begrimed red Lotus screeched suicidally down the rutted drive. God help any kitten or small child rash enough to linger on the road.

For a moment none of us moved. A sound broke the pall of silence. An unearthly wail that gathered, mounting into agonised, suffocating sobs as Sylvia howled her anguish. Ashen-faced, Michael drew her to him. Tamsin too began to cry.

In the West, above the valley brim, the evening sky was ablaze, livid streaks, sickly yellow, crimson flames, as the darkness welled up around us.

'There's no serious damage.' Al appraised the drawing room. 'Nothing that can't be put right easily enough. A lick of paint mostly.' He lowered his voice. Michael and Tamsin had taken Sylvia upstairs, out of earshot, but somehow it seemed as if the house were in mourning.

I felt ill. 'We could all have been killed.'

'But we weren't.' He drew a deep breath. 'All in all, one shit of a day.'

I realised he was absently cradling one hand in the other. 'Are you hurt? You're burned!'

He waved away my concern. 'It's nothing. A couple of blisters, that's all. At least you can all relax, now he's gone.'

'Unless he keeps his promise and comes back to burn us in our beds.'

'Yes. There is that. Maybe none of us are going to get much sleep.'

'Will you stay? Stay the night. I need you.'

I watched the conflict in his face. 'Kate—'

'You want to get back, find out what's happened to Kim.'

He shrugged, apologetically. 'The possessive brother habit is hard to break. You could come up to Annwfyn with me? Get out of this place.'

'I can't leave Sylvia.'

'She has Michael and Taz.'

'I know, but—'

'The possessive cousin habit?'

I managed a smile. 'You know how it is.' I watched him go, then trailed up to my room, anger and anxiety fighting within me. A miasma of dark, conflicting emotions filled the house. Sometimes it subsided to a throbbing undertone, sometimes it burst out afresh. Christian could have killed us. He hated his mother that much. He'd *spat* at her, for God's sake. He had gone, but for how long? Sylvia's love had been tested to breaking point, but it would repair itself, as it always did, and he'd be back, again and again and again. Why couldn't he just die? He was driving in such a state, why couldn't he just hit a tree and set us all free?

I lay awake, listening for the growl of the Lotus returning. Was that it? An engine. Definitely an engine's growl, but not the Lotus. Al's Land Rover. Going out, looking for Kim. Leaving us that little bit more defenceless. Silence. Too deep a silence. I began fancying I heard a crunch of gravel, the creak of a door. I breathed slowly, waiting for the whiff of smoke.

The unmistakable sound of a door, when it came, was so close it shot through me like gunfire, though it was careful, quiet. Soft footsteps in the corridor, on the stairs. I sat up, taking deep breaths. It was Michael, going down.

I should have felt relief, but instead a sense of dread tugged at me. I got up, reached for my dressing gown and followed him. It was pitch dark, past midnight.

Michael was already in the kitchen, his coat on,

searching for keys in a drawer.

'What are you doing?' I whispered.

He glanced up, too preoccupied to be properly startled. He looked terrible. 'Kate. Did I wake you?'

'No, I couldn't sleep. Where are you going?'

'Um.' He rubbed his brow, car keys in his hand. 'I have to see if I can find him.'

'Why? Let him go! It's too late, Michael, he's been gone hours.'

'It can't be too late. I've got to try. For Sylvia. I can't let everything be destroyed.'

I could feel his urgent need to be out there, even if he accomplished nothing by it. He needed activity to sooth the torment. I watched him start the Volvo and ease it quietly out of the courtyard, into the darkness.

My anger against Christian only increased. It wasn't enough to wound his mother in every way he could. He had to tear Michael apart too, a good man who deserved better than to be forced, like cannon fodder, between Sylvia and her son.

Just die, Christian.

I was never going to sleep. Too much adrenalin in my system. Al was gone, Michael was gone; I should be retreating indoors, drawing the bolts, keeping us safe, but I didn't want to be locked in. I wanted to be out, confronting demons. I stepped out into the cool air, listening to the night wind in the trees, the rustling of nocturnal creatures. With bare feet I skirted the house, crossed the terrace, down into the meadow. The grass had grown since the Fayre. It was long and cold and damp around my ankles. The moon was up, casting the shadow of the house, black on grey, across the meadow, and I waded out to be free of it.

I couldn't escape the shadow of Christian though.

Maybe I should do as Michael had done, get in my car

and drive away from this place, so that I wouldn't be in this unforgiveable situation, sitting at Sylvia's table and wishing her son dead.

But no, there was Sylvia, probably weeping in her sleep. I couldn't leave her. I turned and padded back to the house, climbed to my room, listening for her sobs, but all was silent. I towelled my feet dry, forced myself to lie down—

—and felt it.

Unmistakable. The maelstrom revolution of self-pity and self-loathing, and a growing paralysis of fear before the slow, darkening slide into oblivion.

My head swam. The bile rose; I dragged myself to the bathroom and heaved.

What had I done? I had killed him. I had killed Christian.

I didn't know how or where, but as cold and harsh as I had ever done, I felt death.

I felt death.

21

Five o'clock. The sun not yet over the horizon but the sky unforgivingly bright. Somehow, the damage looked worse by daylight. The furniture in the drawing room was scattered, cushions tossed, carpets rucked and rolled, the sooty scorch marks wider, more ominous in the cold light of the morning. The place still stank, despite the open windows.

Michael was standing on the terrace, his phone to his

ear. I'd heard him return from his nocturnal expedition after a couple of hours, creeping into the house, after which we had both lain silent and sleepless, till the first glimmer of dawn. He turned at the sound of my feet on the gravel and if he'd looked terrible in the night, he looked worse now.

'Good morning, Kate. Come to inspect the mayhem?'

Christian's mayhem, or mine? Killer Queen. Death's summoner. I wanted to confess my guilt, but Michael looked so ill, I couldn't burden him. I couldn't burden anyone, not until concrete news reached us. Instead, I stared at the fire damage, and cleared my throat. 'Al says it's all superficial. Are you phoning the insurers?'

He looked at his phone. 'Christian. He's not answering. I've tried his flat.'

I looked at him, appalled. Of course there would be no answer. 'Michael, please don't—'

'I know, I know.' He flipped his phone shut and thrust it in his pocket. 'I need to be thinking about this place. Should I ring the insurers, do you think? It's not good, is it? But better than blackened beams and a scorched shell. We'll need to get it cleaned up. I don't want Sylvia having to look at it.'

'How is she?'

'She's – over the shock. Just needs picking up.' His voice trailed away, his gaze settling on the rooks in the distant, misted tree tops.

'I'll take her out,' I volunteered, as if tending to Sylvia would somehow make amends for what I had done. 'Down to the sea.'

'Good idea.' He pulled himself together. 'I'm sure Tammy and the boys will give me a hand while you're out.'

Sylvia was in the kitchen, holding the kettle. If she had intended to fill it, she seemed to have forgotten.

Like Michael, she'd grown old. The glow had gone, her face was heavy, her eyes red.

'Come on.' I took the kettle from her. 'Tea can wait. You and I are going down to the sea.'

'Oh.' She looked round listlessly. 'No, I really should—'

'Dr Bradley's orders. The place will get crowded, so let's go while the morning's cool and we have it all to ourselves.'

She meekly followed, lacking the energy to fight, and sat listlessly for the short journey, saying nothing but heaving the occasional sigh. No traffic yet on the roads. We reached the beach and found it empty, all ours, the vast expanse of dark, glistening sand, the tide far out, curls of white foam where the distant ripples were breaking in a faint shsh. Across the bay, harbour houses glowed like dull gems, still slumbering. Gulls were the only voices. The cliff tops and distant hills wore a milky haze. The day, as yet, was so innocent. I took Sylvia's hand, leading her down the beach, towards the cleansing lap of the waves, and she walked as if asleep.

'Take your shoes off. Get the sea on your toes.' I set the example, wishing that it could really wash me clean, as we paddled, jeans rolled up, the water sharp and clean and icy round our ankles. It helped Sylvia at least. She began to look around, seeing the present, not the past. Just please, I prayed, don't start seeing the future.

'Look at that shell.' She stooped and held out a pastel glinting cup, a glimmer of her natural delight returning to her eyes. 'So beautiful when they're wet. I was forever collecting them as a girl, then I was always disappointed when I took them home and they dried out.'

I was determined to reinforce her resurgence. 'Maybe we could have a shell grotto at Llys y Garn. They'd keep glistening with water running over them.'

'Of course!' She seized on the suggestion, while we walked and talked, filling our pockets with shells as we splashed along, and once or twice she almost laughed.

Neither of us mentioned Christian.

'You know what I fancy?' said Sylvia. 'Bacon and eggs.'

My stomach revolted at the thought. 'Nothing like it after a walk on the beach.' So we returned to the car and drove home, damp sand gritty between our toes.

The drawing room was not quite back to normal, but Michael had worked wonders with the help of Tamsin, Al and Pryderi. The room had been swept clean, the furniture beaten, singed cushions removed. The soot had been washed off; damaged wallpaper stripped, the walls hastily repainted. The rugs, freshly shampooed, were out to dry on the parapet.

'Oh, thank you all!' Sylvia smiled, so broadly I could barely see the effort it cost her. 'Now I'm going to make bacon and eggs for everyone.'

So we all ate, pretending there was nothing better in the world than a full English on a sunny terrace.

'Kim did return?' I asked Al.

He gave a bruised smile. 'Finally.'

'You were out searching, weren't you? I heard you go.'

'You didn't sleep?'

'No.' I stared at the smears of egg yolk on my plate, thinking back to that terrible moment of annihilation, and my breakfast prepared a volcanic return to the surface. I swallowed. 'She was all right?'

'Apart from being furious with me, yes. What about you, Kate? Are you okay? You look terrible.'

'Thanks! None of us look entirely bonny, this morning.'

It was true. Even Tamsin looked bleary-eyed, though her first thought was for her mother, and Sylvia in turn worried over her. It gave them both occupation.

After breakfast we made a show of returning to our normal tasks. When Tamsin took tea to the hall, I took a mug along to Michael in his workshop. Sylvia had expressed a desire for carvings in the upper chamber of the hall, and Al had produced designs for the green man, a head wreathed in oak leaves, which Michael had promised he would do something with. He had blocks of wood ready, but they were untouched. I found him staring out of the window, juggling coins in his pocket.

'A nice cup of tea,' I said. 'The great British cure-all. Apparently, it's guaranteed to make everything right.'

He looked at me, bleakly, as if seeing right into the blackness of my guilt. 'Thank you.' He sipped, then looked away. Telling me that nothing would make right what I had done.

I studied the sinister face in the drawings. A devil's face. 'Anyway.' I pulled another piece of paper across it. 'Sylvia needs you back at the house, Mike. Why don't you take a break? You're too tired to work safely.'

He sipped his tea, his knuckles tight on the mug. 'I don't know how to pick up the pieces, Kate. Last night—'

'Last night can't be undone,' I said, then bit back the words, terrified he would ask me to explain. But we all wanted the previous night undone, as his despairing face showed. It was so cruel for him to blame himself for anything, when all the guilt belonged to Christian, and to me. 'Come back to the house, please.'

To my surprise, he meekly agreed, and Sylvia greeted him with a hug.

They were still sitting companionably in the kitchen,

an hour later, when Ronnie arrived, knocking tentatively on the kitchen door this time.

I'd seen him coming from upstairs, so I'd hurried down. If he insisted on the promised discussion about Christian and the drugs, all the grief would start up again. To my relief, the elderly Vicky was with him and I could surely rely on her pleasant sanity to keep things level.

'Ah. Good morning,' Ronnie was saying. 'I am sorry to be disturbing you, yet again. I do so apologise for the little, er – I trust our visit last night didn't spoil your evening too much. Miss Quigley is, alas, a somewhat difficult personality.'

He'd heard nothing of the fire and its aftermath, and no one chose to enlighten him, so we murmured demurral.

'Come in and sit down,' said Sylvia, making resolute conversation.

'Well, er, thank you, but we have really only come to, er—'

'We were wondering,' said Vicky, 'if you've seen anything of Hannah this morning.'

Innocently asked, but the hairs on the back of my neck prickled. 'No,' I said. 'Not since she left us, yesterday evening.'

'Just so,' said Ronnie. 'As I supposed. I'm sorry to have bothered you.'

'She's disappeared,' explained Vicky. 'She came back to the camp last night, terribly upset. Of course, you saw her for yourself. We were discussing calling a doctor but things, well, blew up. Hannah just exploded with the girl she was sharing a tent with and she stormed out before we could stop her. She said she was going to find bed and breakfast in the village.'

I could see guilt in Vicky's eyes that she hadn't been

more forceful in resolving Hannah's difficulties, instead of letting Ronnie prevaricate. Guilt seemed to be the universal emotion at the moment.

'I don't think the Cemaes has any rooms free,' said Sylvia. 'But a lot of the local farms do B&B. I'm sure she'll have found something.'

'Oh I'm sure,' agreed Ronnie eagerly, longing only for calm waters. But Hannah could raise a storm, even by her absence.

'You see, we're a bit worried about her,' explained Vicky. 'Poor girl, she's obviously having some sort of breakdown. She took a few things, her handbag, you know, but she left most of her luggage. She was on foot, after all, and very upset. I know she's an adult and we're not strictly responsible...' Her sidelong glance at Ronnie spoke volumes. 'But I think we ought at least to find out what's happened to her.'

Sylvia was immediately with her. 'Have you phoned the Cemaes? We'll try the farms. I've got some of their phone numbers. Let's see. Oh and Emmy at the post office – she always knows what's going on.'

'I really don't want to bother you,' insisted Ronnie, but the ladies were already in the hall, leafing through phone books.

Michael stood up, his chair scraping on the tiles. 'I'll drive into the village, look around.'

'I'm sure there's no need,' said the professor.

'The girl is clearly ill.' Michael was set. He needed to be doing something.

'You'd better get back to your students,' I suggested to Ronnie. 'Nothing more you can do for now. She could turn up at any moment.'

With visible relief, he followed my advice.

Sylvia and Vicky worked their way through a dozen phone numbers. No one in the vicinity had offered shelter to Hannah Quigley. Most significantly, the lady in the cottage two doors down from the post office hadn't seen her, even though she had a 'vacancies' sign in her window. Hannah would have seen that, surely.

How far could she have walked?

'She was talking about going to the police,' said Vicky tentatively. 'All wild stuff, I know, but I wonder if she could have gone to them?'

'Where's the nearest police station, Sylvia?' I asked.

Sylvia was distressed at the mere mention of the police. 'I have no idea. Newport? Cardigan? Fishguard? I've never thought to find out.'

'She wouldn't have walked all that way.'

'Maybe we should phone them,' suggested Vicky. She sensed our reluctance. 'I'll speak to them. I won't mention all those awful things she was saying last night.'

I smiled gratefully at her, and we left her chatting pleasantly to the local constabulary, as the sound of the returning Volvo took us out to the yard.

'Any sign of her?' asked Sylvia. 'We've phoned around, but no luck.'

Michael emerged, holding up a muddy shoe, its sole partly ripped from the upper. 'Found this. In the grass by the road. Do you recognise it?'

It was a sensible walking shoe, the sort Hannah would wear. Vicky had finished her call to the police. 'I just asked if a Hannah Quigley had contacted them,' she said. 'They have no record of her. But it could be – oh.' She saw the shoe Michael was holding. 'That's Hannah's.'

'You sure?'

'Yes, it was splitting, and she was making a terrible fuss about it.'

The four of us stood staring at it. She surely couldn't

have walked far with one shoe missing.

'When did she leave?' I asked, awaiting the inevitable answer.

'When would it have been? Late evening. Nine o'clock perhaps. Or ten? She and Ronnie came here, and when she came back she was almost hysterical. We were trying to calm her down, then Shelley said something, told her to, well, in so many words, to go away, and she went berserk, grabbed her things and marched out, screaming about finding somewhere to stay, phoning the police, reporting everyone, complaining to the university. We just let her go. Oh dear, we should have stopped her. What could have happened to her?'

We looked blankly at each other, thinking of Hannah marching down the road, just as Christian was storming out of Llys y Garn.

I could see the horror spreading on Sylvia's face, a horror that was the antithesis of the appalling hope edging its way into me. I had felt death in the night. I didn't doubt that for a moment, but suppose it hadn't been Christian, after all? I'd felt ill will in plenty for Hannah, but I hadn't wished her dead. I couldn't be to blame, if it were her.

Hannah's wretched face rose before me, accusing as ever, but I could only shut my eyes and think 'Thank God.'

'I'm terribly sorry we've made things so awkward for you,' said Vicky. Awkward? If she but knew.

'I don't suppose you saw Hannah Quigley last night?' I asked Al, as he took a break. The oriel window was repaired now, a small gem of exquisite craftsmanship, which seemed, somehow, no longer relevant.

'No.' Al stretched on the meadow grass and closed

his eyes. He looked exhausted.

'I thought maybe, since you were driving around last night—'

'I didn't see her,' he said firmly. 'Why is everyone so uptight? Anyone really want her back?'

I sat up, looking away. Was I honestly thinking that her death would be a blessing? 'Back, no. Far away would be much better. Australia? But we need to know if she's dead or alive.'

'Do we? Why?'

His callousness shocked me as much as my own reaction. 'Because she's vanished. A woman has disappeared, Al.'

'Look, she's an adult. She can elect to walk out, any time she likes.'

'In her state? At night? With no luggage, and minus one shoe? Michael found one of her shoes by the road.'

'She left a shoe behind?' Al frowned.

'The police think the same way as you. She's an adult, free to come and go, so they won't do anything.'

'You've been to the police?' He propped himself up on his elbow.

'Michael made the Prof phone them. Which was probably a mistake, because Ronnie managed to make it sound like much ado over nothing.'

'So it is,' said Al, lying down again. Hannah Quigley had been threatening to accuse his sister, and whether her allegations were true or false, he wasn't going to waste sympathy on her. I recalled him removing her arm from me, his fingers gripping her wrist. The bandage she wore afterwards.

'She ought to be found,' I insisted. 'We can't leave it, just because Ronnie failed to tick the right boxes with the police. He told them there was no evidence of a crime and she wasn't threatening suicide or certified insane—'

'She should be.'

'Yes, obviously, that's the point. She was crazy. She wasn't safe to go off like that. But the police aren't prepared to do anything. They might, eventually, but not yet, so Michael's taken some of the students out to search. If the police won't help, we'll have to find her ourselves.'

Al sat up properly and hugged his knees. 'You're serious?'

'She's vanished, Al. And there was Christian. Out there, at the same time. Mad as Hell. Capable of anything.'

'Yes of course. Christian threatened her, didn't he?' Al considered the possibility, dispassionately. 'Which would make him the prime suspect. Well there you are.'

'Where are we? Or rather, where is she?'

'Kate!' Tamsin was calling. 'Kate, where are you?'

I jumped up, hurrying up the steps to the terrace. 'Here, Tam. What is it?'

She came jogging round from the Great Hall, breathless with excitement or concern. 'Oh Kate, they've found a bottle.' She stopped to catch her breath.

'A bottle?'

Al came up behind me. 'What's up?'

Tamsin was too urgent even to query what we'd been doing, down there in the long grass. 'Mike took some of the students to search where he found the shoe, so they were combing along in the verge...' Another pause for breath. She must have run up from the road. 'They found this broken bottle and it's got blood on it.'

'I see,' My heart missed a beat. The scenario painted itself, the lurid sky, the distraught girl walking, Christian's wild drive, two insane people in collision. And then that terrible sinking moment of death. Blood on a bottle. It was so obvious what had happened. 'This sounds bad.'

'Yeah. But no sign of Hannah. Everyone's looking now. Mike's phoned the police again. He says, would you mind warning Mum.'

Blood made all the difference. Neither Al, not the professor, not the police, could continue to dismiss Hannah's disappearance as an exercise in unbalanced free will. It made a difference to me too, to the way I was thinking about the girl. I pictured her murdered, dumped in some ditch, and wondered how I could have felt relief at the possibility. However irritating she had been, the idea of her death was appalling.

While Michael took his team further out along the surrounding lanes, I overruled a still dithering professor and organised the rest of the students into parties, to search the woods. I hadn't heard Chris return in the night, but that didn't mean he hadn't come, silently, creeping through the long grass. Planting a murder victim under his mother's nose was just the sort of malice he was capable of, and I didn't want the slightest risk of Sylvia chancing upon a bloody corpse.

I left her and Tamsin making tea for everyone, while I toured the outbuildings, the empty workshops, the stores. In the Great Hall, I climbed to the upper chamber, empty except for a few tools – Al's crew had been seconded to the search of the woods. I went to check the cellar. No. The door onto the winding stair had been padlocked and nailed shut for safety during the Fayre, and had not yet been re-opened. He couldn't have put her down there. The armoury: it was piled high with timbers, sacks of cement, rubble, tarpaulins, and I peered and poked among them before bracing myself and opening the door into the Great Hall. The doorway with its secret panel. The shadow heaved around me, telling me to flee, but I couldn't. I had to touch the panel, steady my fingers, let them search for the secret catch that Al had proudly shown me. The door to the priest hole swung open, and blackness engulfed me.

Fighting nausea I forced myself to look in, waiting for my eyes to accustom to the dark.

Nothing. No bones, no Hannah.

I quietly let the panelling click shut, then ran for the walled garden, gulping down the clean air as I looked around. The well. That would be an obvious place, wouldn't it? I pushed back the heavy cover and the very notion of losing my balance brought me close to doing so. I peered gingerly down, into the clammy darkness. Daylight reflected as a white disk on the surface of the water far below. No broken body floating.

As I pulled back with relief, sirens split the air, echoing down the valley. This time the police were paying attention, and they were doing so in force.

For the first half hour I was happy that officialdom was taking charge. The minutest of Hannah's details were taken; her property was bagged up; dogs were out sniffing along the lane. I was happy until I, along with everyone else, was questioned. It was a matter of course, they insisted, but even now I couldn't shake off the memory of my childhood interrogation, more than twenty years before. You know what we do with bad girls who tell lies? We put them in prison. The frustration and misery of that day had ingrained an automatic resistance to police questioning.

'So you spoke with Hannah Quigley last night?' DC Phillips, plump and wheezy, was appointed to interview me.

'No. I saw her. I don't think I spoke to her personally.'

'But you heard her? Making allegations.'

'She's been here for weeks, feels like years, and she's complained non-stop from the start. I've never taken any of it seriously.'

'Mm.' DC Phillips tapped his pen on the table top. 'You heard her threatening to go to the police?'

'Yes, but then she also threatened to go to the university, and her MP and *The Daily Telegraph*. Last night it was the police. Today it would probably have been the United Nations.'

'So you don't think she really intended to do so?'

'I don't know her well enough to know if she ever follows up on these wild threats. She's clearly paranoid and she never really makes much sense.'

'Mrs…' He checked his notes. 'Mrs Victoria Ives contacted us earlier today. She certainly seemed to think that Hannah was on her way to speak to us.'

'No she didn't. She was worried because Hannah had stormed off, upset. We phoned all the local lodgings and there was no sign of her, so we were trying all other options. The police were last on our list.'

DC Phillips nodded, tapped his pen again. 'Miss Quigley was alleging that drugs were being sold on these premises.'

'Yes, Dr Bradley is obviously a Columbian drugs baron in disguise.' Why did I say that? Didn't I know better than to joke with the police?

'Dr Bradley is a chemist.'

'Oh come on. Petroleum, not pharmaceuticals. Used to be. Now he's a wood carver.'

'So there's nothing in the allegations?'

'We have a holiday cottage, students coming and going at the dig. I can't swear there aren't reefers being smoked in the woods or tablets being swapped behind the Portaloos. But *I* haven't seen anyone trading anything illicit. If I had they would have been out of here like that.' I snapped my fingers.

'You've never suspected drugs were being used by the travellers, camping on your land?'

'I am one hundred percent certain that Al would do everything in his power to keep hard drugs out of their camp,' I said firmly. There was no need to mention Molly's cakes and tisanes. But it didn't help; Al's crew were doomed, once more, to be the focus of police attention.

'Mr Alistair Taverner,' said Phillips, consulting his notes again. 'He has quite a violent record, of course.'

'A bit of a barny at a protest?'

Phillips looked deadly serious. 'Quite apart from that assault on a police officer, he also put an informer in hospital. Fractured skull. A very serious assault; nearly killed her.'

'Rubbish.' Al had told me he'd removed Kim's drug dealer. Removed. Christian had said – but Christian was a liar. I remembered the sorry little would-be mugger in Hyde Park, the blood running from his nose. 'Rubbish,' I repeated.

Phillips sat back, not arguing but gauging my reactions. 'Did you see Mr Taverner, last night?'

'I – yes, he was here when Hannah descended on us.'

'As was…' The notes again. 'Professor Pryce Roberts, Dr Bradley, Mrs Callister, Tamsin Callister and Christian Callister?'

'Yes.'

'And Miss Quigley was threatening to report, let me see, Christian Callister, Mr Taverner's sister, and Dr Bradley?'

'She was accusing anyone and everyone.'

'Christian Callister left the house shortly afterwards?'

'Yes, he was driving back to London.'

'After the accident. I understand you had a fire?'

'Yes, Sylvia's oil lamp. Yes, it was an accident.'

'And apart from Christian Callister, everyone else remained at Llys y Garn?'

'I was upset by the fire, so I went to bed. As far as I know, everyone else went too.'

'You heard nothing?'

'I'm a sound sleeper.'

'Very well, Mrs Lawrence.'

Released from interrogation, I went and sat on the steps down to the meadow, to calm my nerves. Kicked myself for my infantile determination to say nothing and tried not to rerun everything that Phillips had said, but I couldn't help myself. Al had put a police informer in hospital with a fractured skull because he saw her as a threat to his sister. That was far more than twisting a wrist. Now Hannah had been threatening to inform on Kim. He did go out in the night. His indifference to Hannah's fate had already struck me as uncomfortably callous. Could it really be…?

Oh but this was utter rubbish. Al? Kill Hannah? No. Absolutely not. Swat her out of his way, maybe, but he wouldn't kill her, no matter what she said about Kim. I could imagine him killing Christian without compunction, and I wouldn't even blame him for doing so, but not Hannah.

I would tell him, I decided; warn him of the things the police were insinuating. But when I tried to find him, I was too late. He and the rest of his crew had already been rounded up for their session with the police. Instead, I walked to the archaeology camp, imagining that, with a police investigation under way, a hint of hysteria and anxiety might have set in. Not a chance. I

256

was met with a theatre of excited prurience. They were all delighted to be facing police interrogation.

Vicky gave me a helpless shrug. 'Do you know, I think some of them are actually enjoying it.'

'It's probably just a game to them.'

Vicky winced. 'Oh why didn't we stop her last night? We should never have let her go.'

'But she was – is an adult. How could you have stopped her?'

'We could have tried. The police are contacting her mother, but apparently they didn't get on – her stepfather – I don't know. She'd lost her job recently. And there doesn't seem to have been a boyfriend. There ought to be someone to worry about her.'

'Yes of course.' There should have been someone to worry about her a long time ago, and now it was too late. Now there was nothing left to worry about, except finding her body.

And when that happened, still there would be Sylvia to worry about. No matter what happened, there would be Sylvia to worry about. I had wished her son dead; that would have been bad enough, but now she was going to learn that he was a murderer and there was no way I could protect her from it.

For a moment, when I returned to the house, I thought the moment must have come. Sylvia was in the kitchen, sobbing uncontrollably, with Tamsin hopelessly trying to comfort her.

But Tamsin's first words told me nothing was that simple. 'You won't believe it. The police have taken Mike.'

'Mike?' I was floored. 'Where?'

'To the police station. For questioning.'

'What are they charging him with?'

'I don't know,' wailed Sylvia. 'What can we do?'

'It's stupid!' said Tamsin hotly. 'What's him being a chemist got to do with anything?'

'Oh Tammy.' Sylvia hugged her daughter and raised guilty, tearful eyes to mine. 'I told them that he went out last night – well he did. He was worried. He went after Christian. Chris was so wild when he left, Mike was worried maybe he'd have an accident. I couldn't tell them that, could I? Not about Christian. I can't put the police onto him again. So – oh why didn't I keep quiet? I should never have said anything.'

'Hush.' I soothed her, realising that my own prevarication on the subject had been utterly pointless. 'Michael probably told them himself.'

'And then they wanted to know, did he have any witnesses to finding the shoe? And why did he move it? And why did he have everyone out contaminating the crime scene? And he said he'd had everyone out searching because the police hadn't given a damn, and that's when they took him away.'

'Sylvia, stop worrying. He's annoyed them, so they're going to annoy him, but Mike can look after himself; he's not a child. He won't let himself be bullied by big bad men. After all, we don't even know for certain that a crime has been committed. Maybe it wasn't a crime scene.'

'But the blood—'

'We don't know that it's Hannah's.'

'Whose else could it be?' She looked at me, in panic, and I gave up trying to argue. Hannah was dead, and the police should be tracking down Christian. Not Mike, for God's sake! Christian was the first, the only suspect, the one name that should be forced on the police. I couldn't ask Sylvia to do it. Even after the fire and Christian's loathsome behaviour, every maternal sinew in her screamed against repeating that betrayal.

But I should have spelled it out myself, instead of letting others be suspected.

'They're so stupid!' repeated Tamsin. 'Michael! Honestly.'

'Let's keep calm,' I said. 'They can't keep him for ever.'

They didn't. It wasn't long before he phoned. 'Can you pick me up, Kate? I'm in Haverfordwest, and the police don't provide a taxi service.'

'I'm coming now.'

He was waiting for me, as agreed, in Morrison's car park, and jumped into the passenger seat quickly, shaking off the dust of the town, with angry vigour.

'Stupid people!'

'They're not planning on charging you with anything?'

'No. Let's go.'

I let him simmer. 'I told them to look for Christian,' he said, as I circled a roundabout. 'Why are they so bloody determined not to listen?'

'You told them to look for him?'

'Of course I did.' He stared angrily at the hedgerows. 'He's got to be found.'

'Sylvia—'

'Yes, I know, Sylvia thinks that the police must never hear his name mentioned. I might as well not have bothered. They're convinced I just named him to divert suspicion from myself.'

'They can't seriously think you had anything to do with Hannah's disappearance?'

'God knows what they think. That I'm manufacturing methamphetamine in one of the workshops, with Christian as my distributor, and I eliminated Hannah because she threatened to expose our empire?'

'That's too preposterous. But it doesn't matter.

However stupid they are, sooner or later they'll find Hannah and then there'll be something real for them to work on.'

'Can we wait?' Michael thumped the dash board. 'How long is that going to take? They can't track her. The dogs followed her trail to the point where the blood was found, and then it stops. It doesn't help that I let a mob loose on the scene.'

I winced. Our students may have been trained to handle archaeological finds clinically, but the bloody bottle had been passed casually round the entire neighbourhood, before the police arrived. 'If the police had come when we first reported her missing, it wouldn't have happened. That's what this was all about, wasn't it? We stepped on their toes, by organising a search first.'

He shrugged. 'There was the discrepancy about time, too. I told them I went out at one. Sylvia told them it was three or four.'

I thought, he was still out when I felt Hannah die. But Michael? Don't be ridiculous. Absolutely out of the question. 'Sylvia has no idea of time,' I said.

'I think she had an idea it would sound better for me. What did you say? You probably didn't even make note of the time. I did, because I was watching the clock, so I knew it was one, but if all three of us gave different versions—'

'I told them I didn't notice anyone going anywhere.'

'But you saw me go. Good God, Kate, why did you lie about it?'

'I know, I know. I couldn't bring myself to explain about our trouble with Christian.'

'Kate, a girl is missing. We can't afford – look, we both know what Christian is capable of doing. For God's sake, this isn't the time to prevaricate.'

'I know! I'm sorry. But I just clam up, when I'm being bullied.'

'Were they bullying you?'

'No. Sorry. I don't know why I did it. Instinct. Old habits die hard.'

He was no longer listening to my pathetic excuses. 'The girl's been murdered, or, at the very least, abducted. Christian's either dumped her somewhere, or he still has her.'

'Yes.' He wanted my agreement, so I gave it. I could at least do that right.

'They need to look for Christian. Look for him now! Drop everything else and search for him. Kate, you've got to help me persuade them he's the one they've got to find. Now, without any more delay!'

I was so focussed on Michael, so violent in his insistence, that I nearly swerved into a ditch. He put a hand to the steering wheel. 'Watch the road.'

'Yes.' I pulled myself together. 'Yes, I'll do it. I'll tell them. Sylvia will understand, won't she?'

'God knows,' he said, staring at the road ahead. 'But there's nothing else I can do.'

Neither of us said more. I knew he must be replaying that scene of unbearable hurt and hatred in the drawing room, Christian sitting, burned and snarling, spitting at his mother.

Now we'd reached the last act: Christian was a murderer.

22

The sun was sinking as we turned into the drive of Llys y Garn. Sinking into grey murk, a colourless contrast to the infernal fiery sunset of the day before. Was it really only the day before?

Sylvia was out on the drive, watching and waiting, and I geared myself up to do battle. She was going to have to report her son to the police, again.

Her face brightened at the sight of Michael. 'You're back. Thank God. Everything's so crazy. I don't know what to do.'

'What's happened?'

'They've arrested Al and Molly and everyone at Annwfyn.'

'What!'

'They took them all away. Al had a bandaged hand, and it turns out he was out last night too and, oh, it's all so ridiculous. The others were getting a bit loud, so they took them all in. Isn't it absurd? I'm going mad! I don't know what's happened to the girl, I don't know if it's something really terrible, but if they're going to look for someone, it must be Christian. Mustn't it?'

So one battle was over before it started, but another was begun. If even Sylvia could see it was Christian, how stupid could the police be? It wasn't Al. His hand was bandaged because of the burns. He had gone out in the night to look for Kim, not yet home from Aberystwyth.

Michael's own encounter with the police hadn't cowed him at all. 'Bloody fools! I'm going to find out what's going on.'

I joined him in his quest, but despite the omnipresence of the police, pinning one down was next to impossible. Eventually I caught Phillips as he finished with one of the students.

'Why has Al Taverner been arrested?'

'Not arrested, ma'am. Just helping police with their enquiries.'

'He has nothing to do with Hannah Quigley's disappearance.'

'You are quite sure of that, ma'am? You can provide him with an alibi?'

I hesitated. 'No, but surely you lot realise it's Christian Callister you want to talk to?'

'Indeed, ma'am, that name has been brought to our attention.'

'He's capable of anything. And probably high as a kite—'

'So he was using drugs on these premises?'

'Yes. Almost certainly. That's why we threw him out.'

'So his mother has said. Mrs Callister has amended her statement.'

'Well then. Why have you arrested the others?'

'Just making enquiries, ma'am. Looking for evidence. We still don't know precisely what crime's been committed. Assuming that drugs are behind this, you must be aware that Mr Taverner and his companions have a history of—'

'Yes, Kim was an addict, and now she's clean. If you test her, that will prove it.' What made me say that? I knew that Christian had been targeting her.

'We have yet to trace Miss Taverner,' said Phillips. If Kim had been out all day, she probably knew nothing of our drama. 'Do you have any idea where we might find her?'

'None. Kim just turns up whenever she feels like it.'

'I trust you will notify us if she makes contact, Mrs

Lawrence. Hannah Quigley specifically linked her with Mr Callister in the matter of drugs, according to Professor Pryce-Roberts, so we are anxious to speak to her.'

'Hannah said a lot of very stupid things, all utter nonsense! But did the professor also tell you what Christian said to her in return? He said "I'm going to get you in the night." Have you got that in your notes?'

'Would you say he was serious when he spoke those words?'

I hesitated. I had dismissed it as a silly jibe at the time, but that was before he had hurtled off into the twilight, with murder in his heart, along the lane where Hannah was stumbling in her paranoid outrage. 'I know he was deranged and violent.'

DC Phillips sat back, folded his arms and looked at me. 'You didn't mention this when you gave your statement earlier, Mrs Lawrence.'

'No. I – I hoped he'd just driven away. My cousin has a very difficult relationship with her son and I didn't want to be the one to accuse him. I thought it would be so blindingly obvious I wouldn't need to. How was I to know you were going to be arresting everyone else in sight?'

'Not arresting, Mrs Lawrence, just making enquiries. And don't worry, we are looking for Mr Callister. You'll probably not be surprised to hear the Metropolitan Police are also quite interested in his whereabouts.'

'No. I'm not.'

As I came away, I realised I'd learned virtually nothing.

Michael was having no better luck. We pooled our efforts, attacked the phones, and charged at anyone who might be in a position to give us information. After an hour, Michael put the phone down and raised a hand at me. 'Tenby.'

I hung up on my stone-walling desk jockey. 'Tenby?'

'They're all at the police station there. Being held for the night, apparently.'

'Why Tenby?'

'God knows. I'm going to phone the station, make sure they get a decent lawyer.' He was already dialling.

I waited, trying to make sense of a one-sided conversation. No, Michael couldn't speak to Al, no, no one was charged yet or in need of medical attention, yes, note was taken of his offer to provide a lawyer.

Michael looked as frustrated as I felt. 'Sorry, Kate. Looks as if we'll just have to wait till tomorrow.'

I debated driving down to Tenby, but what would have been the point? I would be of more use at Llys y Garn. As darkness fell, I walked down to the lodge gates, with an idea I might catch Kim before she strolled in, unsuspecting, on the entire regional police force. But I could see that she wouldn't even make it to the gates. The lane was a scene of crime, blue and white tape flapping along the hedgerows, officers and dogs still sniffing in the undergrowth and in adjoining fields.

I glanced at the lodge. Our holidaymakers were home for the night. What were they making of all this? As I turned to face the cottage, a curtain twitched hurriedly across the window.

At least they couldn't complain their holiday lacked excitement.

It wasn't quite a dawn raid. No crowbars and battering rams, but the police arrived early with dogs and vans. I hurried downstairs to find Inspector Wiles showing Michael his papers. 'We have a warrant to search the premises, sir.'

'You don't need a warrant,' said Michael. 'We want the girl found, so please look. But would you mind starting off downstairs? Sylvia's only just got to sleep. I'd rather she had another half an hour, before you start to harass her.'

'Tamsin's going to be in for a shock.' I dragged a reluctant smile from Michael.

'Not to worry, sir. We'll be starting with the outhouses. Any locks? We wouldn't want to have to break down doors.'

'No locks. We don't have any secrets to hide.'

Michael was wrong. There was a padlock on the large chest freezer in one of the unused workshops. It was locked and weighed down with a crate of bottles to aid the perishing seal, but the police were immensely interested, even when it was found to contain only half a lamb, bags of damsons and a pack of butcher's sausages.

The dogs were hugely excited in Michael's workshop. I thought of the stash of drugs I'd given him a few months before for safe-keeping, and I turned to him, aghast. His mind must have followed the same path; he was looking ill, but when he caught my gaze he hastily shook his head. 'Disposed of,' he whispered, his face creased with pain. Those bloody drugs. Why hadn't we reported Christian back then?

The dogs took some convincing that there was nothing to be found, as everything was taken apart, work scattered, potentially lethal tools bagged. In the end, they moved on to Sylvia's workshop, and proceeded to dismantle her pottery, while Sylvia, unable to watch any more, shut herself in the kitchen, leaving Michael and me to bear witness.

A young officer hurried along from the walled garden. 'We've found something, sir.'

'Where?'

'There's a well, sir. We've found something in it.'

Michael and I looked at each other, appalled, then followed into the garden. Policemen were clustered round the crumbling parapet of the well, its protective covering hurled aside. Alsatians were straining at the leash.

'Oh good God, she's not in there, is she?' Michael asked.

A policeman shooed us back. 'Please return to the house, sir, madam.'

'You can't have found her there,' I blurted. It was impossible. Unless someone had dropped her down it since I'd peered into it. Someone else on the property, with a vehicle, with access to the well where the builders worked. No, it wasn't possible.

'Come on, they're not going to give us an answer, Kate.' Michael drew me along, back to the house. He was swearing under his breath in frustration, while I walked in a daze. It couldn't be her.

Sylvia, whisky in hand, was waiting for us. 'What's happening? Has anything happened?'

'The police seem to think there's something in the well,' explained Michael. 'We don't know—'

'Oh no!' Sylvia's jaw dropped. Her eyes widened, her free hand flew to her mouth.

'Now it's all right,' he soothed. 'We don't know that it's Hannah.'

'But it isn't! Oh no. Oh dear. Oh, Mike, what have I done?'

Michael blinked, then said calmly, 'Sylvia, darling, what have you done?'

'Those drugs you took from Christian's car. Oh dear.'

Michael winced. 'I'd forgotten, they're in the safe. I'd better tell them.'

'No, they're not in the safe. The police were so obsessed with drugs yesterday, when they took you away, I got in a panic. I thought if they found them here, they'd think—'

'Sylvia, don't tell me you threw them down the well.' I was ready to kiss her. It wasn't Hannah.

'I thought no one would ever think of looking there. Oh dear! I didn't think – what have I done?'

Michael placed his hands on her shoulders. 'Calm down. It can't be helped. I should have got rid of them, first thing yesterday.'

'But now they'll think—'

'Hush. At least it isn't Hannah's body.'

I was almost laughing, swinging from terror to cock-sure confidence. 'We'll tell them we suspected Christian might have hidden some drugs around the place. Let them think he put them there.'

'Don't you think it would be better if we just told them the truth?' asked Michael.

'How's it going to sound? Sylvia's already changed her statement once. Let's not rush. I'll go back and see what's happening.'

I strode back to the walled garden, ready to take on the world. A constable stopped me before I could enter, but Wiles strolled over to speak to me.

'Have you found her body?' I demanded.

'No, not yet, Mrs Lawrence. But we have made an interesting discovery in the well. A wash bag.'

'A wash bag? How bizarre.'

'Packed. My educated guess is cocaine, skunk and E. We'll be able to confirm it when the labs have taken a look, but quite a haul.'

'Good God.'

'Any idea how it might have got there?'

'Christian Callister! We keep telling you he's

268

involved with drugs. That's why Dr Bradley threw him off the property. Christian could have stashes hidden all over the place.'

'Christian Callister. Yes.' The inspector gazed thoughtfully at the Great Hall. 'Professor Pryce-Roberts tells me your builders frequently make use of the well.'

I swore internally. 'They want water; it's a well; yes they use it.'

'You don't think they might have hidden drugs there?'

'No I don't! Why are you so fixated on them? Christian's the one responsible. Isn't that obvious? Why don't you get out there and look for him?'

'We are looking, ma'am. We're also looking for Hannah Quigley.'

'Yes. Of course. Do you know yet if that blood was definitely hers?'

'I'm not at liberty to confirm or deny anything just yet, ma'am.'

'Oh for God's sake!'

I stormed back to the kitchen. We were in the midst of a murder enquiry and no one would tell us what was happening, what was suspected or what had been eliminated. It was unbelievably frustrating. The fact that I'd been telling the police as little as possible either was neither here nor there.

'They've found the drugs,' I told Michael and Sylvia. 'I mentioned Christian, but they prefer to think it must have been Al.'

Michael gave a fatalistic smile. 'Sylvia's explained she dropped the whole bag in. It contains several packets; I checked them, so my fingerprints will be all over them.'

'Oh lord,' wailed Sylvia.

'At least that will clear Al of suspicion,' said Michael.

'I don't suppose it will make any difference,' I said. 'They seem determined to pin something on him. How long can they hold him? Assuming they're not trying to get him for terrorism?'

'I'll ring the station again,' said Michael, fetching the phone. 'They have no business keeping him in at all.'

'Why are there two policemen in the bathroom?' asked Tamsin, entering indignantly.

'They think we've flushed Hannah Quigley down the pan,' I explained. 'What can you do with these people?' I thought of the damage already done in the workshops by the police search. 'I think I'd better go and back everything up before they get to the office. They'll probably smash the laptop and confiscate our files.' The police hadn't yet started on the ground floor, so I had the office to myself for a while, securing what I could and sorting out the accumulated paperwork, before it was thrown to the winds. My heart wasn't in it. When I'd done all I could face, I returned to the kitchen to see if Michael had made the slightest headway with the police station.

Sylvia and Michael were waiting for me to appear.

'Kate. Oh dear,' said Sylvia.

Michael glanced at me, then turned away to the Rayburn.

'What now?' I asked.

'Oh Kate,' said Sylvia, giving me a hug. 'It's about Al.'

'What's happened?' I pictured him hanging in a cell.

'I phoned the station again,' intervened Michael, before Sylvia could raise the panic level. 'Al and his team will be on their way back here quite soon.'

'But that's good!'

'Yes, of course it is. I repeated my offer to provide them with a lawyer, but it turns out they have their own.'

'They're probably used to all this.'

'Oh Kate,' repeated Sylvia.

Michael hushed her. 'It seems Al managed to text Kim.'

'She has a mobile? Good. So she evaded arrest then?'

'Oh Kate,' said Sylvia. I resolved to tape her lips shut if she said it again.

'Kim turned up at the station late last night with their own solicitor.' Michael busied himself with the kettle, then stopped and resolutely turned to face me. 'She's handling the situation. Mrs Josephine Taverner.'

His mother, I thought. But his mother's dead. Josephine – Jo – Mrs?

'Oh Kate,' said Sylvia.

'You mean Al's wife?'

'He never told us he was married,' complained Sylvia. 'Did he, Mike?'

'I don't suppose it ever came up in conversation,' I said, coolly, my mouth dry. 'Did he ever tell you he wasn't married?'

Michael frowned. 'I think his behaviour has suggested it, don't you?'

'Well, they're free spirits. I'm surprised he settled for something quite so conventional, but we all have our weaknesses. As long as she's managed to spring them from Alcatraz, that's the main thing. I'm just going…,' I made for the stairs.

'Oh Kate!' said Sylvia.

'Sylvia!' I retorted through clenched teeth and ran.

A policeman was searching my room.

'Hell!' I retreated, running up the back stairs to the attics. The first door I opened – of course it was that door. It had to be that door. The shadow of fear and resistance pounded into me as I hurtled in, unthinking, almost lifting me off my feet and hurtling me out again. Out, out, out!

'All right, I'm going!' I kicked the door, as I slammed it shut. Slipped into the adjoining garret, where there was nothing to stop me wallowing in misery, resentment and self-pity. Perhaps my emotions were worming their way into the fabric of this room now. They were strong enough. I wanted to curl up and shut out everything…

I stopped and slapped myself at the thought of this pathetic behaviour. It was a joke, wasn't it? I should be laughing. Not so long ago, I was sharing my favours between my husband and my lover. Now my husband had gone to his pregnant mistress and my lover was back with his wife. Yes, it was all one bloody joke. Ha bloody ha.

Thump, thump, thump on creaking boards, doors opening, one after another, and then mine, a policeman's head peering round. 'Sorry, love, but…,'

'Yes, help yourself. There's a mouse hole if you're interested.' I pushed past him, slithering down the narrow stairs, half expecting the woodwork to give way beneath me. After all, everything else had. Then I was on the ground floor, with nowhere further to sink. I headed for the front door, in need of fresh air. Preferably a cold wind, pouring rain – a brutal dose of reality.

I stopped short. Michael was in the drawing room, alone, his head in his hands. He looked up when I came in, that terrible look of anguish again.

'Kate,' he said, pulling himself together immediately. 'How are you?'

I sat down, ashamed of my own wretchedness. Michael had endured more than I could begin to imagine, watching his wife die, succumbing to grief and despair, and a new life with Sylvia was supposed to have brought him peace and salvation. Instead, our wretched family had embroiled him in this mêlée of sordid squabbles, spite and now murder. What did my pitiful romantic troubles matter? 'I'm fine. Really. I'll survive. We'll come through this, Michael. Somewhere beyond all this there'll be calm waters again.'

'Yes,' he said. Not believing it. He glanced around the room, at the newly painted wall, the curtainless window where Christian had fallen, and stared at the spot for a moment. 'Sylvia's gone to speak to the police,' he said. 'She insisted. She wouldn't let me go with her. She seems to think she can put things right.' The words rang hollow.

'She shouldn't have gone alone. They'll tie her in knots.'

'Tamsin's gone with her,' said Michael. 'She just wanted her daughter.'

I was feeling more and more uneasy at the cloud of gloom surrounding him. We couldn't let him slip back into the depression that had brought him down once before. 'She wasn't cold-shouldering you, Michael. She was trying to protect you by not involving you. I know it won't work, but Sylvia always means well.' A thread of thought hung between us. And some people always mean ill. 'She'd do anything for you, just as you'd do anything for her.'

He stared at me and opened his mouth to speak. Then the sound of an engine, grinding gears, slamming doors down the lane, made us both turn to the window.

'I suppose that's Al,' I said.

Michael nodded. 'I think so. Would you rather—'

'I'll go and see them,' I said quickly. 'Nil carborundum.'

He managed a smile. 'The good old British stiff upper

273

lip, eh?'

'The Kate Lawrence pride, more like.' I took a deep breath and strode resolutely to the courtyard.

A garish minibus was parked at the end of the workshops. By the time I reached it, the occupants had been disgorged. I found Al and Kim, face to face in their usual sibling angst. 'You just never listen,' Kim was saying. 'I'm nearly twenty one, Alistair. I'm not your baby. I don't need you to protect me.'

'What was I supposed to think when the Quigley woman said she saw you—'

'Saw what? Saw him pushing drugs at me? He's been pushing them at everyone, in case you hadn't noticed. And I told him where to shove them, okay? You seriously think I'm incapable of saying no?'

'No, of course.' Al saw me and stopped.

Kim saw me too. 'For God's sake, get him off my back, Kate.' She stalked away in frustrated rage.

'Kate? You're Kate. I've heard about you. I'm Jo.' The Wife bounced forward, all bright smiles. Slight, flat chested, close cropped sandy hair and freckles. No one's definition of radiant beauty, and yet she did radiate. She oozed attractive energy.

'How was Peru?' I asked politely.

Jo Taverner laughed. 'Forgotten already. Hell, I don't know. I thought I'd be back a week or two, before I had to get my husband out of a police cell again.'

'Again?'

She grinned. 'He does have his own take on justice, does Al. Any other mischief he's been in, since I've been away?'

'None that Kate knows of,' said Al. He looked depressingly guilt-free.

'I hear you've let them build their round house here,' said Jo. 'I knew he'd find some poor sucker to let him

274

do it eventually. What about the yurt problem, by the way?'

'It's fine,' said Al.

'You fixed that bit about attaching the lining?'

'Yes, I fixed it.'

'Good, because we don't want to be sued.' Jo smiled at me apologetically. 'Sorry. I'll nag him later. You've got rather more pressing problems on your hands than Al's cocked-up instruction leaflets, haven't you? Any news on the missing girl?'

'None yet.' I had become the outsider in someone else's ongoing domestic saga.

'And the pigs rampaging everywhere, I suppose. If you need a resident lawyer for the duration, just call. I've already drawn up battle lines with the buggers. Pat!' She summoned the other new face in the crowd, Padrig I assumed; eight feet tall, with a plaited beard and a beaded head band. 'Get the beer. I'm not ready yet for Molly's tisanes.' She was shepherding them all, for the haul up to the camp. The minibus would never make it up the track. 'I'll just get us settled in, then I'll be back,' she promised me. 'See if I can be of any help.'

They set off, leaving me standing alone with Al. He seemed to recognise that an explanation was in order.

'I'm glad they released you,' I said stiffly. 'Did they give you a hard time?'

'No more than usual.'

'Just as well your wife turned up when she did.'

He shrugged. 'They couldn't have held us for much longer anyway.'

'She's very nice.'

'Jo? Yes. Sweeps all before her.'

I glared at him. 'You could have told me you were married.'

'I didn't keep it secret. I thought you knew. You talked about Jo and Padrig.'

'That doesn't mean I knew Jo was your wife.'

He raised an eyebrow. 'You introduced your husband as a family friend. Took me a while to catch on.'

'That's different. We were separated.'

'Jo and I were separated. By the Atlantic.'

'I meant emotionally, not geographically.'

'Okay,' he conceded. 'So maybe we were too. We'd agreed to have some time out. She went her way, I went mine, to see how things would work out.'

'Oh I see. A trial separation. She goes off to Peru with a Celtic sun god, and you toy with the amusing goods round here.'

He leaned against the wall, his arms folded. 'I figured that was pretty much what you were doing. Trying the water to see if you really wanted your husband back? Sorry your reunion didn't work out. Mind you, you'd have been wasted on him.'

'Don't you dare!'

'Come on, Kate. I like you. I like you a lot, and you like me. It's no great catastrophe, is it?'

'Does Jo "like" Padrig?'

'Yeah, probably.' He laughed. 'They have a lot in common. An interest in the rights of indigenous farmers. I'm not a possessive guy.'

'Evidently.'

'Look, Kate, come up to the camp with us.'

'And we can be a liberated foursome? No thank you.'

He shook his head with a laugh. 'I mean, come up and get away from all this.' He nodded at a police car gliding silently by. 'Chill out for a bit.'

'Chill out! With Hannah Quigley still missing?'

'You don't have an idea where she is?'

'No, of course I don't.'

'I thought, maybe, you could feel something?'

Feel what? The fading out of existence in the dark hours of a sleepless night. I knew that death had occurred, not where or how it had happened. 'I'm not a bloody clairvoyant!' I snapped.

'Sorry.' Al put an arm round my shoulder. 'You're having a rough time. But you'll come through it.'

Great. Did he think his positivity was transferable? It wasn't. I wasn't feeling positive about anything anymore. I no longer knew where I was or what I was doing.

'I've got to get back to Sylvia.' I watched him set off up the path to the camp. Then I turned in the opposite direction and wandered down into the meadow. I needed a moment to breathe, to wipe my mind clear of its helter-skelter chaos.

Tamsin was in the kitchen when I returned, busily filling the kettle, setting out crockery. The sight of such voluntary domesticity took me aback.

'I've sent Mum to bed' she said. 'She's looking terrible. I'm making tea. Do you want some?'

'I'd love some. How did she get on with the police?'

'It was awful. But she was determined to do it. Poor Mum. Dropping drugs down the well! I ask you.'

'I know. She panicked.'

'She's always in pieces when Chris upsets her. I wonder if they've found him yet.' She was diligently warming the pot. Every iota of the tea-making ritual was going to be done correctly.

'I haven't heard, but then they're not telling us anything.'

'At least they've got the drugs in the well sorted out. But would you believe, they've still got this idea that Mike's the real drugs dealer, not Chris. Just because he was a chemist. How dumb can you get? At least it gets

Al off the hook, I suppose. You heard about Al? Being married? Isn't he a rat?'

Tamsin looked merely miffed. A week ago I would have expected a stronger response, but the last few days had given us all new priorities.

'I've just met his wife,' I said. 'Jo. She's very nice.'

'When they talked about Jo and Padrig in Peru or wherever, do you know, I thought they were talking about a man. How embarrassing is that?'

'A mistake anyone could make,' I said, soberly.

'And she turns up and finds them all under arrest, for nothing at all! Can you believe this? Chris is here for a couple of days, and suddenly we're all under suspicion.'

'I'm sure he'd appreciate the devastating impact he's left.' I watched her laying a tray. One bone china cup and saucer – I hadn't realised there were cups and saucers in the house – one lacy plate with biscuit. If niceness cured, this would heal Sylvia for certain. 'What about Michael? Isn't he with your mother?'

'No, I said I'd keep his until he came back. They're searching the Hall now, and the dungeon is locked up. They asked him to go and open it so they wouldn't have to break down the door. I think they were hoping to break it down, but he's got the key and a screwdriver.'

'Oh, can't they just leave us alone? Look, keep my tea, Tam. I'm going to see how much more damage they're planning to do.'

Damage. I hadn't thought of it in such literal terms, until I entered the hall. The door to the undercroft had been opened for dogs to sniff among the cobwebs, but it was the linenfold panelling, at the far end, that was currently commanding the attention of Wiles and his cohort. The very obviously new panelling, Michael's beautiful craftsmanship, so jarringly different, in its coloration and patina, to the surrounding, older work.

'You could have asked me to open it!' Michael was saying. He was shaking. The secret door into the priest hole had been wrenched and prised off its hinges. 'There was no need for this.'

'Well, I'm sorry about that, sir,' said an unrepentant Wiles. 'But we had to check all possible hiding places. Known and unknown. The rest of the panelling. Are there other opening sections?

'No,' I said, more conscious of Michael's distress than of the distant seething shadow. 'There's the one priest hole. The rest is solid wall.'

'But all those panels have been replaced. Why would that be?'

'Because those were the rotten ones that needed replacing.' Michael was tearing his hair, as he ran his fingers through it.

'It's solid wall,' I insisted. 'I saw it when the old stuff came off.'

'You understand we have to check. We *are* looking for a body.'

'Don't be stupid! Those panels have been in place for a month now and Hannah Quigley's been missing two days. She can't possibly be behind them!'

'We'll soon see.'

Even as Wiles was speaking, a police officer with a crowbar stepped in.

Michael gripped my hands in desperation. 'Kate, can you believe these people?' He flinched at the sound of cracking wood. 'Why in God's name are they doing this?'

So furious I couldn't speak, I put my arm round him and we listened to the smashing and splintering of all his work.

'Come away, Michael,' I managed to say at last.

279

'Let's get away from this.'

He spoke through clenched teeth, his eyes shut. 'There's nowhere left to go.'

Michael sat at the kitchen table, staring into space, his hands round the mug of tea he hadn't drunk. I'd placed a glass of brandy beside his mug. He hadn't noticed it yet. For a moment, in the hall, I'd thought he was going to collapse on me. He hadn't, but collapse wasn't far off.

Tamsin wasn't helping with her indignant sympathy. 'That was a totally shitty thing to do. All your work and everything. Did they find anything?'

'Of course they didn't,' I said, pouring a brandy for myself. 'They were just…' Repeating my opinion of the mindless destructiveness wasn't going to do anything to ease Michael's fragile state of mind. 'Let's not think about it. I've called Al. He's coming down to see what he can do with–' With the splinters of matchwood? '–the panels. I'm sure he can make them good.'

Michael began to laugh. It was a laugh that made even Tamsin uneasy.

'They're so stupid!' she fumed. 'If they really want to find the Quigley, why don't they just ask you, Kate?'

'What?'

'Well, you can feel things, can't you? Bodies and ghosts and so on?'

'No!'

'I bet you knew about Bertie and the Bride before they found them,' she insisted.

'Tamsin, please!'

She gaped at my distress. 'Sorry. It's so weird, your thing. I know I don't really get it.'

'There's nothing to get. Honestly. Tamsin, I'm sorry.

I'm not a clairvoyant.'

'Well, I think you'd do a better job of finding the Quigley girl than the stupid police.' She stood up, shrugging. 'I'm going to see how Mum is.'

'Good. Yes. I hope she's feeling better.'

As the door closed on Tamsin, I felt Michael's eyes on me. My niece's unwelcome ramblings had, at least, diverted him from his inner turmoil.

'Did you know?' he said.

'Sorry?'

'Did you know there were bones in the priest hole? The bog body?'

'No! Of course not. How could I know?'

'Sylvia thinks you have some sixth sense or something. An ability to feel bad things.'

'Aren't we all feeling bad things at the moment?' I tipped back my brandy. 'Sylvia likes the idea of ghosts and spirits.'

'Peter thinks you feel things too. He said you knew there was a body in the bog.'

'No! I just – come on Mike, you're a scientist.' Science was good. Science would steer him back to safety. 'How would a scientist define me? A delusional hysteric?'

To my relief, he managed a smile. 'That's the last way I'd describe you, Kate. But what is it you think you have? An ability to sense corpses?'

'I never told Peter there was a body in the bog. I merely told him I could sense something terrible had happened there. I could feel emotions. Very intense and distressing emotions. We were standing in a bog. There was one fairly obvious explanation.'

'You didn't tell us about it.'

'Tell you what? That I didn't like the feel of the place? I never, for one moment, imagined that people

281

were going to poke around there, any more than I expected us to uncover a forgotten priest's hole.'

'So you have no idea why they were there?'

'No. Truly I don't. I am surrounded by mysteries and I don't have the key to any of them. Why would someone be left to suffocate slowly in a priest's hole? A murder? An accident? I've no idea. Why would somebody have been deliberately drowned in that mire? Your guess is as good as mine. I could sense such animal savagery up there. A lynching maybe?'

He nodded. 'That would make sense of the way they found him. Face down, bound, stones piled on him.'

'Not a sacred altar of sacrifice, just a place of vengeful execution. That's what I felt.'

Michael smiled bleakly. 'Justice calling out to you?'

'That's dangerously close to theology. I'm looking to you for a scientific explanation.'

'I don't want to dissect your sixth sense, Kate. Whatever it is, it must make your life bloody difficult. It's not for me to believe or disbelieve. At least, I'd say, you have an intuitive awareness of what might have happened in a place. You instinctively noticed that the end wall in the hall was exceptionally deep, as if something might be concealed inside. You recognised the bog as a likely place for a lynching. You observe and your subconscious interprets.'

'I'll happily settle for that.'

'And you have no instinctive thoughts about what happened to Hannah?'

'Only the same instinctive thoughts as everyone else.'

'No clues where to find her?'

'None. I know there's been a death, but—'

'You know?' His head shot up.

'Yes,' I said, and wished I hadn't, but it was too late. 'Instinct or whatever, I felt death, the night she vanished. But that doesn't mean I have any idea where to find her body.'

He started to speak, stopped, looked at me with bleak, dead eyes. 'Hannah's body.'

'Who else?' I couldn't help him. The girl was dead and there was no hope of shielding Sylvia from the certainty that her son was a murderer.

'Then let them just find her,' he said, barely audible. 'Is there nothing you can tell them?'

'Michael, I promise, if anything I felt would help them in their search, I would tell them. Whatever the cost. But just sensing death – how could I begin to explain that to the police?'

'No,' he said dully, throwing back his brandy and staring into space. 'How could any of us begin to explain?'

23

'I've made all this toast,' complained Tamsin. 'Aren't you going to eat any of it?'

We tried to do better. We'd gathered, more to draw up the wagons, than to eat breakfast.

'It's wonderful toast.' Sylvia seized a piece and buttered it enthusiastically. 'And Meg's quince jam. Lovely. Have some, Mike.'

'Yes of course.' He helped himself and sat looking at the charred crust.

'This bit's not so burned.' Tamsin swapped the slice in front of him.

He nodded, then pulled himself together, smiling at

her. 'Thanks, Tammy.'

She opened her mouth to correct him, then changed her mind.

'Thanks, Taz,' I said, spreading butter. We were going to eat if it killed us. 'I…' Find a topic, any topic except corpses, suspicions, destruction and an overwhelming sense of doom. 'I wondered if we could do with a shopping trip. Are we getting low on anything?'

Silence.

'I don't think so,' said Sylvia.

I wouldn't give up. 'Maybe we need to get out. Walk on the beach? Something?'

'Yes.' Sylvia forced enthusiasm. 'That would be lovely.'

A tentative knock on the kitchen door put paid to any attempts at normality. What now?

Now was Mr and Mrs Pretty from the lodge, nervously supporting each other at the mouth of the dragon's den.

'We didn't want to interrupt your breakfast;' said Mrs Pretty.

'Not at all,' said Sylvia. 'Would you like coffee? Tea.'

'Oh, er, no, that is—'

'How can we help you?' I enquired. As if I needed to ask.

'Well, the fact is.' Mr Pretty, under his wife's anxious gaze, sounded desperately reasonable. 'We're in a bit of a difficult position. It's a lovely cottage. We've enjoyed it very much. But now—'

'Oh I know, that poor missing girl,' sympathised Sylvia. 'It's terrible, isn't it? Oh dear, it must all be an awful disturbance for you.'

'Well it's not very nice, is it?' Mrs Pretty came to the

boil. 'Police everywhere. Questioning us! I mean, of course we heard things, shouting and doors banging and people roaring off in the middle of the night, but it's nothing to do with us. We don't want anything to do with it.'

Mr Petty hastily toned down her outrage. 'The thing is, we don't know what to think, who to trust. There's all this talk of murder, and drugs – and we have children to think of.'

'So you'd like to leave?' I suggested, to save time.

'I know we booked until the weekend, but we think we'd rather go now.'

'Oh dear,' said Sylvia, tears welling.

'We quite understand,' I assured them. 'This can't be at all pleasant for you. Would you like us to find you alternative accommodation for the rest of the week?'

'Oh, no, no, we don't think so,' said Mr Pretty.

'The weather's going to be turning, according to the forecast,' put in his wife. 'So we thought we'd just go home.'

'Of course.'

'And there'll be a refund? Compensation?'

'I'll write you a cheque now,' I said. 'For the whole two weeks. Is that all right?'

'Oh. Well, yes. We… Yes. Thank you.'

Tamsin followed me to the office. 'You know that's all crap? They've been loving it, filming it, asking to talk to the police. And they've had nearly two weeks already. I don't see why they should have all their money back.'

'Believe me, Taz, I'll gladly give them twice as much if it gets rid of them.'

She watched me writing the cheque. 'I bet they only want to go because of the weather forecast.'

'Quite likely. It doesn't matter. We've got enough on

our plate, without having guests to worry about. Best for all of us, if they just go away.'

I returned to the kitchen and handed Mr Pretty the cheque. He looked apologetic, but his wife smiled triumphantly, as she led him away.

'Of course they want to leave.' Sylvia gave way to her tears. 'Who'd want to stay here? Not safe for children. Everything's ruined, isn't it? We might as well all just curl up in a corner and die!'

'Oh come on, Mum.' Tamsin chivvied her. 'It's not that bad. We've got other guests coming, haven't we?'

'But will any of them want to come now?'

'God knows,' said Michael, his head in his hands.

We were still clearing dishes when Fran Garrick arrived, her Range Rover blocking the light from the kitchen window, her dogs erupting into the courtyard.

'Sylvia!' Fran boomed. 'Terrible business. Heard all about it.'

'Have you? Well it's lovely to see you, Fran. Come in and—'

'Can't stay. Just wanted a quick word with Ronnie. Thought I'd better mention this business though. Expect it will all be cleared up in no time. I was saying to Clive, at the post office, nobody believes half this nonsense about Michael. Absurd, of course.'

'Yes it is,' said Sylvia. 'Both halves, whatever they are.'

'And you know, when this is all over, you'll be quite welcome at The Manse. Now, where is that brother of mine?'

Sylvia watched her stride away, then looked at me. 'Probably gone to make sure we haven't murdered him.' She sounded more bitter than distressed. 'Someone tell her to move that bloody truck.'

We abandoned the idea of a walk on the beach. We abandoned the idea of doing anything except waiting for the next piece of bad news. I took three phone calls from the press about the police search. There was nothing I could say to feed their rapacious appetite for sensation, but if I said nothing, my silence seemed to confirm all the most sinister rumours. I was running out of noncommittal nonsense, desperate to decamp, but that would leave Sylvia to cope with them. Again the phone rang. I sat watching it malevolently for a moment, while it trilled and screeched and nagged. I could just hurl it out of the window. Instead I picked it up.

'Good morning, Llys y Garn.'

'Kate! That is you?' Peter.

'Hello,' I said calmly.

'Kate, I've heard. About the missing student. Have they found her body yet?'

'No. No they haven't found her, because they're too busy crawling over Llys y Garn, destroying everything they light upon, instead of getting out there and searching properly.'

'Do you have any idea where she is, Kate?'

'No! For the last bloody time, I'm not a clairvoyant. If you want to know where she is, ask Christian. Which is something the police can't be bothered to do.'

'Christian? You certain?'

'She left, Christian left, neither have been seen again, so what do you think?'

'Good God. I'm coming down.'

'Why on earth would you want to come down here, Peter?'

'I can't just leave you to cope with this.'

'Yes you can. I am coping perfectly well. How is

Gabrielle?'

'Fine,' he said, brushing the subject off hastily. 'But you need—'

'Is she having the abortion?'

He hesitated. 'No. No, she isn't.'

'Well then. You'll make a lovely couple.'

'Yes, but—'

'Don't worry. I've got other things on my mind at the moment, but if you want to arrange the divorce, I'll just sign on any dotted lines. Give you time to make sure Baby Lawrence bears your name.'

'Kate! Please—'

'Now just bugger off, Peter.' I put the phone down.

There was a knock on the office door.

'What!' I snapped.

'Hi.' Jo Taverner put her head round the door. After Peter, it would have to be Al's wife. 'You okay? Well obviously not. Who would be?' She came into the room. 'This probably isn't a good time, but when is?'

'Come in, sit down,' I said. My mouth tasted like battery acid. I could feel the disorientating onset of a migraine creeping up on me.

Jo sat and looked at me with a sympathetic grimace. 'Shitty world. Al's giving the fuzz an earful about their vandalism, so I came to see if there was anything I could do.'

The phone rang again and I automatically answered. 'Yes... yes it is. ... No, that is incorrect... Yes, as far as I'm aware... No, sorry, I have nothing to add.' I put the receiver down and turned back to Jo. 'You fancy dealing with the press?'

'Easy.' She reached down and tugged the phone connection from the socket.

'That won't keep them at bay.'

'It will for five minutes. You just need five now and

288

again to regain your balance. Next time, offer an exclusive. Negotiate. Nothing less than six figures.'

'We don't want their money!'

'You don't have to keep it,' said Jo, cheerfully. 'Give it to charity, and tell them whatever hogwash they want. You don't think the press want the truth, do you? Make it up.'

I smiled. 'I'll think about it.'

'Right, so that's the press sorted. I really meant, can I help with the police? I do know how these things work, you know.'

'We're all beginning to learn. They've got Michael pegged as an East End gangster, I think. It's so...' Words failed me.

Jo nodded understanding. 'The thing you have to understand about the police, is they're all gits.'

'Is that your professional legal opinion?'

She grinned, her freckles dancing. 'Of course. So what are your thoughts about this girl, Hannah? Molly says she was unbalanced.'

'Plain crazy and obnoxious is what I would have called her. But I can't say that now, can I? Yes, she was seriously unbalanced, poor girl.'

'It sounds as if the fuzz are really gunning for Doc Bradley. Al assures me they're totally out of their tree and it's inconceivable that Bradley could have murdered anyone. I take it you concur with that?'

I covered my eyes, my migraine preparing its sharpest knives. 'Truthfully, I've begun to realise that all of us could commit murder if we were pushed into the wrong corner. But Michael? Al's right, it's inconceivable. He could never, in any circumstance, have murdered Hannah. It's not in his DNA, and anyway, he had no motive. If he were the overlord of a drug empire, then maybe, but he's not. He's just Michael, a sweet man who loves Sylvia and wanted a quiet, polite, creative life, and now—'

Jo patted my arm. Was I really getting that worked up? 'Just what Al said, but his judgement's always skewed by anyone who can handle a chisel. I just wanted to be sure. So basically, it's your nephew, isn't it? Is he your nephew?'

'Technically, my second cousin. But, yes. It's Christian. He drove off the same time Hannah quit the camp and he was every bit as unhinged as she was. He must have met her on the road, they fought, she was hurt, he drove off with her and killed her. God knows where he dumped her. He could be anywhere in the country.'

'Well, the police are looking for him. Not only on suspicion of murder. They're just longing for a big drugs bust.'

'Oh yes, we've figured that one out! And Christian can deliver, I'm sure. I try not to imagine what he's mixed up in, but he's probably the lynchpin to an almighty international racket.'

Jo grinned, shaking her head. 'Lynchpin? No way. He's a small-time dealer and courier, and it's no surprise he's gone underground. It's not just the police. There are some seriously nasty guys on the war path.'

'I think I've spoken to some of them. They keep calling. I'm terrified they'll descend on Llys y Garn and knee-cap Sylvia, if she refuses to give him up.'

'Wouldn't put it past them. They'll get him in the end, you know, if the fuzz don't.'

'How did you find all this? The police won't tell us a thing.'

'Nor me. They'd choke on it.' Jo shrugged. 'But Al has contacts. Through the clinic.'

'Clinic?'

'The Taverner Clinic? Battersea? He more or less finances it. You'll have heard about Kim's troubles, I suppose. She was destined for the RCM, poor kid. Instead, she finished up in rehab. Al was so preoccupied with his bloody restoration work, he didn't realise the problem until too late. He's never forgiven himself. It's why he's so dead set on covering her back, even now. I tell him, he can take it too far.'

'The police claim he put someone in hospital with a fractured skull.'

Jo sniffed. 'Tracy Miller? And whose fault was that? She was Kim's supplier. Al told the Bill and it turned out they were running her as an informer. They wanted him to keep quiet, not rock the boat, would you believe? Al was so mad. He tried warning her off, then he came home one day and found her, cool as a cucumber, in our kitchen with Kim. So he marched her to the door and threw her, well, pushed her out. Wouldn't you? She went flying, hit her head on the steps. He was the one who took her to hospital. And then we made sure she was outed, big-time. The police had to whisk her off to some safe house when she came out. Wouldn't forgive Al of course.'

'I see.'

'That's why he sticks like a limpet to Kim. Doesn't trust the authorities to protect her. It's what the nomad lifestyle is all about, of course. Where Kim goes, he goes. I keep telling him, she's on her feet now, and if he doesn't stand back, she's going to run and he'll never see her again, but you know Al. Anyway.' She beamed at me. 'It's nothing to your problems, all this shit happening here. So let me help.'

I cursed inwardly. On top of everything else, why couldn't Al's wife be a sour bitch? Why did I have to like her? 'Please do,' I groaned. 'Everything we say to the police just makes things worse. We got off on a lousy start with them earlier in the summer, with the bog body.'

'Yeah, the bog body. I heard. And bones in the crypt. You do seem to have had an extraordinary run of stiffs. Molly will tell you it's the ley line.'

'No, I think it's me.' I tried to smile.

Jo laughed. 'I bet every place as old as this has half a dozen grisly secrets buried away, but no one thinks of looking. Restoration work, then archaeologists, now the fuzz. If they keep digging, you'll probably finish up with a load more.'

'Don't! I don't think we can take any more.'

Jo glanced at the window, wrinkling her nose as rain began to patter on the panes. 'You've taken more than enough already, I think. The doc must have been pretty cut up about the panelling.'

'Cut up is putting it mildly. I'm really worried about him. All that work destroyed for sheer spite, I swear.'

'If it's any consolation, Al is really sweating the police about it. It was way out of order. They could have used radar if they were genuinely suspicious. Didn't have to rip the place apart. He's got them grovelling.'

'Al's the last person they'd grovel to. They've been itching to lock him up and throw away the key, ever since they found him here.'

Jo grinned, hugely amused. 'Yeah. Can't have smelly gippos littering up the countryside. But that was before they spent a day rifling through his laptop – company stats, interviews, all that correspondence with HRH. Not to mention the OBE; that's always a killer.'

'What OBE?'

'Officially it's for the drug rehabilitation stuff, but it did come very quickly after the Windsor job.'

'Windsor?'

'Yeah. Come on. Wasn't that why you called in Taverner Restorations for this place?'

'We called Al in to knock a hole in a kitchen wall,' I said, sourly, realising that Al Taverner, OBE, of Taverner Restorations by Royal Appointment, had taken on our little lodge solely because he wanted our land for his experimental round house. We were the poor suckers of his dreams. 'He doesn't really live in a yurt, does he?'

Jo giggled. 'Not full time. We've got a place in Hampshire, when he can sit still for more than five minutes at a time. The company makes the yurts, as a sideline, you know, and Al reckons that using them when he's out on projects is good advertising. Besides, he's always enjoyed being eccentric.'

'Lucky him.'

She raised her eyes. 'He's a terrible poseur, you must know that.'

'Yes,' I agreed. 'Isn't he.'

The rain set in, running off in torrents and overflowing the drains. I was lying on my bed, with a damp towel over my throbbing eyes, listening to the tattoo beating on the window, when I heard tyres on the gravel and the merciless clang of the front door bell. I staggered down and found DC Phillips and a policewoman standing on the slate step, framed by a grey veil of rain.

'May I speak to Mrs Callister?' said DC Phillips, quite politely.

'Does she need a solicitor?'

'I don't think so, ma'am. We'd just like a word, about her son.'

I stepped back. 'I'll fetch her. Come in.'

Sylvia was in the boot room with Michael, stringing

up the laundry they'd hauled in quickly when the rain had started to tip down.

'The police are here again. They want to speak to you, Sylvia.'

'Oh.' Her hand was at her throat. 'Is there news?'

'Don't worry.' Michael took a sheet from her and dropped it back into the wicker basket. 'I'll come with you.' I could see him steeling himself as he took her hand. Let this at least be an end to the doubt, I thought, as they followed me back to the drawing room.

'Good afternoon.' Sylvia was fighting to compose herself, waiting for the bombshell.

'Sorry to disturb you, ma'am. I'm hoping you can confirm some details about your son's car?'

It caught us by surprise, but Sylvia quickly got a grip on the subject. 'It's red.'

'Yes, ma'am.' Phillips suppressed a smile. 'A Lotus, I think you told us? Do you recall the model?'

'Elan.' Michael was on edge. 'SE Turbo. Convertible. Two door.'

'Good.' Phillips made notes. 'You don't recall the registration?'

Sylvia shook her head helplessly. She couldn't remember her own registration number.

Michael shook his head. 'I should have made a note of it.'

'Something E L,' I said. Something other than H. I remembered seeing it and thinking that HEL would be more appropriate for Christian.

The police officers nodded at each other.

'Can't you check with Swansea?' asked Michael.

Phillips shut his little book. 'There's no car registered to Christian Callister. However, we have found a red Lotus Elan—'

'You've found it?' Sylvia gasped her relief. 'Where is

he?'

'I'm afraid we haven't yet located Mr Callister himself. The car was found abandoned at the side of a road out towards Rhayader. Mid Wales,' he added, as we stared uncomprehending.

'But what was he doing up there?' asked Sylvia.

'You don't have any idea?'

'He drove away,' I said. 'We assumed he'd be going back to London, but he could have been heading anywhere. He has contacts, unpleasant ones, but we don't know who they are.'

'But his car,' said Sylvia. 'Why would he abandon it? What's happened to him?'

'It would appear he ran out of petrol, ma'am,' said Phillips.

'And then?'

'Maybe he hitched a lift?'

'But surely he'd have come back for it by now?'

'Probably not if it wasn't really his,' I suggested, watching Sylvia's face cloud with anxiety. 'Was there any sign of Hannah Quigley?'

'She wasn't in the car,' Phillips conceded. 'Nor any of her clothing or possessions. Forensics are investigating.'

Michael, who had listened in silence, walked over to the window, leaned on the sill, then turned back to face the officers. 'Didn't you find anything in it?'

'No luggage. Whatever he had, he took with him.'

'Drugs. You found no drugs?' insisted Michael. 'Nothing? I know I'd confiscated most of what he had, but maybe… Anything?'

The officers were noncommittal. 'There may have been possible traces. Too early to be sure. Again, it's something for forensic examination to reveal.'

'Oh this waiting!' Sylvia paced the room, her eyes

brimming. 'Please find him.'

'We intend to, ma'am.'

'Tell him, whatever he's done, he's got to face up to it, but I'll stand by him.'

'Oh Sylvia,' I said.

'Yes, I know.' She smiled through her tears. 'Maybe he's done something too terrible even to think about, but I'm still his mother. Nothing can alter that. I'm his mother and I'll be there if he needs me.'

'Yes, ma'am,' said Phillips, sounding almost human.

'That is so like him,' said Tamsin. 'All that fuss about being low on petrol and then he forgot to fill up. And it was a crap car anyway. He thought it was great, all that noise it made, but I think the exhaust was just about to fall off.'

'That sounds like Christian,' I agreed. 'Do you have any idea where he might have been heading?'

She shrugged. 'You know Chris. All that boasting about business deals. I bet it's all drugs really. Mike nicked all his stuff, so maybe he was looking to get some more. He talks about having contacts all over the place. He had something to do once in Manchester. And Hull. I don't know. Who cares, as long as he isn't here.'

'But we need to know what happened to Hannah.'

'Yes, of course. Though nobody liked her, you know.'

'Even so!'

'But she was a pain, wasn't she? Yes I know it would still be horrible if she's been murdered. Chris is so stupid. I mean, why bother murdering her? Even if she'd gone to the police, they wouldn't have taken any notice of her, would they? She's the sort of person no one wants to listen to.'

Tamsin was right of course. I watched her making herself an elaborate sandwich. It involved peanut butter,

Thai green curry paste and a banana. I decided not to look closer. 'Shall I tell you something awful?' She licked smears from her fingers.

'Go on.'

'I sometimes think it would be better if Chris died.'

'Oh Tammy.'

'No, seriously. I told you it was awful, but it's true. He just makes everyone's life a misery and it's not as if he's happy himself. I think he's really unhappy, don't you? Like deep down, he's afraid. And he's so horrible to Mum.'

I swallowed, shell-shocked by her brutal honesty. 'But imagine how she'd feel if she discovered anything had happened to him?'

'But that's it, you see. It's like she's been expecting it for years. With the drugs and his horrible friends and the stupid things he does, like he can't help himself. That's why she's always so worried about him. Expecting the worst. If he just got on with it, she wouldn't have to worry about him anymore. Oh, I know she'd be heartbroken. We all would. But she'd get over it. Don't you think?'

What did I think? I didn't dare to analyse my thoughts. One way or another, things were going to be bad for Sylvia, but Tamsin was right; it was the endless waiting, the not knowing that made everything a hundred times worse. Me and my unique "gift," my ability to tune into death; what had I ever achieved by it? Al, Peter, Tamsin, Michael, they'd all suggested that surely I could use my magical powers to uncover the truth, and I'd brushed them aside, irritated by their lack of understanding, but perhaps they were right. Could I do more? I could at least try. If anyone could find a body, surely I could.

I drove. For two hours, my migraine still nagging, I drove. Phillips had grudgingly agreed to show me on a map where Christian's abandoned car had been discovered, so I was able to find the spot at last, an empty verge of an empty forest road, police tape still tacked to the trees although the Lotus had been carted away for inspection. It was a road going nowhere, from nowhere, in the middle of nowhere. I parked, got out, looked around, into fathomless, sepia depths of regimented firs. What on earth had Christian been doing here? Where had he been, to put him in this empty wilderness? Standing in the silence, I knew the answer. He was here because he was lost. Utterly lost. He'd been lost for a long, long time.

I covered my eyes, remembering our recent encounters, his child's terror, so palpable, even while he threatened me. Had he really intended to kill Hannah? She hadn't died when they'd collided on the road outside Llys y Garn, I knew that. It had been hours later when I'd felt death. Maybe he'd kidnapped her to teach her a lesson, and she'd just died on him. Or maybe he'd brought her this far, to the point where his car failed him, and then, in sheer malicious aggravation, he'd killed her because he had to punish someone. Either way, here he had been, stuck with a dead body and nowhere to go, no friends to turn to: this was as lost as he could get.

What could he have done with her? Tumble her straight into the nearest trees? I stepped over the police tape, searching in the dimming light. It was impossible to go far. Low branches, lifeless and brown, stabbed and scratched at every step, except where the police had thrashed them down. They'd already searched this spot. Hannah wasn't here.

I returned to the road. So he'd carried her. Not uphill.

I followed the road down, as it wound round a steep hillside. Down and round and on forever, with nothing but trees, closing in, suffocating.

Hannah, tell me where you are.

Why wouldn't her body speak to me? I tuned into death when I would give anything to avoid it, but now that I needed the gift, I was empty.

I had walked along the road half a mile, in misty, pattering rain, when I came to a gate, an overgrown track that led down into the unrelenting plantation. A ruined stone shed stood by it, slate roof sagging, and though the interior had been claimed by nettles and brambles, the great stone lintel of its doorway offered me a margin of shelter from the drizzle, while I considered my options. I could go tramping on along the darkening road for ever, or I could turn down that track into the muffling comfort of the woods.

Either choice was utterly hopeless. I was deluding myself. Suddenly, I was overwhelmed by miserable weariness, a desperate longing to be home, to be back with all the petty trials and tribulations whose tedious certainty offered the only comfort there could be. I wanted to sleep, to be out of it.

All I had discovered was a confirmation of my own futility. Christian might have dumped Hannah's body long before he'd reached this place. Nothing spoke to me, one way or another. Silence. Pointless.

It would be night soon. The light was fading, the darkness of the forest seeping out onto the narrow deserted road. I left the derelict hut and trailed back to the car, steeling myself for the long drive back to Llys y Garn. We would wait, and wait and wait, and there was nothing I could do about it.

24

The physical search of our neighbourhood revealed no further clue to Hannah's whereabouts. Police enquiries continued, leaflets went out, posters appeared in shops, hotels and guesthouses were contacted. An appeal was made on local radio. Nothing. There was talk of a mention on *Crimewatch*.

The press ran with the story, but Hannah wasn't a sympathetic subject. They couldn't engineer any glowing quotes about her popularity, her personality, or her promise, there were no tearful relatives to be besieged, and Jo warned them that portrayal of Llys y Garn as an opium den would result in a libel action.

It didn't stop the rumours though, among the customers at the Cemaes Arms, who came to swap tall tales of our diabolical ways: we were cooking crystal meth in the out-buildings; we'd killed Hannah and stashed her away so we could 'discover' yet another body for publicity; we'd silenced her because she'd discovered The Truth about one or other of us – and doubtless more. All we could hope was that people would soon find a new titillating scandal and move on.

Sylvia still wouldn't accept that her son could be a cold-blooded murderer.

'I can't believe he meant to do it. He's not a mindless killer. He loses his temper and just – yes, I know. Whether he meant to kill her or not, it was unforgivable. I'm not running away from it, and he can't either. He must face the consequences. But I have to be there for him, whatever happens.'

Michael put his arms round her, to give her a hug, and I saw the agony in his eyes.

Then it happened.

I was in the walled garden, picking mint at Sylvia's request, when the gate from the orchard swung open and the professor peered through. Many of his students had been summoned home by anxious parents, but he lingered on, ever hopeful. He saw me and advanced portentously. Vicky followed, waving furiously. Something was up and my heart sank.

'Ah,' said Ronnie. 'Good. I thought you would want to know – and it's all totally inexplicable, can't understand it, but I knew you'd—'

'She's alive!' interrupted Vicky. She paused just long enough for me to blink, before rushing on with her explanation. 'She went to a friend and the friend heard the police appeal this morning, and got in touch. Well, apparently…'

She talked, and my mind was spinning, until it plunged into the black hole opening for it. Hannah was alive. And yet I'd felt death. There were times when I no longer knew what I was feeling about anything, but I had that one certainty: I had felt a death.

Not Hannah.

Christian.

It was just as I had first supposed, that long night, as I'd lain, riddled with guilt about my murderous thoughts. My demonic powers seemed a self-obsessed fantasy now. Something far more tangible that my evil thoughts must have finished him. Something like a knife. A Ray Mears knife. Wielded by someone who'd kill Christian without compunction. Someone who'd been out on the roads north of here when it had happened.

My eyes turned automatically to the Great Hall, where I could hear the clatter of work continuing.

'Anyway,' Vicky was bubbling with happiness, 'we

knew you'd want to hear at once.'

'Yes. Yes, thank you. It's wonderful news. I'll go and tell Sylvia now. She'll be so relieved.'

Sylvia and Michael were in the kitchen, brooding over the ingredients for a dinner none of us really wanted. She looked up as I entered and gasped at the sight of my face. 'Kate! What is it?'

'Hannah is alive,' I said.

For a moment there was stunned silence.

'She's alive,' I repeated. 'She wasn't attacked.'

'Ah! Ah!' Sylvia's shrieks were a mixture of laughter, shock and hysteria, as she grabbed the table for support. 'He didn't kill her. I knew it. I knew it!'

Michael lowered her into a chair before she collapsed, still in a daze himself.

I tried to talk calmly, rationally, explaining for his sake, because I doubted that Sylvia was taking in a word of it. 'When she ran off, her shoe broke and then she cut her foot on a broken bottle, and sat down to cry by the side of the road. That's where a couple found her. Tourists. Just moving on to the Brecon Beacons. They gave her a lift somewhere. Carmarthen, I think Vicky said. Nobody seems to know precisely how she got there, but she finished up at the house of an old school friend in Northampton.' I resolutely talked on, as Sylvia rocked, hands over her mouth, and Michael stared, blankly. 'She was gibbering that everyone hated her and was trying to poison her and steal her toothbrush. So, for the last few days she'd been in hospital, receiving psychiatric evaluation and tetanus injections.'

'I see,' said Michael. Sylvia was groping blindly for his hand.

'Vicky can explain more. I think she's going to come here if she can persuade Ronnie to get back to his

302

students.' I looked at the two of them, adrift in shock and confusion. 'I'll leave you two to talk. I'll be upstairs.'

I would be upstairs because I needed the privacy of my own room, time and space to face up to a new horror.

Why couldn't it have been Hannah?

What was I thinking? Poor girl, it had been obvious all along that she was having a breakdown. She'd arrived already in its throes and the summer school had merely exacerbated it. None of us had thought to help her, because she was just an unwelcome nuisance, impinging on our far more interesting lives. No one had bothered to ask what traumas had sparked her collapse. If we had, that might have been all the therapy she'd needed, but nobody cared to listen. She'd been left to drown in our contemptuous indifference. I'd even laughed when she was exiled from her prized place at the professor's side. That must have doubled her sense of exclusion. Christian's malicious presence would have been more than enough to unleash her most paranoid ravings.

She was a sad, pathetic creature and I felt rightly guilty. I should have felt pity too, but it was no good. I could only wish Hannah at the bottom of the ocean.

I stood at my window, watching the wind running through the long grass of the meadow, watching the trees bend and shiver. I had once thought, triumphantly, Al could kill Christian and I wouldn't blame him.

I pictured it. Al, driving in search of Kim who had gone to Aberystwyth. Chancing upon Christian as he was trying to hitch a ride, in the black of night, in the middle of nowhere. Christian, the malicious little drugs dealer, who would always be a threat to Kim and her like. Christian, whose removal could only make the

303

world a cleaner place.

Al wouldn't have given it a second thought, would he? Any more than he'd thought twice about throwing Kim's dealer down stairs. Any more than he'd hesitated about bloodying a little mugger in the park. Al has his own take on justice, Jo said.

Violence had always disgusted me. I'd tasted too much of its shadow to find it anything other than despicable, and yet – and yet I'd uncovered uncomfortable equivocation when it came to Al and violence. The allure of the alpha male? It might have amused me once, but now the thought of Al murdering Sylvia's son, in cold blood, made my own blood ran cold.

What was I supposed to do? Tell the police? Avoid him like a leper? Or pray that he got away with it?

He wouldn't have a moment's regret for what he had done, I was sure of that. But Sylvia would. Oh God.

'What am I going to do, Kate?' said Sylvia, topping up her wine for the fourth or fifth time. Our dutiful supper had turned into a celebration feast, and Sylvia was celebrating with a vengeance. She was already a little too loud, a little too voluble, even for Sylvia. 'I have to settle things with Christian, you see that, don't you?'

'Mum, don't,' said Tamsin, to no effect.

'No, but listen,' said Sylvia. 'Look at Hannah, you see! She needed help. We should have helped her, shouldn't we?'

'Sylvia—'

'And Christian's the same. He needs help. I'm going to help him. I keep wanting him to love me, you see. That's the mistake. It doesn't matter if he doesn't love me. It doesn't matter if he hates me, just as long as I help him, 's long as he gets better. That's all that matters, isn't it? If only we could find him.'

'I'm sure…,' I began, and stopped, not knowing what to say. I met Michael's eyes, and saw, in them, my own despairing conviction. Of course. There had been a death, I'd said, and he'd believed me. He understood, as I did, who it must be. Part of me was grateful that I could share this appalling secret. Another part was terrified that he too had identified the murderer. But I could see in his grieving eyes only concern for what awaited Sylvia. The who or how was of no importance. All that mattered was that Sylvia's dreams of restitution were utterly doomed.

'I don't suppose the police will bother looking for him anymore, if he's not a murder suspect,' said Tamsin, running her finger round the cream bowl.

'Oh but they have to find him. They must. I'll report him missing. That's what I should do, isn't it, Mike?'

'Yes,' he said, leaning across to kiss her cheek. 'That's what you should do.'

She laughed. 'Such a weight off my shoulders, knowing the worst isn't true. I mean, how could I have believed it? My own son. Well, I'll make up for it. I know things are going to be difficult but I'm going to do it, sort him out and never let anything like this happen again. And you're going to help me, aren't you, my love?'

'Yes, of course,' murmured Michael.

The farcical feast over, Sylvia was too unsteady on her feet to attempt the washing up. 'I'll do it,' I said, rescuing glasses from her.

'Yes, come on, Mum.' Tamsin guided her. 'Come up with me. I've got to get tweeting, tell them the Quigley's safe and sound after all.'

'All right, all right. I'm all right.' With Tamsin's support, Sylvia made it up the stairs, singing.

305

Leaving me looking at Michael.

'The Quigley's safe and sound,' he repeated softly.

'Yes.' I began plunging cutlery. 'That's good news, isn't it?'

He was silent for so long, I thought perhaps he hadn't heard. Then, 'Yes. Of course it's good news. But you know someone died.'

I was scrubbing compulsively. 'I don't know. I'm a mad woman. Sometimes I think odd things, and the next moment—'

'You were certain someone died that night?'

I gave up. 'Yes, that's what I thought then.'

'It wasn't Hannah.'

'No it wasn't Hannah.'

'So it was Christian?'

'Yes. Perhaps.'

'It was Christian.' He paused. 'I've always known it was Christian. He's dead and she's waiting for him to come home.'

'I know.' I clutched at a handful of forks. 'Poor Sylvia, what's it going to do to her?'

'It will destroy her.'

'There's nothing I can do.'

'No. Nothing. It's all too late. Nothing can be undone.'

'And all because – oh damn it!' A plate slipped from my fingers and smashed. 'Damn, damn, damn!'

'Leave it,' said Michael. 'Kate. Leave it. Go on up. I'll sort it out.'

'Are you sure?' I wanted nothing better than to escape.

'Yes,' he said softly. 'I'll finish it.'

I lay on my bed for a while, in the dark, listening to rain beating on my window, lashing the panes in torrential gusts, as I wallowed in my guilt. Guilt for wishing Christian dead, guilt for not thinking how Sylvia would be devastated, guilt for recognising a murderer in Al and not condemning him.

But how could I condemn him? I couldn't really know for sure that Christian was dead, let alone that Al had killed him. Except that I could picture it so clearly, it seemed impossible I hadn't witnessed it. At what point had Christian realised that this was the end, that he couldn't talk or bully or threaten or wheedle his way out of this last confrontation? Had he been terrified? It was Christian's fear that came back to me now, not his loathsome malice. If I'd been a drug dealer, alone in a dark place with Al, I would have been petrified.

How had Christian got to be like that? We'd watched him change, over the years, the gold tarnishing, the promise wasted, the hopes deflating. Why hadn't we done something to stop the rot? Sylvia had tried, oh how she had tried, but she'd never got it right. She'd failed because she was alone. I'd stood by and watched his fall with disdain; I'd wished him dead.

I was overwhelmed by pounding regret, a longing to undo what could never be undone. Hopelessness, darkness, shame, despair; it sucked me down. I'd done nothing to reach out to Christian, even though I'd felt his fear. I'd felt it because that was what I did. I was tuned into people's emotions, not just their deaths. I felt…,

I felt people's emotions.

I was tuned in.

Stupid woman! I sat up, so abruptly my head span. Stupid, stupid woman. Of course I was tuned in, but I hadn't had the wit to see it. So wound up with my own feelings, didn't I realise that all this guilt and despair washing around me wasn't mine? How long had I been walking in another's agony? The murderous anger, the guilt and grief, the sense of Hell. All doubts within me evaporated like water in a hot pan, sizzled away by the sudden blinding understanding of what had been going on. I took one small step to the side and, in an instant, everything was aligned, everything dropped into place.

It wasn't Al.

It was Michael.

I didn't know what he'd done, but I knew that he'd done it. And was living with it, regretting it, torturing himself with it.

I got up, heart pounding. Months before, I'd felt Leo's lurch towards death from halfway across London and I'd failed to acknowledge it until it was too late. I'd felt my mother's slow slide into oblivion, grieving for my absence, from a hundred miles away and there had been nothing I could do. This time, surely, I could react. I could do something.

How long had I been wallowing there? Long enough for Michael to have come up to bed, except that he hadn't. I'd have heard him, but the house was silent except for the beating of the rain.

I ran downstairs. The kitchen was empty, dishes left drying on the draining board. I opened the drawing room door, taking in the rumpled cushions, Tamsin's discarded trainers, Sylvia's magazine. Everything just as it had been earlier in the evening, except for the letter, white as a ghost, on the mantelpiece. I picked it up, my fingers shaking, and read the clear lettering, Michael's hand, made studiously neat for this final purpose. To whomsoever it may concern.

For a second my finger hovered, ready to rip the envelope open, then instead I thrust it in my pocket. What did a letter matter? It was Michael I needed to find now, not an explanation.

Where? I thought of the Great Hall, the pointless vandalising of Michael's work.

Splintered panelling was piled, a mound of black in the enveloping darkness of the hall. No Michael. I groped inside the black interior of the exposed priest hole, brushing aside the horrors within as easily as swatting a fly. Let them exhale! I no longer cared about them. It was Michael's new fresh agony that mattered. The ancient horror parted before me, faded and sank back into the stonework. But the priest hole was empty.

Where else? His workshop?

I stumbled in the dark, in icy rain, without a torch or a coat, running up against something sharp as I groped for the light. The workshop was empty, that was what I cared about, not the chisel that had ripped my jeans and drawn blood from my thigh. Where then? In God's name, where?

The river. No. Please. I was already racing down the drive when it came to me. The place where Michael would be, because I'd told him it was the place to be. A place of execution, I'd called it.

He was there, as I knew he would be. The overhanging rocks and trees held the mire in a cup of impenetrable darkness, but as I reached the place, scratched and torn and panting for breath, the rain eased, billowing clouds parted and moonlight streamed through. A gibbous moon. Shadows seeped and shifted, as the clouds boiled around it.

'Michael?'

He was sitting, his back against a tree, legs crossed, one hand on his heart, the other extended, like a Buddha set in this shrine to misery. As I spoke his name, his eyes moved slowly from the oily waters to me. 'Kate.'

'What are you doing here?'

309

'It's too late, Kate.' His voice was dreamy, distant, as if the cold and the rain had seeped too deeply into him.

'No. No. It isn't. Michael, whatever you did, don't shoulder all the blame. Listen. Christian's been doomed for a long time. Sooner or later, he was going to kill himself, or his friends would catch up with him, or—'

'No excuse.' He bowed his head for a moment, before raising his eyes back to mine. 'Do you know the worst of it? I caught myself wanting the girl dead.'

'Yes, I know. I understand, Michael. If Christian had murdered her, that would have been justification—'

'No justification!' He was almost fierce for a moment. 'How could I have let myself imagine there could ever be justification? You see, Kate, when corruption sets in, it destroys all decency. The girl's alive, and Christian isn't a murderer. Just a pathetic boy. He was always just a pathetic boy.'

'Yes, he was a pathetic boy, who was bent on killing himself. Perhaps that's what he did, Michael. Perhaps he killed himself. You can't know that you were to blame.'

The clouds closed in again. Out of the darkness came his voice. 'I killed him.'

'How?' I had an idea that if I just kept talking, we would come through this, he would return to the house, we would sort something out.

I heard him sigh. A reluctant sigh, as he forced himself to respond. 'His secret stash you gave me. When was that? Years ago, it seems. I made up some tablets. Lethal. Quick. Painless, I hope.'

You planned to kill him even then? I was about to ask, but I already knew the answer. He'd had no thought of killing Christian when he'd made those little doses of death. For safe-keeping, I'd given potentially lethal drugs to a man I knew had suffered from

310

appalling depression. He'd analysed them, because he would, and idly, without precise intent, he'd constructed the perfect suicide pill. Because he could. He'd made them for himself, I was sure of that. Not with any thought of using them, but just in some abstract memory of his worse suicidal moments. A memento, because he was no longer suicidally depressed; he had Sylvia and all her life-affirming joy.

And then he had Christian, and the darkness swept back.

'I understand.'

'He *spat* at her, Kate. He was bent on destroying her and everything she had. I couldn't take it. I couldn't let him continue to hurt her. It came over me, such a rage. And then I remembered these.'

The moonlight was back, dancing like devils in the dell. In his outstretched hand as he opened it, I could see two small oval pills.

'You put one in his car when you confiscated that bloody wash bag?'

'Yes. Pushed into the passenger seat. I knew he'd be desperate before too long. I'd taken his supply but he'd look, he'd hope…' His words died away.

'He'd hope you'd missed something?'

'Just one,' said Michael. 'Not enough for him to sell. Just one.'

'And almost as soon as he'd gone, you regretted it. I know you did, Michael. You drove out to look for him, you phoned, you were desperate for the police to look for him. That's what counts.'

'No. All that was too late.' He was staring at the two pills in his hand.

'What are you going to do with them?' I tried to keep the panic out of my voice. 'Why don't you give them to me?'

He slowly shook his head, then, with an effort, flicked them out into the mire. They settled, sank, and were gone.

I heaved a sigh of relief. 'Thank God. Michael, leave it now. Come back to the house. We can talk there, but come away from here, before you catch your death.'

He smiled. In the ghostly light, I could see him struggling to keep his eyes open. 'Too late, Kate.'

'No! There were only three, weren't there? Michael! How many tablets did you make? Tell me you only made three.'

'Four,' he managed, with an effort.

I'd been kneeling near him but, with my heart pounding, I leapt to my feet. I should have realised he'd already taken one. I groped in my pockets. A letter but no phone. The camp. It was only two or three hundred yards down the hill. I stopped before I'd run half a dozen steps, remembering, Jo had taken them off to some get-together in Narberth. She'd invited me. Nobody would be there.

Then I would have to fight and scramble and blunder my way back to the house, just as I'd fought my way here, in the dark through the trees, losing my way, ripping and tripping and twisting ankles, so that I could phone.

I could go down and call for help that would arrive too late, or I could stay with Michael.

The answer was obvious. Just for once, get it right.

I turned back.

'Michael? I'm here.'

25

The stones were cold, so cold that my skin no longer registered the minute grains and undulations biting into my back. My legs no longer felt the wet, wiry prickle of the turf. This was eternity; no feeling, no sensations, just empty stillness.

The darkness had faded, pallor seeping out to the distant milky smear of the sea, long before the sun edged up over the hills behind me. The valley below was a sea of white, engulfing trees, houses, farms; rivers of mist flowing into every crease and fold of the land. I heard birds, a raven's harsh croak and cows lowing, the occasional panicking bleat of sheep, a dog's bark. Somewhere, down in the valley, a cockerel. No humans. No voices, for once no traffic. This was a world, briefly, without Man, and therefore a world without evil.

It didn't last long, this cold, still emptiness. From somewhere came the hum of a passing car, then another, then the cough and moan of distant machinery.

A man appeared, at the top of the track leading from the excavations. Al. Clear of the trees, he paused, peering along to the stones hunched behind me, his hand shading his eyes. He was looking into the sun, the molten brass disc that I had not yet turned to acknowledge, although its glow was full on him, spilling colour across the empty moors.

He saw me, raised his hand in greeting, and strode towards me.

'Kate? Are you all right?'

I couldn't break out of the silent stillness to answer him. I merely watched as he approached, urgency in his step although his face registered wary relief. He looked down at me, figuring how to cope, then he dropped beside me as if to enjoy the view.

'Been here long?' His fingers tested the wet grass, as his eyes took in my sodden clothes. He already knew the answer.

'Some time,' I said, though it wasn't true. No time: that was the meaning of eternity. One endless moment, without beginning or end.

He pulled off his sweater. Hand knitted. The frizz of the wool felt alien against me, as he tugged it round my shoulders. Warm. I didn't want to be warm. His arm around me prevented me from shrugging it off.

'What's the matter, Kate? What's happened?'

I was going to have to break out of this capsule of isolation. Move. Speak.

'Sylvia called me,' he explained. 'She's worried. Michael never came to bed and when she went looking for you, you weren't there either. She's in a panic.'

'Yes. Of course. Poor Sylvia.'

'Have you been out here all night, Kate?'

'No. Not all night.'

'It rained. You're drenched. And hurt! Look. You're scratched and bruised and there's blood on your leg.'

I looked down at torn, soaked denim. 'Oh. Yes. I walked into something.'

Al was looking me over for worse damage. 'Maybe you should come down now?' he suggested softly. 'You're like ice. We don't want hypothermia.' Cluck, cluck. This was how he worried over Kim.

I would have to go, to humour him, but my limbs wouldn't move. Had the stones claimed me? I didn't mind. It was a good place to stay.

He gathered me up, raising me to my feet, rubbing life back into my arms and legs. 'I searched around, then I thought of the stones. Kate, why are you here?'

'Keeping company,' I said. My jaw was frozen.

'Have you seen Michael?'

'Yes. Yes, I was with him. He's dead.'

I felt Al's body stop. The brusque warming caresses, the natural shift and stirring of life all stopped. He froze. Only his heartbeat continued, faster. 'Are you certain?'

'Oh yes.'

'Dead.'

'Yes.'

He'd recovered from his shock, concentrating once more on the crisis that was Kate Lawrence. 'Explain later. I'm taking you home.'

Very manly, I thought, as he lifted me up like a child. Romantic novel hero. Rough trade, mystic quester, murder suspect, company director, yurt maker to the Queen, OBE. Alistair Taverner, poseur. No posing now as he strode down the slope. I watched his Adam's apple constrict, and felt his anxiety.

Somewhere inside me, some motor coughed back into life. I felt my blood flowing, the shivering, the aches. 'Stop,' I said. 'Put me down.'

'Kate, you're in no—'

'I'm all right. I'll be all right. Really.' I pushed his chest, forcing him to set me down. I shook my hair and stood straight, to convince him I was capable. 'I need to take you to him. It was what I was waiting for, I think. I couldn't manage on my own. Come.'

I set off along the slope, skirting boulders, tussocks, mud and dips, as instinct carried me over all the pitfalls. It was Al who stumbled, racing to keep up with me.

The trees showered us as we passed under them, brushing our way through, down to the chapel gloom of the pit.

Michael was as I had left him, still propped against

the tree, stiff, cold, lifeless. I'd held his hand as he died, just as I'd held my father's hand all those years ago, in childish innocence, but this time I knew death when it came. I recognised the moment when the guilt and despair found their final release and it was no longer Michael that I held.

Afterwards I'd crawled up to the stones. Up to the silent stillness that devoured and forgave everything.

The dell, in daylight, was an empty place. Al and I were lumbering intruders, but we had to be there. Things had to be done.

Al pulled me back, interposing himself between me and death, as if I were too delicate for such a concept. I, of all people.

He felt for Michael's pulse. Too late by hours. He drew back, eyes closed, breathing deeply. Then he steadied himself. 'Come on. Let me take you down to the camp. There's nothing we can do for him here.'

'Yes there is.' I pulled free from his touch. 'We can carry him down.'

'I don't know. Should we move him? The police will have to—'

'The police aren't going to dictate what happens to Michael!' Anger growled within me. 'No!' I knelt, lifting an ice-cold hand, aware of my own physical weakness. I didn't want him dragged like a sack of coal. 'Can you fetch the others?'

Al hesitated for a moment, then gave in. 'Okay.'

As he ran, I faced that dark place. No horrors now. Michael's death had imprinted nothing on the overhanging rocks. His quiet resignation had gone with him. There was nothing left.

Nothing but that last thing, the emotion I couldn't name, but it was here still, a faint whisper at first, a flicker, a shadow of a shadow, and in the silence and the waiting it grew, until it echoed from the rocks, seethed from the green waters, hissed among the trees. What it was, I didn't know, but it was at war with this scene, with Michael lying dead. We were being rejected, Michael and I. I could almost feel a force expelling us.

'Kate?' Al was back, with a sombre cortège; Thor, Baggy, Padrig. Jo slipped her arm around me. 'Come on, love. We'll look after him. Come down and get yourself dry before you catch pneumonia.'

Molly was waiting to usher me into the yurt. I was guided like an invalid into a cane chair heaped with embroidered cushions, while she peeled off my clammy clothes. She tucked a quilt round me and put a mug of steaming tisane in my hands. There was an occasional sob from a white-faced Kim, but no one spoke. I'd never heard the camp so silent. It was as if the trees themselves were in shock.

Then we heard them coming with Michael; speechless tramping. I stood up, belting up the baggy velvet pants, the tie-dye top and the shawl Molly had pulled on me. A clown. Comedy and tragedy in one. 'Will you keep him here?' I asked. 'Just for quarter of an hour or so? I must go down to tell Sylvia. Give me a moment with her.'

Jo laid a hand on my arm. 'We'll take care of him.'

*

Sylvia was in the lane, arms clasped round herself. She watched my approach as if she already knew.

'He's dead, isn't he?'

I'd been wondering how to say it but she made it horribly simple. 'Yes.'

Sylvia looked at me, blankly. 'Why?'

I shook my head.

'I shouldn't have gone to sleep. I should have waited

317

for him.'

'No, Sylvia, it wouldn't have—'

'Yes!' She screamed. 'Yes! Yes! Yes!' She sobbed and I held her to me. 'Why?' she wailed. 'Why did he leave me? Why couldn't he have talked to me? We always talked. We told each other everything.'

How could I explain that that was what had killed him? He could never tell her the one thing that he needed to confess: that he had killed her son. That was something she should never know, so we hugged each other without words, sobbing into each other's hair.

'Where is he?' she asked at last. 'I want him here.'

''They're bringing him down, Sylvia. They're bringing him home.' I turned her back, towards the house, feeling her weight slump against me, grief and disbelief consuming her.

Tamsin was at the kitchen door, anticipating the worst. 'Mum? Mum, oh Mum.' While mother and daughter hugged each other, I thought, now, enough of this self-indulgence, Kate Lawrence. You're the practical one. Be practical.

When a doctor arrived to confirm Michael's death and attend to Sylvia, I had a moment to retreat to my own room and change out of my clown outfit. Molly had brought down my sodden clothes, and as I pulled them from their canvas bag, I felt again the crumpled letter, still in the pocket. I drew it out, ripped open the soggy envelope and unfolded the paper. The ink had run and blotted in places, but it was still legible.

'*I, Michael Bradley, am solely responsible for the death of Christian Callister. I was not prompted or encouraged by any other person...*' All that followed was a chemistry dissertation, pure and simple. There was no message of love or excuse, no quest for absolution, just a full explanation of means and methods. He hadn't been interested in justifying himself, but solely in ensuring that no one else would be blamed.

Only now that it was too late, did I appreciate the extent to which I had been drinking in Michael's emotions over the past weeks, from the moment when Christian had killed the dog and that fatal thought had crept into Michael's mind: if only he were dead and she were free. Michael's thoughts, my thoughts. Perhaps it was because they were so similar that I'd failed to understand I was reading his soul, sharing his shocked perception of hell and damnation, the knowledge that in a moment of impulsive fury, he had crossed beyond excuses, into the abyss.

He'd sunk ever deeper, until Hannah was found alive and all the desperate little excuses finally petered out. Sylvia was steeling herself to sort out the disaster that was her son, and Michael, in that momentary, black determination to set her free, had robbed her of the hope of ever doing so.

I had sat beside him, whispering that he was not to blame, that he was forgiven, but who was I, racked with my own guilt and worries, to offer him absolution? The monstrous penalty for murder that killed him was that sense of damnation, the unbreakable taboo broken, trust betrayed, love ruined. The only judgement that Michael cared about was his own.

I folded the letter back into its envelope, and hid it in the depths of my underwear drawer. If and when Christian was found, if and when some innocent person stood accused of killing him, then it would be the moment to bring it out. Until then, no need for anyone to know.

'He used to suffer from terrible depression,' Sylvia explained, rocking herself on the sofa, drowsy with sedatives. 'When Annette was dying. His children never understood that. Oh God, his children. Someone's got to tell them. I know they never bothered with him, but I ought—'

'Shsh,' I reassured her. 'I've made sure they're being told.'

'They thought he should have helped their mother kill herself, you know. But he couldn't.' She sobbed, despite the drugs. 'He couldn't kill her, but now he's killed himself. Why didn't he talk to me? Why wouldn't he let me help him? I knew the depression was back, he was so low.'

That was the eventual verdict. Depression. Jo played up the police harassment, his wronged reputation and the barbarous destruction of his craftsmanship. All she got from them was a grudging expression of regret, but she had provided the explanation. Michael had a history of mental illness: he had, after all, thrown away a lucrative career to whittle wood in a Welsh backwater, and that couldn't be the action of a sane man. No suicide note was found, but the distresses of his last few days surely explained it all.

Everyone was sympathetic. There was genuine sorrow. I shielded Sylvia until the sedatives and the hysteria wore off and she subsided into numbing grief. By then she didn't care what she or other people said or did. She would never have harmed herself deliberately, but Tamsin stayed with her, day and night, holding her hand, making tea, crying with her while I did all the rest, answered the phone, made the arrangements.

And all the while there was no news of Christian. But no one was looking for him anymore.

'You'd have thought he would have come,' said Sylvia. 'For this.' It was the day of the funeral, that awful ritual of British restraint and dignity, before the state of limbo could end. We'd waited an eternity, with the inquest and so many complications to resolve. Vicious battles politely fought.

'I know they didn't get on,' she said, 'but surely Christian could have forgiven him now. No.' She sighed, as I squeezed her hand. 'I should know better. But I can't help hoping. A mother never lets go, you know.'

'I know.'

Sarah, Sylvia's elder daughter, an American trip cut short, kissed her mother and gave me a helpless smile. 'It must have been awful for you,' she said, as I relinquished Sylvia to Tamsin's care, and took brief charge of baby Liam. 'I don't know how Mum has coped. Poor Mike, such a lovely man. And you've had ghastly troubles of your own. I mean, I don't know of course, but I heard, sort of—'

'What? Oh, yes, Peter's back with Gabrielle and preparing for fatherhood.'

'Oh, poor Kate.' She looked at me guiltily as I bounced her baby on my arm. Innocent blue eyes – just like Christian's.

'We won't begrudge Peter his babakins, will we, Liam?'

Liam blew a raspberry in reply.

'Quite so.' I smiled at Sarah. 'No call for taking sides. I'm not expecting you to draw swords against Peter. He's still Phil's friend. It really wasn't an acrimonious parting. I wish him well.'

Sarah, a younger version of her mother, grimaced sympathetically. 'Good for you. But it's such a mess.'

The drawing room was crowded. We could have used

the Great Hall, but even though Al had made an expert job of repairing and replacing the splintered panelling, it still remained a monument to the futility of Michael's life.

Our party might have been even more cramped, but Michael's children, chill and disapproving in their elegant black, had announced, after the short secular service at the crematorium, that there would be sherry and refreshments at a Tenby hotel for any of Michael's *old* friends who chose to attend. Some of his former colleagues from industry felt obliged to go. His later friends, from the bohemian world of galleries and crafts, followed us back to Llys y Garn.

Dewi Hughes was there, in his chapel suit. 'He was a good man,' he said. At least he'd forgiven us for the sin of Murk, though the repercussions rolled on; they'd told me at the post office that Dewi was going to live with a sister in Lampeter. His heart was no longer in the farm, now that he was all alone, so Hendre Hywel was up for auction.

Ronnie came. The summer school had been wound up, but the professor told me he hoped to publish their interesting findings. He didn't mention the bog body which was, in the circumstances, very wise.

Al and his team were there. Annwfyn was dismantled, only the round house remaining, abandoned to the badgers and foxes. They were moving on, Molly told me, to a New Age community in Scotland, but they would stay for the funeral.

Al came across to join me. 'How are you?'

'Fine, really. Thanks for coming.'

He gave me a quaint look.

'Sorry,' I said. 'Of course you came. I'm just in a groove of polite nothings. It saves having to think.'

'Funerals can be numbing.'

'Yes. But this one shouldn't be, should it? Michael deserves a bit better. I feel I should have arranged a fanfare or something.'

'You've done just fine,' said Al. Sylvia had joined us and he gave her a kiss. 'Keep the faith, sister.'

She laughed, then cried, and he hugged her.

'I wish they could have…,' She sniffed, waving her hands vaguely. 'I wanted to scatter his ashes among the standing stones, but they want them buried with their mother's. I suppose that's right, but I wish – I wanted to say goodbye. I don't feel I've said goodbye. It doesn't feel right, any of this.'

'Come on,' said Al. 'Out of that black dress. Put on your brightest rags, Sylvia. This is a wake, a celebration. Michael wants you laughing. That's what he loved in you.'

He was right. Everyone there felt he was right. Those who wouldn't were sipping sherry in Tenby. So we had a wake for Michael; Kim played her violin, Padrig played the tin whistle and Molly had a bodhran. Drink appeared from nowhere. Everyone laughed and sang and danced, and we all got very tipsy. Michael's sculptures were brought out of the woods to the lane, as a parade of honour, and because the Windhover, which had embodied Michael's spirit, was wrecked beyond repair, we made a pyre of it. With the moon rising, we carried the ashes up to Bedd y Blaidd, to scatter them as Sylvia had wished.

'She's laughing.' Tamsin took my arm. 'I'm so glad. I thought she was never going to laugh again. It's all been so shitty!'

'Yes, it has.'

'I'm thinking I might not go back to Bristol.'

'Tammy, why not?'

'I don't like leaving Mum and I don't want you to feel

you have to take responsibility for it all.'

I looked at my niece. She'd grown up. Not the way I would have wanted it to happen, but we can't always dictate our rites of passage. 'What your mother wants, most of all, is for you to go back to university, spread your wings and prove you haven't been irrevocably damaged by all this. Get your degree and then worry about her, if she needs it. Until then, she's got me, and I'm not going anywhere.'

'But it doesn't seem fair on you to have to cope.'

'It is fair,' I insisted. Not that caring for Sylvia would be a punishment, but if it were, it would be no more that I deserved. Maybe the only sensible penance was to help others to pick up their pieces.

'I'm glad we did this.' Tamsin looked round at the drunken crooning crowd. 'It seems right, doesn't it?'

'It does.'

'And you know the best bit? My brother hasn't turned up to spoil it all.'

He was there though. Haunting the proceedings. Haunting me, at least. I'd always claimed I didn't see ghosts, but it hadn't stopped me helping to create them.

'You look as if you're about to opt out of the party,' said Al.

I forced a smile. 'No. Thanks for helping with this. It was exactly what we needed.' We walked along the hilltop, looking down on the treetops, the dark hollow of the valley, the gleaming roof slates far below. 'And thanks for getting the hall sorted out.'

'My pleasure.'

'Your business, you mean.' I thought wryly of the website I had belatedly discovered. Taverner Restorations. Screeds of technical details and endless photographs of Llys y Garn under 'Recent Projects;' new beams being pegged into place, Thor fitting the last stone into the oriel window, Nathan repairing intricate lead guttering. Plus a full page on the round house. 'At least we provided you with good advertising. Alistair Taverner, OBE.'

He smiled. 'It really was my pleasure. What will you do now?'

'I don't know. There seems to be endless tidying up. Michael didn't leave a will, which means all his money and shares and suchlike go to his children, and I have a feeling they'll want every last scrap that can be identified as his.'

'What about the house?'

'Mike and Sylvia were joint owners, so she gets it. Of course that is one of their little resentments.'

'Of course.'

'I'm sorry about the round house. The planning department is adamant.'

'Don't worry about it. The squirrels were going to get it, anyway.'

'Would you prefer to take it down, yourself?'

'No, let them have the satisfaction. Small pleasures for small minds.' He could shrug it off, now his experiment was over. Doubtless he had new projects lined up. He was probably on his way to rebuild Balmoral.

'When are you leaving?' I asked. This was after all the end of the summer. In every sense.

'I'm off to London tomorrow. Business to see to; the Kent job to tidy up. Then it's on to Denmark.'

'Denmark?'

'A major project. I really need to be there from the start.'

'But Molly said you were all off to Scotland.'

Al smiled. 'Molly, Pryderi and Kim. They're the devotees. The rest of us are just honest labourers, going where the work takes us.'

'Honest labourer. Ha! You're letting Kim go alone this time then?'

'Yep. I'm letting go. She's been pretty shaken up by Michael, you know. She liked him. We all did. Anyway, she's talking about applying to college again next year, so I'm going to stand back and let her work it out for herself.'

'That's wise. And brave. You'll be a long way away from her, in Denmark.'

'I know, but Jo will be on hand. She's joining a firm in Newcastle, so she'll keep an eye on her.'

I glanced across at Jo who was laughing drunkenly into Padrig's beard. 'I see. She's not going with you.'

'I did tell you her trip to Peru was a trial separation.' Al gave his wife a friendly wave. A brotherly wave. She waved back in a sisterly fashion.

We stood silent for a moment, watching the moonlight blaze silver on the distant sea. All things were finishing. Ends needed tying.

'Al.' I half turned to him. 'Could you have killed Christian?'

I'd thought the question might surprise or shock or offend, but it did none of those things. 'No need,' he said easily, hands in his pockets. 'You think he's dead, don't you? Wouldn't surprise me. Someone was going to get him in the end.'

He hadn't answered my question. Better, perhaps, if I never knew.

26

Sylvia and I sat alone in the kitchen, listening to the clock ticking. Tamsin had reluctantly returned to Bristol, Sarah and Phil had gone home, Taverner Restorations had moved on, the holiday season was over. No visitors any more, apart from occasional voyeurs, peering up our drive, eager for a glimpse of the Hammer House of Horrors.

Sylvia was marking the pine table top with her knife. She was thinking of Christian, I could tell, but I wasn't prepared for her words. She sighed deeply, but with no sign of incipient tears.

'You know, I think Chris is dead. I knew he'd do it one day.'

I swallowed. All this time, waiting for news that his body had been found, wondering how Sylvia would cope with one more terrible blow, and now she was accepting the notion as if it were something she'd been quietly living with for years. Just as Tamsin had predicted.

'He'd have been in contact, wouldn't he, if he were still alive? If only to ask for money. Ken hasn't heard from him. No one has. I think he must be dead.'

She had to explain, to a world that wasn't listening. 'I was so convinced I'd find a way of saving him. But I didn't have a hope really, did I? He would never have let me. Poor Mike understood that.'

I took her hand and squeezed it. Perhaps there'd been a part of Chris always calling out for some parental hand to rescue him, but always there had been his monsters, snapping at any proffered hand, withering any hope of salvation. Sylvia was convinced his death must be suicide, and perhaps, in a sense, she was right.

Suicide by proxy.

'And he was in such terrible debt,' she said. 'I can't believe it. All those big plans. He was going to be a millionaire by twenty one.' She heaved another sigh. 'Well, I just hope…' Her voice began to crack. 'If he had to choose that way out, I hope it was quick.'

How much should I reveal? Now that Sylvia seemed reconciled to his death, would it be better if his body were found? Reinterpreting my feelings when I'd driven north in search of Hannah's corpse, I was as certain as I could be where Christian would be.

He'd driven off in hatred and pain, heading God knows where, probably not knowing himself, only knowing that he didn't dare return to London and the 'friends' who would be waiting for him. His car had been facing south, the police had said, so somewhere, out there in the dark, his spite had dissolved in hopelessness, and the little boy had turned to come home. To the mother he'd spat at, because she was all he had. And the car had run dry, like everything in his life.

He'd abandoned it, but only after ransacking it for any pill or resin or speck of powder that might have escaped Michael's confiscation, and he'd found it, one little capsule to ease him from life.

I'd walked the route he'd taken, and I'd felt the ghost of his hopeless weariness, his desperate longing to be out of it all, trapped in the stones of that ruined hut where he, like me, must have sought a moment's shelter. Had he already taken the capsule? Was death already starting to thread its way through his veins? Go no further. Rest now and sleep. Somewhere down in that silent, serried plantation of firs, he'd come to a halt and curled up to wait for the escape a little pill promised.

If I said nothing, his body might lie there forever, slowly buried in fir needles, absorbed into the acid soil and no one would ever know. If, one day, chainsaws and bulldozers cleared the plantation, his bones might not even be noticed. His disappearance would remain a mystery forever.

Like all the others. Life was full of them; deaths unexplained, disappearances unresolved, murders undetected. Why was a man drowned in the bog centuries ago? Why was another left to suffocate and starve in a priest hole? What tragedy left the imprint of some servant's death in an attic bedroom? What would account for human remains, unearthed in a fir plantation?

I had the power to resolve that last riddle. I could have Christian's body brought home to Sylvia. But then, if pathologists deduced murder, I would have to produce Michael's letter.

Sylvia accepted Christian was dead. That was enough. The truth would remain my guilty secret, the shadow of my own making that would follow me wherever I went, for the rest of my life. No escape from that, ever.

My stomach heaved.

It was Sylvia's turn to clasp my hand. 'Poor Kate.' She looked at me with motherly sympathy. Perhaps that would be her salvation: my sickness. It was constantly with me now.

I tried to smile, watching her sympathy turn to concern, then to doubt, then to wonder, then – could it be delight? For a moment, the old Sylvia was there, face lit with eager joy. 'Kate!' she declared, emphatically. 'You're pregnant!'

Nonsense.

Utter nonsense. Surely. Except…

It was absurd. How could I detect the end of life with

such precision, and yet have no sense of its beginning? When I lay, dawn after dawn, sick with the guilt that assailed me, it hadn't occurred to me to question the reasons for my nausea, and as Peter had been fond of pointing out, I was irregular to the point of bloody-mindedness.

'I can't be,' I said, but Sylvia would hear none of it. Of course someone so life-affirming could detect what I hadn't even suspected. Through her dull grief came a flicker of her resurgent vitality. For a moment she was almost impish and I could see a question hovering on her lips.

An unforgiveable question. Sylvia was about to ask me whose it was, and in all honesty…

A jolt. A surge of fierce hunger. Suddenly, in a blinding revelation, I recognised that nameless sensation that had nagged at me, echoing from the rocks of the bog. That unidentified feeling that had clung on when all the anger had been washed away. The feeling that fought against the nihilism of Michael's death and my despair, because that was exactly what it refused to accept. It wasn't fear, or hatred, or desolation, not any of the crushing emotions that I soaked up so easily. It was the reverse: an indomitable will to live, a determination to overcome and be free, so strong that it seemed to grasp me under the armpits and toss me upwards. Life. My life and life in me. Triumphant survival. 'Face the sun,' it screamed, 'and shadows fall behind you.'

I burst into fierce laughter. 'Before you ask, yes, I do know whose it is.' I stood up, ready to take on the world. 'She's mine. And this time she's going to live.'

Sylvia hugged me and at last we dared to laugh.

***

330

If you enjoyed **Shadows**, try its companion and prequel.

Long Shadows
ISBN 978-1788762816

A brief history of the ancient mansion, with three novellas that resolve the mysteries Kate detects at Llys y Garn.

1884. *The Good Servant* tells the story of Nelly Skeel, unloved housekeeper whose only focus of affection is her master's despised nephew.

1662. *The Witch* is the story of Elizabeth Powell, living in an age of religious bigotry and superstitions, who would give her soul for the house in which she was born.

1308. *The Dragon Slayer* tells the tale of Angharad ferch Owain, expendable asset in her father's narrow schemes, who dreams of wider horizons, and an escape from the seemingly inevitable fate of all women.

Other books by Thorne Moore

A Time For Silence
Published by Honno 2012
ISBN978-1906784454

Gwenllian Lewis married John Owen in 1933. Seventy-five years later, their granddaughter Sarah comes upon the ruined cottage where they had once farmed, and the discovery inspires her to investigate her family history. But when she unearths a shocking secret, her interest becomes an obsession. Escaping from her own tragedy, she immerses herself in an older one; a tragedy that overturns her fantasies of an idyllic past, for the story of Gwen and her husband John Owen was anything but idyllic. When the full unpalatable truth dawns on Sarah, she finds herself rethinking her own life.

Motherlove
Published by Honno 2015
ISN 978-1909983205

In 1990, three women are anticipating motherhood. Gillian is childless, and desperate to adopt, but should she? Heather, with financial worries and a young toddler, is stressed by the thought of a second child. Lindy is a desperate teenager, homeless and pregnant.

Two babies are born in Lyford hospital. For two women it's a dream come true. For one, it's the start of a nightmare.

Twenty two years later... Kelly is a happy young woman living on a smallholding in Pembrokeshire. Vicky is a resentful medical student in the home counties. They are worlds apart, but those worlds are about to crash into each other, when they set out to discover who they really are.

The Unravelling
Published by Honno 2016
ISBN 978-1909983489

A bleak January evening and Karen Rothwell returns home from work. An apple falls from a bag and rolls into a gully. An insignificant and undramatic event, but it sparks memories of a school friend Karen hasn't thought about for thirty-five years.

Serena Whinn.

Why has Karen's forgotten childhood crush suddenly sprung into life - and what is it she is still not remembering? Karen cannot rest until she finds out. But then, she's never been able to rest – she's too damaged. And she is not the only one. Will the truth heal, or only serve to open old wounds?

Perhaps it will even inflict new ones.

Moments of Consequence
Available on Kindle

Short stories, including comedies, tragedies and histories, though it is not necessarily easy to decide which is which.

The collection also contains three stories designed to add a little extra colour to some of the novels.

A Time To Cast Away casts a light on the background to *A Time For Silence*

Hush Hush illuminates the life of a character fleetingly mentioned in *Motherlove*.

Green Fingers, Black Back explains how a myth arose in *The Unravelling*.

About the author

Thorne Moore grew up in Luton, but in the 1980s she moved to Pembrokeshire, which provides a rich souce of inspiration for several of her books.

Besides working in libraries and the civil service, she also set up a restaurant with her sister and runs a business making miniature furniture.

Her novels usually centre on crimes, concentrating on their cause and their consequences down the years, rather than the intricacies of forensic investigation.

www.thornemoore.co.uk

Lightning Source UK Ltd.
Milton Keynes UK
UKHW010002270419
341672UK00001B/11/P